W9-CBF-561

Rococoa

Edited by Balogun Ojetade

Copyright © 2015 Balogun Ojetade

All rights reserved.

ISBN: 0991407342
ISBN-13: 978-0-9914073-4-7

DEDICATION

To the authors who submitted Blacktastic works to a Blacktastic anthology. You helped define Rococoa within these pages and now, a fun, original, powerful new subgenre in fiction has emerged and stands proudly between Sword and Soul and Steamfunk as the 'Holy Trinity' of Afroretroism.

CONTENTS

INTRODUCTION

During the 2012 *Mahogany Masquerade: An Evening of Steamfunk and Film*, I inquired about the era that sits between **Sword and Soul** – the subgenre of African-inspired epic and heroic fantasy that is usually set before colonization – and **Steamfunk**, retrofuturistic science fantasy, which normally is set between 1837 and 1901. I asked if anyone had a name for that time because it is a time that fascinates me; a time of revolution – in particular, the Haitian Revolution – a time of pirates and swashbucklers; a time of reverence for art and science.

No one at the event had a name for the era, however, everyone agreed the time possessed that "cool factor" found in Steamfunk and Sword and Soul.

Curious by nature and a researcher by choice, I immediately began my quest of discovery, fueled by my determination to find a name for this era that fascinated me so.

After a brief bit of research, I stumbled upon Rococo…and, to my surprise, Rococopunk.

Rococo is derived from the French word *rocaille*, originally meaning the bits of rocky decoration sometimes found in 16th-century architectural schemes. It was first used in its modern sense around 1800, at about the same time as baroque, and, like baroque, was initially a pejorative term.

The earliest rococo forms appeared around 1700 at Versailles and its surrounding châteaux as a reaction against the oppressive formality of French classical-baroque in those buildings. In 1701 a suite of rooms at Versailles, including the king's bedroom, was redecorated in a new, lighter, and more graceful style by the royal designer, Pierre Lepautre (1648-1716).

In the world of painting, Rococo style is characterized by delicate colors, many decorative details, and a graceful and intimate mood. Similarly, music in the Rococo style is homophonic and light in texture, melodic, and elaborately ornamented. In France, the term for this was *style galant* (gallant or elegant style) and, in Germany, *empfindsamer stil* (sensitive style). François

Couperin, in France, and two of the sons of Johann Sebastian Bach – Carl Philipp Emanuel Bach and Johann Christian Bach – in Germany, were important composers of music in the Rococo style.

Rococopunk is – like Dieselpunk – a sibling of Steampunk, set in the earlier Renaissance era, primarily in the high-class French community of the time. Participants in this movement wear outlandish makeup and hairstyles and sport bold, brightly colored clothing. Think *Amadeus*, *Pirates of the Caribbean*, or *The Adventures of Baron Munchausen*. For darker Rococopunk – think *Last of the Mohicans*, *Perfume: The Story of A Murderer*, *Brotherhood of the Wolf*, or *Sleepy Hollow*.

Okay, I had a name for the era. Now, I needed to come up with a name to define the *Black* expression of Rococopunk; a name to define the subgenre so that – as author and publisher Milton Davis says of Steamfunk and Sword and Soul – "when you hear or read 'Steamfunk' or 'Sword and Soul', you know exactly what you're getting."

Before I could come up with a name myself, the brilliant Briaan L. Barron, artist and owner of *Bri-Dimensional Images* and graduate from Sarah Lawrence College, did it for me with her release of the animated documentary, *Steamfunk and Rococoa: A Black Victorian Fantasy*. While there is not much talk of Rococo or Rococopunk in the documentary – it is mainly about Steampunk and Steamfunk and features Yours Truly – the spelling, **Rococoa**, was perfect!

Thanks, Briaan!

So, with a smile on my face, I sat down to write my first Rococoa story, *Black Caesar: The Stone Ship Rises*, featuring the famed Black pirate. Later, I wrote a story about the legendary Jamaican freedom fighter, *Three Finger'd Jack*.

Around that time, my wife took an interest in Rococoa, as she is fascinated by all things Revolution and Revolutionary. It is she who suggested I publish an anthology of Rococoa stories.

Thanks, Iyalogun!

I sent out a call for submissions.

They came in slowly. So slowly, I thought the anthology was not going to happen, but little did I know the authors were quiet because they were busy crafting their stories. Milton Davis was the first to send in his submission which opened the floodgates and submissions poured in. I reached out to a few great authors for stories. They showed up and showed out.

Now, nearly a year later, you hold a miracle in your hands. A work I am immensely proud of. A work I have full confidence you will enjoy from cover-to-cover.

Dear reader, I present to you a new and oh, so cool subgenre that marries science fiction and fantasy to historical fiction and alternate history.

I present to you *Rococoa*!

Viva la Revolution!

Viva la Resistance!

Viva la Retrofuturism!

CANE

Milton Davis

The merchant ship *Chrysalis* sat low on the ocean waves, her cargo hold packed with the fruits of a generous Mythrian harvest. Thaddus Lean, her owner and captain, did not usually trade for grain; it was perishable and usually low profit. But the Winds had conspired this Cycle and created a once in a lifetime opportunity he couldn't pass up. While the farmer folk in Mythria complained of low prices because of the bounty, the hapless folks of Gebrel suffered from their third year of drought, their fields barren. The mountainous nation had wealthy gold reserves, but what use is gold when there is nothing to eat? With a pound of grain trading for the equivalent of a pound of gold, Thaddus Lean was about to become the richest merchant between the Spires.

He was about to let loose a laugh when the voice caught his ear. A chill ran from his cheek to his spine. For a moment he considered ignoring it. It was probably a bird in the distance, a stray graywill pushed too far from shore by callous winds. But then he heard the melody, the soft sweet words drifting over the gentle sea like a lover's call.

"Siren," he whispered.

"Siren!" a sailor shouted from the crow's nest.

The merchant ship exploded into activity without one word from Thaddus. Any sailor worth his money belt knew what the song meant, even if he did not understand the language. Musketeers climbed the sail ropes then took their perches. Cannon ports were opened and the guns rolled into position. They were a merchant ship, which meant they would be outgunned. But they had to be prepared. Thaddus Lean was not going to lose his fortune without a fight.

The ship waited in silent tension as Siren's schooner approached. It was a small ship, but it was armed to the teeth with cannon and men. The masts bristled with musketeers and the deck seethed with armed men. As she sailed closer Thaddus saw her, sitting like a princess out on an evening jaunt, her beautiful brown face tilted toward the sky as she sang. Despite the desperate situation he found himself entranced, listening to her voice as she sang of love and loss.

The spell was broken by the call of his name.

"Thaddus Lean!"

Thaddus blinked. Siren no longer looked into the sky. Her eyes were locked on him.

"I'm sure you think we have come to steal your cargo," she shouted. "But that is not so. We have come to buy it."

Thaddus's first mate, Kelan Gould, appeared at his side. The tall, bronze man was also the senior guildsman and had a personal stake in the cargo.

"Don't listen to the wench!" he said. "She's here to steal our cargo and end us!"

Thaddus looked at the man as if he was a giraffe.

"And what do you expect me to do, fight?" he said.

"Of course!" Kelan replied.

"Let's hear your offer," Thaddus said. The ships were now close enough for Thaddus to see her smile.

"Twenty gold crowns!" she shouted.

It was far less than Thaddus would receive if he delivered the cargo, but much more than he would have received under normal circumstances. Add his life into the deal and it was well worth it.

"We refuse!" Kelan shouted. "I am Kelan Gould of the shipper's Guild. Twenty gold crowns is an insult. We can get three times as much in Gebrel!'

Siren's smile faded. "Thaddus, does this fool speak for you?"

"No," Thaddus said quickly.

"Kelan Gould, apparently you have mistaken this as a negotiation," Siren said. "It's not. Brak!"

A musket barked and Kellen jerked then fell to the deck, a musket ball in his forehead. Thaddus looked up to see a burly bare-chested man in Siren's crow's nest lowering his musket to reload.

The ships were close enough for boarding. Siren and a dozen pirates swung over on ropes. Siren sauntered to Thaddus then pulled a leather pouch from her waist belt.

"Half your payment," she said. "You'll get the remainder when we reach port."

"Which port?" Thaddus asked.

"Don't worry about it," she answered. "My men will take the helm. Go to your cabin and rest Thaddus. We'll handle it from here."

Siren was walking away when Thaddus called out.

"Why pay me?" he asked. "You could have taken it."

Siren turned then smiled. "Fighting would have damaged the cargo. I need it intact."

Thaddus watched her swing back to her ship, a song on her voice. He looked at Kelan's body on the deck and realized that it could have been him lying there instead.

"I'll be in my cabin," Thaddus said. He would take Siren's advice. He had a bottle of rum that needed his attention.

Siren watched Thaddus until he disappeared below then set about securing his ship. She had waited months for him. Her plan would fail without his cargo. Now that it was secure she could go about working on the next part of the plan. She had a good, brave and hardworking crew but she needed more. She was not the trustful sort, but circumstances drove her to push the limits on her ways. There was no better time than now, and time was of the essence.

It took three weeks to sail to Bracken's Cove, one week longer than she anticipated. No person rules the sea; the saying went, a quote proven true during their journey. But she would not dwell on what she could not change. It was time to work on the second part of her plan.

Malik, her blood brother, sauntered up to her. He was shirtless as always, his pantaloons gathered around his waist with a wide belt. He wore his sword, which was rare. He hugged her waist and she smiled.

"You're wearing your sword," she said. "You never liked the Cove."

"It's not that I don't like it," he said. "I don't *trust* it. Too many of us here."

"They are not us," Siren said. "Remember that."

Malik laughed. "We've been at this for ten years. I think it's safe to say that we are the same as them."

Siren gripped the bulwark, her arms trembling. "We'll *never* be the same as them."

"So you're mad at me," Malik said.

"And I don't want to be," she replied. "Everything we've done has been according to plan, even coming here."

"For a moment I thought you'd forgotten our plan," Malik said.

In truth, she had. So many years wasted running away from a promise, but they were not all wasted. She was a captain now with a reputation that resonated far beyond her territory.

"I'm back now," she answered. "I could never forget the cane."

The ships eased into the docks closest to the tavern district. She was to meet a man, one who would support her plan for his own reasons. Siren went below to Thaddus' cabin.

"Come with me," she said.

"So you're to kill me now?" he asked.

"Don't be in such a hurry to die," she said. "I need your company."

"I knew you'd succumb to my charms," Thaddus said.

Siren was surprised Thaddus's words made her smile.

"I was told you were a humorous sort," she said. "Follow me."

Siren led Thaddus back on deck.

"Brak! Knife! Malik!" she shouted. "Come with me. The rest of you stay with the ship. We'll only be in dock for one night."

She ignored the groans of her crew as she and the others debarked then made their way to *The Cradle*. The streets teemed with men and women, most drunk and the rest lurking with serious intent. She hated the Cove as much as Malik, but these types of hovels had been their life ever since they escaped. Anything was better than the cane. Anything was better than slavery.

The Cradle's entrance was filthy and crowded as always.

"Brak, stay here and keep a lookout for him," Siren said. The hulking man nodded then positioned himself beside the dilapidated door. Their group caught the attention of the Cradle's patrons as they entered. Siren received more than a few leers and lewd comments as they made their way to an empty table near the rear of the crowded tavern. A thin man in a flowing shirt, leather pantaloons and dingy apron followed them.

"Welcome back, Siren," the man sang as they sat.

"Barron," Siren said. "You're still alive I see."

Barron, owner of the Cradle, smiled.

"This place hasn't killed me yet, although many of my patrons have tried."

"Keep your pistols loaded," Malik said.

"That I do," Barron replied. He cut a mean glance at Thaddus.

"So you're hanging with merchants now?"

"For the moment," Siren replied.

Barron waddled away then returned with a steaming cup of coffee that he placed before Siren. He was about to put down a cup of sugar then stopped.

"I almost forget," he said, a hint of fear in his voice. "Forgive me."

Siren grinned. "No worries. It's been a long time."

"I'd like some," Thaddus said.

"No you wouldn't" Barron said.

He took the sugar then hurried away.

Thaddus was frowning when he looked at Siren.

"So you don't like sugar," he said.

Siren sipped her coffee. "It tastes like blood."

Realization came late for Thaddus.

"I'm sorry," he said. "How insensitive of me."

"Ha! There she is!"

The lean man pushed his way to the table then sat before Siren without an invitation. Knife and Malik rose from their seats but she waved them down.

"What do you want?" she asked.

"I want to sail with you," he said. "Name's Mattew Jan."

"I have no need for more crew," she said. "Be off with you."

"I spent six years on the Griff under Captain Braddock," he said. "They don't come any tougher than him, or me."

Siren smirked. "You ever worked the cane?"

"Yes!" he said.

"Brak!" Siren called out.

Brak entered the tavern, pushing aside people and tables as he made his way to Siren. Mattew eyes widened and his mouth went slack as the hulking black skinned man came closer.

"I'll leave you be," he said.

Siren unsheathed her machete then laid it on the table.

"You'll stay where you are."

Brak stood beside her, his sword scars heaving with his chest. He stared unblinking at Mattew for a long moment.

"Brak, this man says he worked the cane," Siren said.

Brak laughed hard and loud for at least a minute. He grabbed Mattew then pushed him down face first into the table with his right hand. With his left he ripped of the man's shirt. Siren stood then looked at the man's bare back.

"I thought so," she said.

She turned her back to Mattew then lifted her shirt. Ragged keloid scars marred her dark skin. Brak grabbed Mattew's hair, pulling back his head so he could see the gruesome sight.

"This is what the cane does to you," Siren said. "There is nothing harder than the cane."

She dropped her shirt then walked back to her seat.

"You can go now, Brak," Siren said.

Brak shoved Mattew's face into the table before he walked away. Mattew's nose bled as he lifted his head.

"Every man and woman on my ship has worked the cane," she said. "Hell is a relief to us, Heaven a place we'll never see"

She picked up the machete then pointed it at Mattew.

"Now I ask you again. Have you worked the cane?"

"I'm...I'm sorry," Mattew said. "I'll leave you be."

Siren's movement was swift. She cut off the tip of the man's little finger then pressed the machete's edge against his throat before he could cry out.

"A souvenir," she whispered.

The man ran from the Cradle. Siren sipped her coffee, ignoring Thaddus's stare.

"He lied to me," she said, answering the question she knew was on his mind.

Brak entered the Cradle again. He was not alone. A man with skin like night followed him, as tall as the brooding pirate but not quite as broad. A cutlass and a dozen jeweled daggers hung from his wide waist belt. A leather jerkin fit tightly against his broad chest. He smiled at Siren and she smiled back.

The man turned his chair backwards then sat at the table.

"Jonas, you came," she said.

"I would never refuse you, Queen," he said. He took a dagger from his belt then placed it on the table. The blade was pure silver fitted into a hilt of carved ivory decorated with rubies and emeralds.

"I had this made for you in Carmalin," he said.

Siren picked up the knife, admiring the

craftsmanship.

"It's beautiful," she said. "Not very practical, but beautiful."

Jonas laughed. "Not as beautiful as you."

Malik's eyes narrowed as he sucked his teeth. Jonas looked his way and his smile faded.

"Malik, how are you," he said. "I didn't notice you there."

"You never do." Malik stood. "I'll take my leave. Thaddus, come with me. These two have business to discuss."

Malik leaned close to her.

"I don't trust this snake," he whispered. "You know what he wants."

Siren looked directly into Jonas' hazel eyes.

"Of course I do," she said aloud. "I'll be fine."

Malik glared at Jonas then led Thaddus to another table.

"That one fancies you," Jonas said.

"Malik is my brother," she replied. "By bond if not by blood. He looks out for me. You are the one that fancies me."

"As do half the corsairs that sail the True Sea," he said.

"Yet none of them came with you, did they?"

Jonas frowned. "No they didn't. Most would give up half their treasures to bed you but not their life," he said.

"Bedding me was never part of the bargain," she said, her voice tinged with anger. "I'm not a whore." She snatched out her machete again then slammed it on the table.

Jonas raised his hands. "I never meant to imply that, Queen. There is no other person, man or woman, that the Black Brotherhood respects more."

"Yet again, they did not come," she said.

"Let's be practical," Jonas said. "What you plan yields no gold or booty. Besides, the Dalmatin coast is treacherous, especially this time of year."

"I know that coast," she said. "I've spent years studying it. I know every bay, inlet and harbor. I could sail it with my eyes shut."

"You can, but we can't," Jonas replied. "Which leaves you with me."

"And why are you here?" she asked, even though she knew the answer.

'I came to give you the dagger," Jonas said, grinning.

"We sail in the morning," she said.

"I'll be ready," Jonas said.

Jonas stood then took a deep bow before striding from the tavern. Malik and Thaddus returned soon afterward.

"So how many will come?" Malik asked.

"Only Jonas."

"Then we must end the plan."

"No!" Siren said. "The conditions are perfect. It's now or never." She heard her voice crack when she said the words. She knew Malik heard it, too.

"We can't do it with only two ships," Malik said. "We'll have to make arrangements for the others," Malik said.

"Yes we will," Siren said. "Come, we have work to do."

The two of them stood to leave the tavern.

"What about me?" Thaddus said.

"Enjoy the rest of the night," Siren said. "Tomorrow, we go to war."

Black sails crested the horizon, hidden from the shoreline watchtowers by dense fog. Though the harbor guards could not see the approaching vessels, Siren knew well the shore she approached. It had once been her home, if a plantation could be considered such a thing.

She turned to Brak, who stood bare-chested beside her, exposing his collection of scars.

"Let's get to the boats," she said.

Together they marched to the bulwark and joined the others. These were the elite of her crew, men and women who had proven themselves time and time again in battle.

"We won't have much time," she said. "So stay focused. They won't know we're coming so do the best you can to get them out. And remember, we only have so much room. Bring back only those you need."

Everyone nodded. She looked about the deck before spotting Malik.

"Malik!" she shouted.

The lithe man hurried to her side.

"Are the cannons ready?"

"Yes, Siren," he said.

She glanced over his shoulder. The Kraken, Jonas's heavy ship, kept time with them. She could barely see him in the crow's nest but she knew he was there.

Her attention came back to Malik. She raised her arm as he did, the two of them setting the wrist clocks attached to their leather gloves.

"Begin the bombardment in ten minutes," she said. "We should be to shore by then."

"Yes Siren," he said.

They touched foreheads and shared a smiled. Malik was her oldest and dearest friend. There was no one she trusted more.

"Bring them back, Akini," he said, using her little name.

"I will, Ajamu," she said.

They touched each other's cheek then broke away to their duties. When she faced her landing crew her smile was gone. She climbed over the bulwark then sat in the first boat hanging over the side. The others boarded and the boats were lowered into the choppy sea. Conditions were bad for a boat landing but perfect for her plan. They rowed to shore with eight boats; three fill with the landing party, three empty and two filled with supplies.

Ajamu's timing was perfect. The cannons roared as the boats ran aground. Siren leaped over the side with the others, drawing her sword and pistol.

"Get the rifles and follow me," she ordered.

In moments they ran across the misty field, her memory unflagging. The cane appeared abruptly and old memories of pain and drudgery hit her like a physical blow. She remembered her thin arms clutching the cane stalks, the leaves cutting her skin like razors. The brutal work from sun up 'til sun down, then trying to stay awake as mama soothed her wounds with butter and kisses. The horror of finding a dead worker among the stalks, another soul worked to oblivion. She stumbled but her burly friend caught her.

"Are you alright, Siren?" he asked.

"I am, Brak," she replied. She pulled away from his grasp, angry at her weakness.

They met the first overseer halfway through the fields. He turned suddenly, his eyes wide when he recognized what was happening. Siren drove her sword through his throat before he had the chance to shout. The second overseer stood by the slave houses, too close to kill silently.

"Brak," she shouted.

Brak raised his musket and then fired. The man's head jerked then he crumpled to the ground. Moments later the alarm drum rumbled.

Siren and the others quickened their pace. The other overseers appeared with muskets, swords and maces. They were no match for Siren and her sailors. Siren shot her pistols empty then used them as clubs in concert with her sword as she cut through the inept guards.

"Find your loved ones!" she shouted. "Our time is short."

She ran directly to the hut where her family lived. She burst inside and was greeted by their fearful faces, faces that transformed to joy when they recognized her.

"Akini!" they shouted.

Her mother was the last to come to her.

"You said you would come back," she said.

"And I have. Now come. We must hurry."

"I can't run so fast," her mother said. She opened her ragged cloak, revealing her swollen belly.

Siren's entire body burned. "Is it his?" she asked.

Her mother didn't reply.

She grabbed her mother's hand, pulling her from the hut.

They met the others running back to the boats with their families, passing those who did not have anyone to rescue them. A group of her sailors stood in the middle of the village with the wrapped bundles. Siren went to them, her family in tow.

"Listen to me!" she shouted. "I wish I could take you all with me but I can't. But I will not leave you here defenseless."

The men opened the bundles. There were muskets, pistols, swords, knives and bags of gunpowder and musket balls.

"You can die in the fields, or you can risk your life now for freedom. Those who wish to risk it should head due west. There is a city on the coast that will take you in. Your life there won't be easy, but it will be better than this. May the Goddess guide you!"

The workers surged at the weapons as Siren and the others fled to the boats. Siren and her men kept watch as the others clambered into the boats; then Siren's cohorts boarded the last one and set off. Once she knew everyone was secure she strode back to the huts.

"Where are you going?" Brak called out.

Siren didn't answer. She loaded her pistols and then picked up and loaded a musket which lay beside one of the dead overseers. She found a horse, climbed on it then kicked the beast into a full gallop down the trail leading to the grand house. The horse galloped between fields of unharvested cane, much of it on fire from the relentless barrage from the ships. The cane disappeared, replaced by fields of vegetables and various other crops. The master's loomed before her and her anger grew. As she neared the front gate she spied militiamen running towards her. Siren pulled the first pistol from her belt then slummed against the horse's neck. She slowed the horse to a trot as the militiamen came near. The first to reach her stood before the horse, mistaking her as a slave come to warn them.

"What's going on girl? Is it pirates?"

Siren jerked upright, a pistol in each hand.

"Yes!"

She shot the man in the forehead and the other militiaman in his chest. Siren rolled off her horse onto her feet, using the beast as a shield for her right flank as she confronted the two men on her left. Both went down, musket balls in their heads. By the time the other militiamen rounded the horse she held her last pistols in her hands. The men raised their muskets; Siren dropped to her knees then took aim at each man, firing simultaneously into their groins. She dropped her pistols then took theirs.

Siren was climbing onto the horse when she heard a musket fire in the distance. A second later a musket ball slammed into her shoulder, knocking her to the ground. Light flashed before her eyes as her head struck the mud. An image appeared; she was a girl, surrounded by the opulence of the master's banquet room, singing for his guests. She looked at him and he looked back, the expression on his face terrifying her. It was that day she decided she would escape. She was already his work tool; she would not be his pleasure tool as well.

Siren shook her head then struggled back to her feet. She climbed onto the horse, wincing in pain. The musket fired again; this time the shooter missed. Siren spied him on the porch of the grand house. She took her musket from the saddle straps, using the horse's neck to steady her aim. The horse jumped as she fired, the musket smoke blinding her. When it cleared she saw the musketeer sprawled on the porch.

No one challenged her as she rode through the gates to the stairs leading into the home. Pistol in her right hand and sword in her left, she shoved the door open and then entered the home. She instinctively dodged to the left, avoiding the ambush she knew awaited her. The foyer rang with the pistols' report; Siren waited for the smoke to clear before shooting a militiaman point blank in the face. She raised her sword, blocking the downward stroke of another militiaman before plunging her dagger into his gut. She spun away as the man fell, facing the only person remaining in the room.

Graeme Kell, her former master, stood before her, armed with sword and dagger, a malicious smile on his face.

"Siren," he said. "So you are the cause of this."

They circled each other, Siren's face twisted with hate.

"You've grown into a beautiful woman, as I suspected you would," Graeme said. "You would have made an excellent concubine."

Siren screamed as she attacked. Graeme was skilled, but not as skilled as Siren. His smile faded with each cut inflicted; soon his eyes were wide with desperation as he fought off Siren's assault. Siren ignored every wound, her mind filled with one purpose. Her sword finally found its target, plunging just below Graeme's ribcage. Siren twisted her sword sideways then ripped it from Graeme's body, causing a wound that couldn't be healed.

Graeme tumbled to the ground. Siren stood over him as he died. She screamed again then spit into his face. She turned away, stumbling toward the door as the toll of her wounds overtook her. She was about to fall face first into the floor when two strong hands caught her. She looked up into Brak's stoic face.

"We must flee," he said. "More militiamen are coming."

She leaned against Brak as they ran to her horse. He helped her onto her horse and then, together, they rode to the shore to the waiting boats.

Siren, Malik, Brak and Jonas climbed the steep slope, their heavy breathing and sweaty clothes a sign of the difficulty of the climb. Siren reached the summit first then sat hard in the knee high grass, letting out a relieved sigh. She took her water bag from her waist belt and took a long swig; by the time she lowered it the others sat beside her in various states of exhaustion.

"Was this absolutely necessary?" Jonas asked.

"You said you wanted to see the island," Siren said. "This is the best place to see it."

She stood and then pulled Jonas to his feet. Her shoulder ached from the wound she received at the plantation, the musket ball still inside. Once everything settled she would have a healer remove it. They stood side by side, the entire expanse of the island visible to their eyes.

"I'm impressed," Jonas said. "Very impressed. How did you find it?"

"I studied the old maps in Great Zumbawa," Siren said. "I was searching for an island far from the main sea routes, somewhere we could be hidden from the world. This island was considered a legend, but I discovered it to be true. We are not the first to live here."

She pointed due west of their position.

"There are ruins there," she said. The people who once lived here were great builders."

She pointed north. "That's where we'll settle. The land is good and it's far enough from the coast so not to be spotted by any passing ships. We'll build a fort on this summit as a lookout for any approaching ships and set up a signal system to warn us."

She then pointed to the east.

"That's where we'll grow the cane. The conditions are perfect for it."

Jonas looked surprised. "Grow cane? I thought that would be the last thing you would do."

"Some of us still have a liking for it," she said. "It will also be a reminder of what we endured and what we must never let happen again."

"I'm impressed," Jonas said. "And what will you call your little paradise?"

"Serenity," Malik said.

"No," Siren said.

Brak nodded. "It is a good name."

"I don't agree," Siren said.

"I like it, too," Jonas said.

The three of them stared at her. Siren tried to stay stern but a smile creased her face.

"It's a possibility. But the people will decide."

They began their descent. Malik and Brak walked ahead while Jonas and Siren walked together.

"So is there a place for a wandering corsair in this wonderful land?"

Siren cut her eyes at Jonas.

"That's up to the corsair. But don't expect to be asked. I have no intentions of being anyone's wife anytime soon."

Jonas scowled. "After all I've done for you?"

Siren sucked her teeth. "All you've done for yourself. You were paid, quite well I must add."

Jonas laughed. "I suspect you'll marry someone one day and have a dozen children."

"I wouldn't wait on that day," Siren said. "My days on the sea are not yet done."

Jonas' eyebrows rose. "Really?"

"We weren't able to rescue all of them," she said. "I plan to."

"Then I will help you," Jonas said.

"There will be no pay in this, corsair," she said.

"Consider it an investment," Jonas said.

Siren smiled. "So be it."

They reached the summit base and the trail leading to the village. Siren was about to catch up with Brak and Malik when Jonas grabbed her arm.

"One more thing," he said. "What is your real name?"

Siren said nothing, amused at Jonas' attention.

"Please, you must tell me!" he pleaded. "I can't stand Malik knowing something I don't. Besides, you owe me that much."

Siren laughed. "Akini. My name is Akini."

"Akini." Jonas rubbed his chin. "A lovely name, but I prefer Siren. It's more mysterious."

Siren rolled her eyes. "Whatever. Come, we can discuss our plans as we walk."

"As you command, Akini of Serenity!"

He took a deep bow and Siren laughed. They hurried to catch up with their companions.

SEA-WALKER

Carole Mcdonnell

It is well-known, though not officially recorded, that a sea captain from one of the western islands had a strange, disabled child.

This son – Nohay, by name – was the only child of his beloved, deceased wife and the captain cherished him as his own peculiar treasure and would allow none but the kindest eye and warmest heart to look upon him, for the boy's body was twisted and bent and his mind slow and the child lacked all ability speak. So the father kept his son hidden away in the uppermost floors of his lodgings, filling those rooms with rare joys that he had discovered in his journeys – strange delights that a child of limited understanding might enjoy. Always he would resort thither, after his day's duties, to play with his son.

With the exception of one kindly old matron whose task it was to care for the boy whenever the captain was at sea, the boy had no other human friends. Mark me: I say not that he had no friends, but that he had no *human* friend. For I will tell you now that he was not entirely solitary.

When he was some ten years old, his father became castaway on one of the Caribe Isles. For two years he lingered thus, alone and exiled, his thoughts turned in on himself. And in the third year, a passing fae chanced to hear him muttering to himself and, being curious about the captain, endeavored through various means to befriend him. This he did by pretending to be a castaway himself. Thus the captain befriended the fae – or, as he supposed, the dark native – and the two became fast friends. The captain taught his new friend all that he thought befitting of a man of such limited understanding of the world: the language of the English Isles, and how to go and fetch for him. Perhaps he thought it good fun. Perhaps he only wanted to see how far the matter would run until the story was played out, but never once did the fae correct the captain or challenge his "master's" assumptions. At last, after three months passed, what should appear on the horizon but a ship to return the captain to his native lands?

It has been said by many that the fae was responsible for this happy turn of events – and it is very likely that he was. But whether this be true or not, the fact remains that the captain returned home. And not himself alone but with a dark native at his side.

When the fae arrived at the captain's house, he saw the human child (and as is often the habit and wont of faes), befriended him. Soon after this, the child's rooms began to be filled with paints, canvases, and musical instruments of diverse sort. Through some fairy magic, the boy – although he could not speak – began to be expert in painting and music. He painted scenes of foreign lands that neither the matron nor the captain had visited, and drew conveyances that no man on earth, save the great Da Vinci, had seen or devised. The music he played on flute, viol, citre, or oboe had an airy quality that hinted at worlds humans had never entered.

Being an astute man, the captain soon began to believe that an entity was influencing his son and – afraid – he set guards to watch the windows, balconies and doors of the boy's rooms. Soon enough, it was reported to him that the Caribe native he had befriended was nothing more or less than a wood fae and instead of washing pots and scrubbing floors as was required, the fae was often accustomed to visiting the child's balcony. From there, the fae would call out. In response, the boy would come running to him. Indeed, as he stood on the balcony, the fae never wore the bedraggled rags his master had provided but was often dressed in cotton tunics of green and red.

The fae's description and mien was reported to envoys and emissaries throughout the British and Caribbean isles. At last an answer came: the boy's visitor was Prince Hark, a forest fae from the southern seas. More importantly, this fae prince was reputed to be kind and trustworthy and prone to playing tricks on unwary humans.

The captain was of course angry at the deception but being persuaded by those who understood such matters that Prince Hark had no desire to steal his son or replace the boy with a changeling, the captain begrudgingly allowed the friendship. Even so, because he now understood that he had been the fae's fool, he no longer commanded the fae as he once did. And the fae, in turn, stopped residing in the cottage.

Thus the fae and the captain dealt with the situation and with the boy as if the other did not exist. And this arrangement suited them for quite some time. (Although the captain did seek out a physician who would examine the boy weekly to see if the fae had done the boy any physical harm.)

But one night some weeks after the boy's twenty-fifth birthday, the captain returned from the sea and found the fae sitting cross-legged on the third-floor balcony. With some trepidation, he wondered why the fae should suddenly desire to speak with him. He stood, wary and bowed, awaiting some word from his former friend.

"Do I have permission to speak, Master?" the fae asked.

"You have permitted yourself much already all these years," the captain answered. "Why should you ask my permission now? And we both know that I am not your master, Prince Hark."

"True," Prince Hark answered. "But know that I cannot take your son away unless you give me permission."

"Take my son away?" the captain echoed. "But why. . .?" His voice trailed off and he studied his son's face, a face that seemed to yearn for greater things outside of his confined rooms.

"Soon, Nonny will begin to speak," the fae continued. "And you will of course be curious as to what his voice, what his humor, what his intelligence. You will wish to have long discourses with him. You can do that all in good time. But first, I must travel with him to regions far away."

"Nonny?" the captain said, more to himself than to the fae. For it had not occurred to the father that his son might have a nickname. He shook his head. "No, Nohay cannot travel with you."

"I have not asked very much," the fae said. "Give him to me for seven years. After that, he shall be yours forever."

"Are you the one who will make him speak?" the captain asked. He studied the crippled form of his son's body. "And will you heal him entirely?"

"It is not I who will heal him," Prince Hark answered. "The Good Lord of Light will. I have seen that he has already answered your prayers. But I have determined that I also wish to help the boy."

"Help him?" the captain's voice dripped sarcasm. "And what will your benefit be? What will you require or gain for this help of yours?"

The fae laughed. "How shrunken-hearted you humans are! And remember, it was not I who called you 'servant' when we were on the island, but you who determined I was your inferior. I want nothing but to acquaint your son with the world he will find himself in."

"When you say 'acquaint him with the world,' what exactly do you mean?" the captain asked.

"I will teach him your mores, your etiquettes, your histories, your geographies, and sciences. Only that."

The captain had no trust of faes but because the fae looked impatiently on him and he wished to be well-rid of him, he answered thusly, "Well, Prince Hark, if you wish, you may take my son. But only for seven years. Then return him safely to me. And give me a week to prepare both my son and myself for our mutual separation and loss."

"I will give you a day," the fae prince said.

"What an intrusion you have been in my life!" the old captain cried out.

"You did not consider me much of an intrusion when I was your dark servant," the fae answered and left, promising to return the next day to take Nohay. But that night the old captain called upon his friend, a duke who had long ago befriended him because he had heard of his adventures during his watery exile. The duke took the boy and hid him in one of the dungeons of his castle, where the echoes of the waves could be heard thundering against the brick walls. As the duke closed the door upon the father and son, the gnarled body of the young man suddenly straightened itself like a tree spreading out its limbs to heaven and Nohay suddenly spoke.

"Father?" he said. "Why have you brought me here?"

Those were the first words the child spoke.

The voice was not what the old man had expected. He had not expected the first words from his child to be a challenging question either. But what perturbed him more than having to answer to his son was the sight of a suddenly well-formed, muscular young man. The old captain could only stare into the dark room with perplexed eyes. What manner of creature would his son turn out to be?

The young man asked again, "Father, why have you brought me here?"

The old captain managed to speak. "To protect you from the fae," he answered, not knowing how much his son comprehended.

"The fae?" the young man asked. "Is that what his people are called? I had surmised, even in my unusual mental state, that he was not like us. For he had hair the color of moss and heather and skin dark as the night. But I did not know that his people were called 'the fae.' Are there many like him?"

"They are many indeed, my boy," the captain said, "and it is unclear whether they serve the good Lord of Light or not. Therefore I have determined he will not remove you from me."

The boy looked at his fingers. His thumb touched his little finger, then methodically counted through the others. "But he has not hurt me these fifteen years," he said.

"You know mathematics, My Nohay?" the old captain asked, smiling sadly.

"That I do," the boy said. "The one you call a 'fae' taught me much."

"But how could he teach you so much?"

"He has joined my mind to his in such a way that I can see clearly the thoughts in his mind. In this way, I have learned much."

"Indeed?" the old man said. "Such strange intimacy indeed! But has he harmed you in anyway?"

"'Harm?'" the boy echoed. "What is 'harm?' It is not a word you have used often in my presence."

"You do not understand the word?"

"I do not, Father."

And so the old father explained the meaning of the word and the many kinds of violence that men can use against each other and against young boys, even to the point of death.

Nohay listened, a look of deep surprise on his face. "No, he has not harmed me. Nor did he tell me that men could harm or steal from each other. But he has told me about death and other such matters."

"Has he?" the old father answered. "About death? Why would he tell you about death?"

"When he explained to me that I had no mother," Nohay answered. "And that she had gone to live in the sky. He thought I should be made to understand why she was not at my side."

And there was more the boy knew. So much more that the captain was both thankfully impressed and fiercely, jealously suspicious of the fae's influence on his son. They spoke at length for much of the night.

Having power and wealth, the duke had warriors and armed guards assembled roundabout his castle, and from the highest turrets to the dungeon. For although the deception was hidden from the fae, it was well-known that such deception could not be long hidden.

The captain spoke with his son until dawn, discovering all manner of truths about the boy. Then when his son fell asleep, he rose and waited for the sun to rise to its height. At noon, the fae returned to the captain's cottage. And how powerfully he returned! For Prince Hark arrived upon a mechanical dragon from whose mouth dense fiery smoke issued. Beside them was a winged horse with flesh and blood like any other.

"I have come for your son," the fae prince said. From within the dragon loins, a slat opened and after a series of rhythmical clatter, a series of steps unfolded. The fae stepped upon them and lighted down from the dragon. He stood on the last step looking at the captain.

"He is not here," the captain answered, quivering in fear. Whether from fear of the dragon or from the fearsome skill required in making such a dragon. For the thing was about three times the length and height of the cottage and it gleamed black like the blackest of oils on a bright blue lake.

"And where might he be, if not here?" the fae prince asked, with a calm that would have startled the hearts of most human men.

But the captain only answered. "What does it matter where he is? All that matters is that I have sent him away because I will not allow him to go with you on your travels."

The fae prince smiled. An angry smile. "How shrunken-hearted you humans are!"

The old captain muttered under his breath. "If you had such a contraption, why did you not use it to rescue me from that forsaken deserted isle?"

"Are you one who expects a dark one to tell you all his secrets?" the fae prince answered.

"You should have told me you were not human like the others of the Carib isles," the captain retorted, still seething that the fae had deceived him.

The fae answered, "Old man, I am older than you by three thousand years. I have power to crush you. And you dare talk to me as if I am still your servant? Are you out of your mind?"

With that he left, and as if he had known the young boy's dwelling all along, he and his dragon flew toward the duke's castle. There, the fae prince once again descended those steps of wood and iron. Having arrived in the courtyard, he pushed past the duke and the armed guards and down the stairs of the castle to the dungeon where the young man was. Then, without key or word, he lifted his hand and opened the dungeon door.

None approached or challenged him as he took the young man by hand and walked into the courtyard. Seconds later, young Nohay sat astride the pegasi and Prince Hark atop the dragon. And within moments, they had taken to the skies.

Nohay and the fae prince travelled together for half the day, Nohay lost in thought. At last Nohay said to the fae prince, "How are fae and humans different and why does my father fear your kind so much?"

"We are more alike than unalike," the fae said.

"But in our unalikeness, there is nothing of me that you can understand."

So, Nohay was silent again, thinking. And all his thoughts were known to the fae, but few of the fae's thoughts were privy to him. Still, enough of the fae's thoughts were known and Nohay could understand much in the world without opening his mouth to ask a question.

They travelled for many days, Nohay's eyes being full of sights he had only seen second hand through the fae's mind. The day came when they arrived at a great river in which the sky of our dear Lord was so keenly reflected that it seemed as if the very sky and water had met.

"See there," the fae said, pointing at the bright blue water.

Nohay peered downward, the brightness of the water almost blinding him.

The fae directed him toward an inlet near the river's edge. "There," he said. "What do you see?"

Nohay saw two human children swimming, their heads under the lake. Without knowing how he knew, he now knew that the boy was seven-years-old and named Pel. And the other, his sister, some five years older, who was named Onada.

"Shall we descend?" the fae asked.

Nohay nodded. Immediately the back of the mechanical dragon opened –its mechanical scales sliding along slots and grooves. The fae gestured for Nohay to join him within the creation. When all – Nohay, Hark, and the pegasi were inside – the juncture closed around them with a thunderous but efficient clatter. Nohay found himself in a dimly-lit chamber through which he could see the sky and land. Yet only dimly, for the skins and scales of the mechanical creature were like a highly-polished metal glass. Before Nohay could sigh his delight, the creature plunged headlong into the lake. At first the little chamber grew dark but after several seconds the room was filled with the biofluorescent lightings of crustaceans from the deep or from the skies. On the walls, which were formed by the creature, shells glowed. Through the skin and scales of the dragon, the sunlight reflected through the water.

Prince Hark directed Nohay's attention to the swimming siblings. The boy swam with his eyes opened. Not so his sister Onada. She was perhaps too mindful of dirt and filth, for the lake was very near the gardens and farmlands of the rich folk of that region.

Now this was the girl's thought as she swam with her brother, her eyes closed, "If I am to grow up for hard work, I should have no aversion to the water-weeds, the scattered mermaid scales, and the countless flotsam and detritus that float around me. For I and this scum are one and the same, carried about by the uncaring waves of time."

"Why have you shown me this?" Nohay asked. "And why intrude on the girl's musing?"

But the fae did not answer.

So Nohay grew silent and listened as the girl's brother attempted to convince her to open her eyes under the lake.

"Open your eyes!" the boy commanded, although he was some years younger than she. "True, your eyes will burn a bit. But after a while what wonders you will see!"

The girl did not open her eyes. She only remembered with a shudder a moment when a water fae threw a half-eaten fish into the lake. She imagined herself swimming in fish-meal and mer-folk dung and she shuddered. And because Prince Hark felt her shudder – although he was far from her and resting in his sub-mariner – Nohay also felt the shudder.

"How she scorns your people!" Nohay observed.

"As much as your father scorns the dark people of the Caribe," Prince Hark said. "But listen and look."

So Nohay turned his attention again to the siblings.

"Open your eyes," the brother ordered the sister.

She opened her eyes. And Nohay saw through the thoughts of the fae that the water did not sting as much as she feared. Yet, Onada could not see the beauty of the pond; she only imagined herself surrounded by a sewer.

Her eyes adjusted to the brackish water. Plant

sludge floated past her. Nohay watched in silence, waiting. Then, in the distance...he saw little creatures, about an inch long, each with two tiny fins or arms and two feet flapping underneath treading water. Onada saw these as well and could only imagine newts, tadpoles, or leeches. Whatever it was, it disgusted and terrified her.

She lifted her head above the waves but looked in the opposite direction of the creature. "Over there!" she said, directing her brother's gaze at the creatures behind her. Her brother lifted his head above the water line. "What swims there?" she pleaded. "Look and tell me what it is!"

"But you should look, Sister. Turn your own gaze!"

"I won't."

Onada imagined leeches. She feared to see their heads and eyes, peering up at the water. The fear controlled her. And she began to think that she did not like being controlled by a fear. So, with a force born of a desire not to be controlled, she turned her head toward the creatures. And as she turned to look, she saw the little creature gasping for air and attempting to keep its head above the water. Then in the midst of its struggle, suddenly – quite suddenly – it rose above the waves of the lake...a tiny humanoid creature. Suddenly airborne and with wings!

"Have we. . .?" Onada stammered, "just seen the birth of a fae?"

"We have! We have!" her brother shouted. How

delighted they were – clapping their hands in the air and shouting in joy. And at that moment, Onada cared little about the murk of the lake or the dung of mermen and waterfolk.

But Nohay too clapped his hands in delight. "How lovely the world can be!" he shouted.

The fae did not respond, but the joy of that experience stayed with Nohay for many months.

Some days later, in the early morning in the dark gray winter, in the winter morning and white winter sunlight, with white soft snow covering the hard brown ground, Prince Hark and his flying dragon took Nohay to a little village in the southern continent.

"I will show you," he said, "a little woman who is the bringer of dreams."

They came upon a little bent old woman walking through the village pulling a cart. "Is this the swatch lady, the bringer of dreams that you've told me of?" Nohay asked.

"How long she has lived here not even the faes know!" the fae prince said. "And how often she creates dreams! Always, always she brings dreams."

On her cart, the woman carried baskets of flowers, flower bulbs, small shrubs. Other items too. Fine porcelain cups, painted and fired in white. Iron cooking pots, black as coal against the white snow. As she entered the village square, old women – brown-skinned, pink-skinned, black as night, or pale as snow – left their houses and gathered around her. To some she gave shrubs, bushes. Flower bulbs, pots, cups and kittens were given away. The cart grew emptier and emptier. Only to be refilled with cloth scraps and swatches, made from old kimonos, kente cloth, and hanboks. Cloths of green, red, gold, painted all with flowers, fruit, animals, household goods.

"Ah, so that is it?" Nohay said. "Is this how they show her their wishes?"

The fae nodded as the old woman placed the swatches in her cart and returned to the edge of the village to her little house in the middle of a great big yard.

At home she climbed three steps then opened her door. Inside, she rested while milk thistle tea brewed on the stove. Then, when the tea grew boiling hot, she poured it into a porcelain cup and walked to the back of her big large yard where she sat on a wooden table, snow all around. There, she gathered the swatches from her cart, looked at each cloth scrap intently then frowned or smiled.

As Nohay watched, he saw that the swatches were many: Blades of green or yellow grass, scenes of flowery meadows, chrysanthemums, fruit, lilies, trees. But there were other swatches as well, of man-made objects; cups and babies and houses woven expertly or exquisitely...or rudely painted on cloth. The old woman studied them all until night fell. Then the moon rose high and she chose several swatches and threw them into the air.

And suddenly, fruits and vegetables on the cloth

swatches became real. Oranges, apples, strawberries began to fall from the sky. Parsnips, beets, and radishes too, fell in a shower like ice and snow atop the snowy ground. One swatch depicted a meadow, and when thrown into the air, it scattered, split apart and suddenly seeds of many flowers fell into the cart and the woman's yard was transformed into a meadowland. Nohay watched as the old woman gathered them all and placed them inside a clay pot, along with fruits, bulbs, and plants into baskets. But for herself, she also took one of each item. One beet, one parsnip, one radish, one strawberry, one apple, one orange, one apple tree. Then she lay on the grassy meadow smiling.

"But, this is not the normal working of the world, is it?" Nohay asked the fae. "Have you not taught me about the workings of gardens? That human men dig and toil and plant and reap? Why have you shown me what is not true?"

"But it is true," the fae answered him.

The next morning at early dark dawn the old woman traveled again to the village center.

"This is hard work," Nohay said.

"But this is how the woman makes her living," Prince Hark answered.

Again, the old woman gave the village women the fruit of her hard labor. Again, the women gave her swatches. This time some swatches depicted farmhouses, farms, farm animals. Other wishes as well, as a young barren woman gave the old woman a swatch depicting a little baby. But all the while there were villagers who did not seek the old woman's help.

When the old woman returned home, the swatches were once again transformed. This time, farmhouses, and cows, goats, fell from the sky. The farmhouse fell as brick and mortar, the cows as baby calves, the goats as fluffy baaing sheep. Outside in her back yard, the old woman perused the swatches given to her. One piece had gold coins on it. She burned that. The other rejected swatches she threw into the air above her head. They disappeared into the night. As for those swatches she liked, a cat, a citre, a flute, and a little baby floated down from the sky. The woman retrieved the baby from the sky and placed him in a little basket/cradle. She put the cat in her arms and lay under the night sky.

The next morning, she pulled her cart of bricks, mortar, calves, and goats into the village. The baby she held in her arms. The barren woman approached the old woman despairing, not seeing the child for it was visible only to the old woman, Nohay, and the fae. The swatch woman put the invisible baby inside the woman's belly and said to the barren woman, "Believe."

Then she returned to her home. With his telescope, Nohay caught glimpses of the women who had received their gifts. An old woman in her home watched a kitten chase mice near her stove. The barren woman told her husband to create a baby cradle. Another woman gave her son the flute and the child joyfully retreated to the family garden to play it.

Over and over the daily trips were repeated and Nohay watched the village as it changed, thatched roofs turned into large beautiful farms.

"I have learned much," Nohay said.

"What have you learned?"

"That the old are powerful," he said. "But only a few can see their power. For although the village is full of people, only a few seek the old woman's help."

"She will quit this place soon," the fae said. "For she is no longer needed here. And perhaps she is no longer needed in the world."

The next day, a smiling beautiful young man arrived with the village women. Whether he was fae or not, Nohay could not tell. He watched in silence as the man gave the old woman a transparent cloth. Intrigued, she took it and studied the boy's youthful face. Meanwhile, a frown appeared on the faces of one of the women who had to walk away empty-handed.

The old woman gathered the swatches given to her, then looked back at the smiling young man with a look of bewilderment. When she returned to her home, she threw the cloth into the air. Slowly nothingness unfolded and enveloped her. Slowly she vanished into it leaving all the swatches the women had given her.

"Was that the old woman's dream?" the fae asked. "And what did she give to gain it?"

"I will try to understand this," Nohay answered.

"Of the gifts the Gracious Lord gave you, which will you choose to perfect?"

"The gifts? The two gifts of music and painting, do you mean?" Nohay asked.

"Are those the only gifts he gave you?" the fae asked.

"I think so," Nohay answered. "But tell me, when will you teach me about our Gracious Lord? The captain, my father, has told me to ask you."

"Does he trust me to teach you?" the fae asked.

"He has said that there are a people whose view of God is only of His majesty, His meticulous control, His Power, His sovereignty. But for us, God's basic essence is Love."

"Has he told you all that?" the fae asked, laughing. "Perhaps I have already told you about this God of love."

"Have you?" Nohay asked.

"I have."

Nohay sat inside the mechanical dragon watching the world beneath him. Strangely, he found himself loving all that his eyes saw. Human, mer, and fae. The rich and the poor. The pale-skinned and the dark. Male and female. Adults, children, the aged. Sick, healthy, or lame.

"And what is the gift you will use most from our Lord?" Prince Hark asked.

"I will love and honor all as I love and honor myself, and as I love and honor our Lord," Nohay answered. "For has the Good Lord of Light not made me and all creatures to be as an excellent machine as this dragon of yours. And am I not an Instrument of God to show His love to all?"

"Indeed," the fae answered, "you have learned much. And will you be strong enough to commit to this love?"

"Perhaps I would not have been strong if I had not met you, Prince Hark. But the things I have seen! The hearts I have seen!"

FOOL'S ERRAND

Gerald L. Coleman

The morning heat might have been oppressive and stifling, were it not for the cool breeze blowing in off the sea. The city of Alhamara hugged the coastline like a small child clutching her mother's leg, at the very northernmost tip of Senegal. It was actually a kind of cape, sticking out into the ocean just south of the Western Sahara. The French held sway in Senegal. The Europeans were carving up the continent like it was a loaf of bread. So, though Alhamara sat on the western coast of Africa, it was as much a French city as an African one. The city smelled of spice, molasses, and saltwater. It was early, so the sweet smell of freshly, baked bread filled his nose. His stomach growled. Nothing made him hungrier, faster, than the smell of recently, baked bread.

While it was still early, the streets of Alhamara were not deserted. Hannibal passed merchants on their way, presumably, to the docks. Most were overweight Frenchmen dressed like peacocks. Brightly-colored silk strained at the seams while the sweaty merchants huffed and puffed down the street. Some had their hands full of rolled pieces of parchment, while others were busy fussing at bowing servants. Hannibal sucked his teeth at the sight. He despised men like that. A tall, pale, chubby fellow, with a double-chin, in a ridiculously oversized, black hat with a red plume, caught his eye. He wore a black, wool coat and tunic with a red, silk shirt. White stockings ended in black, leather shoes, with a large, silver buckle. The man looked Hannibal directly in the face as he approached. He had been berating a young woman who was carrying several packages, while, simultaneously, trying to duck her head. Hannibal must have been scowling because the man swallowed hard and, immediately, crossed to the other side of the street. The oaf walked on in silence, at least until Hannibal was out of earshot. He sucked at his teeth one more time and tried to put it out of his mind. Rounding the corner, of the cobblestoned street, Hannibal passed a bakery, cheese shop, and wine merchant before reaching his destination. With a slight smile, replacing the scowl he had been wearing on his face, he ducked into *La Course de Fou*. It was time for breakfast.

Ebrima ran a nice, clean establishment. The Mandinka was of average height and several shades darker than Hannibal. There was an easy smile on his face, which showed nearly all of his bright, white teeth, as Hannibal stepped through the open doorway. The tavern Keep dressed like a Frenchman. His shirt was bright green beneath a white apron. He nodded to Hannibal from behind the dark-stained, wooden bar.

Hannibal found an empty table in the back, where he could sit with his back against the wall. Lowering himself into the padded chair, he removed his wide-brimmed, gray, felt hat, placing it gently on the table. He turned it so the purple plume, sticking out from the wide band, pointed away from him. The hat's buckle, decorating the front of the silk, gray band, gleamed as it caught a stray ray of light from the open windows. Without thought, he adjusted the matching set of wheel-lock pistols, stuck in the sash at his waist. Leaning back in the chair, he pulled up on the large, rectangular, buckle of his leather belt. It made the hilt of his slightly-curved saber cant forward a bit on his left hip. With a sigh, Hannibal lifted his leg, and placed a booted-foot in the chair to his left.

It did not take long for a serving maid to appear at his table. She was an attractive, brown-eyed girl named Nyima. Nyima was also dressed in the French style. A short-sleeved, tight-fitted, white blouse, which tied up the front, was tucked into a long, brown, pleated skirt. The young woman did, however, have very non-French, shell-covered, leather bracelets around her wrists. She smelled of frankincense. After telling Hannibal her name was Nyima, she took his breakfast request. With a curtsey, fit for a European court, Nyima flashed him a smile before heading to the kitchen. It was not long before Hannibal was sipping coffee out of a small, porcelain cup. It was a strong Ethiopian brew, to which he added a bit of sugar. Soon, breakfast followed. Nyima brought him a plate with a square of sharp, yellow cheese, a thick slice of dark bread, and a small bowl of hot oats with honey. It was simple fare, but it was prepared well. The oats were not too thin, and the bread was fresh.

The tavern was only half-full, but Hannibal glanced around the main room while he ate. The windows were open so there was plenty of light and fresh air blowing in. The tables were sturdy and spaced nicely. There were paintings on the walls. Several young women cleaning and waited on the tables. And while the mood was neither raucous or unruly, a large, brooding fellow sat near the door. It was the opposite of a lot of the places Hannibal visited. Taverns were usually darkly-lit, cramped, smelly affairs. But while Ebrima may have taken on European airs in his dress, he had not adopted the tendency to neglect his place of business in order to extract every ounce of coin from it. La Course de Fou was well-kept. Even the serving maids seemed happy.

Nyima appeared out of nowhere to refill his cup with coffee. He returned her smile as she turned to leave. While he sipped the strong, sweet brew, he took note of the other patrons. Alhamara was a port city, so it was no surprise that the clientele was diverse. Hannibal spotted two French sailors, three Senegalese men who might have been from the countryside, and a few merchants. Everyone seemed busy with their own discussions. He noticed smoked fish, olives, and wine, bread and cheese with mead, as well as plates of soft, boiled eggs with bread and tea.

Hannibal finished his own breakfast. He did not

have to wait for more than a few moments before Nyima was there to whisk away his dirty plate and pour him more coffee. As he brought the delicate, silver-wrapped cup to his lips for a sip of the freshly-poured brew, a young couple in traditional Berber robes entered the tavern. The woman was on the small side, but she moved with an air of authority. The young man was a little bit taller. He wore a large, red kaftan, covered in gold brocade, over a blue shirt with matching, billowy pants. His soft, red shoes curled sharply at the toe. A red and gold head wrap was wound around his forehead, covering his head, down to his neck. The young woman was dressed just as colorfully. Her shirt and long skirt, were blue with gold brocade covering it in intricate designs. She wore a very short jacket with long sleeves. Gold brocade covered the sleeves, from wrist to elbow, and then picked up again at the shoulder. Her black hair hung down her back with a headdress, made of golden chain with tiny coins hanging, at equal lengths, across her forehead. Her wrists and fingers were decorated with gold bracelets and rings. Their complexion was somewhere between the very dark-brown of Ebrima, and the light-brown of Hannibal's own.

The new arrivals stood in the doorway while they scanned the interior of the tavern. After glancing over the tables, they found an empty one in the corner. Hannibal watched as one of the serving maids made her way to the table. The young couple looked over their coin and then spoke briefly with the maid. She smiled and nodded before heading for the kitchen. Hannibal turned his own attention back to his cup. As he turned the cup up to empty it, he noticed a small group of rough looking men enter the tavern. They took one look around before their gaze landed on the young couple. They smiled among themselves. Hannibal already knew what was coming.

Placing his hat on his head, Hannibal rose quietly from his chair. He moved calmly toward a spot between the young couple and oncoming group of what looked like sailors fresh off their boat. Hannibal was not sure why the young couple had gotten their attention, but they did. Maybe it was her jewelry. Maybe it was the fact that they were clearly new in town. Whatever the reason, these louts had decided to do something about it.

They were ahalf-dozen paces from the young couple's table when Hannibal bumped into them, spilling what was left of his coffee on the man in the lead. He threw the coffee forward as he feigned bumping into the man so that he did not get any on his own coat. Hannibal's long coat and matching tunic were made from expensive wool and he would have hated to need a cleaner after this was over, especially since purple was a difficult color to make, according to his clothier. It would be difficult to remove coffee stains without affecting the color.

One whiff told him the men were just off their ship. They smelled of rum and the need of a long overdue bath. He had seen the type often enough. So what came next was as predictable as the tide.

They all stumbled to a halt. The fellow he spilled

his coffee on, presumably their leader, looked down at his filthy shirt, as if he could tell the difference between the coffee stain and the other grime on it. It must have been white at some point, but that was a long time ago. The man was almost as tall as Hannibal. His dull, brown hair was matted. His teeth were rotting in his mouth. His clothes were frayed around the edges. When he spoke, it became clear that he was British.

A hand on a British merchant ship then, Hannibal thought. Their captain was likely a small cog in a larger merchant wheel. Had their ship's master been an independent contractor they would have been paid better.

He gave Hannibal a shove, chewing up his words as he spoke, "Alright then. What have we here? A ruddy fool, what doesn't look where he's going!?" The man took a step toward Hannibal, poking him in the chest for emphasis as he continued, "I've a right mind to teach you a lesson, blacky. Haven't I."

The man's companions, who were just as seedy looking as he was, spread out to flank Hannibal on either side. There were five of them in total. Hannibal smiled and said, "How about a bath first?"

They looked at each other, their faces turning red with anger.

Hannibal ducked under a sloppily thrown right hand. As he stood back up, he kicked the leader in the groin as hard as he could.

The man crumpled to the floor like an empty burlap sack.

Hannibal took two, full steps back, to give himself some space to maneuver. When he did, he pulled both of his wheel-lock pistols from his sash, cocking them in the process. He aimed one at the leader's head. The man was on his knees, clutching at his groin. He aimed the other at the groin of the nearest man to his left.

The men all froze in place, rusty sabers half-drawn. Hannibal had seen only one flintlock pistol. It was still tucked behind the belt at the leader's waist. The rabble stood there, slack-jawed, with wide eyes trying to look at their leader and Hannibal at the same time. No one made a sound. The sound of a blunderbuss being cocked seemed incredibly loud in the silence. Hannibal saw Ebrima, standing behind the bar, with the short barrel of the weapon aimed at the head of the man nearest to him.

Hannibal paused to let them figure out that they were in an untenable situation.

The men looked anxiously at one another.

Hannibal smiled calmly, giving each of them a good, hard look.

They were bilge rats. They were not hardened soldiers or pirates. They were the kind of men who liked to fight when they had the numbers on their side and thought they faced someone unwilling to fight back. It was likely that they saw the young Berber couple on the street and decided they were easy pickings.

Looking down at the leader, Hannibal flashed him his most wicked grin. He had a few different one-liners. He decided against using his usual *I'm crazy enough to do it* line. A little gleam in the eye always added just the right touch. Once he had their undivided attention, he said, "I haven't shot anyone in awhile. Maybe it's time. If for no other reason than to clean out my guns. What do you think?"

The leader looked around at his fellows with a quick glance, saw Ebrima with his blunderbuss, and said, "Now, we was just having some fun, weren't we? No need to loose them pistols, cap'n. No need." With one hand still on his groin, he slowly waved the other in surrender.

Hannibal let his voice go cold. "You have about as long as it takes Nyima to bring me another cup of coffee to be out of this tavern and on your way. Or we start shooting."

The leader looked up at Hannibal with raised eyebrows. Hannibal motioned toward the door with the pistol he was aiming at the man's head. Without a moment's hesitation, they turned and ran for the door, climbing over each other to get out, like crabs in a bucket. They left their leader to bring up the rear, hobbling for the door while clutching at his crotch. Hannibal watched them go before uncocking his pistols and sliding them back behind his sash. Sparing one more look toward the door, he walked slowly back to his table. Dropping his hat, where he sat it before, he lowered himself back into his seat. Nyima was there, even as he was sitting, with another cup of coffee and an even brighter smile. He smiled right back at her. He barely had time to take a sip before the young couple approached his table. They both bowed their heads, but only the young man spoke.

"My thanks, good sir. We are in your debt. We made the mistake of taking passage on their ship. They harassed my sister, Massinissa, for much of the trip. We thought we were finally through with them when we made port, but they must have followed us from the docks."

The young woman's voice sounded like music. It was light, soft, and lilting, when she said, "Thank you, good sir. Thank you."

Hannibal smiled at them both and said, "No thanks is needed. I have seen their kind often enough. It was my pleasure to give them a taste of their own medicine. Please, join me." He stood and motioned to the other chairs at his table. They bowed again, the woman's headdress making a soft jingling sound as she moved. It was only after they sat that she raised her head to look at him. He inclined his head and smiled. She returned his smile, revealing beautifully white teeth.

Nyima returned to ask after the two Berbers. There was a lot of bowing heads as they asked for tea. Hannibal sipped at his coffee while they talked with Nyima. When they finished he cleared his throat and said, "I am Captain Hannibal Black." The two of them nodded. The young man placed his hand over his heart and said, "As I mentioned, this is my sister Massinissa. I am Anaruz. We are blessed to make your acquaintance." Hannibal nodded. "No, the pleasure is mine. May I ask why you took passage?"

The young man's face changed. The smile slowly slipped away. It was replaced by a grim frown. "Yes, Captain. We are from Sali, in southern Morocco. The Barbary pirates began raiding farther and farther south. We thought we were safe from their slaving raids. They had never raided so far down the coast. But two days ago they attacked Sali. Our village was devastated. Many were carried off to the pirates' ship. It is our understanding that they will be taken to the Canary Islands to be sold into slavery."

The young woman's head dropped again. Anaruz stared off toward the wall, his expression blank. Hannibal spoke softly. "So, why did you come south?"

Massinissa raised her head. She had a defiant look in her eyes. "We came looking to find men who would help us retrieve our family. We drove what was left of our village's cattle to the market at the port and sold them. We have money. All we need are sailors willing to take the job."

Hannibal sat back in his chair. He had never heard of the Barbary pirates raiding so far south either. But it did not surprise him. At some point pirates discovered the slave trade and how lucrative it could be. Some of them even worked for the countries involved. Every European power was invested. He drank from his cup as he did the calculations. It was likely that their fellow villagers were already on the Canary Islands. But they might not have been put on ships bound for their final destination just yet.

Hannibal looked back across the table at the young woman. "Did you happen to hear the name of the ship, or see the colors they were flying?"

Massinissa nodded slowly. "We were hiding at the villages edge, on our way back from the fields when they attacked. We were afraid. But we forced ourselves to watch. I heard a name. I think it was their ship. It was *Whydah Galley*."

Hannibal leaned forward quickly. He nearly spilled his coffee. He gave Massinissa a hard stare. The woman did not even flinch. Absently, he thought, he was starting to like her. Hannibal said, "This is important, Massinissa. Are you sure they said, Whydah Galley?"

With her lips pressed into a hard line, the young woman returned Hannibal's level gaze, and nodded. "I am sure Captain Black. I had never heard the name before. It sounded so different that it stuck in my thoughts."

Hannibal sat up straight in his chair. Tilting back his cup, he finished his coffee. "Then we haven't any time to spare. Come with me." He stood, dropped some coin on the table for his meal, and flipped Nyima a full piece of eight on his way out with the two Berbers in tow. Nyima smiled her gratitude at him as he left. His own smile only lasted long enough for him to get several paces down the street from the tavern. Hannibal did not believe in omens. But maybe the name of the tavern should have given him pause. La Course de Fou, was French. It translated to, *Fool's Errand.*

Hannibal despised the pirates of the Barbary Coast. They did not hunt merchant ships on the open sea, for treasure. They were slavers. They raided the coast, from northern Morocco to Tripoli, for people. They raided villages, captured people, and sold them into slavery. Hannibal had become well-known for hunting *them.* He was called a pirate too. But Hannibal did not hunt merchant ships, he hunted pirate ships that turned to slaving. Hannibal, along with his crew, attacked Barbary pirate ships, freeing the captured people and plundering the ships for gold, silver, rum, salt, or whatever other treasures they invariably carried. It was a lucrative business. But the treasure was never Hannibal's true motivation. It kept his ship well-supplied and repaired, and his crew fat and happy. Hannibal's reward was seeing the people set free and the pirates made to pay.

As long as he had been hunting pirate ships there was one that eluded him. The Whydah Galley was one of the most notorious pirate ships in the entire Atlantic. She raided up and down the Barbary Coast. But Hannibal knew the name from a much older history. The crew of the Whydah was brutal. Her captain was cunning. They filled their coffers with the blood money made from shattered lives. Hannibal was itching to get his hands on them. There were wounds to repay and the crew of the Whydah Galley was going to repay it all with interest.

Hannibal turned toward the docks. Reaching into his coat, he retrieved his long-stemmed pipe. After filling it from a pouch he removed from a different pocket, he scanned the street vendors as he passed. A lovely, plump woman in a green tunic was grilling fresh fish. It smelled heavenly. Only a full stomach allowed him to resist. But he was able to prevail upon her for a lit piece of straw. Hannibal puffed away to get the tobacco in his pipe bowl burning nicely. With a flick of his wrist, he smothered the flame, leaving the piece of straw smoldering on the ground.

Alhamara was a typical city for the Senegalese coast. It sat on a rise, with its reddish-brown stone dotting the landscape of the coastline like an anthill. The stone was well-laid. It was only when you walked the streets that the anticipated brightness of the Senegal aesthetic became evident. There were arches everywhere. Building fronts were inset with colored stone arranged in squares and rectangles. A darkly-stained door was surrounded by white stone in the shape of an arch. The white stone was surrounded by a square of red, which was engulfed, in turn, by a rectangle of blue tile. A few paces farther down the street and the walls exploded in bright yellow, green, and blue tile, arranged in dozens of small, multi-colored circles. Even the streets were laid with stone tile in amazing colors and designs. It was a beautiful city. Hannibal liked it for two reasons. It was far enough south, along the coast, that it was generally safe from pirate activity. And it was clean. Alhamara was one of the cleanest cities he had ever visited. He enjoyed being able to walk down the street without smelling days-old refuse or having to weave around puddles. He certainly did not miss people heaving dirty water from second story windows. Hannibal left a trail of pipe smoke behind him on his way to the docks. He was not trying to ignore his walking companions on their trip to the docks but he needed the time to think.

Overhead, Hannibal saw arctic terns flittering about. The birds were white with black beaks and heads. They would soon be darting from the sky, into the water along the coast, catching lunch. Hannibal watched one catch an updraft of air. It went straight up with barely a flap. His mind went back to a late night, many months ago. It was on one of his earliest trips to Alhamara to resupply *the Gambit*. He and Ebrima were beginning to get to know one another. The Gambit had arrived late, so Hannibal arrived at the tavern just before closing. Ebrima was kind enough to allow him to stay, fixed him a late supper, and sat with him, drinking rum late into the night. In a moment of candor, Ebrima told him no one had supported his dream to open a tavern in the city. He was told again and again that it was a fool's errand. Ebrima grew up in a family that herded goats. While it was a good living, he had always wanted to be near the sea, in a city. He ignored the naysayers and opened his tavern. When he did, he named it *Fool's Errand*, so he would never forget. That story stuck with Hannibal. He used it to remind himself of his own purpose whenever he began to doubt himself. The search for the Whydah Galley had begun to feel like a fool's errand. Maybe, it was just that. But like Ebrima, he was going to find out for himself.

When he arrived at the docks, he could see three of his crew, at the end of one of the piers, waiting for him in the longboat. Just before stepping onto the pier, Hannibal ducked into a nearby merchant's shop. It was a sundries shop. Though they did have a lot of candles. He was only interested in using some writing materials. He left Massinissa and Anaruz on the street outside the shop. For a single, silver coin, the husband obliged him with a piece of parchment, a quill, and ink. When he finished, he picked up his companions again at the front door and continued on to the docks.

As Hannibal approached his crew, he saw that two of them were seated in the boat, with oars in their hands, while his First Mate stood on the dock watching him approach. If he knew Safiya, she also had an eye on the street behind him. Normally, pirate ships had Quartermasters serving as second in command. But Hannibal never wanted his crew to think of themselves as pirates in the traditional sense. Though they were neither a merchant ship, nor a military vessel, he still preferred the more respectable chain of command. The Gambit had a Quartermaster, but Salke was third in command, behind his First Mate Safiya.

Safiya was probably the finest sailor Hannibal had ever met. She had a sharp mind, a deadly sword hand, and, more importantly, was loyal to a fault. The woman was also a tough chess partner. She snapped-to as he approached. Pirates did not knuckle their foreheads, but she liked the show of respect for her Captain. When he nodded, she relaxed. Safiya had a beautiful, brown complexion, with matching eyes. Her hair was a long, black, curly explosion that covered her head like a giant bundle of soft wool. She was nearly as tall as Hannibal. Her white, silk shirt was buttoned to the neck. She wore a light-blue tunic, with red embroidery around the button holes, over the shirt. The tunic belted, with silver buckles on brown straps, across the chest. She wore a red, silk scarf around her neck. It matched the much larger, silk sash around her waist. The brown, leather bracers, covering her forearms, matched the spauldrons on her shoulders. Her forearms were resting easily on the butts of the set of flintlock pistols tucked into her sash. They were gifts from him, and similar to his own. The beautiful woodwork was accentuated by silver trim, covered with flowery engraving. Safiya also carried three knives and a saber, which hung from her leather belt, buckled over the red sash.

Hannibal nodded for Safiya to get in the longboat. He took a few moments to speak with the dock master. Hannibal gave him the sealed parchment and a gold coin to make sure it found its way to the right person. Janic was not above a bit of graft on the docks but he was a man of his word. The missive was safe in his hands. Hannibal crossed the docks to the longboat and motioned for Massinissa and Anaruz to hop in. His crew did not even blink an eye. After a brief conversation with Safiya, about the other two longboats he sent ashore for supplies, they were on their way out to the Gambit. She sat, at anchor, out in the bay.

The Gambit was a Man-of-war class ship. She had once served as a ship of the line in the British navy. Now, she was his ship. As the longboat approached, Hannibal puffed on his pipe and took in the view. No matter how many times he saw her from a distance it still gave him pleasure. She had three masts, each with four sails. She was fitted with seventy cannons, ranging from thirty-two pounds to twelve. There were thirty on each side, two fore, and eight aft. She could carry more, but he did not want the added weight. He led a crew of three-hundred and ten. The Gambit could carry another two hundred crew easily but Hannibal liked the added space. And so did his crew. He preferred that there was room for his crew to keep themselves freshly bathed and for them to have sufficient room to sleep. He did not like stepping over sailors as he made his way around the ship. Hannibal also liked keeping the Gambit fast.

As the longboat closed on the Gambit, Hannibal could see the crew preparing for departure. The other longboats were stowed so the supplies must have already been stored. Safiya was an exemplary First Mate. It was not long before Hannibal was stepping down onto the deck to shouts of, "Captain on deck!"

The men and women of the Gambit were all African. A handful had come with him from his posting on a previous ship. The rest of them had been liberated from pirate ships aiming to sell them into slavery. The overwhelming majority of the people Hannibal freed went home. But sometimes they chose to join the crew. Hannibal made his way past the main mast, and up the steps to the stern castle. The crew smiled at him as he passed them. Hannibal did not have a half-hungry, inebriated, barefoot crew. He kept them well-clothed, well-fed, and they could leave at anytime with a pocket full of coin. They liked having wool tunics and leather boots. But most of them stayed because they enjoyed burning slave ships to the water-line. The crew also had smiles for Anaruz and Massinissa.

Hannibal found the Quartermaster, Salke, standing amid ship. With some quick reassurances, he turned the two Berbers over to Salke with instructions to provide them with a cabin and anything they needed. Before they left, Massinissa tried to pass Hannibal a pouch full of coins. Holding up his hands, he told her it was unnecessary. They had been looking for the Whydah Galley. He thanked her for the information about the ship's whereabouts and assured her that no payment was needed. With a bow of her head, and a bright smile, Massinissa allowed Salke to lead her and her brother below deck.

The main deck was clean. Ropes were being coiled, while men and women moved about the ship with purpose. Hannibal made his way to the stern castle, just above the short deck with the ship's wheel. He leaned against the rail, puffing on his pipe, while watching his crew. Safiya came into view down below him. She was standing before the mast. As if she knew he was ready, she looked up toward the stern castle. Hannibal pulled his pipe from him mouth. Raising his voice, he bellowed, "Weigh anchor!"

Safiya turned to the crew and barked, "Weigh anchor! Prepare to get underway!"

With a practiced ease, the crew of the Gambit jumped to their stations. Within moments, the anchor was raised. The sails were lowered, and immediately billowed taut with wind. Hannibal felt the Gambit surge under his feet. In the meantime, Safiya made her way to the helm. She was standing just behind, and to the right of the helmsman. From that perch she could see most of the main deck. She was only a few feet below Hannibal as he stood on the deck of the stern castle. Hannibal said, "Set your course north, by northwest. Seven knots please. Make for the Canary Islands."

Safiya barked, "Aye, Captain! Helm, make your course north, by northwest." At her instruction the helmsman turned the wheel. Safiya took three paces to the rail of short deck and shouted down to the main deck, "Hoist the main mizzen and make for seven knots!"

Hannibal heard the responses as voices were raised to shout, "Aye!"

As he looked on, taking another draw on his pipe, the main mizzen was lowered into place and snapped full of wind. The Gambit picked up speed. Seawater sprayed into the air and his ears filled with the sound of ruffling sail and boots thumping along the wooden decks. He could not have stopped himself from smiling if he wanted. There was nothing like a stout ship and a brisk wind to sail her by.

A few more puffs on his pipe told him he was out of unburned tobacco in the bowl. Stepping to the back of the stern caste, he emptied his pipe over the rail. The water below churned with the passing of the Gambit. He could tell they were nearly at speed. In the distance, the coastline of Alhamara began to recede. While he watched, the coast thinned into a fine line on the horizon before, finally, disappearing altogether. In no time at all there was nothing to see but blue water in every direction.

A quick glance down on the main deck assured Hannibal that everything was in order. Making his way to the steps, he headed down, past the helm. When he did, he said, "Safiya, you have the helm."

With a sharp nod, his First Mate said, "Aye, aye, Captain."

Hannibal hit the main deck and took a sharp right. He opened the door that lead to the rear section, aft, beneath the stern castle. There were several cabins on either side of the hall, which ended in his quarters. He opened the door to his cabin and stepped inside. It was the biggest cabin on the ship. Along the wall, to his right, was his bed. He had relieved the captain of a pirate ship, flying the flag of Portugal, of his new Queen Anne bed. It had dome-shaped, carved head and footboards, with cabriole legs. It made him sleep like the dead. The rear wall was actually the very rear of the ship. Small, square, glass panes, inset in wood, made for a large window. In front of it was one of his prized possessions: A French writing table, made by Charles Cressent in Paris. It was a full four paces long and two wide. It was oak and pine, veneered with satiné rouge and amaranth. The mounts were gilt bronze and it had a leather top. It was one of the most beautiful pieces of furniture he had ever seen. Every now and then, when he captured a slaving ship, there were a few surprises in the cargo hold. It was, undoubtedly, headed to some wealthy man's estate. The armchair behind it was Italian, made from rosewood and kingwood, with looping armrests and blue, back and seat cushions, covered in a finely woven thread. Against the wall to his left was blue and gold Turkish bed he used as a couch. The floor was covered in Persian rugs.

Hannibal closed the door behind him and walked over to his writing table. It was covered in maps and his plotting tools. He sat. Taking a deep breath, he reached for the crystal decanter on the right side of his desk. It was filled with a lovely Armagnac. He relieved the captain of the *Salty Dog* of a dozen hidden bottles. It would have cost Hannibal a heavy bag of gold coin to buy such a supply. If Dandy Rand Doggert had not been busy swimming for his life, he might have cursed Hannibal for raiding his cabin. He poured a glass of the amber liquid into a heavy matching crystal glass. It went down smooth. A warm glow began to spread across his midsection. With a smile, Hannibal sorted through his maps until he found what he was looking for. *The Canary Islands*. After another sip of the brandy, he set about looking for an edge.

Hannibal twirled his steel divider by one of its legs. Someone knocked on his cabin door. He leaned back in his chair as he said, "Enter." The door opened and

Safiya stepped into his cabin. After closing the door behind her, she stepped to attention. He smiled at his First Mate and said, "As you were, Safiya. How are our guests?"

Safiya relaxed. She walked over to his writing table. Leaning over the maps, she glanced at what he was studying. Her voice as calm as the sea without wind or wave. "They are doing well Captain. The young man keeps to himself, but he's pleasant enough when you speak to him. The young woman is as curious as a school of dolphins. She asks twenty questions in as many minutes. But the crew doesn't mind."

Hannibal took a sip of his brandy and nodded. Good, his crew was always well-behaved. "What's our course and speed?"

Safiya nodded. "Aye, Captain. We are maintaining our heading: North by Northwest. And we are continuing at seven knots. I just checked our speed before coming down. The wind is good, no storms on the horizon, and no ships sighted."

Setting down his divider, Hannibal nodded again, and said, "Very well. Now lets talk about what's to come."

Safiya listened intently as Hannibal explained his plan. She pointed to the map a few times, and unsurprisingly asked some incredibly good questions about her captain's plan. But once they were finished, Hannibal was sure she was clear about what needed to be done. She stepped back from his writing table and asked, "Will that be all Cap'n?"

"Yes, Safiya. That will be all. Continue on our present course until its time for our first course correction and make for twelve knots."

His First Mate turned her lips into an excited grin. "Aye, Cap'n. This is going to be fun."

Safiya's smile was infectious. When she left his cabin, he realized he was smiling too. He poured another finger of brandy into his glass and stood. Turning from his writing desk, he leaned on the window in the back wall and stared at the wake of his ship. It did not take long before he heard the sound of pounding boots on the deck. As Hannibal watched the foaming water in the wake of the Gambit, he could feel her pick up speed. The last of the sail was certainly lowered and full of wind. Things were going to get dangerous. But Hannibal had a crew and a ship he trusted. He hoped his plan worked.

Several hours passed with Hannibal in his cabin going over his calculations. As the sun dipped low in the west, he made his way topside. Climbing the steps to the stern castle, he heard Safiya bellow, "Captain on deck!"

The evening air was brisk, but invigorating. The sound of the sea, as the hull cut through the water, made Hannibal feel alive. He leaned against the forward railing, watching his crew keep the Gambit at speed. He took a moment to fill his long-stemmed pipe. Safiya appeared at his side with a long, lit, piece of straw. She covered the pipe with her hand, while holding the flame just over the top of the bowl. Hannibal puffed several times until the tobacco was glowing bright red. Safiya walked to the port side of the ship and tossed the burning straw overboard. Hannibal reached into the pocket of his tunic. The gold chain, he tugged on, slid from his pocket with his watch on its end. The pocket watch had a gold back, impressed with intricate circles. The face revealed all the gold-plated inner-works, which clock makers called complications. One glance at the watch face told him it was time. He gave his First Mate a single nod. It was going to be a long night.

####

The Gambit sat about five hundred yards off the shore of *Lanzarote*. The Canary Islands were not actually a single entity. While there were basically two different provinces, Las Palmas for the western islands, and Tenerife for the eastern, each island had its own *Cabildo Insular,* or Island Council. That also meant that each had its own economy and concerns. The major islands made wine and sugar cane, trading with England and the Americas. But the poorer islands, like Lanzarote, at the northernmost tip of the islands, were left out of that lucrative trade. Sadly, they decided to participate in the slave trade. So Hannibal brought the Gambit up past the most western point of the islands, past Valverde and around the tip of La Palma. But he kept her well out at sea. The Gambit's sails were black, for just such an occasion. They were running dark and quiet. Earlier in the day he plotted their course for maximum coverage of the islands. They moved the Gambit, using dead reckoning, from point to point, searching for any sign of the Whydah Galley. Hannibal had his crew lining the rails of the main deck, with spyglasses in hand, scanning the sea.

They wove their way around Gomera, up the coastline from the south, and around Tenerife. They quietly sailed south past Canaria, before swinging east. They took a wide birth around Fuerteventura. Staying closer to the African coast, than the eastern shoreline of Puerto Del Rosario and Arrecife, the finally ended up north of Lanzarote, just before dawn. Peering south, they found her. The Whydah Galley sat at anchor, just off the shore of Lanzarote. Hannibal set the Gambit, with her port side to the Whydah, guns loaded, upwind from where the pirate ship was anchored.

As the sun came up in the east, one of the mates, a charming, young man named Issa, climbed up the stairs to the stern castle. He brought Hannibal coffee, in a porcelain cup and saucer. The set was white, with blue and green flowers winding their way around the exterior. He thanked the young man. Walking to the rail, on the port side, Hannibal took a sip of the coffee and gazed across the calm, morning sea at the Whydah.

The Whydah Galley was a Carrack class ship. She had four masts and was built to cross an ocean. She was a sturdy ship. Her captain was notorious. Captain Randall *Jolly* Redhook refitted his ship to carry both cargo and cannon. The man gave up some space for slaves in order to better arm his ship. It likely worked because the Whydah did not make the trip to the Americas, but spent her time along the Barbary Coast. Hannibal knew what that meant. Redhook made more runs to make up for smaller numbers in the hold of his ship. That was all about to change.

Hannibal would rather have just sunk the Whydah and headed for open sea. But there might have been captured people in the hold. He had one other reason, which he kept to himself. Any other crew would have been loudly questioning his plan, maybe even on the verge of mutiny. But the crew of the Gambit trusted her captain. Hannibal took one final sip of his coffee, and then he said, "Safiya, give her a single shot across her bow. Let's get her attention."

Safiya said, "Aye, Cap'n." She turned and walked to the rail, facing the main deck. Looking over the rail, she barked, "One shot, across the bow, Salke!"

Hannibal could not see the Quartermaster from where he was standing by the port rail, in the stern castle. But he heard the man relay his command. As Hannibal set the cup back down on its saucer, a loud *boom*, echoed from beneath him. Canon smoke drifted up, dissipating in the breeze. Over near the Whydah Galley, he watched the sea erupt in a violent explosion of water. The cannon passed over their main deck before splashing into the sea. Hannibal smiled as the deck of the Whydah flailed to life with activity. He waited a few heartbeats before telling Safiya, "Send the message."

Without hesitating, Safiya said, "Aye, Cap'n."

His First Mate relayed his order and soon, a female crewman was standing on the foredeck, signaling the Whydah with a flag in each hand. The message said they were to surrender, or be sunk. Hannibal was pretty sure he knew what the answer would be, but he wanted to try. He watched as the crew of the Whydah scrambled to get her anchor up and her sails lowered. When the Whydah lurched forward, with her sails filling with wind, Hannibal shouted, "Raise the colors!"

Safiya echoed him, "Raise the colors!"

The flag of the Gambit shot up the line from the deck, unfurling overhead. When it caught the wind, it snapped taut. Hannibal did not fly the Jolly Roger. He left that to traditional pirates. The Gambit flew a skull, but one made of shards of various colors, on a field of red. Just below the skull was a black set of shackles, broken in the middle.

Hannibal watched as the Whydah tried to gain speed. She was downwind. Her captain knew they were at a serious disadvantage. Hannibal barked, "Port-side guns, fire at will. Hard to port! Lay in a pursuit course. Bring us up on her rear." Redhook hoped he could get to speed in time to be out of the range of Hannibal's guns. He shook his head as the Gambit's port guns blasted away. The Whydah's main deck exploded from its fore section. It was not long before the Gambit was in pursuit. The Whydah, rather than heading south, along the coastline, made for what appeared to be open sea. But Hannibal knew that she was headed straight for Tenerife.

Hannibal should have laid down raking fire. Generally, ships were the most vulnerable to attack from the rear. Just like the Gambit, they had large windows in the officer's quarters. Raking fire would run through the ship, length-wise, from stern to bow, causing maximum damage. But Hannibal was still trying to damage the Whydah as little as possible. Cannon fire blasted into the sea to the port side of the Gambit. The Whydah was firing her aft cannons. There were only two cannons in the Gambit's fore, while Redhook likely had as many as six in the Whydah's aft. Hannibal would have to rely on the second part of his plan. He shouted down to Safiya, who was standing next to the helm, "Keep us outside the range of his cannons!"

Safiya nodded. The Gambit slowed as Safiya gave the helmsman orders. After several more volleys from their aft cannons fell short of the Gambit, the Whydah stopped firing on them. Redhook focused his efforts on running.

Hannibal sent for another cup of coffee while he watched the Whydah tack for wind. She was fast. They were making about ten knots. The Gambit could still overtake her, but Redhook would not know that. Man-of-wars, fully outfitted, generally rated for eight to nine knots. The captain of the Whydah would have no idea that the Gambit was only outfitted with half the guns and crew, and that she was sailed by a captain who knew how to get two or three extra knots out of his ship. Hannibal let her run. It was a waiting game now. Redhook knew that there would be other slaver ships in the Canary Islands, or at least a few Spanish or

British Galleons he could call on for assistance. He was running his Carrack full out trying to reach the waters near Tenerife. Even Hannibal knew there were likely other ships off shore. And even if there were not. There would certainly be cannons along the shore.

Issa returned with another cup of coffee and a nod. Hannibal saw the young man, out of the corner of his eye, look at him just before he left the stern castle. He was measuring his captain. Hannibal smiled to himself. If all went according to plan he was going to have a story to tell. It took another twenty minutes, but the call came down from the crow's nest. "Sail ho!"

Hannibal looked in the direction the crewman in the crow's nest was pointing. Sure enough, there was ship making for the Whydah. Hannibal barked for a mate from the main deck. A young woman came running up the steps to the stern castle. He handed her his cup and saucer before taking her spyglass. Raising it to his eye, he honed in on the approaching ship. She was already flying her colors. It was a skeleton, dancing on a field of black. Hannibal knew that mark. It was the Salamander, captained by Percy *three-fingered* Vane. It did not take long before the Whydah began tacking, to come about. Redhook had found his support. He was turning to fight.

Hannibal put down the spyglass, and pulled out his pocket watch. Closing his eyes, he ran through his calculations. He could feel the eyes of his First Mate on him. It was a sure bet that nearby members of the crew were watching him too. A small part of his mind knew what they would see. Sometimes, Hannibal moved his lips while he ran the numbers. He could hear the ticking of the pocket watch in his hand. He could smell the salt water of the sea, as spray leaped into the air. He could hear the snapping of black canvas as the sails of the Gambit played in the wind. But his focus was on the calculations. Wind speed, current, longitude and latitude, all ran through his head. In the back of his mind he knew that the Whydah and Salamander would be in range of the Gambit in moments. *Wait*, he thought. *Just wait.*

Hannibal's eyes snapped open. "Now!" he shouted down to Safiya. In quick succession, the Gambit fired seven shots, then three shots, then seven more.

He barked, "Come about! Hard to port!"

Rigging strained and canvas snapped, as the helmsman made the course-correction. Crewmen scrambled on the deck and in the rigging, adjusting the sail. The Gambit leaned into the turn. Hannibal held onto the rail and watched her turn. The sea exploded with cannon shot where the Gambit had just been. As she started to straighten, Hannibal roared, "Starboard cannons, fire!"

The starboard side of the Gambit exploded and the heavy cannon volleyed. The Salamander took a direct hit on its fore deck. The Whydah was hit on her starboard side. Hannibal bellowed into the wind, "Make for twelve knots!"

In moments, as cannon fire hit the water all around them, the black sails of the Gambit surged with wind. The cat had become the mouse as the

Salamander and Whydah Galley, chased the Gambit. He had the aft cannons fire without stopping. And then, as the numbers popped up in his head again, Hannibal lifted the spyglass and began laughing. Given their bearing, he knew he was seeing Las Palmas ahead, on the horizon.

As soon as he saw land, he turned the spyglass south. And there they were. "Come about!" he shouted. "Come about!" The helmsman hesitated. Safiya pushed the man aside and spun the wheel, yelling up toward the rigging as she did. The Gambit leaned into the sea again. Once she was fully turned and heading directly for the Whydah and Salamander, Hannibal had another message sent. When the crewman, leaning at the fore of the ship, finished waving the flags, the cannon fire stopped. Hannibal slowed the Gambit to just a few knots as the Wanderer, Flying Dragon, and Fortune came alongside. When he decided to go after the Whydah, he sent messages to their captains telling them to meet him at dawn off the coast of Las Palmas. He sent three invitations in the hope that at least one of them would show. Hannibal was gratified to see all three. It should not have surprised him. The Whydah Galley was the most notorious ship in the Atlantic.

The Salamander and Whydah surrendered without a further fight. It was only when Hannibal boarded the Whydah that he saw that her crew had mutinied. Captain Randall Redhook was trussed up like a pig for slaughter, before the mast. In short order, Hannibal freed the one hundred men and women who were chained in the hull. His crew looted the Whydah's hold. They pulled the ship close enough to the shore of

Las Palmas to give the crew a chance to swim ashore. Hannibal had Redhook placed in his brig, below decks on the Gambit and set the Whydah on fire.

While the crews of the Wanderer, Flying Dragon, and Fortune raided the Salamander, Hannibal stood on the stern castle of the Gambit and watched the Whydah burn to the waterline. He allowed Safiya to oversee the dividing of the spoils from the Whydah's hold.

The only thing Hannibal wanted from the ship, he retrieved while its crew was being thrown overboard.

Slowly, with trembling fingers, Hannibal flipped through the pages of the Whydah's ledger until he came to the name of his father.

BLOODLINE

DK Gaston

West Africa

Equafo Kingdom

Year 1694

Moon barely made it out of the Dutch fort alive with his prize, an allegedly mystic bone knife. He would been tracking its owner, a shaman named Cadoc, for months and finally caught up with the sorcerer there. Unfortunately the Dutch West India Company and the British Royal African Company were in the midst of a war over trade rights. From what he could gather, Cadoc had gone there to take advantage of the escalating tide of death to build an army of the dead.

In the many years since escaping slavery from the Colonies, he had taken refuge with buccaneers and eventually became a member of their crew. Moon had seen many strange, unexplainable things as he travelled the world, going from one perilous adventure to the next, seeking fortune and glory. But he had yet to see the dead rise and found the notion laughable.

Still, even he could not deny there was power that surrounded the shaman. When an opportunity arose for him to collect the bone knife without a face-to-face confrontation with Cadoc, he had taken full advantage of it. While the sorcerer was in some type of deep trance, Moon had acquired the treasure and slipped away into the night.

He had been negotiating the land, avoiding man and beast, gaining distance from the Dutch fort and the battle for several days to meet up with other members of his crew. Yet, he could not shake the odd feeling that he was being pursued. His suspicions became reality when he caught movement in the corner of his eye.

Moon made himself small, positioning his body into a crouch, wishing the grass was taller to hide his six foot frame behind. His breath, heavy with exhaustion and the pounding of his heart, filled his ears as he waited for more signs of movement. Had he journied all those hard miles only to be tracked and caught when he was so near to his waiting shipmates?

He would not allow himself the luxury of panic. Closing his eyes, he held his breath and took in measured gulps of air. His heartbeat slowed. Listening to his surroundings, Moon should have at least heard swarming insects and the rustling swish of tall grass, but there was nothing at all. It was as if the night had drawn all sound away into a void.

Opening his eyes, he spied the signs of morning and was grateful that dawn drew close. Though the moonlight provided enough illumination for him to trek through the tangle of grass and trees without a torch, it was not enough to see past a few feet ahead of him. As the sun slowly emerged over the horizon, Moon strained to find the source of his anxiety. It was the stench of rotting flesh he noticed first, followed by the low moan within a spitting distance of his hiding place.

Moon searched through the thick foliage and caught the outline of a hunched beast of some kind. Its huge silhouette undeniably that of a two-legged beast, perhaps an ape. He had heard rumors about wild simians plaguing humans who had come too close to their habitats, but he found no evidence of being in ape territory.

He doubted he could outrun the beast and even if he could, Moon recalled apes typically moved about in a group, or shrewdness, as it was commonly called. With one ape, he had a chance of escape, but with more, the odds would weigh heavily against him. The only thing in his favor was the fact the breeze blew downwind of the animals, masking Moon's odor. He slowly moved away, trying to put some distance between them.

Slow, measured steps became Moon's world. He avoided sound as best he could. The task seemed impossible because his heart pounded too loudly inside his chest and he feared he would be heard. His clothes clung to him and his skin was damp, more from nervousness than from the stifling African heat.

The rotting odor gradually diminished as he withdrew.

Though he could no longer see the hunched silhouette of the predator, Moon had the sense his every movement was being tracked.

The sharp crack of a twig to his right confirmed his fears. The time for hiding was over.

Moon scampered through thick prickly undergrowth. Thorns as sharp as knives scratched his bare cheeks and forehead and eventually found his skin through his clothing. The rising sun made it easier for him to avoid running into obstacles. Unfortunately, barring a nocturnal beast with inadequate daylight sight, it would aid the predator that hunted him with its relentless tracking.

Several times it closed on him and pulled away. Ape or not, whatever animal it may be was much faster than Moon and seemed to be toying with him, enjoying the thrill of the chase. He found the notion strange since most animals hunted for food or protection, not sport – a particular proclivity of man.

Moon spotted tall trees ahead and considered for a moment about scaling one. Most two-legged creatures indigenous to the region would have the ability to effortlessly climb a tree and would be on top of him before he made it a foot off the ground.

Perhaps I don't need to climb the tree, he thought.

He drew his only weapon, the bone knife, from its sheath.

Days ago, Moon had to abandon his normal accompaniment of weapons, which included a sword, pistols and daggers. The only way into the fort was to pretend to be a local laborer. The self-important Europeans would not notice another black man in their midst, but would, without delay, become conscious of one possessing small arms.

He dodged behind a wide tree and flattened his back against it, clutching the strange knife tightly in his hand. It pulsed gently with a uniformed rhythm as if a heart thudded beneath the bone exterior and it seemed to generate an unnatural warmth.

Is the damned thing alive? he thought.

He fought the instinct to drop the knife on the ground, though every fiber of his being beseeched him to do so. The smell of death suddenly intruded on his internal struggle. Moon willed himself to peer around his hiding place. In the dawning glow of the sun he could clearly see what had been stalking him.

Something that was once a large man of more than six feet came hulking gracelessly out of the tall grass. It stood slumped as if fighting to keep its balance. The tattered remains of its clothing was that typically worn by a man of Dutch heritage. The fabric hung ill-fittingly on its physique. All color had been drained from its skin, giving the thing a pale hue that matched the hilt of the bone knife. Its eyes were milky white and dull – its ominous gaze stared directly at him.

Grabbed by a strength born of horror and desperation, Moon struggled to scale the tree, his feet barely finding purchase as he climbed and he had to rely mostly on the muscles of his arms. The creature pounded toward him. Moon doubled his efforts, using the bone knife as a makeshift anchor.

If the crew saw me now, they'd laugh and taunt me 'til my dying day, he ruminated.

The extremities of a putrefied hand that looked more like talons than human fingers swept past Moon's foot, catching his boots. He heaved himself up a thick limb, narrowly being pulled back down. The boot was pried loose and plummeted to the ground. He stared down to see the creature staring back up with that milky gaze, its fingers opened and closed reflexively like it was waiting for Moon to fall into its waiting outstretched arms.

"You've have to wait until hell freezes monster," Moon yelled.

The creature lowered its arms and began circling the tree. Whatever tendrils of humanity it had left in its brain obviously figured out its prey had no place to go. All it had to do was wait him out.

Becoming the creature's quarry was a prospect that Moon did not care to face. He needed weapons that he could use without being forced to toss his single knife at it. He was sure his aim was good enough to place the blade between the thing's eyes, but he could not be sure it would destroy it.

His answer surrounded him – the tree.

Clopping at a nearby limb with the knife, he began fashioning it into a spear. The branch broke off easily. He used the sharp edges of the blade to cut away at one end of the wood. There were enough branches he could reach that he felt confident he had more than enough to finish off the creature. Movement from above caught his attention.

A cuckoo-hawk far larger than Moon had ever seen was perched on a high branch. The raptor's keen eyes had settled on him. The bird's gaze ranged freely up and down Moon's body as if studying him. Then the hawk turned its awareness to what Moon was doing, spying the limb being forged into a spear. Moon saw fury and something else in those eyes that disturbed him more than the creature below him, intellect.

A sound emitted from the animal that was not the characteristic kaw or shriek or even cluck one would expect a bird to make. No, it was human. "Kill the thief," the cuckoo-hawk cried out. "Take back what is mine!"

"By the gods," Moon gasped. In his life he had seen many strange wonders, but nothing at the magnitude of which he faced now.

Clawing and scratching came from beneath him,

tugging him out of his stupor. Below, the creature had leaped onto one side of the tree and dug its talon-like fingers deep into the bark. It climbed skyward inches at a time. He turned back to the bird. "You somehow control this monster don't you? What are you?"

"I am Cadoc," the hawk answered. "And you have my knife. You will give it back to me!"

"The witchdoctor?" Moon whispered. He stared at the hand holding the stolen bone knife and back down at the unearthly creature scaling the tree. "It's true then. You can bring the dead back to life."

The value of the blade was far higher than the price he agreed upon to steal it. Assuming he survived to stand before the man who had hired him, Moon would make sure the recompense was quadrupled for his troubles.

The dead thing's hand reached up and around the thick branch Moon had been perched searching for purchase. Its mouth spread open far more than could be humanly possible, as if it planned to swallow him whole. Hefting the spear up over one shoulder, he hoped the tip was sharp enough to break skin. The foul stench of death filled his nostrils, making him nauseous and he nearly lost his sense of balance. In a flash, he was the escaped slave again, whom his former Virginian master had simply named Moon. At the outset of his days at sea on the pirate ship, he suffered from an overwhelming wave of seasickness. He had learned to deal with his queasiness then as he would now.

Moon forced his mind back to the present. "Get away from me," he shouted defiantly.

Steadying himself, he thrust the spear. The point entered the creature's open mouth and exited through the back of its head. Its hand fell away from the tree limb and gave itself, unwillingly, to gravity.

The living corpse struck the ground with a sickening slap. It flailed this way and that but appeared unable to rise up.

"The spear," he said, realizing the tip had lodged itself into the dirt, in effect trapping the dead creature where it had fallen. It was now or never for Moon to make his escape. He started down the tree.

"No," came an inhuman cry from above.

Moon glanced up in time to see Cadoc fly up into the air. He took a moment to digest the witch doctor's power. Not only could he bring the dead back to life, he could change himself into a bird. He thought aloud, "What else can you become? And what other dark magic do you possess?"

Scrambling down the tree, he landed softly behind the thrashing creature and stared at it in amazement. There was a word he once heard from one of his fellow pirates who came from the Congo, *nzambi* – it was used to describe dead men who continued to walk the Earth. Moon thought it was only the fabricated tale of a drunkard. Obviously he had been wrong – nzambi, were very real, brought about by a witchdoctor who could change himself into a giant bird.

Moon recovered his pilfered boot and rapidly slipped it on. He decided not to linger, but he refused to run without first ensuring the nzambi could not free itself from the spear and come after him. Taking the bone knife, Moon knelt beside the flailing dead creature and began sawing off its head.

Moon ran for miles until he came to a fresh water pond. Before embarking on his venture to the Dutch fort, he made sure he knew the locations of drinkable water along the trail. Fish swam in the pond and he wanted to take the time to catch and cook one. But after catching his breath and rejuvenating his body with liquid, he realized just how lucky he was to still be alive and did not want to push his luck any further.

He had just downed a handful of water when he heard movement and voices headed in his direction. The language was familiar to Moon.

"The Dutch," he cursed under his breath.

Both the Dutch and the British had established camps throughout the Equafo Kingdom. Obviously, one of these sites was stationed close to the pond and the Europeans came to collect water as he had.

Moon filled his leather canteen and ran off in the opposite direction of the voices. In his haste to avoid detection, he was not as careful as he should have been when he stepped into some high grass. Losing his footing, Moon tumbled and slipped over the edge over the lip of a drop. Against his will, in an unflattering sequence of somersaults and skids, he rode down a muddy, steep incline, smashing through thick grass and shrubberies.

"By the gods," he yelled once he burst through the last of the undergrowth.

At the end of the slope was a severe overhang. He desperately tried to take hold of shrubs or vines to slow his descent but everything broke away in his hands. He rolled off the crest of a vertical drop and fell. His arms wind-milled and his legs paddled. He felt as if his stomach would explode through his throat. Before he could let loose a scream he splashed down, face first, into water. Its coldness shocked his exhausted senses into full awareness.

I couldn't have reached the shore yet, he thought, *I still have miles to cover.*

Moon swam up to the surface and stared at his surroundings. He appeared to have fallen into a small lagoon, hidden within a valley. He thanked the gods for his luck, because he could have just as easily smashed against the rocks. Moon stared up at the sky. A dark shadow flew overhead.

"Cadoc," he said through gritted teeth.

Almost before finishing the witch doctor's name, rifle reports and human screams of horror rang out from somewhere above. It was not hard to conclude that the Dutchmen were being attacked, likely from one of Cadoc's monsters.

Moon swam toward land and crawled out of the cool water onto dry ground. He lay on his back to catch his breath. His exposed skin was a patchwork of scratches and every inch of his body ached. If the evil shaman did not manage to kill him, the jungle certainly would.

He had hoped he lost Cadoc or that he had given up his pursuit, but the circling giant bird in the sky said otherwise. Exhausted, hungry, and unsure how he could best the monsters that pursued him, he feared he would never make it to the crewmen waiting on him. Feeling totally defeated, the buccaneer was tempted to hand over the bone knife and pray the shaman felt generous enough to let him live.

Disheartened, Moon crouched, shivering, colder than he had ever been. *Do I feel this way because of the chill of the water or because I am frightened?* Doubts filled his thoughts. He questioned everything in his life that led him to steal the bone knife. Retrieving the blade, he stared down at it and thought about the riches he would receive if he should survive. The thought of his reward pushed back much of his fears.

The giant bird let out a longing cry, as if Cadoc could see the bone knife from where he soared. *Perhaps he can,* Moon considered.

A heavy splash ahead of him in the lagoon drew his attention away from the bird – something large had fallen into the water and sank to the bottom like a stone. His gaze went up the crest where he had tumbled from. Nzambi Europeans and Africans alike came tearing through the thickets, sailing across and down the edge into the water. Some crashed into jagged rocks becoming impaled, yet still their limbs moved with life.

"Time to go," he said as he rose to his feet. And for some reason that confounded him, Moon held the bone knife defiantly over his head and shouted, "I will bury this blade into your dark heart demon!"

"We shall see," Cadoc bellowed back, his voice sounded strong as if he stood next to him.

That sent another chill up his spine and gave him something tangible to cling on to. He would survive if for nothing else but to defy the shaman. Moon was not accustomed to fear and futility; he refused to let them rule him. Glancing at the water, he noticed that none of the nzambi swam. All of them sank. Apparently, simple tasks for the living, like swimming, did not carry over into death. Cadoc must have realized it as well because his anguished screams echoed throughout the valley.

Moon laughed as he ran off. He crossed grassy fields, wandered through overgrown woods and climbed up the side of a rock face. By the time he cleared the small valley his clothing was dry and the sun was starting its exodus. He needed to rest and to eat. Moon came across the half-eaten carcass of an antelope. He must have scared off a leopard in the middle of its feeding, but he was sure it was close, watching. It would not be long before the startled cat regained its courage.

He cut away meat from the dead animal, but not enough to infuriate the cat. The last thing he needed was to be hunted by leopards.

After finding a place he thought was secure, Moon started a fire and heated his acquired meat. He was not too worried that Cadoc in his bird form would see the blaze. The canopy of trees above him was more than adequate to hide the light of the fire. He took off his boots and left them near the flame. The lagoon had filled them with water. Though the exterior was dry, the interior was another matter.

His stomach full, he closed his eyes planning to rest them for only a short time. By the time he awoke, the fire had died and night fully engulfed the jungle. "How long have I been asleep?" Moon cursed under his breath. Without the fire to protect him, he was vulnerable to both animal and human.

He groped for his boots in the dark and put them on. He had the sudden feeling of being watched. Had the leopard followed him? He watched and listened for a long time. Nothing. He wondered if his fear shadowed him rather than any predator. Looking up at the trees, the canopy worked both ways it seemed – Cadoc could not see the ground below to spot Moon and he could not see the stars above to direct him safely out.

Fumbling around in the darkness, he eventually managed to rekindle the fire and then fashion a couple of pine knot touches. He was glad the bone knife's blade never dulled, even after he used it as a hatchet, saw and a knife. He lit one of the torches and began the trek once again.

After an hour, the canopy opened up and the crescent moon stars revealed themselves to him. With the entire universe as his map, he would navigate using the stars. He doused the flame from his torch in case the shaman was nearby and began his work of charting. It did not take long for him to get his bearings. He was not far from his meeting place with his crew and he could be there within an hour.

Using the moonlight as his lamp, he set out on the last leg of his journey and hoped it would be uneventful. He was twenty minutes into his walk when he heard a familiar voice call out.

"Moon."

He spun on his heels toward the caller, startled to see his shipmate hidden half in darkness. "Tobias? Is that you?"

"Yes," Tobias replied, but he sounded off like he was having a difficult time speaking.

"What are you doing here old friend? Did you encounter danger?"

"Yes."

Moon grew cautious. Tobias was known to talk far too much, even when he slept. There was also something about his posture that was not right. He was hunched like he was having difficulty standing, which was different than his typical tall and proud stance. "Are you wounded, friend?"

"Yes."

"Come toward me so I can get a better look at you. I need to see your injuries in the light."

He staggered out of the shadows. Half of Tobias' face was gone. His jaw fell open, hanging loosely be a thin thread of skin. "You must give me back the bone knife," came a completely different voice.

"Cadoc, what have you done?" Moon demanded.

Tobias swayed back and forth in place. "You must have known there would be a heavy price to pay for your thievery. Your friends are also culpable. Lucky for me I discovered them as I searched for you."

Moon stared at his friend. Tobias' wounds were fresh, some still bled and although his pigment had dulled, color yet remained in his eyes. He was not an nzambi... At least he did not think he was. "Is he still alive?"

"Presently yes, but without my knife, I cannot bring back the dead, but I can leave them suspended between life and death," Cadoc replied. "Give me the blade and I will be merciful and let your friend slip into oblivion."

"And me?"

What might have been a misshapen grin gradually stretched across Tobias' damaged face. "I shall kill you quickly."

Cadoc had placed Moon in a precarious situation. If Tobias had been made into an nzambi, he could be justified in cutting off his friend's head. As it was, he still lived and if there was any way he could save him, he would.

Another problem struck him. Where were Roche and Thomas? They were the other two crewmembers that waited for Moon.

His answer came from behind him. The two men clambered out of the thick foliage – they, too, looked as if they had been mauled by some animal. They staggered toward him.

Tobias closed in on him as well.

Their movements were clumsy and slow like they were struggling to wrestle free of the shaman's control over them.

"You are still alive and have free will," Moon shouted to them. "Fight whatever he's doing to you! Don't make me kill you!"

A menacing laugh rang out from the trees. Moon could just make out an abnormally big ape hunkered on a thick limb staring back at him. The primate displayed his sharp fangs in a toothy smile, but its eyes were dull.

"You waste your time with your pleading," it explained. "They are nothing more than puppets."

"By the gods," Moon yelped.

His suspicion about the shaman being able to transform into other animals was confirmed. He cursed under his breath and brought the torch close to his face. He hoped it still carried some faint embers. He blew on it desperately trying to reignite the flame. The torch came alive in his hand.

He thrust the torch crosswise at Tobias hoping it would force the man to back away. It did not.

To Moon's dismay, Tobias boldly staggered headlong into the hot blaze. His shirt lit up into flames and fire quickly engulfed him.

"No, I did not mean to..." the rest of Moon's words got trapped in his throat.

His friend screamed in agony; terror was reflected in his eyes. Whatever Cadoc had done to Tobias obviously had not blocked his sensitivity to pain or the awareness of what was happening to him. Still, he pressed forward with his charge in an attempt to grab Moon.

Moon canted to one side. His body reacted automatically, following his dodge with an elbow into his friend's ribcage.

Tobias hit the ground, a smoking fireball and stayed there, no longer screaming.

Moon wanted to mourn the man, but there was no time.

Roche had drawn his sword in an attempt to stave off the flame.

Moon brought his torch front on guard, and parried, easily knocking the sword away. A maneuver his crewmate should have avoided with no trouble. The shaman's control over Roche's movements clearly lacked a swordsman's skill.

Clumsily, Roche came in with a thrust.

Moon countered by slashing the torch at his opponent's stomach. He hoped Cadoc would not want his slave dead and would instinctively have him give ground.

Roche retreated several steps.

Thomas, however, came in from another direction, forcing Moon to divert his attention to him. He, too, had his sword out. In a blur of steel, the blade clashed against the torch. Metal proved to be more formidable than Moon's timber; the torch was hacked in half, its flaming head plummeting to the earth.

"Yes, now slay him," Cadoc roared in a pale imitation of a human voice

Moon kicked as hard as he could, launching the lost torch flame into the air and right into Thomas' surprised face.

Thomas dropped his sword as he unconsciously reacted to the sudden attack.

Moon flung himself into him, lifting the man off

the ground and slamming him onto his back. For good measure, he slammed the sole of his shoe down onto his crewmate's ribs, which was followed by an audible crunch. Controlled or not, Thomas was still human and it would take time for him to recover, even at the shaman's magical prompting.

Moon whirled around to face his last standing opponent. Roche lunged forward with his blade at Moon's chest. He barely had time to sidestep the attack.

Roche's attack was true and found a mark, slashing Moon's left arm. The wound was not deep nor life threatening, nonetheless it burned with a fierceness.

Moon hurled the remaining piece of his torch. It struck Roche in the face forcing his head to snap back. The momentary reprieve was enough to give Moon time to pick up Thomas' discarded weapon. He deflected a second attack from Roche.

The men's swords crossed and they stood facing each other.

"Kill... me," Roche said in a strangled breath. It was his voice and not that of the shaman. He had always been bullheaded and did as he pleased even when it countermanded Moon's orders. It appeared even Cadoc had difficulties commanding him.

"Fight him," Moon insisted.

"Can't... he's t...t...too strong."

"Slay him," Cadoc shouted. "Slay him now!"

The two men slowly circled each other, their blades still locked. The warm glow of flickering flames reflected off their somber faces as Tobias' corpse continued to burn. Sweat ran down Roche's forehead as he fought to resist the shaman's grip. His eyes pleaded for help.

Moon wrestled with what he knew must be done. "I can't."

"Then... we are both... dead men," Roche replied as his eyes turned cold.

He pushed Moon's sword away and followed with a vertical slash, cutting a straight line through his shirt. If Moon had not jumped back in time, his guts would have been all over the ground. He let his sympathies get the better of him and nearly got himself killed because of it.

Was this Cadoc's doing? he considered, *Did he let Roche's mind free only to distract me?* Flames revealed the shaman's fanged grin in the shadows, validating his thoughts.

Roche slashed and thrust his sword countless times.

Each blow was parried by Moon, but it was only a matter of time before one of Roche's strikes got through his defenses. Where his crewmate did not seem to tire, Moon could not make that same claim. He was already at his limits end from days of travel with little food, water and rest. Perhaps that was the reason the shaman had not immediately attacked him after he had stolen the bone knife, he wanted Moon at his weakest.

No, he thought, *it had to be more than that.*

Cadoc had power; that was obvious. Yet instead of directly facing a man he should be able to easily defeat, he chose to send his undead creatures and Moon's crewmates after him, while he stayed a safe distance away.

Again, Moon allowed himself to be distracted. Cold hands grabbed both of his ankles. "What the..."

He glanced down to see Thomas, on his belly, glaring up at him. Thomas' arms were stretched out, his fingers digging into Moon's limbs, preventing him from moving.

Moon gave up on his conviction that he could save his crewmates.

Without hesitation, he plunged the point of his blade deep into Thomas' right eye socket. The man's hands tore away from Moon and he rolled to his back reaching urgently for the metal invader to pry it out. A torrent of blood sprayed out as Moon wrenched the sword from his crewmate's face. His body jerked like a fish out of water, silently shaking as his chest rose and fell in short gasps.

Moon glanced up to see Roche stampeding toward him.

Moon quickly drew the bone knife from its

sheath, took the blade by its edge and threw it. The bone knife soared through the air and punched through Roche's chest and into his heart.

"Thank you," Roche gasped before he toppled backwards.

"No," Cadoc roared. He leaped down from the tree, landing gracefully onto the earth. His gaze locked on the bone knife jutting from Roche's chest.

Moon's focus was also on the blade. He tossed his sword away, knowing it would do little good against the shaman.

Cadoc and Moon glanced up at one another. "A race then," the ape growled.

Both rushed toward Roche's body. In a back and forth mixture of hops and sprints, Cadoc, who was further away from the body, closed in much faster than Moon could in his fatigued state, but he refused to let the shaman best him. For the first time in his life, he prayed for the gods to grant him strength, not caring which deity answered his pleas. One must have been listening.

Moon grabbed the hilt of the bone knife just as the ape glided down from a desperate jump, eclipsing all light from the heavens. He uprooted the blade and rolled to the left just as Cadoc landed heavily next to the body.

"No," the shaman screamed.

Cadoc whirled around to face his prey. His body

began to shrink and his features slowly became more human-like. In seconds, a sinewy, tall man, with skin as black as dusk, stood before Moon. He wore long, thick braids on his scalp that danced freely with his every movement. He wore nothing but a loincloth wrapped around his waist. Inked drawings of devotion and strange symbols covered all of his exposed skin.

Cadoc squatted so that he was level with Moon's prone body. "Are you wondering what these symbols mean?" he asked in a casual tone. Without waiting for a reply, he answered. "They signify life and death. They show devotion to my master Legba, who granted me his magic over two hundred years ago."

Legba, Moon knew, was the gatekeeper of the dead. That explained much about how the shaman could create the nzambi creatures. What surprised him more was Cadoc's age, he looked no more than fifty, yet he was claiming to be over two centuries.

"I tell you this," the shaman continued, "because this same gift can be granted to you. All you need do is hand over the bone knife." He proffered his hand, his palm facing the sky.

Moon gaped down at the knife, noticing for the first time his crewmate's blood dripping off from its blade. He looked up, first seeing the vanishing flame from Tobias' baked corpse, next the body of Thomas which lay in a pool of blood, and finally at Roche who had a hole in his chest – all dead because of him. He felt a dark cloud envelop him.

"I want nothing from you or your deity, except

for your death at my hands," Moon replied.

The shaman lowered his arm in defeat. "You know you cannot win against me, boy."

Right before Moon's eyes, Cadoc transformed from one large carnivorous predator to the next before reverting back to human form. "I am a god weighed against you."

"Then kill me," Moon dared him. He righted himself, standing to his full height of six feet. "Come bring me this death you've been promising me."

Cadoc stood as well, his gaze darted to the bone knife and then into Moon's face to meet his eyes. "Don't be a fool."

"I told you I would pierce your heart with this blade and I will do just that." He paced forward one step and the shaman took one back, maintaining his distance. "Do you fear me Cadoc?"

"I fear no man."

"Then why not attack me? You are obviously far stronger than I. Attack me now!"

Cadoc took another apprehensive step back, placing even more space between them. His expression suggested he was thinking of something to say. Finally, he gestured to the bodies. "Your fellow thieves called you Moon. Not a name native from our land. Were you a slave? Did some white master give you that name, boy?"

The question had taken him aback. His mind flashed back to a time when he was shackled in metal chains, torn away from his mother's arms forever and tossed into a carriage on the night of a full moon.

Repeatedly, the young son of the white man who had taken him kept referring to him as Moon. A name he never bothered to change after he escaped, because he no longer remembered his birth name.

He shook off the unpleasant memory. "Why do you care?"

"Because I want to end the Europeans' régime of our land, which has always been my goal. With the bone knife, I can build an army to slay the white man and return our land to its once proud heritage," Cadoc explained. "You've interfered with that plan by stealing my knife. Give it back to me and I can save our people from slavery."

"Save our people?" Moon repeated, thinking about his mother, who may be alive, still a slave in the Colonies.

Cadoc must have read his thoughts. "You want to save someone you love, yes? I can do that for you."

It was a tempting offer and for a brief moment, Moon considered returning the bone knife to its true master. But the bodies of his crewmates, the friends Cadoc killed, made him reconsider.

Is my mother worth all the lives it would take to free her? he mused, *And could I ever look her in the eyes knowing that?*

"Your price is too high, shaman," Moon blurted.

Cadoc's expression changed into a furious mask. "I will revel in making you one of my undead slaves, Moon."

Despite having the magical knife, he had his doubts he could defeat the shaman, at least while he stood alone against him. "If only my crewmates were still alive to help me," he whispered. The bone knife pulsed in his hand.

All at once the three corpses sat up, all looking directly at Moon. At first he thought it was the shaman's doing, but from the fear emitting from his eyes, he knew immediately he was wrong.

"No," Cadoc exclaimed. "This is impossible."

Roche, who was closest to Cadoc, grabbed the shaman's legs. Tobias' smoking corpse got up and jumped onto his back. Thomas' lumbered toward his prey and clutched him by the throat and began squeezing.

"How are... you doing this?" Cadoc managed to choke out. "How?"

Moon had no idea. Perhaps his friends felt their lives were stolen from them and they thirsted for revenge. Maybe the gods saw fit to stop Cadoc before he became so powerful that they felt he would one day become a threat to them. The answer did not matter; in the end, all that mattered was that, somehow, Cadoc would be stopped.

The shaman transformed into an ape, followed by a tiger, and finally, a rhino. His efforts were fruitless because the nzambi were relentless, ripping and tearing at his flesh.

Finally, Cadoc changed back to a man. The nzambi dragged him deeper into the jungle. If he had lightning bolts in his eyes they would have been hurling bolts at Moon.

"This is not the end, Moon! This only delays my plans! I am forever and I will have the bone knife back," he promised. "I curse you and all your descendants. I shall be a plague upon your family until there is none left to torment!"

The shaman's threat hit a nerve. Moon's father had been savagely murdered trying to liberate his wife and son from slave traders. And Moon had no idea whether his mother was still alive or had borne any other children in the Colonies. For all he knew, he was the last of his lineage and the only hope of continuing his bloodline. That thought did not sit well with him. He raised the knife preparing to end the shaman's life.

Cadoc's eyes grew to the size of silver coins, conscious of Moon's intent. Trapped by the nzambi, unable to shield himself, he cried out to his deity, "Master save me!"

Moon waited for something to happen, expecting the earth to shake or the heavens to be lit by storm, but there was nothing. "It appears your god, Legba, has deserted you, shaman."

"Has he?" Cadoc shot back.

Without delay he charged at the shaman intending to cut open the man's throat with the blade. He was within reach when it felt as if he ran into a wall of stone. Moon bounced off of some invisible barrier and then went sailing backward in the air.

His world went black. After the cobwebs had cleared from his head, he felt dirt and grass against his cheek.

In the distance, Moon heard the shaman's screams of elemental fury and triumph.

Moon searched around. Cadoc and his dead crewmates were gone. He climbed out of the black pit that was his mind, realizing too late that Legba had come to save his loyal servant from death.

Struggling to sit up, he saw that the bone knife was still gripped tightly in his fist. "I hate magic," he said under his breath. He wanted to rid himself of the blade, get back to his ship and get sloppy drunk to pretend the last few days never happened.

Moon trudged back to his ship in a state that could have had him mistaken for one of the nzambi. Initially, he spoke to no one; he gave the crew vacant stares.

A few days after they set sail, Moon finally came out of his shock. His captain and crewmates questioned him for hours about Thomas, Roche and

Tobias. He told them the truth – a mistake on his part.

Upon hearing about the nzambi and the retribution Cadoc promised, his crew wanted nothing more to do with him or the bone knife. They provided him a week's provisions and a boat and set him adrift in the middle of the ocean. He could not bring himself to be angry with them because had the roles been reversed, he would do the same thing.

The bone knife sat beside him next to his right leg. The raw, malevolent pulsations from the blade were palpable. He fought the urge to drop it into the ocean. The shaman would dog him until he got the knife back. Yet, it was Moon's only protection against Cadoc, so in the end, he knew the knife would stay by his side for a while yet.

Cadoc's words about being a plague to his family echoed in Moon's mind. Staring down at the enchanted blade, he wondered about other magical treasures that might exist. "All magic can't be evil," he said aloud to convince himself. If he was to live out his days and someday bear children, he and they would need some way to safeguard themselves.

It was then he promised to dedicate his life to finding other enchanted relics and he would pass on the tradition to his children and them to theirs. Cadoc may think of himself as some immortal, but he still feared death, which meant he was not a god.

For three more weeks he floated in the ocean, surviving a tremendous storm that nearly drowned him. A bit of food and fresh water, and a lot of will, allowed him to survive. Dehydrated and starving, he was not long for this earth.

He had just about given up hope when he spotted a ship in the distance. The crew of the vessel must have spotted him because it turned toward him.

He used what little strength he had to sit up. Perhaps it was his imagination, but he thought the ship floated above the water.

Moon tumbled backwards, no longer able to keep himself upright. The crew collected him from the small boat. All the while, he clutched to the bone knife like his life depended on it.

Once aboard the ship, he was give food and drink to recuperate. After settling Moon into a bunk to recover, the skipper stopped by to identroduce himself, "I am Captain Hendrick Van der Decken. I see that you are looking better."

"Y-yes. Th-thank you for your hospitality," Moon strained out.

"Don't thank me yet, lad. Recompense for saving your life will cost you time and hard work serving on this vessel." The man grinned, but his smile did not reach his eyes. "Once you have fully recovered, you will be dispensed your duties."

Relief flooded into him. The thought of working on a ship appealed to Moon. He was at home on the sea. One day he would have to tell the skipper about the enchanted bone knife and the coldblooded shaman who would stop at nothing to get it back. But that could wait. He was saved and for a short time, at least, he could forget all about the supernatural.

"I understand," Moon replied. "I will do my best not to be a burden to you or your crew."

"Very good, lad." The captain said, folding his arms behind his back. He then turned and marched away.

Before he exited the cabin, he glanced over his shoulder and said, "Welcome aboard the *Flying Dutchman*."

AN OMNIBUS RIDE IN SCARLET

Nat Turner

The warm stolid air in the old rickety red omnibus stank strongly of absinthe and vomit. The gears and weights that ran the bus clicked and whirred, straining against the tremendous combined weight of its sixteen passengers.

To one such as her, the smell was far worse to her than to inferior human nostrils. Her heightened senses had come in handy many times in the past, even saving her from destruction on the one occasion when the hunters had come creeping, sneakily slithering their way into her home, but on other occasions, like tonight, she would give her wisdom teeth (after all, they served no purpose now) for a set of nose plugs.

She'd purposely sat at the back of the Omnibus

so she could scan the travelers seated within. Unfortunately, this also meant that she was seated among all the drunks and the burps, grunts, farts and profanities that erupted from them, as well as the various odors – or "oh, dears," as she called them – they brought.

Normally, she would travel in style – by carriage, or by the new, spring-powered dirigibles that were all the craze, but on leaving New York and her bloody trail behind her, she feared that the hunters would once more come looking in another attempt to banish her accursed soul back to the Abyss.

The Abyss awaits every life stealing, immortal horror, bent on causing chaos, death and destruction. The Abyss is patient and always gets what it wants, but only if you're careless; careless enough, that is, to get yourself killed. While oblivion is inevitable, the pleasures of feasting on humanity outweigh the bitter and agonizing end.

She planned on remaining *untoten* – undead – for as long as possible. To do this, she had to keep a low profile some of the time, especially when her killings brought curious eyes, seeking the cause of the many deaths. *I should really flee this country for a while*, she thought. She had relocated many times but the prospect of setting up coffin somewhere else abroad vexed her. Creating fresh aliases and finding new places to live was dirty and mundane. She hated it. Besides, a little risk kept her sharp and stopped her from becoming overconfident in her approach. So, instead, she decided to take a simple trip down south, taking a carriage from Manhattan to Southampton County, Virginia and then jumping on an omnibus that would take her to a small town called Jerusalem. The village was a small hamlet of approximately 175 people, with only three stores, one saddler, one carriage maker, two hotels, two attorneys and two physicians. It was located nine and a half miles away from the omnibus station. This was where she had one of her many safe-houses, places to lay low when the heat was on.

It had actually been several months since she'd last devoured a human, draining his spirit through his veins. She had killed last night, however.

She thought she was safe, hunting in the shadows of the trees of Bowling Green Park in Manhattan, at the end of Broadway. She had tailed a man wandering home whom she guessed, from the look of him, to be nothing more than a lonely middle aged man – an easy kill! It turned out the man was a master and teacher of Savate, a French martial art that uses the hands and feet as weapons, combining elements of boxing with graceful kicking techniques. And although her inhuman strength and speed eventually proved too much for him, the kill lasted far longer than she had estimated. By the time she'd ripped open his chest with a powerful strike from her clawed hands, a young couple, romancing the night away in the bushes nearby, were alerted to the man's shouts and she had to leave, unfed, before the two lovers got too close and witnessed her malformed state. Of course, she could have killed the two of them as well, but that would undoubtedly set suspicion levels soaring, and suspicious killings could easily bring a hunter snooping.

That was not an option.

From early on in her untoten life, she learned that hunters should be avoided at all costs. Within the first few days of being reborn as one of the undead, the vampire who made her had told her many tales of how hunters used sneaky, underhanded, dirty tricks and tactics to destroy vampires. He told her many horrible stories of careless vampires he'd known that had been destroyed by the bedraggled rabble. He even told her horror stories involving a hunter that some of the more superstitious vampires thought to be true. They were nothing more than stories used to scare young vampires who thought themselves unable to be harmed by mere mortals. The one known as "Nat Turner" was rumored to be able to track and kill a vampire by means that were unbelievably fantastic, bizarre and impossible.

In the last twenty four hours, a terrible hunger had grown inside her; a hunger that demanded to be sated. She found that such hunger interfered with her thoughts, and though it didn't make her clumsy or slow, it instead turned her more animalistic in nature and aggression. In such a mood, she might simply rip out the throat of some passer-by and not give a care about who might witness the act.

The trouble with leaving too many slain victims, or worse still, witnesses, was that more attention would be drawn, and with such attention, hunters always followed. What she needed right now was a lowlife – a down and out fellow that no one would miss; someone weak and feeble. She had at first considered an elderly victim. These were easy to come by and even easier to kill and dispose of. But she did not like the taste of old folks. Their blood was bitter, with a hint of cottage cheese and mothballs. Even in a desperate situation like this, she would not stray higher than a sixty year old.

Composing herself, she began to scan the omnibus for a potential meal. Her eyes slyly scanned back and forth, weighing up each potential victim. Eventually, she settled on a young woman that she guessed to be in her mid twenties. The young woman sat in the middle of the Omnibus, chatting away with the man sitting beside her.

Using her superior hearing, the vampire listened as the woman ranted. It appeared that the man beside the young woman was her boyfriend, Kevin, who, according to the woman, was nothing more than a lowlife, cheating scumbag who was not worth bothering with. The vampiress smiled as she heard the woman's teary voice tell Kevin that she was not coming home tonight as the thought of sleeping in the same bed as a slimy, sniveling, poor excuse for a worm, let alone man, did not appeal to her. Instead she was going to spend the night at her mother's house. *Perfect*, the vampiress thought. She prepared to make her move and introduce herself to the young woman, perhaps by asking her if she was alright and sympathizing with her predicament. The omnibus slowed down.

Having finished a run for Samuel – *Master* Samuel, his enslaved Africans called him – Leroy now waited patiently in the cold dark night at the omnibus stop. He hated riding the omnibus. Being a Black man, he was not supposed to ride the vehicle at all, but his so-called owner was powerful, so he was allowed to ride in the omnibus' undercarriage...with the luggage.

The omnibus stopped. The driver, whose name he did not know, but whose stone-mask face had leered at him many times, nodded.

"How do, suh?" Leroy said, forcing a smile.

The driver nodded again.

Leroy yanked on a handle on the exterior frame of the bus and a horizontal door slid upward, exposing several trunks and leather bags. He squatted and then stuffed his lean frame into the undercarriage. He pulled the door down behind him and was cast into darkness.

After several minutes, the omnibus still had not moved.

Suddenly, the panel door slid upward. The driver squatted before him. He was smiling.

"Forgive me, sir," the driver said. "You can ride inside the bus."

Leroy poked his head out of the undercarriage

and studied his surroundings, ensuring no mob waited on the road with a noose. Certain of his safety, he slid out of the undercarriage, hopped to his feet and followed the driver onto the omnibus.

The Omnibus was packed. No one seemed to notice him, though. The sole Black man on a "Whites Only" omnibus? He shrugged and scanned the vehicle for an empty seat.

Luckily, he spotted one in the middle of the omnibus, next to an elderly man with dead eyes that rolled around in their sockets. Good, the old man was blind. He should be okay and be able to avoid any unwanted confrontation as long as he kept his head down.

He shuffled to his seat and sat down, staring at the floor.

The omnibus pulled off again.

There wasn't much to see on the floor, just scuffed wood, but it didn't matter, he kept his gaze downward. He just had to remain as indiscreet and as quiet as possible. This way, with any luck, no one would bother him.

As the omnibus continued on, the noise of the rabble mixed with the slow ticks, clicks, whirs and hums of the clockwork engine began to melt into one another within Leroy's head. The aches and pains of a long day's work were massaged by the omnibus' slow, rocking gait. Leroy's eyelids fluttered and then closed as sleepiness overcame him and he drifted off into his wild and troubled dreams.

"Hello there", said a sweet singing voice that made Leroy suddenly jump awake from his short-lived slumber.

"You from around here, are you?" continued the voice.

Leroy, now fully awake, realized that someone had come and sat by him while he slept. The blind man was gone and, somehow, this person had scooted by him and taken the window seat without rousing him.

The voice, he quickly noted, belonged to a woman – a young WHITE woman. This was bad. A Black man, on a "Whites Only" omnibus, sitting next to a white woman? He couldn't shrug this off.

"I um...sorry, what? I mean yes. Yes, I live in Jerusalem!" Leroy said, turning to the young woman. A dark haired woman, dressed in a long, full, conical skirt with large, "leg of mutton" sleeves, a narrow, low waist – achieved through corseting – and lace coverings, draped over her shoulders, smiled back at him.

The girl introduced herself as Claudia and told him that she too was traveling to Jerusalem. She then went on to tell him that she had just come from up North. As she spoke to him it became clear that the she was pleasant and charming and also seemed genuinely interested in him, and before he knew it, he found himself enjoying the conversation.

His brow furrowed as he scanned her emotions, but he detected no lie, no underhanded trick, no scheme thought up by the woman to trap him.

After talking for a few minutes about her life, she suddenly said to him: "Anyway, that's enough about me. Tell me about yourself.

"To tell the truth, there's not much to really tell," Leroy said. "I deliver messages, pick up packages and shop for my master. And that's about it, really."

"Come on Leroy", she said with a wink and a smile. "There must be more to you than that. What excites you? What's inside the man sitting beside me? There must be more to you than just work. You're more than just some slave boy!"

Leroy gave a nod. "Well, I *do* have a few hobbies".

"I'm intrigued," Claudia said. "Tell me."

"Well I...I'm interested in the supernatural," he said."

"You mean ghosts?" Claudia asked.

"Yes, ma'am," Leroy replied. "Ghosts, monsters, creatures from the black depths of the sea and from the blacker depths of space, people with extraordinary abilities and magic artifacts. I'm interested in it all."

"Interesting," she said. "Tell me more."

"There are things out there", he said. "Things that walk our world, things we don't understand, things we were never meant to understand. In the last fifteen years, I've made it my personal mission to collect the things, oddities and curiosities that we were never meant to see".

"So you're telling me you know of monsters and the like," she said, with not a trace of sarcasm in her voice. "This is fascinating, Leroy! And what's more, you've been collecting the evidence. Building up a menagerie of proof. Incredible! Tell me more!"

"I'll tell you everything I know," he replied.

####

The vampire listened with faked interest as her prey ranted on. *Claudia May Broaddus, you've really gone and picked a right one this time*, she thought. The man was Black, a little intelligent, it seemed, but also a bit crazy – all slaves were at least a little crazy, she reckoned. They were, after all, away from home, abused, and robbed of their culture – enough to drive anyone mad.

When Leroy was done talking about life on the plantation and the things that go bump in the night, Claudia put on her "Wow...how fascinating"-look once more.

"Just this morning", Leroy said, shaking his head and laughing. "Just after Pearline had served Massa his breakfast and slipped me the extra biscuit, A knock came at Massa's door. This scruffy looking man, who goes by the name of Lyman, tried to sell Massa something in a dirty brown carrier-bag that he called the *Great Discarnate Fundament of the Undead Lord and Savior.*"

"What?" Claudia said, forcing a chuckle. She was tempted to release her glamour on the passengers and driver and watch them tear Leroy apart for daring to "sneak" onto and "defile" their omnibus, but she so wanted to drink his spirit, so she kept everyone enthralled as she listened.

"He claimed that in 1776, giant monsters – demons the Founding Fathers called them – broke free from Hell and stalked the Colonies," Leroy said, shaking his head. And wherever the beasts roamed, towns and villages would crumble under those terrible and humongous fiends. So, a plan was formed by the Founding Fathers, Lyman claimed."

Leroy leaned toward Claudia. He lowered his voice to a whisper, as if he was going to share something even crazier than what he was already telling her. "Benjamin Franklin created a giant lightning rod, but this rod was built of materials that would attract power from the realm of spirit. He drove the rod into the head of a huge stone that sat in Pennsylvania's town square. A stone that was to be sculpted into a statue of General George Washington. The Founding Fathers fasted for a fortnight and then prayed around the stone for a day and a half and, lo and behold, a bolt of red lightning came down from the heavens and struck the giant stone. The big rock became soft, like clay. It whirled and folded in upon itself. A few minutes later, a one hundred foot tall Jesus Christ stood where the giant stone once was.

Big Jesus plodded toward the demons, eager to do battle with the monsters. Things went well at first, with the giant Jesus demolishing the monsters with his big holy fists of power. However, after each fight, giant Jesus got weaker and weaker, until, by the time only one terrible monster remained, giant Jesus was barely able to stand on his two mighty divine legs. And this final monster, who was the biggest and most powerful of the bunch, attacked Big Jesus, all claws and fangs."

Claudia could not believe what she was hearing. As a vampire, she knew there were powerful spirits the Christians foolishly mistook as demons – she had even been called a demon or a devil once or twice – but giant Jesus? She was going to savor consuming Leroy; he was certainly a rarity in this land of dullards.

"A terrible battle ensued," Leroy went on. "But in the end, the monster was killed, and giant Jesus stood triumphant, his brilliant holy eyes shining with the light of the sun as the Founding Fathers fell to their knees and gave praise. Alas though, giant Jesus had been dealt a mortal wound and died the next day as the Colonies celebrated the fact that no more horrid monsters would eat them! For three days and three nights the celebrations went on, but on the fourth day, a new terrible menace arose to once more threaten the Colonies. Giant Jesus had come back to life, though now one of the undead...and he was hungry for brains!"

A snicker escaped Claudia's lips. She composed herself, straightened her face and said, "Tell me more."

"More terrible than all the monsters put together, giant, undead Jesus went about killing and destroying all before him!" Leroy said. "Again, the Founding Fathers got together to come up with a solution for ridding the world of their terrible creation. They invented an immense grenado and fired it from a cannon at the giant undead Jesus. On impact, the grenado blew up and killed the undead giant Jesus. The only thing of undead Jesus to survive was his left buttock."

"And you believe this story, do you?" Claudia asked.

"Lyman was, without a doubt, quite mad," Leroy replied. "But he seemed a harmless soul nonetheless. When Massa kicked Lyman out of his house, I caught up with him and paid him five silver coins – half my savings – for it."

Claudia dreaded her next question but knew that she needed to seduce the fool a little more, as less than a couple of miles remained before they reached Jerusalem. "Can you tell me more?"

"Of course," Leroy replied.

"Claudia had no clue Black men could talk so much. They always hung their heads around white people and spoke only when told to, but this Leroy fellow was different.

The omnibus came to a screeching halt, as did Leroy's rambling.

"Looks like we're here," Leroy said. "It was a

pleasure to meet someone else who has a mind for the stranger things."

"I am staying not too far from here," Claudia said. It's dark, would you be so kind as to escort me home?"

"Well...I don't know," Leroy said. "Massa expects I'll be home directly."

"I'll pay you ten silver coin for your trouble," Claudia said.

Leroy nodded.

####

As the two started walking, Claudia knew that she had no place to stay in Jerusalem – she had planned to kill some old couple and take their home – but now she had a better idea; she needed to be invited back to Leroy's plantation – she would kill his master and take over the plantation, which would provide her with many slaves from which to drink; hopefully, they all were as exceptional as Leroy. She decided that if Leroy was going to invite her, then he needed a little push.

"So, this collection of the strange and unusual that you've amassed, it must be a wonderful thing to lay eyes upon," she said.

Leroy nodded, saying: "I am mighty proud of it."

"I'd love to see it, Leroy," Claudia said, batting her eyes. It would be easy to enthrall him, but enthralled prey tasted bitter and left her with a terrible headache. She would do this the old fashioned way.

"Really? Well okay," Leroy stuttered. "I was going to invite you back but it's not the way."

"The way?"

"Well, yes. A slave inviting a white woman to his plantation? I ain't trying to get myself whipped and burnt at the stake!"

Claudia gave a laugh. "Oh, don't worry about that. Who will ever know? We can do whatever we like. I won't tell, if you won't."

Leroy stared at the ground, blushing. He peeked back up at her. She gave him a smile.

"Okay, then," Leroy said.

####

"Here we are", said Leroy, waving his hands about at the entrance to the expansive estate. "My cabin is over there. Go on in and make yourself at home. I just have to go tell Massa I'm back"

"Alright," Claudia said. She rubbed her hand down his arm. "But hurry back."

Leroy blushed again. He turned on his heels and jogged toward the mansion that loomed in the distance.

Claudia entered Leroy's cabin. She was happy with what she saw. A small, one bedroom cottage, with a little garden at the front. There were other cabins on either side and behind it, but only a couple of them had the flickering of candlelight coming from their windows. On the walk to the plantation, they had not encountered anyone. Leroy had rambled on some more about his collection but Claudia had been on the alert, her eyes constantly searching, hoping to see no other wandering souls. She was very pleased with the way things were going.

On the mantelpiece, she noticed a jar with some small brown thing floating in it. The label read "Franz I's Lost Nose." On another jar containing a whitish liquid, a label read "Ectoplasm," and a small glass box with a piece of brown moldy fur within, was branded with the words "Yeti Hair."

Suddenly Leroy appeared behind her. Claudia turned to face him and gave him a smile. She sauntered toward him. "There's one thing you should know, Leroy."

"What's that?" he said as she stood in front of him.

"Yeti's and ghosts and giant undead Jesuses don't exist. It's an altogether different type of undead that you need to worry about!"

"What? You mean wraiths? Revenants?" Leroy said. "By the way, ghosts aren't actually undead. They're actually just *dead* and..."

With blinding speed, a deformed swung out and, with inhuman strength, slapped Leroy on the side of the head.

The blow knocked him senseless, and he fell to the floor not moving.

"Enough of your prattle!" Claudia said with a snarl as she looked down on her food.

She needed to act quickly now, Leroy wouldn't stay unconscious long and if he awoke too soon a few more blows from her may well finish him off before she could feast.

####

When Leroy did awake, he found himself sitting in his rocking chair. The chair had been dragged into the center of the room. Before him, sitting in his dinner chair, was Claudia, grinning.

"What...What happened", he said shakily. He tried to stand up but found that his legs and arms were tied. "You're robbing me? Is that it, Claudia? You want my collection of oddities? Take them!"

She narrowed her eyes at him. "Your collection. You actually think anybody with half a brain would be interested in your little collection? You really are a nigger! In all my years traveling this world, I've met some fools; believe me! I've met some of the stupidest, most ignorant pieces of walking feces to ever grace the planet! But you...you are the dumbest of the lot. Imaginative, but dumb. Entertaining, but dumb! Over the last hour that I've gotten to know you, I've really, really, really, grown to hate you. And believe me, I'm not someone that you want to piss off!"

"Listen, just take what you want. Just don't hurt me."

"Oh, my dear Leroy", she said, her mouth twisted into a wicked grin. "I intend on not only on hurting you, but to skin you alive and to feed you your own flesh. With this she gave another wicked laugh.

Leroy struggled with his bonds.

"Now, now, dearie," she crooned. "Stop your struggling or I'll rip off *your* nose and add it to that Franz I jar to make a pair."

Leroy stopped his struggles immediately.

"Besides", said Claudia, leaning back in the dinner chair. "You'll find it hard to escape. In my line of work, and in over the past few hundred years, I've become something of the knot tying expert."

Leroy remained still and quiet.

"Still though," she went on. "I suppose I may as well take your collection up to the main house. I'll find a room for it."

She rose from her chair and bent forward until her face was less than a finger's length away from his. "Tell me Leroy...in all your time researching all that unbelievable nonsense that adorns your grim little hovel here, have you ever learned much about vampires?"

"Vampires! Well, I know a little," Leroy replied. "In fact I once tried to buy a cane from a man in New

Spain who claimed it was the very cane carried by the Vampire Lord Ruthven and..."

"Lord Ruthven is a fictional character from a book", Claudia sighed, interrupting him, the annoyance clear in her voice. Then she calmed herself, her voice becoming sweet and angelic once more: "Tell me though, Leroy, if you believe in Lord Ruthven, then you must also believe in other vampires as well, right?"

Leroy nodded his head.

"Well for once", continued Claudia with a sudden dark gleam in her eyes. "You'd be correct!"

As Leroy sat tied and helpless, a horrible transformation began to take place before him.

Claudia's eyes became large and catlike, the white skin on her face faded and decayed to a deathly gray, her face stretched downwards to accommodate a new set of huge sharp teeth as two exaggerated fangs hung down past her chin. The rest of her body twisted and elongated as fingers became claws, her torso and neck stretched, making her weave and sway, serpent like. Now, in her true form, she gazed at the horrified little man before her as the hunger inside her grew. It was tempting to kill him right then and there. Eat his miserable soul and be done with it, but she planned on having her fun first, the food could wait just a little while longer.

The loathsome terror before him reached out and grabbed Leroy's face with its claws. "Tell me Leroy", Claudia's voice had lost all its beauty. "I know you wanted me before. Do you want me now?"

Leroy did not speak.

Having received no answer, the vampire squeezed its claws into Leroy's cheeks. Blood flowed down his jaw in rivers. Leroy screamed in agony.

"You will answer me in words or in screams," Claudia said, smiling wickedly. "Understand?"

Leroy fell silent again.

The vampire, gave Leroy a slap across the face, busting his lip and nose.

"When I ask you a question, you will answer me or suffer. Do you understand?"

Leroy nodded his head.

"When I'm dead. Once you've killed me, will I become like you?" Leroy asked.

Again, the vampire gave out a hideous laugh before drawing itself up to its full height in front of him. "We vampires are truly evil. Even when we existed as pathetic humans, our hearts and thoughts were of a design of pure wickedness." She then pointed to the jar on the mantelpiece saying: "Franz I for example, now he had potential. You however, don't! You are a moron, a simpleton, a plain and simple nigger." Then she brought her face down angrily to his, and with a vicious snarl, said: "Don't you dare suggest that a little nigger like you could ever become something like me! Vampires are of the noblest malevolence."

She then sat back in the dinner chair, the anger removed from her face; replaced by the terrible mask of hatred that she'd first sported. "But come on, Leroy, surely you must have learned something of my kind when investigating all the poppycock you love to drivel on about! What about, say, the way we eat, not just on your blood like some overgrown mosquito, but on the spirit that resides within the blood – sucking out your soul and devouring all that you are. You mean to tell me that you haven't learned any of this?"

The vampire shook her head in mock disappointment. "What about hunters? You never heard of them either? Vile lowlife scumbags with nothing better to do than to hunt vampires. No? You never heard of the so-called legendary vampire hunter Nat Turner, said to be able to hunt and kill vampires with inconceivable skill and fearsome techniques? No?!"

Leroy shook his head. The vampire sneered at him.

"So basically", continued the vampire. "You've learned only the dullest, saddest, dumbest drivel that the morons of the world have dreamed up. And what is worse, you actually believe it!" Claudia sprang to her deformed feet. "Let's take a look at this amazing collection of yours, shall we?"

The vampire spun Leroy around in his chair so he faced the mantelpiece. "Let's see. Franz I's missing nose." She picked up the jar and unscrewed the top.

Then reaching in with her long sharp claws, plucked the brown floating ball out of the vinegar inside. Putting it to her nose, she gave it a cautious sniff. "Hmmm. My acute sense of smell can definitely say that this, even for the many years it has been smothered in vinegar, is certainly not of flesh. I would say that what we have here is most definitely a walnut!" And with that, she popped it in her mouth, chewed and swallowed. "Oh, by the way, that's another myth that vampires can't eat food. One of the highlights of being undead for so long is that I have had the privilege of sampling all types of delicacies from many countries over many years. It's just that every so often I've got to eat a human as well!"

She flashed a smile at Leroy and then returned her attention to the mantelpiece. "Now then, let's see. What shall we look at next? Ah yes, Yeti fur."

Smashing open the glass box with a sharp rap from her gnarled knuckles, she pulled out the small piece of long brownish fur. Raising the fur to her nose she gave another sniff. "Well, well, well! This piece of fur that you've got here is indeed, I believe, most probably from Tibet. However, as anyone but yourself might guess, it's not the fur of the mysterious and non-existent Yeti. It's actually Yak fur." Placing the small piece of Yak hair atop his head, she then gave a slight guttural chuckle as she gazed down at the sad spectacle that Leroy presented.

"Last, and probably least, we have this. Ectoplasm!" She held up the tube with the white, gooey liquid inside. She took a sniff. "Paste...made from sea water and flour." Giggling, she poured the gooey white liquid all over the top of Leroy's Yeti wig.

"Now, you really look as pathetic as you actually are. But don't worry, soon I will snuff out your misery. Should we see what other precious junk you've collected?"

The creature scanned the room, a sneer stretched across its wicked mouth. "Where are the rest of them? Where is that...Jesus buttocks thing?"

"In my bedroom," Leroy croaked. "The chest at the foot of my bed."

The vampire darted off, with frightening speed, through the door. Seconds later, the creature darted back into the room carrying the chest under one arm.

Leroy shook as the vampire stared, unblinking, at him with unkind eyes that enjoyed his plight. The creature took a firm hold of the old wooden chest's lid and tore it off, nonchalantly tossing it to one side of her. She then gazed down at the contents. "What's this?" she said, pulling out a pair of white woman's knickers and shaking them at Leroy. "You have one or two secrets perhaps that you haven't told me about?"

"They belonged to Lavinia Fisher," Leroy said. "She murdered dozens of men at the *Six Mile Wayfarer House,* a hotel owned by her and her husband, John"

"Boring," the vampire crooned before tossing the bottoms aside and continuing her hunt.

She drew a large, gray convex disc, that

appeared to be carved from stone, from a brown leather bag she pulled from the chest. "The undead Jesus thing, I presume?"

The vampire opened its mouth, filling the room with its evil guttural laugh and the stench of rot. "I still can't believe that a grown man believes in all this rubbish", said the vampire, once it had finished laughing. "Are all niggers this dumb?"

"Perhaps we are," Leroy said with a hint of venom in his voice. "Though I do find it hard to take criticism about my belief in the unexplainable from a goddamned vampire!"

"Look at you!" Claudia said, rising up to full height and opening her huge eyes wide. The gray disc was still in its clawed hand. "The nigger has grown something of a backbone. You dare answer me back! Just for that I'm going to tear out your..."

The vampire stopped mid-sentence. It looked down at the gray disk it held. The hand holding the disk began to shake. Claudia opened her hand in an attempt to release the disk but it was as if it were glued to it. The creature grabbed the disk with its free hand and tried prying it away. Both hands became glued to the disk.

The vampire screamed. Pinkish-white smoke billowed up from its clawed hands.

Leroy slowly rose from his chair, pushing the still knotted ropes that once bound him to the floor.

Smoke billowed from every orifice on the

vampire's body and even from under its fingernails. The horrible scream from the beast shook the cabin. A moment later, a pile of ashes lay on the floor where the vampire had stood.

A few whiffs of smoke swirled up from the pile of blackness. On top of these ashes lay the *Great Discarnate Fundament of the Undead Lord and Savior.*

For a time, Leroy just stood, gazing at the ashes and the gray disc. Slowly, he went about cleaning up the mess. He bowed slightly over the pile of ash and spoke:

"Apologies, Claudia; I forgot to give you my real name. That was very ungentlemanly of me, but my clients do pay me well for my discretion, as well as my skills. I am Nat Turner...pastor; freedom fighter...monster hunter."

THE ADVENTURE OF THE SILVER SKULL

Deanna Baran

From ten until close, with a short break for *la sieste*, Louis Cailloux was Monsieur l'Horloger, the finest clocksmith of Cap-Français. But although he kept his doors tightly locked and his windows closely shuttered, regardless of the stifling heat and humidity, from dawn until ten he was at his workbench as M. l'Mécanicien, in the employ of the most infamous buccaneer in Les Caraïbes.

Today, however, there was an urgent knock at his door. Cailloux tried to ignore it, but the rapping continued. He swept his project aside into a secret cupboard – an experiment in brass and wood and lethal-looking steel blades – and moved to the door.

"Good morning?" he inquired politely through the solid wood, beginning the complicated process of releasing the elaborate system of locks which secured the premises.

"Bonjour, M. l'Horloger," came a youthful voice from the other side of the door. "It is I, Ismael."

"It's rather early, child," said the free man of color, opening the door to admit the boy. At sixteen, Ismael was hardly a child; indeed, there had been very little of the child about him at the age of six. "My condolences to you upon the death of your father."

Ismael slipped in and found a stool upon which to perch. "Things are growing uncomfortable at the estate," he said. "I'm surprised I haven't been sent off to Aux Cayes to lay the rails. There has been talk." He spoke casually, but Cailloux knew it was a deadly serious danger. The colonial administrators of Saint-Dominigue desired to somehow link the scattered coastal settlements. Heavy losses to privateers and pirates made the shipping lanes unreliable. Forbidding mountains, thick jungles and marauding Taíno made the travel through the interior hazardous. Cailloux, despite his protests and distaste for the work, had personally been tapped to develop the draisienne prototype that would soon reduce a week's hard journey to a day. In the meantime, countless lives on the rail-laying teams were devoured by yellow fever, poor sanitation, and extreme working conditions. The grieving widow of the Couvent Estate would not have hesitated to sacrifice her husband's bastard son to the costly dream of the gleaming silver track.

Cailloux expressed surprise. "You mean, your

father didn't arrange for your manumission upon his death? But he always told you..."

Ismael held up a grinning silver skull, with a large key fastened to the chain. "This was what he left me before he died," he said, his voice glum. "After the accident, he was barely conscious enough to speak."

"It's quite a fine dial," said the clocksmith, with a forced show of cheer. "Not bad at all. Few can afford a watch, let alone one of such a fine caliber. I'm familiar with it. I've handled it before, when M. Couvent had a difficulty with the spiral balance spring last year."

He flipped open the jaw of the skull, which served as a cover for the dial face. Possessing only one hand, in the fashion of the last century, the face was a delicate confection of gilded brass and steel, adorned with Roman numerals, the half-hours being marked with fleurs-de-lis.

"Ah! But he's made a change to it since I saw it last. He's given it a motto," said Cailloux. "'Vigilate et Orate.' Very nice touch."

"What does it mean?" asked Ismael.

"It's Biblical," explained Cailloux. "It means 'watch and pray.' It's a reference to the Garden of Olives."

"I see," said Ismael, who didn't. "He always told me to visit his grave and pray for his soul."

"Have you?" Cailloux asked absentmindedly. "Hum. The mainspring is in need of a bit of winding. Allow me. Eh...what's this? The key doesn't fit," said

Cailloux, with a frown. He pulled the key from the chain and examined it more closely. "It's far too large." He pocketed the mismatched key, set the watch aside on his workbench and pawed through a drawer in search of a key or crank that might be of similar size to what was needed.

At that moment, the door to his workshop flew open, without the courtesy of a preliminary knock. Isaac Couvent – the free-born son of M. Couvent's lawful wife – and a pair of friends entered the shop like a trio of young, wild wolves.

"Excuse us, M. l'Horloger," said Isaac, brandishing a silver-topped walking stick. "I apologize for your having been intruded upon in this manner. He has other tasks that have brought him to town this morning. He has no business bothering you in your workshop. I see he has shown you my father's watch," he added, snatching it up and secreting it in an inner pocket, where it bulged unattractively. "It should never have left the house. It was dishonest of him to remove my family's possessions, and he will be punished for it."

Ismael's eyes snapped with fire but he was master enough of himself to remain silent. Freedom was difficult to obtain on the French side of the island. He had hoped for something far more valuable than a mere bauble from their shared father, and yet he found himself suddenly deprived of even that memento.

"Your errands in town did not extend to bothering

M. l'Horloger," reprimanded one friend. "Don't act as if your time is your own."

"There is no room for a slave who cannot be trusted with time or with goods," agreed the other, like a Greek chorus.

Ismael stood up and gave a stiff bow. "Thank you for your time, M. l'Horloger. I must tend to my duties."

"Vigilate et orate," said Cailloux cheerily, pulling some of the draisenne plans towards him in a pretense of activity. As the door shut behind Ismael's retreating form, he turned towards Isaac. "My condolences on the loss of your father. I attended his funeral. What a rare honor to be buried beneath the floor of la chapelle de Saint-Rémy. There is no art to match it on the island."

"Yes, he was its most important patron," said Isaac. "He financed the construction of the chapel and commissioned almost all of the artwork within from the finest artists of Paris. His passing was a great loss to everyone, but he left them a stipend in his will for its continued maintenance."

"What a considerate man," murmured Cailloux. "I usually attend the services at the mission nearby, but I will have to stop by Saint-Rémy and admire your father's generosity with new eyes."

Two weeks later, Cailloux found himself on the Couvent Estate to tend to the mechanisms of a clockwork carriage. The gear assembly had gone awry, and it had taken the better part of the afternoon in getting it disassembled and reassembled. Ismael had been tasked with assisting him and had been given permission to carry the great man's tools back to his shop.

The boy's hands trembled a little. "I will be sent to Aux Cayes tomorrow," he said in a low voice. "They think I do not know. But I will not go. I will hide in the mountains and join an outlaw encampment before I permit myself to be taken to Aux Cayes."

"Let us go tell your father goodbye," suggested Cailloux kindly. "We will pass Saint-Rémy on the way back to town."

It was a small little church, its bright whitewashed walls nestled in the vibrant green hills. The windows were thin and narrow; they would not have survived hurricane season otherwise. But the interior more than made up for it in a riot of bright color: saints and angels and Biblical stories richly illustrated the walls and ceilings in vibrant golds, heavenly blues, and rich crimsons.

M. Couvent was buried beneath the stern gaze of St. Rémy, off to the side in the transept. As Archbishop of Rheims, he stood with mitre, balancing a floppy red cap upon his crosier, carrying an edifice securely in his hands. Roundels illustrating vignettes from his life surrounded him: the fire of Rheims, the resurrection of the woman, the baptism of Clovis and his army. Ismael knew nothing of St. Rémy; slaves were not encouraged to attend services or seek a greater Master. He threw himself on the smooth, cold marble of the floor, a cross and a name indicating the spot of his father's interment, and cried quietly. Cailloux wandered through the church, admiring the art and politely ignoring the muffled sounds of sorrow and distress.

He eventually made it back towards the image of St. Rémy once more, and spent a few minutes staring hard at it. By this time, Ismael had controlled himself and sat back on his heels, rubbing his red, swollen eyes.

"Ismael, tell me. These paintings – everything in this building – were commissioned by your father?"

"Yes," said Ismael. "He had very specific ideas as to what he wanted within the church. The priests had other wishes, but they went along with his ideas in the end. He even dictated his own burial-place."

"Then tell me," said Cailloux. "Why does Saint-Rémy have two hats? He has a mitre, which you'd expect on a bishop, and that red thing is a Phrygian cap, which has quite a different meaning. And normally, when you see a bishop holding a building, it's an image of his cathedral. But that's not a church in his hands. Tell me if that building looks like a building you've seen elsewhere?"

Ismael scrubbed his eyes one more time with his knuckles and stared blearily at it. "It has three red doors and that funny roofline. It makes me think of that one building – it's on la Rue des Trois Chandeliers – doesn't it look like that one building? With the three red doors?"

"The middle door is marked with a star," said

Cailloux. "Do you suppose your father is asking you to visit that building, and perhaps see what is behind that middle door?"

"I don't believe Father ever had any business on la Rue des Trois Chandeliers," said Ismael.

"Let's go see," urged Cailloux. "We watched, and we prayed, and this is our answer. Let us investigate further."

They paused only to drop off his tools at the shop in la Rue Saint Simon. The premises were securely locked and bolted, as he had left them – but something was amiss. Cailloux froze, trying to place his finger on whatever it was that should not be. Had one of the authorities come to ask after the draisienne prototype? Had someone come snooping and discovered certain projects that should not have been discovered?

He heard a step above his head. Someone was in his private chambers. Cailloux reached for a long-barreled pistol, winding it up as he moved cautiously towards the stairs. At a cue from the older man to remain still, Ismael moved only enough to pick up a sharply-pointed clock hand from the workbench, the best substitute for a dagger in a pinch.

Surely the intruder would have heard their noisy entrance and was ready for them. Cailloux moved stealthily upstairs, bypassing the boards that always creaked in this weather. It was important to know who had the audacity to commit such an intrusion.

The curtain at the top of the stairs swung aside to

reveal a tall, dark, elegant figure dressed in dramatic orange silk. "Good morning, M. l'Horloger," drawled a feminine voice. "Please don't shoot. I've come to check on the status of my clock."

Cailloux discovered he had been holding his breath. He let it out in a gusty whoosh of adrenaline and sank down to sit on the stair-step to compose himself. "Madame Saya! Please don't ever do that again. And when the door is locked, it means, 'Come back later.' But I appreciate your pointing out the flaws in my security. If you have any advice, I would be grateful."

"But I was ever so anxious," she pouted, descending the steps and twirling her matching orange parasol by its wrist strap. "And you keep your comfy chair upstairs. Surely you wouldn't expect a lady to sit at your workbench."

"I wouldn't expect a lady to be inside my workshop when it was locked and closed," he returned. "I will be happy to help you with your, um, clock in a short while, but M. Ismael has precious little time left to him, and I have promised to help him see a certain project through elsewhere. I should be back within the hour."

"Certainly not," said Saya. "One thing leads to another, and you're sure to get distracted somewhere along the way. I'll come along to remind you of your obligations to your paying customers."

"As you wish," said Cailloux, shaking his head and suppressing a smile.

They locked the workshop securely behind themselves – how *had* she gotten in? He must remember to make her tell him – and made their way at a quick pace to the building which was their destination. Cailloux used the opportunity to sketch out the sequence of events to Saya; Ismael was not pleased at having the woman drawn into their confidence, but as Cailloux seemed to know her quite well, there was nothing he could do about it.

The sun hung low on the horizon and the sky was streaked in gold and raspberry as they stood before the building with the three red doors and the unique roofline. In life, the middle door was not marked with a star, but the door still stood open at this late hour, and Cailloux led their small contingent inside. It was an apothecary shop; the walls were lined with crockery jars filled with various ointments, syrups, and powders.

Cailloux found the chemist who ran the shop. "Excuse me," he said, "but I was told you might have a parcel from M. Couvent for my young friend here."

"That may be so," said the man gruffly, "M. Couvent was a good friend. He left a box with me a few years ago. He said someone would be by someday with a key."

"M. Couvent had a great faith in his puzzles," observed Saya, arms folded, watching the scene with glittering dark eyes. "He obviously puts more time into planning them than he does in explaining them to others."

"I suspect he would have been plainer if he had had more time at the end," said Cailloux, examining the locked casket which the chemist had produced. "You do have to admit, the government has no interest in making the process easy for a living man. Things are far easier on the Spanish side of the border."

"A living man can accomplish anything he wants to, provided he's willing to do what it takes," said Saya scornfully. "I have no patience for weak men, no matter how rich they may be."

All Ismael said was, "M. Cailloux, do you suppose that key that was too large for the watch might have been meant for this box?"

"Excellent idea! You left so suddenly that night, I had no chance to return it to your keeping," said Cailloux, extracting it from an inner pocket. "It was my intention to return it to you when I saw you today, but I was distracted by our adventure. Please...you try."

Ismael held his breath as he fitted the key into the lock. There was a brief hesitation where it didn't quite seem to fit. Then, with a snap, the mechanism was released, and the lid opened.

Inside were a series of papers, neatly folded, tied with red ribbon, heavy with wax seals. Ismael passed them to Cailloux. Slaves were kept illiterate, on pain of death; there were no such restrictions on free men of color.

"Your father's regrets and request for your forgiveness," said Cailloux, leafing through the pages slowly through the waning golden light that filtered through the window. "I'll read it to you more thoroughly when we are in private. A request to the colonial authorities to begin the legal process for your manumission upon his death. I presume he did not trust to leave such valuable documents where his loving family could find them. And a request for you to travel to Marseilles and seek employment with a certain shipping company there, with whom he has standing arrangements. A banker's draft for your passage and to start a new life."

Ismael's eyes were round and his hands trembled a little as he accepted the stack of precious papers.

Twilight had come and gone and the streets were deserted by the time the chemist had shooed them outside so he could lock up his shop and take his dinner. There was an odd lantern here or there, breaking up the darkness with its inadequate illumination. They traveled slowly enough so as not to stumble, but quickly enough to try and get back to the workshop. Cap-Français was not safe after sunset.

A shadow detached itself from the deeper shadows of a building and stood in front of them to block their progress. There was a glint of silver from a silver-topped walking stick, and a scraping noise, and then a longer, thinner, deadlier gleam.

"All you had to do was carry M. l'Horloger's tools home for him," said a familiar, sneering voice. "And yet here you are, disregarding your duties yet again."

"There is no need for violence," said Cailloux sharply, stepping forward to shield Ismael and Saya from Isaac's threatening blade. "Put your swordstick away."

"I don't think so," said Isaac. "I've been following you all evening. What mischief are you up to?"

"You reek of rum," said Saya, striking her parasol against the pavement. "Go home."

"You only want me to go back so you can send me off to lay the rails tomorrow," said Ismael, stepping forward from Cailloux's protecting shadow. "But I shall not. I shall respect my...*our*...father's wishes. I shall go to France as a free man. You took our father's watch from me, but you shall take nothing else. I bid you adieu, my brother."

He held his gaze steadily for several moments, then stepped around the threatening point of his swordstick to pass by. Isaac stared after him, open-mouthed, for several moments, as Cailloux and Saya hurried after him. Then, he seemed to realize what was happening.

"That's what you think!" Isaac cried, lunging forward to attack the group from behind.

Cailloux reached out to shove Ismael aside. There was a flash of orange and ring of steel as Saya spun around with a parry and counterthrust, all in one fluid motion.

Isaac stumbled backwards at the unexpected interference.

"I have no patience for weak men," said Saya, pressing a button on her parasol. Hidden gears began to grind. "There is no honor in attacking an unarmed youth, man, and lady from behind." Metal slid against metal. The shaft of her parasol telescoped into something longer, spearlike. The ruffled orange silk fell away. A wicked blade latched into place to form a glaive. "I take it you don't know who you threaten?"

Isaac shook his head mutely, the point of his swordstick trembling.

Saya smiled. Her teeth shone like pearls in the darkness. "Few living men do."

"Madame Saya," said Ismael, his voice barely more than a whisper. "Please don't."

"Not in cold blood," said Cailloux.

"But he will cause trouble for you both if he goes free," objected Saya. Her voice was petulant, but the tip of the weapon hovered confidently, inches away from his ruffled jabot. "You've worked hard for your reputation, M. l'Mécanicien."

"You have an imagination," said Cailloux. "Surely you can be more creative than mere death."

"Perhaps," said Saya, considering. Then she seemed to come to a decision. "You will have no need for such fine clothes where we're going. If you would do me the favor of disrobing – ah! That wouldn't be the infamous skull watch that I have been hearing about all evening? If you would kindly drop it to the side, there...yes. Now, gentlemen, if you would please excuse me. I have some business back at the waterfront – no, you have quite enough to occupy yourselves this evening. M. l'Mécanicien, I apologize that I will have to visit you another evening about that...clock."

"It will be ready for you at your convenience," said Cailloux, with an elegant little bow.

FURY

Zig Zag Claybourne

Vingree Ramsee spoke seven languages, had sailed more of the world than most knew existed, and had created weapons and tools so much more useful than the springbow pointed at her face that she almost felt sorry for this man's eventual trip to the hell of his upstart religion.

"You're the seventh man to threaten me today," she said to the addled, violent man sitting across a filthy wooden table from her. The cleanest thing on him was the ornate cross around his neck.

"You must be out of favor with your god," said The Dead Man. Vingree thought it was a foolish name to choose for one's self, but men of his nature were often very, very foolish.

"You don't see any of them standing," said Vingree. She laced her fingers atop the table and leaned forward, making him more afraid than he was. "I do not give others what is not theirs to own," she said. "My alchemist is mine." And, she thought, his potion is late. She had counted the moments as he had instructed her. The little flash bag affixed with the special rubber was supposed to have gone off sixty breaths after she'd quickly placed it upon seeing the gaunt, bleached pirate enter the meal tent. He had spotted her and made straight for her table. He was not alone. Nor was she.

She distracted The Dead Man by speaking, looking directly into his eyes. She worked a needle-thin throwing lance up her wrist and into her palms, another sleight the alchemist had taught her.

The Dead Man's men were distracted by the uncovered legs and bosoms of Astarte and Tanit standing off beside their captain. Both women had curved swords slung at their hips and straight swords strapped to their backs. Both were so dark of skin that it was said that to see the flash of their blades was the last good light one saw in the current world.

Three against three. It was not an even fight.

Vingree leaned back. She had caught the slight jasmine whiff the flash bag gave off as warning. Dead Man caught it too, but, as the scent was designed to do, he was more confused as to its source than wary.

The three women steeled themselves. The flash went off in a loud sizzling flare directly under the table where The Dead Man sat. Vingree threw her body to the side without leaving her chair. The small arrow whizzed the space by her ear like an angry insect. A lance lodged in the pirate's cheek immediately before two long blades flashed in the candle light. There was much cursing, then screaming, then silence.

When it was over Vingree retrieved The Dead Man's bow. There was a large spring in it; made of a metal the Alchemist said was particularly useful to him. The Dead Man had had the metal plated in gold. His calling piece. Even his teeth had been plated in gold. Always gold for fools. "Vital I have it, Vingree," the alchemist had said. Everything was vital to him. She did not like using her treasures as bait for his trinkets, but she did like very much the way his trinkets worked with her own.

"Dead was a fool," said Bilo the alchemist, his voice as deep as his skin was dark, coal like his sisters' who were likely somewhere sharpening blades and trading jokes at his expense. Vingree was soil, rich and alive. "One less fool is not a bad thing." Such a sepulchral voice should not have come from a gaunt, severe body. It was a voice the soil beside him loved to hear in the night.

She brought her leg over his and rubbed an ache in her foot against his shin. She kissed his shoulder. She loved the taste of cooled sweat. "All are fools," she said. "Has a day gone by that you haven't called someone 'fool'?"

"Not," he said, raising enough to find her nipple. Cool ocean air filtered in through the dark of the opened port. He gently kissed her skin. "Since my last suckling."

"All of an hour ago."

"You negate my awful childhood."

"Your sisters affirm daily that *you* were your awful childhood."

"Fools," he said. Vingree felt the smile in his voice. "Are you tiring of hunting things?" he asked. "This metal, with the threads coated in the iron shavings and wound around a proper tube, will propel an object without direct contact. Reaction motion."

"And if big enough it can propel us," she said. "Kiss me again."

He did.

"Again."

He did.

"Now stop talking. The night won't last forever. We must bathe in it. It would be foolish not to, yes?"

"This is why you are *daazeet* of this ship."

"I am daazeet of this ship," she said, moving him into position, "because there is no one better than me."

He considered himself fortunate enough now to know the enduring value of silence.

####

Bilo watched his sisters on deck. Their ship, unnamed, for names were too important to waste, had been crewed by men and women the world over. The tall blonde warriors who complained of heat and thirst always; those from the hidden island who claimed to have studied under Sakanouye No Tamuramaro, the warrior from Bilo's home shore responsible for the Samurai code; the women with the long straight hair from the far far land whose language Vingree had not learned but who had, instead, taught the ship a new sign language; none of them, fine sailors as they had to be to sail with Vingree Ramsee, came near the machine-like efficiency of his sisters. This thought made Bilo smile. He had seen the crude clockwork dolls in Italia that moved limbs or other such childishness. It was only a matter of time before he perfected a clockwork human to replace the more repetitive work demanded on an able ship.

He scanned the horizon. No sign of another ship. Pursuit did not concern him, only the possibility of sudden blockade. There wasn't a vessel with sails enough to pose a threat to Vingree's ship when it deployed its most protected secret. Water was the world, and the ship from Asante currently ruled that world despite the Inquisition's pretense otherwise. There were four papal ships always on the prowl for them, evil ships with gray, scarred hides and always full of bile at being four steps behind Vingree Ramsee of the Ocean.

Bilo admired the sheen of sweat on his sisters' backs. Sweat was work. It was life. Except in cold lands, his sisters preferred the mode of dress from home. They often laughed at the starched and ruffled and overly-laced peoples who used clothing as a shield against ephemeral things. Bodies were as common as grass, sky, and dirt. If clothing was not a tool it was useless.

He carried a tureen of water to them. "Astarte, rest before you become as ugly as me."

Astarte took the water gladly and drank deeply before passing it to her sister. Bilo, who was constantly scurrying, sliding, or crawling to repair, research, or enhance was dressed in his usual alchemical attire: a dirty, patchwork vest and outwardly-rough breeches but secretly inward silk. Two bands of fabric were wound one over the other at his waist and fastened with a system of tiny needles in resin he had devised from studying burrs. Most of their equipment and clothing had squares of these bristly resins strategically placed. They were strong, quickly unfastened and refastened, and kept the hands free at opportune times.

He pulled a notebook affixed in such a way from the small of his back. It was waterproof, sealed, and had a cache for several of his injection styluses. He depressed the syringe on one. A dot of squid's ink appeared at the tip. He opened the book and began writing, maintaining perfect and constant pressure on the cylinder to keep the ink flowing as needed.

Tanit nodded at the book. "He's planning to kill us again," she said.

"What are you writing now?" said Astarte.

"The workings of your back muscles. I see how we can increase the efficiency of the sails. There's no reason we cannot fly on water," he said.

"We already have our scoop wheel," said Tanit. "Next, he'll want to take us underwater."

"It would be a good way to avoid the papal fleet," Astarte admitted. "I am not sure, though, we need to be the test subjects."

"Where do we go next?" said Tanit.

"We need to put into port," said their brother, "so I can build."

There were men born hating. It did not matter what. Hatred was their lens by which all was seen, felt, and understood. For these souls, hatred was clarity in spite of clearer waters. Hatred was dank bits that nourished in spite of food.

Inquisitor Boniface swirled a gilded spoon inside a bowl of thick, gray muck. Bits of his bread dotted the table and it was intolerable that one of his slaves had not yet rushed to brush them away, although the slave's hand was already swooping under the old man's arm with a quickly flicking towel.

The mongrel ship had not been spotted for nearly a month. No one, not pirate or cleric, reported sight of the woman warrior, her crew, or – and even his Grace, the King, freely admitted this – her genius. It was said his inventions had changed the world seven times over already. None of those were in the service of Boniface's betters, and that, the Most High Inquisitor knew, would not do.

Boniface was known as Hell among his lessers, and this pleased him. Hell was all-encompassing, hell was eternal, and hell was very, very vigilant.

Boniface would put into port soon. His mission was not only to patrol for the heretics but also to collect tribute and penance along the way. There was a small coastal town directly ahead, full of acolytes, full of boys, full of girls. Boniface pushed his bowl away.

Hell was a place of hungers.

####

"These coils and this rod on either side of our wheel," said Bilo, "will make us untouchable."

Vingree had seen how his small prototype had zipped when he tested it. "We are already the fastest ship in the world. Why do we need so much more speed?"

"Because those idiots will eventually catch up to our wheel," he said. "This will also generate the power to focus our light through a new lens array," he said, about to pull a notebook from his back.

Vingree stayed his hand. "How powerful?"

"Hot enough to feel as though burning skin."

"I love how you play on their superstitions." She gave him a peck on the cheek and ducked under the long cylinder hoisted beside her dry-docked ship. "Can you make the ship fly?" she teased.

"Not this one...but I do have a design," he said.

"If you reach for that book again I will cut you."

Too late. He held his notebook and waved it at her. "This out-values royal gold," he said.

"As do you. I'm glad of this break. I'm tired of using you as bait to procure the treasures of others."

"Only from the fools who advertise their treasures and mean to do the world harm with them," said Bilo. "We will not allow our world to be dried and plundered."

"No, Bilo," agreed Vingree, and ended with even more finality, "I won't."

"Daazeet!" shouted Astarte. She only used Vingree's official title when there was trouble. "A new slaver, trying to pass. Heading toward the Land, not away."

Vingree looked at Bilo. "Do you need me?"

"No."

Vingree headed for one of their interceptor boats. They were light and fast but their hulls were strategically plated with armor and their prows sharp as stingers. She shouted names as she ran: crew who would make this a quick, victorious trip. Astarte kept pace with her, feeding her information gleaned from their long range scope. The two interceptors were usually moored to the sides of their main ship, giving the appearance of formidable pontoons. They bobbed in the water of the makeshift grotto Vingree and crew had created a year ago, never staying in one long enough to be found or create a pattern.

Slavers received no mercy. One more ship not reaching the shores of her home land was one less damnation for the planet to atone. The merfolk would be well-fed tonight. The last living sight that ship would see would be the Most Daazeet Vingree Ramsee sending ship and crew to be shamed before their ancestors.

She captained one boat, Astarte the other. When they had made sufficient headway they furled sails and dropped swift, silent wheels into the water. The ships surged ahead.

####

He glared at his brother inquisitors.

"No one," snapped Boniface with a sharp rap on the table, "can find them." The inquisitors felt no need to answer. This was not their failing. "Yet they have no problem finding our ships and tributes?"

"It is not often they leave survivors to provide counsel, Imminence," said the captain of the ship Boniface called home, given leave to speak by the tilt of Boniface's grizzled, quizzical visage toward him. "They are ghosts."

"You speak the words of heretics and savages and fools," said Boniface. "Increase patrols threefold. I will have no more of our ships scuttled or I will have all our ships' captains put to death."

"Yes, Imminence."

Boniface ignored the man. He looked at the small, coal dark eyes of War, Famine, and Pestilence: the Inquisitors Three to his fourth. Rarely were they all in the same place, but this summit required a deeper, more prayerful meeting than they could accomplish alone. "Are we agreed?" he asked each, knowing that as Hell he would receive the assent he requested.

"Send word to begin burning all Moor libraries. Kill anyone who speaks of research. This comes from the throne itself. We will not be humbled by a single boat of heathens."

The captain bowed and left.

Hell looked to his brethren. "This ends."

The Apocalypse nodded.

He had grown a rough, beady beard in the three months of building. It looked good on him. Except for when he ate. "We have plenty of food," his sisters teased. "You don't need to save some for later."

Vingree watched a speck of bread dangle at his upper lip as he spoke. The urge to swipe it was overwhelming but she was too animated to interrupt.

"This is propulsion anywhere, my heart! Land, water." He pointed upward at the open sky and nodded at her. "Eventually. It needs nothing but removing this separating barrier to start and stop or regulate speed. I have built smaller ones to power our lights, cooling urns, and the sound boxes."

"I don't like your sound boxes."

"They work over greater distances now."

"I know but there are times I do not want to hear your voice."

"Ha!"

Astarte's head appeared over the side of the ship. She spotted the two on the ground. "Bilo, stop showing off! Our daazeet could have built this herself."

Vingree smiled widely at Bilo. Nothing but teeth.

Bilo, knowing any battle with the ladies was already won by them, touched his heart and head to both.

"I have checked everything," Astarte said. "The crew is learned to my satisfaction."

"Then we leave at first moon. I want it to taste the night before the day," said Vingree. She was quite happy. "It's been a while since we've had a good test."

When night fell, the electromagnetic hum chased the insects away. The ship, freshly tarred and oiled, made no more noise upon the waves than the waves themselves. Vingree didn't want to use the lights until they were major leagues away from their base of operations, but when she did it was glorious. The ocean was lit by dozens of lights bolting outward, positioned in such a way as to be frightening and confusing: a beast of light with eyes of red. The sea was where she lived, and if she was to be considered a monster it would be as one of the old ones caretaking all of creation.

She spoke into the sound box for Bilo in the engine room below. "Bilo... Make us fly!"

She could practically feel his smile through the decking and see him nodding to his disciples as they put their bodies into throwing huge levers and watching tension levels on springs and pulleys. It was a dance to him, a magnificent, life-giving ceremony of thanks to the All. It was no wonder she cherished him so.

All lights on the ship flared a moment, then the vessel kicked at the water and surged so suddenly Vingree lost her footing and wound up laughing on her ass. The ship moved like an eel! She whooped and stood, arms wide to catch the spray. "Faster, Bilo!"

Voyages that would have taken weeks? Mere days now. A fleet of these ships? She and her beloved would change the world. Balance would be restored.

The ship shuddered and groaned a bit until it found its rhythm, then the speed became part of it. The prow lights shone ahead of them, lighting the stygian ocean beneath the canopy of a billion fresh stars and the blade of a crescent moon. The entire crew was shouting and laughing. Even the joy of the ancestors was palpable. Materials would not be so hard to come by now; this ship provided greater reach and scope. The gold and precious metals of both throne and papacy—taken from villages too poor to educate their children beyond servitude—were theirs to take and transform into life. Vingree said a prayer and a greeting to the stars. The Igbo people spoke of their other home somewhere among the sky. *We,* Vingree greeted, *will join them.*

####

When word reached them of the third library burning, Vingree convened their war session.

"How do we fight an enemy," said Tanit, "that does not exist? They are everywhere, and as such are everything."

"They have commanders," said Vingree. "They have ships. We shall seek ships that rarely pull into dock. Large ships. They are not fools. They mimic our wisdom of being constantly on the move. If we shake their nest, they will come out to attack."

"You are sure of this?" said Astarte.

Vingree nodded. "It is what they are trying to do to us."

####

Bilo walked Morocco's dizzying lanes, his head and face wrapped, his loose clothing blowing in an unusually high wind. To any glancing, he seemed to walk alone. Nothing was further from the truth.

The wash of colors here always infused him, not only of people but of cloths, smells, words and even souls. He sensed things here that he experienced nowhere else, not even at home. This mélange was where the gods did business. He listened as he walked.

"...no one knows who is burning our libraries..."

"...cattle slaughtered because they thought Vespucci had something to do with it..."

"...rumors and dangers are being spread..."

A wise one collected information not by treading water but by riding the currents. The wharves were the busiest and liveliest of Morocco's gathering spots. Their interceptor had arrived under cover of night and was well-hidden; even better guarded.

He rounded a corner and ducked into the alcove he'd been looking for, rapping on an ornately carved door with his booted heel.

After a moment a voice issued from behind the door. "Speak."

Bilo kicked again. One rap, a pause, three raps, one rap.

"Do you have a riddle for me?" said the voice from behind the door.

Bilo, still facing outward, eyes scanning for anyone taking undue notice of him, turned his face toward the door and said, "I am the riddle."

"Why?"

"Because I am alive."

Bolts shifted. Many bolts. The door swung inward. Bilo caught Astarte and Tanit's eyes across the way before he spun and entered. The door closed and rebolted. *"Mzee,"* Bilo said, honoring the man's generosity.

The man was not alone. Two burly men and three burlier women formed a semicircle behind an elf of a man: small, wiry, dark yet filling the space.

"Family," said Bilo.

"Family," answered the largest of the men in the old language of alchemists. "Show your face."

"You do not know me."

"Then let me be surprised," the burly man said.

Bilo unwrapped. The women were of the Mongol people. The silent man had the look of the Kushites. The speaker had the tan of a native Moroccan, while the elf...he, Bilo knew, was beyond men and places. His small face and skeletal hands were all that was seen of him; all else was one unbroken, brown robe.

"You know my works," Bilo said. He held his arms out and opened his legs. "I ask to be searched."

"We give trust or death, not both," said the elf. The large Moroccan relaxed a notch.

Bilo withdrew a slim, rectangular box capped by a lens from one of the interior pockets of his tunic. He pressed a pearl stud on the rear of the box. The lens lit brightly.

The elf smiled a bit, turned, then appeared to glide, not walk, away. Bilo, respectfully, made no notice of this. He followed the brown robe down a passage to another door, then down a sloping path, one that went deep before leveling out into a leftward corridor that was lit, Bilo noted, by strings of glass bulbs, not the primitive torches or oils still widely favored. "Your light?" the elf said. "Acids, filaments, woods and metals?"

"Yes, Mzee."

"So small."

"Mzee is small."

"Yes."

"Yet not small." Bilo plotted their course: they traveled under the street itself, away from the house. This was a marvel of engineering. No dank air, not a speck of dirt, and lit brighter than most of the streets in daylight. The corridor branched off at several points but they continued straight.

They entered a room, barren but for a plain wooden table and two chairs.

"Who sits first?" said the elf.

"We sit simultaneously, for we are the same spirit."

The elf clucked his tongue and smiled again. "I like you, boy. You are the monster the crown seeks to flush out. Timing could not speak otherwise."

"I wish no more destruction of our knowledge," said

Bilo. "Your family can help in that. You've done so before."

"Many times," agreed the elf man. "And for eons hence. I have many daughters and sons."

"Then you will help us?"

"You think we are not?"

"Apologies."

"We are why this entire world has not yet burned. We may allow you to become family. We are not certain."

"On what does certainty hinge?"

"On whether or not you can call war upon yourself."

Astarte's hand unconsciously went for her sword the moment the ornate door swung open again. It had been a ridiculously long time in there. She and Tanit had had to take turns wandering from their positions of surveillance to avoid suspicion, keeping in contact when out of view of others by speaking in their sound boxes.

Bilo, wrapped again, left the doorway. They followed at their distance. He sat for a meal. They shopped and spoke with others. He walked toward a less populated area, then an even sparser one, then to the deserted area where he, his sisters, and the four other crew who had been guarding behind the sisters were to meet, uncover their interceptor, and return to Daazeet

Vingree Ramsee to prepare for war.

####

You are authorized, the letter read, *to use all means and resources both available and conscripted. We have lost eight tribute ships and four carriers. We will lose no more. You are expected to succeed. If the widows of your former captains require their children become orphans that your current stewards may find proper motivation, it is a sacrifice lesser are blessed to make in their ignorance. Spain, Brittania and Italy are all reluctant to sail waters that carry the finest ships the world has ever constructed. If there is no safety under my Inquisitors I must question the value of that office. I must question the value of our grace upon your liberties...*

Boniface stopped reading. His job was to collect tribute and sow fear among both populace and pirates. His job was to ensure that the very lucrative flow of trades, human and otherwise, was maintained. His job was not, he thought with bitter acid burning yet more holes into the dead lining of his soul, to ensure that ghosts no longer roamed the Earth. There were witnesses now, men able to make it to life rafts that made it back to the sovereign land. They described being suddenly blinded in the cool quiet of the sea, then eyes approaching fast, straight for collision, but just as suddenly going dark. Then the hard, shattering rams from both sides of the ship. It was as though the beast called forth spirits. Water flowed inward like blood in reverse, for every screaming man on the ship knew this stab was mortal. Even the ones on deck firing their guns blindly at waves and moonlight knew that their lives had ended upon this vast, immortal sea. Then the lights again, a sudden flash astern, aft, port, starboard—never the same place twice, and always a presage of the coming THUD!

Ships ripped to pieces by demons.

There would be one final convening of the Apocalypse.

Then holy war upon the black lands.

By the time word from spies had gotten around to Vingree, four large assault ships and three smaller frigates, all bristling with cannons, had rounded the horn of Africa. It had been a circuitous, non-stop voyage. Hell drove each ship like a flogged horse on pain of death. The demons liked saving the brown and black skins from being taken from their lands? Fine. Let them then tend the fires Hell meant to rain down.

By the time Vingree's ship and the interceptors made it around the horn of Africa, Kismaayo was burning. The city's coastline was a smudge broken here and there by jumping flames. "What can we do?" she said. Bilo said nothing. "Bilo?"

"I'm thinking."

Oil had spread upon the waters a fair distance. It, too, burned, creating a wall of smoke and fire that stung the eyes and nose.

"They had several days journey ahead of us," said Bilo. "We reduced it to hours. The city is still burning, Daazeet."

She had her entire crews standing on decks to show the fishermen scrambling in boats that they were no harm. The efforts to fight the fires on land were futile. The attackers had used shells containing highly flammable unguents. The city was far from lost but it sustained serious enough injury. Vingree did not want to think on the deaths involved.

"We cannot man our hoses," said Vingree.

Bilo nodded.

"They are still here," she said. "Prepare for battle," she said softly to the crewperson beside her. The word quickly, quietly, and efficiently filtered to the entire crew who moved as one mind to their duties. Vingree used her sound box. "Be wary."

Astarte and Tanit agreed. They spaced their interceptors wide so that the three ships formed a great talon upon the water.

"They are behind that wall, Daazeet," said Bilo.

"I know."

"They are idiots."

"They are dangerous. They have no plans to return home if not entirely victorious," she said. "If they want smoke we shall give them all the smoke their tainted lungs can hold." She spoke into the sound box. "All ships, slow sail, random spillage, then ignite."

From the shores it was a sight that generations would remember: three ships as dark as the night sky criss-crossing the bay in wide, unhurried arcs as though forming a web worthy of Anansi's praise. The day the water burned, the thunder fell to rescue it.

The three dark ships all turned to face the thick camouflage wall hiding the inlet. Cannons from the eels cracked the air and sent massive weights whizzing through the smoke, some merely creating loud splashes, many not. Many brought forth the pain of wood splitting.

Hell raced his ship through the flames, the wind at its back and full rowers giving the ship high speed. He had hoped it would appear as an avenging angel, cannons blaring, striking the ghost ship that dared bring a man of his age and station into battle. He, of course, was not on the ship. His instructions were. He and his brethren were well hidden on land with a nearby frigate ensconced from battle.

Vingree's ships scattered, weaving through the smoke and fire like living things. Two other war class vessels emerged from the roiling smoke screen, both at speed and both firing, hitting nothing.

There was nothing to hit.

Merely water.

Vingree and her interceptors rode the smoke like wraiths. They circled behind the war ships and fired, targeting their masts. Wood and sails split. Bilo used his heat lens against the men on decks pointing guns warily outward before Vingree dropped into another billow of smoke. The gunners, touched so suddenly by Satan's hand, did not know whether to curse or pray, looking at each other for immediate guidance. Astarte followed Vingree's course, lobbing cannon shot in her wake. Tanit arced far outward behind the war ship and increased speed, burying her vessel's lance tip into the beast's side and grateful yet again for Bilo and Vingree's shock absorption as part of the lance and hull of the ship. She reversed and quickly pulled away, leaving a hole that eagerly filled. Vingree was already adjusting course to dart past the second war ship. Her vessel was half its size and height but she moved as though she was of the water. Bilo's engines made them too fast for these lumbering oafs, but the daazeet was in no mood to toy, not while homes and businesses burned. Not while there were dead on the shore of a land that had attacked no one. Daazeet Vingree came around and between Astarte and Tanit, who made the same maneuver and followed her out. This was a fight meant to feed open water, the ancestors above, and the sharks below.

The war ships followed.

Cannons boomed.

One of the rounds slammed into the foredeck of Vingree's ship and exited the prow. She cursed and gave the order for bowmen. They took their positions, their arrows already impregnated with flammable gel. "Bilo, be ready!"

"Ready, Daazeet!"

"Fire!" She brought the ship parallel to the offending war ship. Arrows immediately lined its side. She swung around the ship in a circle. Bilo brought his lens to bear on all the arrows, needing ignite only one. A cluster midships flared. Flames raced left and right from center. Tanit and Astarte ran their own circles around the ship, firing away. They veered off, again following Vingree. This ship was dead, it just didn't know it yet. The other war ship had sailed, hoping distance would serve it well, but reserved its fire. The 3 dark ships were too close to its sister ship.

"Let us see," said Vingree eyeing the wall of smoke that seemed as though part of the water and land, "what is behind the curtain." She made straight for the smoke.

A third ship. Meant to engage the battle if the noises of war indicated its brethren were in distress. Captained, however, by a man who felt no need to pointlessly die so far from anything he called home or family. Tendrils of smoke wafted off Vingree's ship as it faced him. She read the war ship's posture immediately and motioned for all stop. She took up her cone and spoke in Spanish to the unseen: "I will allow one ship to leave. Will that be yours or that of your masters?" She knew how this enemy thought. Over-confident and greedy, thus cowardly and cautious. The coastline had enough naturally-occurring inlets blocked by cliffs that hiding even several war ships would not have been difficult.

The captain of the ship calculated his odds. To return home without others to counter their tale was no hardship.

"I need but one finger to point the way," boomed Vingree's voice. Bilo, appearing beside her, scanned the war ship with his binoculars. "I need you," Vingree said to him away from the cone, "down."

"I need to be here," said Bilo. "They have killed and robbed for no reason. I need to see." He looked again. Several uncertain hands were raised on the offending ship, raised and pointing. A coastline with an obstructed view, and none of their signalers on land would be fast enough to warn of Vingree's approach.

Daazeet Vingree nodded. Astarte and Tanit, on their ships, nodded back. The interceptors followed their mother ship at full speed. "Sting them repeatedly," Vingree said into her sound box. The interceptors took point. Gunshots rang out on shore: alarm shots from places of hiding. The three eels angled course outward for visual vantage, then brought their speed inward, homing in on the idiot ship. Vingree dropped back out of cannon range. The interceptors, like the animals they resembled, wove in and out at great speeds as they approached the rapidly firing ship. Astarte and Tanit ordered their protective metal domes set in place, then sent their crews below decks. Firearm barrels could already be seen glinting off the high sun. Astarte and Tanit piloted via rectangular slits in the domes. Shells rang off the domes or the hull of the ships. The ships, immortal, cleaved the water toward the great beast festooned with flags bearing crosses and sigils.

The ships stabbed the beast at the same time, causing all three to churn the waters. They reversed direction on the wheels and pulled out, zipping backward as Vingree shot forward, arrows and Bilo's light firing at the same time. No one on the war ship had ever seen the likes of these three devils attacking it. They feared God, and in fearing God were ingrained with the fear of mystery. Seeing their brethren fleeing did nothing for their resolve either. Each war ship had been told they would have time to harm others at leisure; that the ghost ships would enter a certain ambush of unmatched naval power; that even some of the outlying African kingdoms would assist their holy cause, for much gold and other wealth had already been given in exchange for bodies. They had been told of their superiority.

Their superiority faded as though a flame to a gale.

Vingree raised the cone. "We intend to board your vessel. If we are harmed there will be nothing left of you that would feed a fish." She had a dinghy lowered. She and three crew made the brief row over. They threw grappling hooks over the ship's rail and hoisted upward. When Vingree made the final pull and vaulted over the rail the nervous stares of pale-faced men faced her and her sword. She took a moment to take bearings. The nervous men all calculated the odds between a burning upper hull, three black ships bristling with evils and death, and this dark, bald woman in breeches and long-sleeved tunic striding toward their captain, all pretending that the sound of her boots on the deck drowned out the immediate dangers. She stopped before the captain. She hoped he would not be foolish enough to test her.

"You have sailed where you should not have," she said. "You have angered gods. Speak the names of your betters and I will leave you to die at the water's leisure. Resist and suffer till the end."

"They are on land with a garrison."

"Show me." He did not want to point because he knew they were watched. His hand raised shakily. His finger straightened.

"Die well," said Vingree before turning to leave. "Water or land. You've made no friends here."

"This does not end, devil."

Vingree stopped. She turned to him. Her eyes narrowed and she clenched her jaw as she spoke. "When I find them," she said, "they. Will be. As ash!" Smoke wafted upward like the fear settling on each man present. She turned again and took a step.

"We will bring God to this land and—"

And a sword pierced his chest faster than his next breath. His eyes widened and froze. Vingree held the sword and waited till his body fell to pull itself off her blade. She looked around her, grabbing the eyes of frightened men and turning them without word or motion to hollow, fragile beads. "THIS ENDS HERE!" she shouted. She pulled her sound box from her interior pocket, one more thing for these primitive men to fear. "Bilo?"

"Daazeet."

"Bring all weapons. We hunt." She caught the eye of a grimy-faced war man. "What is the name of he who brought you to die?"

"His excellency Inquisitor Boniface."

"Again," she said, nostrils flaring. The man was looking at her sound box. "Again!" she shouted.

"Hell! He is called Hell."

Vingree frowned. Clearly this was a name used among the lessers as an insult. She had only wanted his actual name spoken again to assure the ancestors marked it. She made for the rail. "Bring him," she ordered. Her people swooped on the man, scooped him by his arms and legs, and swung him over the edge. When they reached the dinghy they fished him out of the water. Somewhere on land there were men heading inward, knowing what was coming for them. Fools hoping the bush would conceal them. "You get to see," she told the wet, gasping man, "your Hell face to face. There will be no more ships taking my people. There will be no raids against my people. I will eradicate your navies. I will give you fires like you have never known. Daazeet Vingree Ramsee is now protector of this land. You will tell Hell you learned of this first." As far as she was concerned, this Boniface Hell was already dead.

Her three ships, dark and shiny, bobbed with the ocean's consent. She was not Yoruba but she wondered if their Orishas worked favorably with her this day. "We hunt Hell," she told them, then used the sound box for Bilo again. "Use the hoses, my love," she said. "Help them." She angled the dinghy toward shore.

"We hunt Hell," she told her treasure again. "And will broke no further evils. This Daazeet Vingree Ramsee promises all ancestors and spirits. Mark it."

Without even thinking about it Bilo pulled the notebook from his back. He jotted the date and three quick words before tucking it back, his mind already racing toward ways to improve their hose system for land-based emergencies.

She is vengeance, he had written. That seemed appropriate. That seemed right for these crimes. She was goddess of this ocean. What was fire to water but pale, useless smoke meant solely for the wind to pull it apart, blow upon it, and make it drift into nothingness. Away.

She was the fury.

She led the way.

TRAVELER'S SONG: *A PULSE PRELUDE*

Kai Leakes

A slight, thudding pain made Fanta aware that she was still alive. Its intense pressure drummed at her temples. She had been in an accident, she was sure of it.

The sound of a loud, *"Bah!"* made her jump. She sat bolt upright, suddenly becoming aware of her surroundings. Her eyes fluttered, clearing her vision. As she moved, she felt dirt under her. She was deeply relieved that she could move without pain, but her vision was milky. Something nudged her. It nudged her again. A moment later, she felt something tugging on her twisted braids. She wiped at her eyes until she could see what the culprit. She let out a shrill scream as she stared into the black beady eyes of several peculiar animals. Leaning back, she blinked again until the hazy things in front of her took shape – a goat and a wolfhound.

The sharp, salty scent of pungent fish accosted her nose. Light water sprinkled over her face and with it she felt her body rock back and forth, making her stomach clench. Back and forth it went. Her hands flew to her mouth to push back the bile rising in her throat. What had felt like grass was filthy, excrement covered straw, complete with plump, buzzing horseflies.

Startled, Fanta pushed herself up to stand, feeling the weight of a bag around her shoulders. A sharp whistle sounded. The wolfhound ran past her. Fanta turned a half circle, following the dog's strides.

"No, damned way," she gasped. "This has to be a dream!"

Crystal clear, turquoise water surrounded her. She was onboard a massive, immaculately carved, dark wood ship inlaid in gold, copper, and shiny steel. Twin, copper gears towered before her, rotating slowly.

Away from her was a large entryway that blocked her view from the rest of the ship. Above her were large, stark white balloons. They were folded together, held by a gilded copper geared belt and thick gold ropes.

She stepped forward in disbelief, then felt herself abruptly snatched backward.

"I'd stay right where I was if I were you," someone behind her said. "Wiggling in a bush only draws bees."

What the hell? Fanta thought, wondering to whom the deep, authoritative voice belonged. The voice was thickly accented in a way that reminded her of her mother. The sultry baritone sent a chill of pleasure and uncertainty down the side of her neck and kept her in her place. She sucked in her breath, too petrified to turn.

"This has to be a nightmare," she muttered.

A deep rumbling laugh traveled through her. Heat radiated from the person behind her.

"I might be a bearer of wicked news, but no, 'tis not a nightmare," the man said. "Alas, bella, it *can* be one, if you make yourself known."

The man laughed.

Fanta felt a chill. She trembled. She glanced down at the long bourbon brown fingers that held her waist. On his index finger was a stunning gold ring, with a ruby stone. An insignia was engraved into it.

The man's grip loosened. Fanta turned. A flash of sun washed over a young face that was very familiar to her. It was the man from her dreams; dreams that had visited her for weeks.

His thick afro bristled in the wind. He sat casually, studying her while still holding her wrist with an amused grin upon his face. A mango lay in his lap. In his other hand, he held a knife, which he used to slice the juicy fruit. He was dressed in a sleeveless kaftan that matched the ships mast. The tunic revealed the man's dense, striated chest. He also wore tailored trousers and black boots. The brother reminded her of a casually dressed dandy in his late twenties.

Fanta scanned him up and down. She noticed that he wore several wheel-lock pistols in his belt and a musket was strapped diagonally against his back. His knife had a jagged, curved blade engraved with intricate carvings on its smooth surface. His handsome face was lined in white stripes that formed angled shapes, horizontal lines, and dots – war paint.

Fanta pressed a hand against her temple. *Where the hell am I and how did I get here?*

"Is this some joke? Did my cousin set this up?" she asked. "Come out, Mikayla!"

"Psst! Tis no joke and stop drawing attention to yourself," the man said. "I must change you out of these peculiar garments before our enemies settle eyes on you and you be strung up." He popped a piece of mango into his mouth.

"Change me out of my clothes? Excuse me?" Fanta said, frowning. She was not about to let this strange guy come anywhere near her.

Licking his full lips, the man gave a slight nod of his head, popped another piece of mango into his mouth, chewed, and then smiled. "Si...and don't echo what I'm saying again. You're like a cockatoo." He chuckled.

"Alas, you crossed over at the wrong time," he went on. "We're in the midst of a battle, Traveler.

Whenever you people pass through, battles always occur or come to a halt."

"Traveler? Who are you? Why do you speak to me as if you know me and why am I soaking wet?" She asked.

Tossing the rest of the mango behind him, the man slid his blade into the side of his boot, then wiped his hands on his trousers.

"I go by many names," the man replied. *"The Afrikan Aztec; the Kemetian; the Senegalese Runaway Rebel,* or *Captain Mbaye.* But in private you may call me Akil Mbaye Nahuatl."

Akil offered his hand. "Welcome to my ship, *the Octavian.* We are in the middle of the Caribbean and I *do* know you. You tumbled into this world at the wrong hour. See, we sorry lots are being sought for bounty as runaway slaves. This was once a slave ship that carried many Africans to the Americas. We liberated it and alas 'tis ours now."

She could not believe this man's words. This was *not* her time. This had to be a dream.

She turned and then made a dash for the edge of the boat. She stopped dead in her tracks. Before her was, trudging toward them on the bright, blue water, was an even more opulent ship with towering, multiple white masts. She staggered backward, bumping into Akil's hard body.

"What year is this?" she croaked.

"You believe now, eh?" Akil said. "You were but a dream to me, also. A strange dream, that followed me from my village overseas to Brazil. Bokonon – High Priests – told me to find you and wait and I did. 'Tis not happenstance that I found you floating adrift on a tree branch covered in odd flower petals..."

His warm words drifted off.

An iron ball whizzed past them.

"Ey...forgot about that," he sighed.

How in the hell could someone forget they are in the middle of a battle? She thought. *Is this man crazy?*

Leading her away, Akil kicked crates to the side with his boot, then stopped near a large door.

"'Tis the year of our Lord seventeen eighty-nine. Now, Senora, you must do as I say...quickly!"

She felt the boat rise then quake. A loud explosion followed. Fanta covered her ears. Akil dragged her into his quarters.

"Before you on the bed are several garments," Akil said, pointing at the African garments on his bunk. "Change into them, then stay here. If trouble comes, I'll send someone to you, si?"

She didn't want to die today in this strange waking dream.

She bobbed her head. "Si...I mean okay."

"Dandy, now act swiftly," Akil said. "Keep your

bag with you and stay hidden." Akil took several strides to the door, then paused. "What is your name?"

"Fanta Awadi," she muttered.

"That is a pleasant name," Akil said. "You are from the same region as my people, I see. Fula." His eyes ran over her in appraisal. "Si, I see it in you; interesting."

Akil swung open the door to his cabin. A loud boom sounded and the ship shook again.

"Keep hidden and tell no one you are a Traveler!" He ordered.

"Why?" Fanta shouted over the clamoring noise.

"Because our people are no longer chattel to be taken," Akil answered. "The Continentals have a standing order that Travelers are to be killed at once or captured. The Travelers are a gift to us and witches and devils to the rebel Colonists. I will protect you, but do stay quiet."

With that, Akil was gone, closing the door behind him.

Fanta snatched off her wet top. The clothes on the bed were rough and scratchy, but they were dry and warm. Sighing, she pulled off her wet dress and slid into a pair of trousers that were somewhat snug against her curves.

Fanta sat on the bed. The shouts from outside continued. Something crashed into the boat over and over.

Fanta stuffed her feet into boots that, thankfully, fit her perfectly. She crawled the bed toward a double pane window. She peeked out.

Before her, were several men and women, of every shade of brown and black, running to and fro, firing weapons powered by gears and pulleys.

Sailors from both sides engaged in masterful hand to hand combat. A petite young woman with low cropped, natural hair, tumbled across the floor. She popped up onto her knees and then whipped her leg in a wide arc, taking down an angry Continental.

The young woman then drew twin copper and wood fighting sticks from the sash tied around her waist. With fluid motions, the young woman blocked blows then advanced, whirling the sticks before her.

A bullet blasted through the window. Shards of glass flew everywhere. Trembling, Fanta hunkered low, covering her head with her bag.

Clinking in her bag drew her attention. She dug into it and found a beautiful knife and a wheel-lock pistol.

Her fingers brushed against something smooth; something that felt like glass. She wrapped her fingers around it and then withdrew a large, pear-shaped object with copper and silver inlaid filigree and coils wrapped around the tip.

"Lotus bulb," Akil's voice came from behind her.

Fanta scrambled to her knees. Akil stood in front of her. His towering shadow draped over her. She noticed that he sweated profusely. Red droplets and soot were splattered all over him.

"You and the lotus bulb are precious to us," Akil said. "In my dreams, I was told it will help us mine the *Pulse*."

"What is going on?" she asked, her voice shaking. "I want off this boat."

"Si, I know you do. Alas, you can't."

"But why?" Fanta asked. "It's crazy for me to stay here. Your enemies could storm in here at anytime!"

"Aye, that's true, but they won't," Akil replied. "I'm keeping you protected as the Bokonon told me to do. If you leave here, you will die. The Colonists will take you and the bulb and that cannot happen. We haven't learned any methods to prevent stray bullets from harming Travelers, so keep clear of the windows."

Akil chuckled.

"Funny," Fanta said with a smirk.

"The goddess Mami Wata says that the world is awakening because of you Travelers. Tethers of natural power that connect us – *Pulse*, we call it – are drawing all timelines and all worlds within this world together for some grand purpose. You will see and understand soon."

Akil bowed and left the room again.

Fanta's face reddened. Her brow furrowed. "I am done with this madness and this madman! Just sit here? Mami Wata?" She vaguely remembered her mother mentioning Mami Wata, but she could not remember what she said or why she said it."

Fanta slipped the bulb back into her bag. *Pulse?* She thought. She withdrew the knife and pistol. She tossed the bag over her shoulder and then slid the knife into her boot. With shaking fingers, she held the gun sideways, studying it.

She had never shot a gun a day in her life. Not even when her mother had given her the old Henry rifle left to her by her father and told her to shoot the angry former Confederate soldiers who raided their Georgia farm after the war, looking to force the now free Blacks to continue laboring for free. Luckily, her mother was a good enough shot for the both of them. No more Confederates returned to their farm after that day. This gun, however, was a bit different from any she had ever seen. It had a thumb gauge, along with a clip in the finger area that connect to gears in the pistol's frame.

She jumped when she heard harsh shouting come from outside.

Akil said stay put; stay low. Okay, I can do that...but he didn't say anything about not defending myself.

Lying flat against the floor, she crawled to the

door and opened it a crack. She peered out. A woman's body fell before her. Life faded from the woman's eyes. Liquid red seeped slowly from the corner of her trembling lips. Terror surged through Fanta as she recognized the face – it was the woman who had fought so well outside of her window. Panicked, she flung the door open, crawling out of the room on her arms and elbows. She lay two fingers against the woman's moist neck. The blood and sweat coating her flesh made it difficult for Fanta to feel the fluttering of her pulse.

Fanta, come on! You're trained for this. You're a nurse. You can do this!

A line of what looked like lightning pierced the hull of the ship. Shards of the ship's deck flew into the air. Everything around Fanta shook. Latching onto the fallen woman's shoulder, she pulled hard and dragged her into Akil's cabin.

"Don't die! Please," she said, searching frantically for the woman's pulse. She sighed through her smile when she found it.

Entry wounds peppered the injured woman's arms, side and right leg. Fanta was not sure where to start, but she worked as quickly as she could. Fanta pulled open the fallen woman's kaftan and then looked around the cabin. On a table near the bed, were several amber liquids, rushing to it, she grabbed the decanters and water in a bucket.

In the fireplace was an iron shovel and a poker. Hurriedly, she grabbed them. Then something – like a fluttering in her stomach –guided her to her bag.

Digging in it, she pulled out what she thought useful – a pair of tweezers; and a blue, glass bottle labeled, simply, *ointment*; She began work, extracting wood shards and iron pellets from the woman.

The woman stirred.

"Stay with me...what is your name?" she asked, tapping the woman's face to keep her awake.

Blood spilled from the corners of the woman's eyes. She let out sharp cries as Fanta worked. Her lips and body trembled from the effort to speak.

"You're a fighter; you can do it! Your name...tell me, please."

"Tulu," the woman whispered. "Tulu Wata."

"Hello, I'm Fanta," she said, continuing to work. "I saw how fierce you were out there. You saved many of your people."

Tulu said nothing. She just stared at Fanta through fading eyes.

Occasionally she would mutter in a language Fanta did not understand and then pass out. All Fanta could do was continue working her hardest to keep the woman alive.

The door to the cabin flung open. Orders were barked at her in Spanish. Swiftly, Fanta grabbed her pistol and squeezed the trigger.

She yelped as a ray of golden light erupted from the muzzle of the pistol. The flames and gleaming lights in the cabin intensified.

The hulking man in the doorway stiffened.

Fanta could see the hallway behind him through the gaping hole in his chest and back.

He collapsed in a smoking heap.

Fanta darted to the open door. Other men bounded up the hall toward her. She pointed the pistol and squeezed the trigger again. This time, balls of pewter shot out of the gun.

The round ripped through the flesh of the man at the front. A moment later, a muffled burp rose from the small hole that the ball punched in his chest.

The man fell to his knees, his bubbling insides running out of every orifice like soup boiling over a pot.

Fanta, appalled, wrinkled her nose. She leaped back into the room and then quickly slammed the door, pressing her back against it.

Tulu lay sprawled on the floor watching her. She shifted her body, bumping agains Fanta's bag. The Lotus Bulb rolled out and onto the floor.

Tulu stared at it, wide-eyed.

Fanta stuffed the bulb back in the knapsack and then checked the bindings on Tulu's waist. "Just stay calm Tulu."

Tulu gazed at Fanta. Tears fell down the corner

of her eyes.

The door swung open again.

Akil stepped into the room, panting and frantically looking Fanta's way. He rushed forward then took a knee beside Tulu.

"Blast the bastards!" he roared.

Akil cradled the woman's head in his muscular arms. Yanking off his tartan, he gently placed it under Tula's head and then stood. "Can you help her?"

"I've been trying," Fanta explained. "I don't know what else to do. I'm a nurse, but there is very little here to work with."

Akil took several strides towards the table. He reached under it, his long fingers feeling for something. When he found it, a slight clicking noise began.

Several gears appeared from under the table, cranking and revealing a massive metal contraption that rose from the floor.

"Tulu is the embodiment of Mami Wata," Akil said. "She prophesied that we will harvest the Pulse for our people and you Travelers will protect the gates from the men who attack us. This special ship was to keep you safe and hidden from them, but they found us too fast because of their traitorous trackers who seek the bulbs...and you."

The contraption that rose from the floor was

what the people of Fanta's time called a *Gatling Gun* – a rapid-fire, crank-driven gun with a cylindrical cluster of several barrels.

Akil hit a button on the edge of the table.

The windows in the room disappeared into their sills. The ceiling opened, exposing the sky. He sat in his chair before the "Gatling" gun. The seat rose, taking him, and the gun, skyward.

"*Negro furtou é ladrão; branco furtou é barão,*" he said. "A Negro who steals is a thief; a white man who steals is a baron."

Rotating the chair he gave Fanta a quick glance. "They call us thieves, but we take to survive; to protect Pulse. They take *us* and take the Travelers."

"I can't let them take the ship or you," he said, staring down the big gun's barrel. "You are a descendant of Mami Wata. Her blood is the key to the gates that bring all the Travelers here. We must keep the gates open for the future generations because if we don't, all is lost and the Colonists will wipe us out."

Tulu coughed. "They will kill those of us who can mine the Pulse and then steal it from us," she said. Her voice was a bit stronger. "Then, they will jump to your time and continue our suffering as chattel. Your...Emancipation, as the other Travelers I have encountered called it, will never happen. I have seen it in my dreams. I have also seen you saving your world."

"I'm just a nurse who awakened in this crazy world. I don't have power," Fanta cried.

"You are still locked in fear and confusion," Akil said. "We need you to trust us; trust yourself. Tulu, too, is Mami Wata incarnate. Her dreams never fail."

Tulu coughed then slapped her hand in the bowl of water beside her.

In the rippling water, Fanta saw images of people locked in battle. They fought using an energy that emanated from the earth. She saw people from her world disappear and then appear in this time on the same mission that she was.

Fanta felt weak. She fell to her knees. Her hand seemed guided to the same bowl of water where Tulu's hand lay.

A translucent, light blue mist rose from the water and then wrapped around Fanta's hand. It traveled up her wrist, disappearing under the sleeve of her shirt. She felt its cool touch spread throughout her entire being.

She heard Tulu whisper, "Pulse."

Fanta grabbed Tulu's hand, sending some of the light blue essence into the woman.

"We are the vessel of Pulse; all shaman and native born around the world," Akil said. "Only we can wield it and we will stop it from being corrupted!"

He fired the big gun. The weapon purred as it spat a maelstrom of iron across the sky.

Fanta stared at Tulu. The light blue essence had

transformed her. Her exquisite, red-brown skin shimmered like the surface of the sea. She had taken the appearance of a sea nymph. She was a god.

"Touch the bulb," Tulu said. Her voice like the sound of a well-tuned harp. "Then cast it into the open. We will protect you, daughter."

Fanta felt everything around her speak to her. The air, the wood of the ship, the fire, the clouds, the water – it all spoke to her and welcomed her to use their gifts. She picked up the bulb.

Akil shot off rounds like a madman from his seat behind the massive gun. "Go, Traveler!"

She grabbed the bulb, then ran to the door.

Heat flowed from her hands into the bulb. Running with it, she sprinted past frenzied men and women who tried to block her way.

"The bulb!" someone shouted.

"Traveler!" shouted another.

Then, "Kill her!"

The sailors on the boat, Akil's crew, protected her. A rope was thrown her way. She grabbed it and held on as she was lifted off her feet. As she rose, she saw Tulu, fighting with her twin sticks as if she had never suffered any injury. A light blue light flashed with each strike she delivered. Tulu shouted. A moment later, columns of water erupted from the sea and struck her enemies, knocking several of the men overboard.

Akil fired on the enemy ship, ripping scores of small holes in its hull.

Fanta looked down at the sputtering bulb. It's blue light had begun to fade. It obviously needed more power, and she was not sure how to recharge it.

"Crazy world I'm in, please, help me feed this bulb," she said, looking skyward.

A bullet whizzed past her. She yelped.

Tucking the bulb under her arm, Fanta drew her pistol and fired a volley of rounds.

Men fell wherever she pointed the muzzle of the weapon.

Akil smiled at her, raising his fist.

Two men charged toward her. She squeezed the trigger again, but the gun did not fire.

"Damn it!" she spat, dropping it.

She took a wide legged stance and, holding tight to the sparking bulb, she swung her fist.

Her fist slammed into a man's mouth.

The man she struck laughed.

Fanta extended her leg driving her instep up between his legs.

The man collapsed to his knees, grasping his

aching groin.

Fanta shuffled her feet in a little dance and then kicked the man in his face.

The man fell on his face. He did not move.

Akil shouted down to her, "Your power! Use it!"

She turned, looking up at the chair. Akil was gone.

Around her, the air rippled. She thrust out her palm. She felt a tug within her, like the atmosphere was pulling her into its embrace, becoming one with her. A wave of water rose and followed the movement of her hand. She thrust her palm toward the second man who closed on her. Tendrils of water speared into each of the man's orifices, drowning him where he stood.

Fanta dropped her hand. She blinked a couple of times and shook her head. She looked around to see if anyone noticed what she had done. Akil's crew was locked in battle. Intermittently, they, too, used elemental powers. Pieces of wood lifted Continentals into the air and then slammed them into other Colonists. Other men combusted into flames and ash.

"My dreams revealed that you can call on lightning," Akil said, felling men with his war hammer as he stepped toward her.

Fanta shook her head, laughed, and then shrugged, "My day can't get any crazier. Okay...let's do this!"

Akil slammed his hammer into the face of a Continental. He peered over his shoulder at Fanta and nodded. His hand reached behind him, brushing against her back. She turned to face him. He turned, leaned forward and kissed her. *Bring on the lightning,* she thought.

A loud crack of thunder sounded. She and Akil leaped back from each other.

Lightning speared through her and into the bulb. All around her, the waves rolled, swayed and grew.

Tulu leaped from the boat. A moment later, the waves swallowed her.

"Tulu!" Fanta gasped.

Tulu's smiling face surfaced. She waved toward Fanta, beckoning her to join her.

Fanta breathed a sigh of relief. She then tossed the bulb overboard, opened her arms wide and plunged into the sea.

Panic swallowed Fanta up with the waves. She sank, following the bulb into the blackness of the ocean. Water burned her lungs. *This wasn't how it was supposed to be,* she thought. But it was.

The bulb landed on a bed of sand deep in the ocean. Fanta landed beside it. Colorful fish swam past her, settling around where the bulb was, as if protecting it. She felt the thumping of her heart stall into a slow rhythm.

Had she not felt the light fluttering under her body she would have let go of the final bit of air in her mouth. She felt her body drift away, leaving the bulb where it lay.

Her spirit danced in her chest. She heard a voice: *Stay or go.*

Stay! She thought.

A mighty blast of blue energy rose from the sand beneath her and sent Fanta flying out the sea. Below her, the seas swirled and swirled. She coughed out the briny taste of water. A moment later, she landed on her side, back on the deck of the ship.

"The ships...they are being swallowed by the sea! Mami Wata's vengeance has begun!" people shouted.

She felt a hand on her back. It gently traveled down her body and then lifted her into the air.

"I was vexed that I would not get to kiss you again," Akil said, gazing into her eyes.

Too weary to speak, she laid her head against his chest.

His crew, including Tulu, gathered on the deck.

A bright light flashed above them. Over their heads, a circle of white power opened in the sky. Within the circle, Fanta could see many islands, mountains and massive stone structures, whose outer surfaces were triangular, converging to single points at their summits.

"You opened a new gate," Akil said. "More will come and more battles will occur. But until then, we have our own journey to go on, Fanta, my precious Traveler."

Fanta held him close. She noticed a gash on Akil's forehead. "I have to patch that up," she said.

"Patch? Hmm...si, yes you do," Akil replied. "Shipmates, we won! Now, home to the Isles!"

Fanta smiled. *Mami Wata, if I'm dreaming, never wake me again,* she thought.

Her dreams had become a sweet reality, one she never wanted to give up, as strange as that was.

THE ADVENTURES OF THE BLACK STAR

Jeff Carroll

One

"Ijeoma why must we go so far from the shore? The Niger is not a fan of our fishing," Aneesa observed.

Both sisters had rich, dark-brown skin. Ijeoma, the oldest, was also the larger of the two girls.

"Never mind the rough waves. This boat is carved from the baobab tree." Ijeoma replied.

"It is not the boat that I fear will not survive these waters, big sister. It is us."

Their boat rocked from side to side in the muddy waters, as the craft passed through a bend in the river. Ijeoma steadied it with her oar, and Aneesa rowed. It was just past dawn and the animals were awake.

Birds flew over the river looking for fish, and large fish hunted the smaller ones.

"Why do you fear the water Aneesa?" asked Ijeoma. "You have been my fishing partner for over a year, yet you do not trust me."

"I am not here because I enjoy the water like you," Aneesa retorted. "I enjoy eating fish, and if I wait for mother to fish I will go crazy."

Ijeoma smiled at her sister. "When father started taking me out on the water, he calmed my nerves by telling me the story of 'The water and the lad'."

"Well, tell me the tale so that my nerves may be calm."

"If you quiet your running mouth, I will."

"Just tell me the story."

"Father explained to me that we are always on water," Ijeoma said. "In fact, it is water which we are made of. Water loves the land. And water surrounds all land."

Aneesa looked interested. "Really? But all I see to the East is land."

"Well beyond our forest are hills; past the hills is water. You can take this river to that great water. Father said: 'Land rests in the palms of Yemoja. She is the Goddess who creates and loves us.'"

Aneesa laughed. "Well I don't want to drown in the hands of this river. Maybe the story was more effective when father told it."

"You need to worry less about drowning," her sister scoffed, "and start gathering the net as we are almost near our fishing spot."

"I am only worried about falling into the water, because you are as big as a man, with arms and legs like an ayyu."

"Oh, so you feel my legs are as fat as a manatee?"

"Yes, a big, fat ayyu."

"Well, it's not my size and strength that threaten the capsizing of our boat. It is your melon head. At least I am balanced, as your head is as big as a manwawi. When you were little, mother said you might need a crutch for your head if you were ever to walk straight."

"You always talk about my head. You're just jealous because the boys like it better than yours. Wait until we get back to the village. I bet Musu helps carry my fish basket. I can't wait for us to get back," Aneesa teased. "He's going to try to kiss me again."

Why must we travel so far from our village anyway? We have passed our land."

"Hush, Aneesa! Father said land is of no one tribe's possession."

As Ijeoma and Aneesa's boat came around the bend, they saw another craft with two boys throwing their nets into the water. One youth was the size of

Ijeoma. The other one was much larger and had longer hair.

Both boys seemed strong. Their skin was as dark as midnight, and their muscles shone bronze in the sunlight. The young men's teeth were so white and shiny they could be seen across the river. The larger boy threw a sharp stick into the water with a rope tied to the end of it.

"Meeng-gah-bou!" said the larger boy as he looked down at his fishing partner. "The women are here early, too! Don't let them see that we haven't caught any fish yet."

The sisters steered their boat up beside the men. "Ga Kojo, I see you came early to see if you can out fish us!" Ijeoma called out. "I'm sorry, but you and Kwame will not be winning today. We have a hungry village to feed."

"You will lose this time!" Ga Kojo said.

"I have a new fishing tool. And we have already caught a few fish." Kojo said.

"Is that why Kwame's net is dry?" the young woman taunted. "Do not lie to me Kojo! You are no better a fisher, than Kwame is a fighter. Let us get on our way then, and see who will be the better team."

Aneesa stood and almost fell, as she threw her fishing net over the side of the boat. Kwame quickly stood and threw his net into the water as well.

"We cannot lose to these girls again Kojo! Enough

with your silly fishing pole! Fishing has not changed since the time before our fathers. Now sit down and help me win this contest."

The two groups fished until sun set. As the river began to darken, they made their ways to the shore. They quickly pulled their boats out of the water, and unloaded their baskets of fish.

"Those are very big fish that you have caught, Aneesa," Kwame said. He smiled slyly. "Let me see one of them." He reached toward her basket.

She balled up her fist, and shook it in front of Kwame's face. "Touch one of my fish and I will toss you in the water!"

The young man laughed. "Look at this small fist." He cupped Aneesa's hand. "It looks like a decoration. What, may I ask, do you plan to do with a little fist like this?"

"I bet this little fist caught more fish than you did."

"Just be glad we let you fish here, in our tribe's water." Kojo retorted.

"What do you mean?" Aneesa bristled. "The river is not the possession of any single tribe. It is here for us all."

"You are as wise as you are beautiful. You will make quite the wife one day. Maybe I will come rescue you away from your poor tribe, and bring you to live with the kings and Nanas of *my* tribe." Kojo grabbed his fishing pole, and placed it next to their pile of baskets.

"You can't even out-fish me, how will you be able to afford me." Aneesa said, while smiling. She dropped her last basket, making her and her sister's total of four baskets one more than Kwame and Kojo's three.

Ijeoma grinned. "We won again! It is always nice to fish with you."

As the four sat down, a twig snapped loudly behind them. Kojo grabbed his fishing pole.

"That sounds like a monkey or something," Kwame scoffed. "Put that fishing stick down!"

The brush behind them was pushed aside. Ten heavy-set white men stepped through. Two of them were holding long rifles. The men wore clothes that fitted around their legs, chest and arms loosely. Their bodies were hairy, they looked dirty and they reeked of body waste.

"Look what we've got here!" the fattest one of the white men said in a language the four barely understood.

"Yes, Cortland," his blond friend replied. "It seems they have also brought us lunch."

"What do you want from us sicklings?" Ijeoma demanded. She spoke the language of whites, once helped by her tribe.

"Dirk, this one knows English!" the fat one exclaimed. "And we're not sick!"

He grabbed Kwame.

The youth flipped him over his back.

Another white man punched Aneesa knocking her to the ground.

Kojo grabbed his fishing pole and threw it into the chest of a white man.

Ijeoma was punched in the stomach.

She returned with a blow to the face of her attacker.

Kojo rose to throw another of his fish spears, but was shot in the chest before it could leave his hand. His body was blown across his boat, landing in the water.

Ijeoma and Aneesa froze, as the other whites pointed guns at them.

Kwame turned toward his brother's motionless body, floating on its back in the Niger's water. "Kojo!"

Rifles were pointed at each of the three friends' heads. They were shackled and led to the brush to a group of other shackled Africans.

They were dragged through the woods and forced to walk the whole night.

The other African captives were so battered, they

could not utter any words.

Just before dawn, they reached a large stone building surrounded by water.

Kwame was separated from the women, who were pushed into a dark room with only a small opening in the top.

The room smelled of human waste and rotten flesh.

They could hardly see each other and could not make out any of the other women.

"Aneesa are you okay?" Ijeoma said.

By now, both sisters were tired and scared.

"Yes. What happened? Is our tribe at war?" Aneesa asked.

"I don't think so. They told us this building was a castle, but it's a dungeon of some sort. This is no war! War is fair, this is a sneaky capture!"

"I wish Kojo had killed all of them!"

"We must calm ourselves, so we can think of a way out," Ijeoma said.

The other women in the room moaned and cried. The sun beaming through the small window, was the only light they had. Ijeoma held her sister close. They closed their eyes and the smells and sounds of their Slavers faded.

####

The wooden door opened. "Bring him four women and one boy for me," said a white, red-haired man pointing a rifle. Two other pudgy men strained to keep the heavy door ajar.

Ijeoma and Aneesa fell back, covering their eyes from the glaring sunlight. One of the men walked through and grabbed Ijeoma, Aneesa and two other women.

"Let me see them first." The red-haired man said.

The captives were pulled to their feet and spun around before the man. Two of the women were thin, and coughed when their clothes were opened.

"I will take these three," the man with the rifle said, as he pointed to all but Ijeoma. "Take this large one back to the hole. She will fetch a high price at the market – that is, if she, or any of these withered animals, can make it."

Ijeoma jerked Aneesa back as they pulled her away. "Get off of my sister!"

One of the pudgy men hit Ijeoma in the back.

She turned toward him, blocking the next blow and two more before the butt of another white man's rifle crashed into her jaw, knocking her to the ground.

"Gentlemen," the red-haired man ordered. "You must stop playing with these savages!" "As you can see, they get quite aggressive when they are from the same tribe or family. That is why you must separate them all. They must not be able to even communicate with each other. We will ready the ship and leave before night fall. Notify the crew that they have two hours to finish up their fornication."

Ijeoma was dragged into another dark room and thrown inside. Before her blurry vision fully dissipated, she saw Aneesa taken upstairs.

Two

Ijeoma rocked from side to side. Her eyes opened and closed. Images of her Slavers, Kojo being shot and Aneesa being snatched away, flashed before her. The screams of Kwame and Aneesa grew in volume, growing louder and louder – so loud her head began to throb.

The screams merged with the moans outside of the realms of her mind. She opened her eyes to find she was shackled to the other female slaves. The smell of salt and the rocking of the room, told her she was in the *Palm of Yemoja* – the endless water only the big men of her village could fish or swim in.

"Wha, wha!" the lady next to her screamed. Ijeoma jumped and nudged another woman in her side. The woman's only response was a soft moan.

"What is this place? Where is my sister? Aneesa! Kwame! Somebody tell me what is going on!"

Ijeoma cried. A chorus of voices answered her.

"We are captives of the Devil, being punished for something we have done wrong!" a man's voice said.

"They are white traders!" another voice exclaimed. "Maybe they are going to sell us to the Arabs or Moors!"

"They can't be Arabs, they did not mention Islam," another voice from the far end of the room said.

"I was taken with my sister, Aneesa, and another boy named Kwame!" Ijeoma said. "We were just fishing!"

"The Arabs don't have boats this big!" the male voice said. "My village was raided by Arabs two seasons ago. We were converted to Islam and I was given the name Kalif.""

"My name is Maremba I was given to them with my uncle. We were supposed to be representatives from our tribe to their tribe. As soon as we got out of the village, we were beaten and shackled."

"My best friend, Kojo and I were taken in by the Mali tribe, after our parents were killed by Arab and Moor raiders," a young male voice said.

"Kwame, the fisherman is that you?" Ijeoma said.

"Yes, Ijeoma! Where is your sister?" Kwame said.

Ijeoma bowed her head. "I don't know." She began to sob.

####

The door of the ship's hull squeaked open and moonlight shone through. Three heavyset white men walked into the center of the room. A thin white man with a long beard followed. He was holding a scroll tablet.

"Amazing," the thin man said, while looking around the hull. "You have taken a three-mask, galley warship and simply boarded up the cannons ports. This ship was designed for the British Royal Navy. It carries eighteen six-pound cannons. It was not designed for human cargo."

"Take the dead blacks, and pile them over here," The largest of the men said, pointing to the right. "We'll wait until morning, and throw them into the water. I like to watch the sharks tear apart their flesh."

The thin man looked shocked. "Commander Millroy, you mean to tell me, you're just going to throw them overboard?"

"Mr. Clarkson, you may have been given permission from the Lloyds' market to work with us," Commander Millroy sneered. "But those prissy businessmen from London know nothing of the trade of these savages. I must remind you that this is a *Dutch* Trading vessel and you could find your*self* fighting off sharks in the morning if you do not mind your tongue."

Clarkson turned red. "Captain Alonso, my employer, is far from a byproduct of Holland! I am well aware of your country's pride and involvement in this Atlantic trade."

"But mind you this," Clarkson went on, "I am not only an inspector for the Lloyds council. My trip is partly funded by the Brotherhood of Abolitionists. Therefore, my dear, Dutch trader, if you want to continue to brave these seas, and make a living in trade, you would be wise to make my return to England a safe one! Or you will find yourself in a British jail!"

The white men inspected the various African captives separating the ones who were dead from the living. The woman shackled to Ijeoma was still moaning when they unchained her. She let out another soft moan when her heavy chains were unlocked.

"What are you doing? This woman is still alive!" Mr. Clarkson said.

"Mr. Clarkson this is not the work for the squeamish," Millroy drawled. "This is a dirty job. You enjoy your tea from the East and sugar from the Caribbean. But you are having a hard time accepting where they come from."

"What does the treatment of this woman have to do with my love of tea?" Clarkson shot back.

"She is rotten and will be jettisoned with the dead. She will die before morning. And if she hasn't already infected these others God, has blessed us. A rotten one like her could destroy entire booty. We are very lucky if she hasn't already passed her disease on."

Commander Millroy grabbed Ijeoma by the arm. "Look! She is next to this strong female! This young one could balance our books and yield a lot of your beloved sugar barrels when we make it to Hispaniola."

Clarkson shook his head in disgust. "I'm surprised any of these people make it anywhere, being treated like this. No wonder the Lloyds only insure one third of your cargo. These people need food and water."

"I have heard enough from you! If you continue to be a nuisance to me, I will have the captain lock you in your quarters for the remainder of the trip. That is something, my good fellow, well within our agreement with the Lloyds."

"Very well, commander Millroy. I will document my observations and you will hear no more from me."

The men continued to examine the African captives in the room, and pull dead slaves out. Then they passed out cups of water, and tossed them bread to eat.

####

"Ijeoma, I do not know what is happening to us!" Kwame seethed. "But as soon as I get my hands free, I will knock one of those rock shooters out of their hands and seek Kojo's revenge!"

"Kwame, I think I have an idea," said Ijeoma, "Do you remember why you have to club a Tiger fish when you take them out of the water?"

####

The next morning, all of the captives were dragged on deck and allowed to exercise. Ijeoma gazed into the waters of Yemoja. She looked on as the sick woman next to her was pushed over the side of the ship.

Ijeoma closed her eyes in horror, when she saw large fish devouring their flesh. She also observed the size of the ship. . . and each of the men working on it. Just when she heard the command to bring them back down to the dark room, the young woman fell to the floor and began moaning.

"What is wrong with this big one?" a pudgy white asked.

"She is too big to have her thrown in the water," another slaver replied. "Give her a second ration of water and bread. Maybe it will strengthen her by morning."

"Very well then."

####

That night in the captive's quarters, Ijeoma moaned and made herself vomit. She lay in the vomit and smeared it over her body. When the men came down to pass the drinking cups and inspect for dead, Ijeoma closed her eyes and lay still.

"Well it seems Mr. Clarkson has brought us bad

luck!" a slaver exclaimed. "This big one has caught the dead disease, from the old one we threw over this morning." He unshackled Ijeoma, and tried to pick her up. He gestured to his pudgy friend: "Dirk grab her legs. . ."

They tossed Ijeoma into the pile of dead. Ijeoma lay motionless until the door was closed again. The she pushed through the few bodies laying over her and stuck only her head out.

Lying in the pile of dead bodies, Ijeoma was reminded of an experience with her father. She was clubbing fish in their boat, and her father asked: "Why are you so passionately killing the fish?"

Ijeoma pointed to her father's leg and told him she did not want the tiger fish to jump out and bite her like they did him. Tiger fish would lay motionless in the boat and, without warning, wake up and hop back in the water or bite the fisherman.

Her father said: "Even a fish has a spirit. It is still a life you are ending. We are fishermen not killers. Killers take lives for no reason. We take lives for food. We honor the spirit of the animal by eating its body and not giving it a gruesome death."

He looked into her eyes. "Be mindful of the taking of life and ending spirits. Even ending the spirit of an animal has an effect on the hunter. If you fail to respect that, you can become a murderer. A hunter – even a *fish* hunter – can be a dangerous person."

After thinking about what her father said, she

asked: "Father, why didn't you tell me this before I clubbed my first fish?"

Her father's face was solemn. "I am telling you this now, so you will only club *fish*."

The smell of dead flesh was nauseating. But not enough to wipe out Ijeoma's fear that she would become the very thing her father warned her of – a murderer.

Dirk and two other men walked down the stairs to the holding room. "We are going to have to call in a claim for this entire booty," Dirk complained, "If we continue to lose slaves at this rate."

"I think the captain enjoys fornicating with the savage women too much and we stayed at the fort longer than we should have," another man said.

Dirk joined in their laughter. "Well you can't blame him for that. I find myself lost in the flesh of these primitives."

The third slaver held a long rifle pointed to the ground, as the two others walked among the Africans. "Just make this fast because I do not enjoy the smell of dead flesh. We only have two weeks left. I won't make it, doing this every day. I'll have to climb the mast or something."

A body slammed against the third man, knocking him into a group of waiting Africans. Ijeoma's legs swung into Dirk, and the second white man.

Kwame caught Dirk and twisted his head. He

squeezed, gritting his bright white teeth until he heard the snap of Dirk's neck.

Ijeoma jumped on the other mate and delivered a blow to his groin.

The mate was only able to open his mouth before her fist connected with his jaw, knocking him to the hard wood floor.

Kwame found the keys to the shackles in Dirk's pants. Free of his shackles, he joined the other Africans. He found another African, named Kalif, struggling with the slaver holding the rifle. In the next instant, the gun was pulled from the white man's hand and the rifle barrel came crashing down on – and through – his skull.

"I say we kill them all!" Ijeoma said, pulling the long rifle out of the fat white man's head. "There are at least 75 of us and fifty are strong enough to fight! Twenty white men remain on the other side of this door! I am going to kill as many of them as my strength allows. I ask that you do the same."

Kwame unlocked Kalif and the rest of the captives. They rushed to the deck, attacking the ship's crew with great speed and stealth.

Raging, the Africans tossed as many slavers as they could into the waiting waters.

"Send them to Yemoja and let the fish feast on their white flesh today!" Ijeoma cried.

Three white men armed with rifles rose up from the

port side of the ship. Ijeoma dove to deck as shots flew over her head.

Kwame charged.

A steel ball hit him in the shoulder, knocking him to the ground.

Ijeoma squeezed behind a hogshead, trying to figure out how to fire the rifle she wrested out of a white man's hands.

Kalif jumped up to confront the men. He grabbed one of the guns and engaged the man in a struggle for it.

Another man aimed his rifle at Kalif. He fired, blowing Kalif over the side of the ship.

Kalif's murderer reloaded and then aimed at another African, but before he could fire another shot, he was overtaken by five gaunt captives.

Captain Alonso stood on the quarterdeck shooting Africans with his pistol. Ijeoma and Kwame watched, trying to figure how to get to him without being killed.

Kwame pressed his palm against his bleeding shoulder. He shook his head at Ijeoma. She pointed, motioning toward a long piece of wood.

"Go fishing Kwame!" Ijeoma yelled.

The wood was long and sharp just like his brother's fishing pole.

Kwame grabbed the wooden pole, stood up and then hurled it through Captain Alonso's chest. As Alonzo fell into the ship's steering wheel, the remaining Africans stood up and cheered.

Three

"Search the ship! Find my sister! Make sure we have killed all the devils!" Ijeoma said, as she finished wrapping Kwame's shoulder. "This should hold you."

"I can't believe something like this has happened!" Kwame exclaimed. He stood up and looked out into the open water. "Where are we, and where were they taking us?"

"I don't know. We are so far out in this water, I cannot see land. We need to get back to our villages and warn others,"

She choked back a sob. *Aneesa, where are you?*

Two Africans dragged William Clarkson out to the main deck. He was dropped in front of Ijeoma and Kwame.

"He says he can help us," one of the Africans said. "He had no weapon. We found him hiding in a room under the captain's room."

Ijeoma looked into Clarkson's sky-colored eyes. It reminded her of her first meeting with a white person – and of how her mother cured their disease. She remembered, too, the blue-eyed man who taught all of the children English.

"You are not like the other sicklings are you?"

"No I am not. My name is William Clarkson. I was on this ship to document the treatment of Caribbean labor transfer."

Kwame stood and walked over to him. He grabbed William by the shoulder and lifted him up. "I heard you talking to the men who guarded us. I believe you. Do you know where they were taking us?"

"You were being transported to a trading port on the island of Hispaniola?"

"Do you know how to get us back to our villages?" Ijeoma said.

"I am not a sailor. Or a navy officer. But if we can decipher the captain's charts, we should be able to figure out how to get back to Africa."

"Where will they be? These charts of the captain," Ijeoma asked.

William pointed behind the wheel. "Please follow me. I'm sure captain Alonzo kept them in his quarters."

Ijeoma and Kwame went with William to the captain's quarters. She asked another African to count how many survivors there were, and get an overall report on the ship while they were gone.

The Captain's room was fitted with a desk and a cushioned chair; embroidered with Adinkra symbols and precious gems. There was also a large rug from Persia, copper pots, Arabian clothes and other European items.

"May I ask how is it that you know how to speak English so well?" William asked.

"There are white people who were given land near our village. They taught us," Ijeoma said. "They were very sick when they came to us. That is why we call them *sicklings*."

"I know how to speak English, because many of the traders who came to our village spoke it," Kwame added. "Can you speak Ga or Yoruba?"

"No," William replied. "I am not familiar with your native tongues. However, I am aware that in the colonies, the laborers have created a patois, of both the Spanish and English languages."

Ijeoma finished her search of the room. "I see no charts. There are valuables from everywhere, but no charts. What would these water directions look like?"

"They should be large, rolled papers," William said.

"What if we don't find these papers?" asked Kwame.

William whipped his head around toward them. He was shaking. He was clearly afraid of telling them his answer.

"It is quite possible that Captain Alonzo was so experienced, that he no longer required charts,"

William said. "And if that is true, then we must set our sails, say a prayer, and hope we drift to land and not into another slave ship."

####

Just before dawn, across the ocean, a dark skinned crewman climbed the mainmast of another ship. He hooked his legs around the thick pole and looked over the water through a long copper telescope. Something sparkled on the horizon. Another dark-skinned crewman stood below him on the deck, holding a back-staff and looking out in the same direction.

"Oh, oh! I see a ship! Tell Captain this morning brings us English booty," the man hanging from the mainmast exclaimed.

The crewman ran across the deck to the captain's cabin. It was an elaborate room with flashy cups and huge gold picture frames on the walls. A large chaise lounge lined the wall, giving the room the feel of a miniature castle.

"Caesar, Caesar! There be booty at sea!" the crewman announced.

"Why, why, *why* do you address me as such?" Shouted a voice from the behind the shadow cast by the morning sun. "And who is this *Caesar* you keep asking for?"

"Excuse me captain! Caesar be the great ruler of the Roman Empire. But you...you be *Black* Caesar, sir – the one and only free man of the high seas. Feared by all who dare to sail the salty waters."

"Aye," the voice boomed. "Caesar is for Rome; *Black* Caesar is for the sea."

Out stepped a block-shaped man almost as wide as he was tall, with skin as black as the night sea. Though Black Caesar stood a little over six feet, he was without doubt a monster of a man. He flashed bright, white teeth with a wide grin in stark contrast to his ebon skin.

"Where is this booty you speak of?" Black Caesar demanded.

The crewman led him to the quarterdeck, where they were both able to see the ship using the telescope.

A smile of excitement and eagerness spread across Black Caesar's face. He threw back his arm holding the telescope into the chest of the crewman. "Well make haste and ready the crew for it's booty we be getting today!"

The crewman smiled, and quickly walked down to the ship's lower levels to rally the other men.

Adams Brown was playing a game of chess with another crewman as Black Caesar approached him.

"Why do you teach my crew these games of conquest, rather than enjoy the real conquest we pursue?" Black Caesar asked.

Adams was clothed in a worn sweater vest, made in his birth place of Virginia. He looked up directly into

Black Caesar's eyes. "I play these games with my fellow crewmen so it will sharpen their strategic minds. This game is a game of moves. You cannot simply win it with one move. You must plan three and four moves ahead in order to trap your opponent. You learn to use your pawns to..."

Black Caesar took in a deep breath and, let out a laugh full of bass. "You are no different than the day you joined our crew! The time you endured as a war captive on that slave plantation has served you well! But listen up...on my ship we have no room for pawns! Now, take your mind away from the artificial and ready yourself for reality. We are preparing to take a ship which seems to be adrift. "

"Captain we are going to seize a ship in the day?" the crewman playing with Adams asked.

"Why not? Do you think we need the cover of darkness to pirate these waters? We cannot limit our actions to the cover of night, whatever we encounter!" Black Caesar bellowed. "We must be able to handle it if we are to truly be the source of fear of these waters."

Black Caesar looked Adams up and down.

"Adams, I see you still wear that ragged vest of yours," he said. "Why don't you put on something more battle-ready, like that black leather coat we took from the last royal ship we sank?"

"This is what my father was wearing the night we ran away from that prison the Europeans call a plantation," Adams replied. "It is all the armor I need in any battle with traders of human flesh."

The crewmen all stood ready as Caesar's ship cruised up alongside the adrift ship.

The ship appeared abandoned. No life was visible on it. There was rope tied to the wheel. And all of the sails were drawn, leaving the ship drifting.

"Caesar, the ship looks to be empty. I see no life aboard," Adams said, as he held the wheel of Black Caesar's ship.

"Maybe a case of scurvy?" another crewman cried.

"Just bring us up close. Everyone stay ready," Black Caesar ordered.

No crew suffering from scurvy would tie rope to their wheel, he thought. *Something is wrong. They wanted the rudder steady.*

Caesar's ship bumped the side of the adrift ship. His men threw anchors connected to thick ropes onto the ship's deck and then pulled the two ships together.

The captain was the first to board the main-deck of the barren ship. He held a flintlock pistol in each hand. Following him were several crewmen holding a variety of daggers, cutlasses and muskets. The deck was stained with blood. They explored the ship, creeping with heightened caution.

Adams – a wiry figure, not as burly as Black Caesar but standing a little taller than the menacing Captain – tiptoed toward the door to the captain's quarters.

Adams motioned with his knife toward a crewman holding a short-barreled musket.

Although Adams was thin he had what he called "a country boy strength," which all of Caesar's crew learned to respect. Caesar often relied on it himself when he needed it. This was one of those times. So, Adams leaned back and kicked the door with the heel of his foot.

The door flung open, revealing an empty captain's room.

Adams stepped in, looking around as he entered the room. The cabinets were open and a variety of charts lay scattered on the floor. A desk with a large gold chair sat in the corner. There was no sign of life.

Adams turned back to announce his findings when an arm wrapped around his neck and a knife's blade pressed against his groin.

"Drop the knife and put the gun down," said a female voice.

Four

Ijeoma walked Adams out onto the quarterdeck.

She stared down Black Caesar and the rest of his crew.

"All of you put down your weapons! Or else I will

cut this man so he will never have descendants!"

The ship decks filled with Kwame, William and all the other Africans who had overthrown their European kidnappers. They surrounded Black Caesar and his crewmen. Shivers slithered up many of their spines, but they still held their ground.

Ijeoma twisted Adams' tall, lanky body down and sideways in order to hold him in her grip. Even twisted he managed to smile at Black Caesar. He turned a little and Ijeoma tightened her grip.

"Hey, sister, ease up!" Adams said. "We're not here to hurt you!"

"You want not to be pointing your weapons at my men," Black Caesar growled. "See, we be pirates. The threat of a conflict is only a turn on for us. You'd be a smart girl to release my first mate and let us go about serving you some food."

Black Caesar gave one of his broad smiles. "It's obvious you liberated yourselves from your captives. And it is also obvious you are lost and rationing your food. So, my dear, put down your gun so no one gets hurt."

Kwame threw his machete down, and walked toward Ijeoma. "Let's see what they have to offer. If we slay them, we will be in no better position."

"Well..." Ijeoma hesitated, "let's *all* put down our weapons."

"Exactly what I was thinking," Adams added. "You

can start by pulling your knife away from my baby maker."

Black Caesar looked around at his men. "Very well then, on three...one; two; three..."

They all dropped their weapons on the floor of the ship.

Ijeoma released Adams.

He grabbed his groin, and stretched out his shoulders, as he stood upright. Then he shook his head and let out a laugh.

Ijeoma stared at him. "What are you laughing at?"

"I haven't been touched by a woman in so long," Adams replied. "I was enjoying your grasp. Allow me to introduce myself. I am Adams Brown, a free man of the sea."

"And who is that?" Ijeoma pointed her gun toward Black Caesar.

"I be the one and only Caesar of the sea," Black Caesar growled. "I be known as Black Caesar — terror of all who trade in my waters. My crew here are liberated booty. They are all men like me, taken from their own families to be used to work as slaves. Just as you here freed yourselves, so did these men."

"Where did you come from and where are we?" Kwame asked.

"By the look of your ship, you were being taken to Santiago, a port on the Island of Ayiti." Adams replied.

"Excuse me but wouldn't that be in Hispaniola and Port-au-Prince be in Ayiti?" William said, as he stepped into visibility of Black Caesar.

Two of Black Caesar's men grabbed William.

"Who is this?" one of Black Caesar's men said.

"My name is William Clarkston, I am a journalist from London. I am of no threat to you —please believe me!"

"Let him go! He's telling the truth!" Ijeoma said. "If he were with these kidnappers, we would have already fed him to the sharks!" The men released William.

Adams put his arm around Ijeoma's shoulder. "Dear lady, the more you speak the more I want to know about you."

Ijeoma shook out of Adams embrace. "So, Caesar..."

"Ah, ah that be Black Caesar to all," Black Caesar corrected.

"*Black* Caesar, we want to get back to Ghana to our families," Ijeoma said. "We just need you to show us how to steer this ship in the right direction."

"That be no problem, but first let us feed your crew and I will have my men ready your vessel." Black Caesar motioned for his men to do his wishes then he walked up onto the quarterdeck and took in the full view of the ship. "This is a fine vessel! You need come and join me in the captain's quarters and I will tell you what you need to know."

Ijeoma, Kwame and William joined Black Caesar and Adams Brown in the cabin, while the crew got to work.

#####

Black Caesar stood looking out the window into the sunlight. It was a clear day and the ocean was calm.

"You are days from the African coast," Black Caesar said to Ijeoma. The current has taken you to the Caribbean Sea. In fact, you are lucky we found you first, or else your revolt would have been in vain. It is best you come with me to The Black Island. There, we can stock your ship and find you a navigator for your journey home."

"Caesar, you would do this for us?" Ijeoma asked.

"*Black* Caesar it is. And yes Black Caesar would be happy to aid you. We will arrive in the morning. This will give you enough time to learn about what's going on in these waters."

"Black Caesar what is this war we are involved in?" Kwame asked passionately. "My village fought no war with Europeans. We've only encountered Arabs and Moors from across the sands, seeking conquest. How did these Europeans come to go to war with us?"

"I am also curious to know who it is that you are at war with." William added. "It is not a war we know of in London."

Black Caesar cleared his throat to begin his story "It is a shame that the details of this war are not known in Africa. But the explanation is simple. There is no war in Africa. The war is in the Caribbean. That is where the crimes are being committed."

"I think perhaps the investors in Europe," the captain went on, "like these Lloyds of London, turn a blind eye, that is to say if they care at all. What I do know is that ships have been transporting we Black people for as long as I can remember."

"They are working us in these death camps, which they call plantations, from America down to Brazil," Adams chimed in. "And every kind of European is involved – Dutch; Portuguese; English; Spanish and French. They are all involved in this war. My ancestors were brought to Virginia from Africa. And I would love to go back and visit...just to see what it's like. But I could not stay, because I have left friends on the plantations that are still being tortured."

"Mr. William, I have met several men like you," Adams continued. White men like you who could not understand the actions of their own kind. If you are true to your heart, you will join us and help end this war. There are many pirates who fought in your country's Royal Navy, but once they see what their government is doing, they can no longer participate."

"Well, if righting this wrong will have me called a

pirate," William said, "then a pirate I'll be."

One of Black Caesar's crewmen brought in a bottle of rum and mugs, and passed them out.

"Here, here then! Let it be resolved!" Black Caesar bellowed. "Adams, we have ourselves a new army. Let's drink, with full cups, some of Jamaica's finest rum to this new ship of soldiers."

Ijeoma raised her glass and drank the rum. She thought about all that had happened to her and Kwame. She pictured Kwame laughing with Kojo while fishing on waters of the Niger river. She felt the warmth and love they had for each other.

Then she pictured Aneesa running and laughing and began to daydream. Aneesa smiled and ran toward her, but before Aneesa reached her, the old white man who traded goods out of the fort near her village grabbed Aneesa around the neck. The old man was not strong enough to hold her. But somehow she could not get loose.

Ijeoma watched as the old white man threw Aneesa to the ground. Ijeoma watched without the power to do anything. The old white man took out a knife, while pinning Aneesa to the ground with his knee.

He looked at Ijeoma and laughed. She tried to move, but for some strange reason she could not.

The old white man said "What are you going to do?"

Ijeoma felt a cold strike of lightning shoot through her body.

The old white man raised the knife high in the air and plunged it into the chest of her sister...

Ijeoma spit out a mouth full of rum.

Kwame threw his arm around her. "Are you alright?"

"Yes," Ijeoma said. "I think the rum was a little strong for me."

After everyone had eaten, Ijeoma, Kwame and William followed Black Caesar and Adams as they showed them details of the ships.

They walked the planks over to Black Caesar's ship – a Schooner with two large masts. It was a massive ship. One main deck had three lower desks. There was another level with nothing but cannons. Ijeoma counted six on each side. Black Caesar had cannons on another level where the crew slept. There were even four cannons on the quarterdeck.

Black Caesar's ship was one big cannon! He had even cut out cannon ports on the deck below his cabin, so he could fire at ships behind him.

By the time they finished learning the operations of the ship, it was dark. Black Caesar pulled Ijeoma aside while Adams showed Kwame how to lower the anchor. William joined the crew for a meal of salted meat and more dried bread. William was eager to hear the stories of the various crew members.

Black Caesar walked with the young woman on the deck of his ship. He leaned on the railing, looking out into the night sky. He pulled out a back-staff and held it out, showing her. "This is what is used to guide ships. But a pirate must learn to read the stars. Being able to read the stars allows you to navigate your ship at night. The brighter and whiter a star is, the better it is for a night reader."

"Are there Black stars?" Ijeoma said.

"Yes there are," Black Caesar replied. "There are the nights when pirates wreak the most havoc on ships that cross the pirates' path. We hang black sails on these nights so we can surprise these ships. The element of surprise and fear are a pirates' greatest asset."

Ijeoma stared off into the night sky and absorbed the immense darkness. She imagined the fear of the crews of the attacked ships. Goose bumps rose on her arms. "How does one become a pirate?"

"That is the question I have been waiting for you to ask," Black Caesar said. "A pirate is not something you can *want* to be. A pirate is something you are *made* to be. I, along with my family, was forced to work in the sugarcane fields of Ayiti. My father worked during the day for the Spanish plantation owners and at night, he worked for the rebellion. One night he said goodbye to us, claiming he was going to build a great citadel in the hills. He said when he returned, he would bring freedom with him. Months later, the revolution started and our plantation was destroyed.

The Spanish Army fought our great leader, Toussaint L'Ouverture and even greater leader, Jean-Jacques Dessalines, in the very fields my family worked. Everyone in my family fought alongside these great leaders in war."

"Separated from my family, my brother and I fled to the sea," Black Caesar went on. "We drifted on a raft until we landed on the shore south of the Spanish colony of Saint Augustine in the land of the Mayaimi Indians. We were taken in and fed by the Mayaimi. My brother was sick and died shortly after. It was there in Florida where I met a man trading stolen goods with the Mayaimi. I don't remember his name but I do remember he was a pirate. I learned from this pirate's crew members that Toussaint drove Napoleon's army back to San Domingo. Many of his crew were younger than me. Boys and some girls just like me but fighters nonetheless. They told me that the war was spreading throughout the Caribbean. They said they were fighters in the war. I decided then that I would become a pirate. I joined with these men and we took two ships in our first year. Now, I command a navy of four ships. We have found several ships like yours, adrift after the enslaved have revolted, but none have had as many survivors as you."

Black Caesar put his arm around Ijeoma and said: "Think hard about your future. What you have experienced since your capture has changed you and what you thought your life would be."

Five

The ships arrived on the sandy beach of Black Island. The smell of rich land and fresh vegetation filled the air. The clear blue water and the swaying of the palm trees made Ijeoma's desire to return home even stronger.

There were buildings made of stone just beyond the shoreline. She stood looking over the side of her ship, taking in the view of this island Black Caesar called home.

There were three other ships in addition to Black Caesar's and Ijeoma's lining the bay. Although it was bright and sunny, there was dark, ominous energy about the place. A hint of sulfur lingered in the air. There were children playing on the beach; but even they looked sad. Their smiles were hard — unlike the children in Ijeoma's village. They wrestled and fought, snatching toys from each other. As a child, Ijeoma would have never fought with another child from her village.

The houses all looked like fortresses. They were run down, but painted in bright colors, faded and splotched with dirt.

The women looked tired and old. They yelled loudly at the children and used foul language. Their clothes were ragged and falling off their bodies.

Ijeoma thought that Black Caesar's men looked frightening, but these women might have surpassed them.

"I see you're already up," Adams said as he walked up behind Ijeoma. "I bet it feels good to be on land."

He handed her a coconut with the top sliced off and a mango. "I brought you some coconut water and some fruit. It will make you feel better. You can drink it while I show you the place. Black Caesar is already setting up a big feast of fresh fruits for you and your crew. It's the best thing to eat after a long trip at sea."

"Let me tell Kwame. I'm sure he would like to come as well," she said.

As she turned toward the door of the captain's cabin, Adams frowned.

"Alright," he said. "But don't you think it is best that he continues to sleep? Maybe he is tired. I could come back for him."

Ijeoma stopped before she reached the door.

"Let me show you this place that the Good Lord has blessed us with," Adams said. "And I can show you a hot spring where you can wash off the ocean salt."

"Okay," Ijeoma said. She followed him off the ship and into town.

####

"Whata-gwan, Adams! Welcome back, my brother!" A voice called from inside a bar, as Adams and Ijeoma approached it.

"Oh no," Adams sighed. He turned and greeted a dark-skinned man wearing a multicolored outfit – green shirt; red pants; yellow scarf. "Good day Brother Coconut, Adams said. "It's good to be back. How are you?"

"Everything is irie, man," Brother Coconut replied. "Much better than if I were in Kingston. I see you and Black Caesar found a beautiful treasure! And what is the name of this sight, warming my eyes?" Coconut asked.

Ijeoma smiled. "My name is Ijeoma. Black Caesar and Adams rescued us at sea. We would have been a dead treasure, if they would not have found us when they did."

"Coconut is the best cook on the Island," Adams said. "He escaped from Jamaica a few years ago and he has been blessing us with full stomachs ever since."

"Well Black Caesar has me cooking for a army today," Coconut said. "I've got your favorite curry chicken and the biggest red snapper you've ever seen. Come see. I'll set you up with you some conch soup, too."

"Get that ready and we'll be back," Adams said. "I want to finish showing her the island."

"Yeah man, do your ting!"

Adams walked Ijeoma down every dirt road in the village. She saw houses, more women with hard looks on their faces, a few older people and more rough children.

"So why do you all call him Coconut?" Ijeoma asked. "Because he is hard on the outside and soft on the inside?"

"No, because he is a fierce fighter," Adams said with a smile. "He earned his name because he is dark like chocolate and fights like a nut."

"Really? He doesn't look like a fighter."

"I am joking," Adams said. "I don't know; I never asked. Everyone here has taken nicknames. My mother named me after my grandfather, that's why I haven't changed mine."

They reached a secluded lake, surrounded by large, smooth rocks. A waterfall poured into the lake on the other side.

"Here you are my African sister," Adams said, "you can bathe here. I will return in an hour."

####

Kwame and William sat across from each other in Coconut's bar, talking to Black Caesar. Both had plates of food in front of them. The crew members of Ijeoma's ship and the other ships filled the rest of the bar. Some white pirates were there as well.

Ijeoma and Adams entered the bar. Coconut rolled out a large barrel.

Black Caesar stood and raised his glass. "As the Buccaneers say: ahoy, matey, here be your rum! Now, grab a mug and fill 'em up!"

Once everyone in the bar had drink in hand, Black Caesar continued. "All you scallywags, raise up your drinks! I want to say a toast to our new friends. It was just a couple days ago when we found you drifting. We thought you to be lost booty, from a ship gone waste from scurvy. But when we walked onto the ship there you were, blimey!"

Black Caesar eyed his audience. "See, I've learned one thing on the seas and in this war – to expect the unexpected. That's what my mother told me. And she be one of the strongest black women who fought in the war of Ayiti. What she told me was to also enjoy your good times, for they are few and far between. So drink up, Ijeoma and all you revolutionaries, for this be a good time. Eat all the oxtail and jerk'd chicken you can. I will have Coconut make some cod fish for your journey back. Maybe I'll get him to throw some ackee in with that cod for you."

It was late night when Caesar walked Ijeoma back to her ship. He handed her a cup of coconut water. They walked slowly and Ijeoma took in the night sky.

"The stars are the same as in my village," she said. "They just seem to be twisted around."

"You have all the makings of a good navigator," Caesar replied. "A good Pirate captain can see the sky, as a hawk sees the earth. To the Royal Fleet's navy men, the sky is just darkness. It is of no use to them. It's as if the stars were black. But the moon and the stars are what guide us. The blackness others fear is what we must learn to use. The sky never changes, only your place underneath. If you can learn to read the blackness, you will have an advantage over those who only know how to chart their course by the sun."

"My father read the sky to know when to plant," Ijeoma said, "and when to fish, but never for travel. This is new to me. Will you teach me?"

"Adams has offered to lead you back whence you came," Black Caesar replied. "You can learn from him. He can read both the black sky and the navy sun charts like the ones found on your ship. He will be a great loss for us. But I send him in hopes he will influence you to return and wage war with us here in the Caribbean."

Ijeoma turned her gaze toward the captain. "I thank you for your kindness, but do not underestimate the war in my land and my usefulness there. If you like, you can follow us and take our ship back with you."

"Your wisdom and foresight continues to amaze me," Black Caesar said. "However, I must decline. Your ship is yours and you must decide its destiny. And as for Africa, I will not journey there until I have won *this* war. Africa, to me, is where we all came from. And to go there may only boil my rage over to where I cannot control it. I allow myself only short trips here to Black Island. I fear if I stay away from the water-war, I will lose my edge. These robbers have learned to fear my black sail. And I never want them to stop."

Six

The African coast was unusually calm, almost welcoming, as Adams steadied the ship for the traders' port. He wore a shirt he had taken from another Dutch ship they robbed. The shirt made him look like a person suited for trade across the Atlantic.

The rear gate of the traders' dungeon opened wide. William stood at the port edge of the ship. He was dressed in the high fashions found in the captain's cabin.

Ijeoma and Kwame stood out of sight inside the ship.

A white man met William as he stepped off the ship.

"Captain!" He exclaimed. "We had not expected your return so early. We have only a few slaves for you at this time."

"Is that so? Let me speak to who's in charge!" William scoffed. "Or else I'll have to go out to the jungle and find my own slaves."

The man led William into the dungeon. He ordered a mulatto slave to fetch him and the captain a cup of water. "I will trust sitting here is okay? Captain ah..."

"William!" William barked. "And this is not acceptable! I will have my laborers teach your half-breeds how to serve a drink."

"Very well, then," the man said. "Please, wait here.

I will wake the Governor and inform him of your arrival."

Kwame stood facing the ship, while Ijeoma's back faced the interior of the fort. She concealed her musket, as she looked out the main gate toward her village.

She had hoped to spot a few children playing or even a woman washing clothes along the beach but so far there was nothing. She smiled as she listened to William continue his slave trader impersonation.

"I'm sorry you had to wait," the governor stammered. "If I had known..."

"Spare me your excuses!"William snapped. "Your aide has informed me that you have no slaves for me!"

"I have only a few, who I've kept for my personal use." He winked at William. "You understand."

"Let me see them," William said, looking down his nose at the governor. "Hopefully, I will find one or two of them of interest to me."

"I assure you that with all of the goods we have stored here, your trip will not be a loss."

"Just show me the women."

The pudgy governor motioned to the men around him. Young girls in torn clothes were pulled out of each of the rooms of the dungeon's upper area. The girls moaned and sighed as they were showcased to

William.

Ijeoma peeked through the corner of her eye as she looked for Aneesa. Her anxiety grew as each girl was brought forth and it was not her sister.

"She is not here!" Ijeoma whispered.

She charged toward the governor, pointing her musket at his chest. "Remember me?" She flipped the long gun around and struck, catching the chubby man flush on the chin.

Kwame stepped aside and trained his gun on the rest of the men.

More men from Ijeoma's ship rushed through the port door. Adams came in and picked up the governor. He held him in front of William.

William spit in the governor's face. "You disgust me! Death is too good for you! But it is a gift I gladly bestow upon you today!"

Ijeoma pulled William back. She pulled a knife from her side and raised it to the governor's face. "Where are the rest of the girls? You took my sister!"

"I will not cooperate with you, savage!" the man snarled, spitting blood onto the floor.

"I expected you would say that!" Ijeoma said. "Let's lock this uncooperative barbarian up!"

Ijeoma grabbed the man by the back of the neck and dragged him toward the cells. She shoved him into the same dark cell she was once held in. The rest of the white men and mulatto slaves were thrown in there as well.

Ijeoma and Kwame searched the rest of the dungeon.

It was in the governor's room that Ijeoma found Aneesa and two other girls. They were weak and thin, lying on blankets in a corner of the room.

"Kwame!" Ijeoma yelled. "She's here!"

####

Adams, Kwame and Ijeoma crossed the road leading to the center of her village, each one dragging a young woman on a two-wheeled gurney normally used to transport the dead from the dungeons.

Ijeoma held Aneesa under her armpit and helped her walk the road.

They saw no men when they entered the village; only children and women.

Ijeoma helped Aneesa sit down on the side of the road.

The women were busy crushing meal in large mortars, sweeping and sowing fishing nets. When they saw Ijeoma they all dropped what they were doing to greet her and her crew.

Ijeoma's mother ran over and embraced her.

"Oh momma I am so glad to be back home!"

"I thought you and your sister drowned fishing!" Ijeoma's mother cried, falling to her knees before Aneesa. She wrapped her arms around Aneesa and sobbed. Aneesa cried with her.

They carried the young women to a house where women of the village brought water and herbs to nurse them back to health. They removed the young women's clothes and cleaned them, combed their hair and gave them new garments to wear. The men in Ijeoma's crew bathed and then joined the villagers.

Ijeoma's mother ushered Ijeoma out to the village center to have an audience with Asantewaa, leader of the village and the other elders of the village council.

Aneesa faced Asantewaa. Behind the Great Asantehene sat her council.

"Nana Yaa Asantewaa, we would like to inform you of the devils who have been trading within the dungeon on the shore," Ijeoma said.

"This man here," she pointed towards Adams. "He is from across the water, from a place called Virginia. He is not from there although he was born there. His parents were from here."

"They were kidnapped and not traded, as we have been made to believe." Ijeoma looked around and saw she had everyone's attention. "My sister and I were fishing with Kwame and his brother when we were kidnapped, and Kwame's brother, Kojo, was killed."

"We were taken to their dungeon," Ijeoma continued. "Kwame and I were separated from Aneesa. We were chained and dragged to a ship, where we met other black people from different tribes. On the ship our white Slavers tortured us. Afraid they would kill us, we fought back and won. Captain Black Caesar, Adams' captain, helped get us back here."

"Your story is familiar to one I heard as a child," the Nana Mother said. "It was of the Europeans who first came here. The Europeans said it was not true, and we believed them. They built these big trading castles. But the Abosom speak as you speak, and they compel me to believe you."

"Indeed, Nana, my story is true!" Ijeoma said. "When we came back, we tricked the white men at the dungeon into believing we were one of their ships! Please come with us we have the men locked away in the cells they locked us in."

Asantewaa brought a few men with her to inspect the dungeon.

Ijeoma walked the Asantehene around, showing her every part of the large dungeon. She opened the cell and dragged the governor out. He was now a sloppy mess of disheveled clothes, sweaty, pale skin and greasy hair.

"Oh, you can throw people *in* here, but you can't

handle it yourself!" Ijeoma sneered.

She raised the governor's head with the barrel of her rifle.

Asantewaa stepped to him.. "You come to us sickly and hungry! We feed you and cure you of your plague and this is how you repay us? You are a devil of a people and you will not get away with this!"

Asantewaa threw her robe off of her shoulder, cocked back her hand and punched the governor square in the eye. The governor fell from Ijeoma's hold.

As his face crashed to the ground, a gunshot sounded.

The ranks of the white men who captured Ijeoma and Kwame, swelled, outnumbering the small number of men Ijeoma and the Asantehene brought with them. "Listen, niggers," one of them snarled, "Now just what do you think you are doing here?"

They quickly filled the dungeon and tried to disarm Ijeoma's crew. Ijeoma reached for her musket but it wasn't there. She then reached for her knife. But by the time she had it in her hand, the butt of her kidnapper's rifle knocked her on her back.

It took only a minute for a full out riot to break out. Even Asantewaa displayed her fighting skills, tossing a man over her shoulder and then stabbing him in the chest with his own knife before he hit the ground.

The governor muscled up the energy to tackle William. The men exchanged blows falling into – and knocking over – crates. Kwame was fired at and had to flip behind a barrel of grain to avoid getting shot. As the slaver reloaded the rifle, Kwame raised the crate over his head and dropped it on the man.

Just then, two other traders jumped him. Adams ran to Kwame's aid, but was hit in the head with a long piece of wood. Ijeoma was pinned to the ground and could not free herself.

Asantewaa was finally overwhelmed by two attackers. Adams and Kwame were subdued. William had gashes all over his face and Ijeoma was now held up against the wall by two of the Slavers.

"Take these jungle monkeys out to the water and shoot them." Nana Asantewaa's escorts and Ijeoma's crew were taken out through the ocean side door of the dungeon.

The governor grinned. "Leave these three in here with me!" He gestured toward Ijeoma, Kwame and William. "Lock them in the breaking room. Girl, I'll show you what I did to your sister tomorrow."

"Hey what is taking so long?" yelled the head slaver. Hearing no response he walked out of the back door. As soon as he turned the corner, he was grabbed in a tight choke-hold. Coconut and three pirates held five of the slavers at gun point. Coconut pressed a knife to the neck of the head slaver, and walked him back to the dungeon door.

The other slavers turned to run out of the front doors and were met by Black Caesar and the rest of his pirates.

"You jungle...!" the Slaver spat.

His words were cut short by a flintlock pistol ball in the head.

Black Caesar blew smoke out of the barrel of his pistol. "I have heard enough from white men outside of Africa; I will *not* hear them speak when I'm in my homeland!"

Kwame grabbed the two men who held Ijeoma and threw one to the floor. Adams did the same.

William delivered a fatal blow to the governor. He then turned to Nana Asantewaa. "Shall we skip your justice process and decide their fate right here?"

Black Caesar flipped open his long coat and bowed to Asantewaa and the rest of the Africans with her. "Black Caesar is pleased to make your acquaintance. Now, let's see the beautiful land Ijeoma told me so much about! "

Seven

The dungeon was very difficult to clean. The blood and tears of the many Africans held there had merged with the structure.

The white slavers' bodies burned in a pile just outside the dungeon.

Ijeoma and Black Caesar sat atop two hand-carved wooden stools. They were surrounded by Kwame, William, Adams and the entire village.

In the center stood Nana Asantewaa and another woman, Iya Aduni, the village's spiritual leader – originally from Yorubaland. Iya Aduni dusted both of their heads with white powder.

"Ashe!" Aduni said.

"Ashe!" repeated the audience.

On the left side were drummers and dancers, and across from them were the village children. Ijeoma's mother and sister were led into the circle by men dressed for war. They sat across from Ijeoma and Black Caesar.

"You have displayed nobility to our people," said Nana Asantewaa. "From this day forward you will be appointed my representatives. This Enstoolment will grant you entry into our places in the here, now and ever-after."

Nana Asantewaa stretched out her hand to Black Caesar. He nodded respectfully. "You, Black Caesar are truly the warrior of our distant tribe. The story of your life is divine prophecy." She turned her head toward Coconut sitting next to the drummers. "And your cook Coconut is skilled with a knife in all of its uses." Coconut offered a wide smile back and nodded his head.

"Sister Ijeoma, you possess fearless leadership. Recent events in your life were no accident."

Everyone cheered and the drummers played louder. The dancers danced a circle around Ijeoma and Black Caesar. And the men dressed in battle garb, lifted them in the air.

They were carried to the shore, followed by a parade of villagers, to the capacious slave-ship that Ijeoma thought would be her tomb, but later became the place she would become a leader.

Iya Aduni threw dust on the ship and turned to the spectators. "Ashe!"

"Ashe!" the crowd repeated.

Nana Asantewaa stood between the crowd and the ship. She turned to face the ship. "Let this vessel be used to carry our warriors to this war in the Caribbean. Let this ship's cannons blow holes in all ships that stand in its way. Let this ship's hull protect our warriors from all who seek to destroy it."

Ijeoma stepped forward and stood next to Nana Asantewaa.

"Ijeoma what name to you give this ship?" Nana Mother asked.

"It will be called *The Black Star*. Night without stars strike fear in the hearts of those whom we fight. So I will use this ship to do the same."

"Who here will assist our new sister in her efforts

to make war at sea?"

Kwame stepped forward. "I will."

"And what is it that you will make your worth?" Nana Asantewaa walked in front of the strong, young man.

"I will protect her from harm at the cost of my life."

Iya Aduni flicked powder over his face.

"Ashe!" Iya Aduni said.

"Ashe!" repeated the audience.

"Are there others who will aid?"

Adams and William stepped forward.

"You have both displayed your commitment. I expect you to help make Ijeoma's efforts come to fruition. Use what you have learned to take *The Black Star* to the heart of our enemies, who use race as their battle lines."

"Who else?" she said.

Out stepped twenty-five other men and women. They were a mix of villagers and people who fought for freedom with Ijeoma. They were all anointed with powder by Iya Aduni.

After being sprinkled with powder, Ijeoma's enstooled crew all shouted: "Ashe!" over and over.

They danced and cheered throughout the night.

Ijeoma stood on the main-deck of her ship and waved as Kwame led the crew in the raising of the anchor. Nana Asantewaa, Ijeoma's mother and Aneesa looked on from the shore. The dungeon now flew a flag with a black star on it, identical to the flag on the ship.

"Everything Irie!" Coconut cried from further out to sea on the deck of Black Caesar's ship.

"It's all good my brother!" Ijeoma yelled back.

As the ship floated into the ocean Kwame joined her on the main-deck.

"We are in the hands of Yemoja, and she will protect us now," Kwame said.

"I'm just glad she will not be protecting the traders," Ijeoma said.

William stood next to Adams, peering over his shoulder.

"You do not need to be so close to me," Adams retorted. "I think I know how to get back to the Caribbean."

"Who said we were going to the Caribbean?" William said. "Have you ever heard of Sarah Baartman?"

THE BANDIT KING AND THE ISLAND OF TEARS

S.A. Cosby

"Up top, Lothar, now!"

A ragged voice screamed down through the hatch. Lothar hopped up off his bunk and quickly climbed the ladder to the deck of the *Lancer*. The Lancer was a cargo ship bound for the Colonies.

Lothar could hear the moans and screams of the ship's cargo as he climbed the ladder. Once upon a time he had been cargo on another ship. But his talent with language had gotten him off the plantation and onto a slave ship as a translator. He could hear a few words of any language and in a day or a day and a half he would be fluent in said language. The owner of the plantation who had sold him to Captain March used to trot him out at dinner parties and parade him around the table speaking French, German, Italian,

Portuguese, but never languages from his home. He was forbidden to speak Twi, Igbo, Amharic or any of the other languages he knew.

He was only allowed to saunter around the table in a little frock coat and powdered wig, saying humorous little limericks in multiple languages like a trained pet.

Lothar reached the deck and took a deep breath. The scent of the open sea was different from the scent of the ocean from the safety of the beach. Lothar could smell blood and salt in the air. The cloying odor of decay mixed with a wild freshness that came from the white caps as the ship sliced through the waves. But nothing could stave off the stench coming from the cargo hold. Lothar remembered those scents all too well. At seventeen, he could still recall the smell of death and despair that saturated the lower decks of the slave ship that had ripped him from everything he knew and deposited him on an island a world away. Lothar saw the First Mate, Archibald, direct the crew as they manipulated the sails and the rigging. Archibald was as cruel as any overseer and as ugly as a boar. A wide stump of a man with bread loaves for forearms. The only difference between Archibald and an overseer was that Archibald was cruel to *everyone*, not just the slaves in the cargo hold.

"Up here, Lothar!" Captain March barked.

Lothar climbed up to the platform where the Captain stood. The helmsman steered the ship's wheel, whistling. He stopped whistling long enough to spit on

Lothar as he passed him. Carnahan was his name and Lothar avoided him as much as he could, for he seemed to take delight in torturing, abusing and raping anyone with black skin; man, woman, or child.

"Look port side. You see that ship?" the Captain asked Lothar. Lothar nodded. He didn't speak unless he was given permission. He had made the mistake of responding to a question his first day on the ship and Archibald had smacked him in the face with the leather sap he always carried. Lothar could see a ship about one hundred yards away. It was a long teak schooner. Huge plumes of stark white smoke billowed from the ship like a cloud had descended from the heavens and enveloped the craft.

"You are gonna go over with Archie, LaGrains and Simmons. If you come across any person or persons you will translate if they don't speak the King's English. Let them know we are taking them to Virginia and turning them into the Crown for a salvage. They are not flying any flag from any nation, so, in my book, they are fair game. Understand me boy?" Captain March said.

Lothar nodded his head and headed toward the dinghy. Anytime off the ship was time well spent.

Lothar gripped the oars tightly as he rowed over to the smoking ship. The ship did not seem to be engulfed in flames but smoke poured from it like spring melt coming down from the mountains.

Archibald yelled from his seat in the bow of the dinghy. "Ahoy! Prepare to be boarded!"

"If ye all ain't dead from the scurvy," he murmured.

Simmons prepared to toss a rope with a metal hook on the end onto the railing that ran around the top of the deck. Archibald put a hand on his shoulder; the other man stayed his throw.

"Look it there. Them be pots of clay burning," he said as he pointed at the bow of the ship.

Lothar craned his head to the right and saw two clay pots hanging from a yard arm that extended from the bow of the ship. The smoke rose from those orange pots.

"Lothar, turn the boat full starboard! We are heading back to the Lancer!" Archibald said.

Lothar did as he was told. The waves lapped at the hull of the dinghy as he struggled to manipulate one oar while steadying the other one.

Once they were back on the Lancer, Captain March came down off the bridge to question his First Mate.

"What happened Mr. Archibald?" he said. "If that ship is empty, she is prime for a salvage! You didn't even inspect the cargo!"

Lothar stood on the deck feeling the fire running up and down his arms from rowing against the open sea.

Archibald stepped closer to the Captain and

spoke in low conspiratorial tones. "Sir, the ship isn't on fire. There be pots that are smoking."

Lothar was no longer listening. He stared at the shirtless, dark-skinned man who had just climbed over the port side of the Lancer. The man was dripping wet. Rivulets of water ran along the lean muscles of his abdomen. He put a long, dark finger to his lips.

Then the shirtless man drew a cutlass from the weathered scabbard on his side. Suddenly, dozens more dark-skinned fellows climbed over the side of the ship. Interspersed with the dark-skinned men were some fellows of indeterminate ethnicity. They sported skin the color of fresh honey and long, lank locks saturated with sea water. Lothar felt his belly twist and turn like a bear caught in a trap.

"Pirates!" a voice cried.

Lothar looked toward the smoking ship. It was no longer without a flag. It now sported the full black flag that was discussed in hush tones by ship captains up and down the coast and throughout the Caribbean. The all black flag belonged to the *Black Angel*, and she was captained by Jabari Masterless. But he was better know on the high seas by his nom de plume: The Bandit King.

The ship turned toward the Lancer and then closed the distance between them at an alarming rate.

Lothar watched as the *Black Angel* pulled alongside the *Lancer*.

Like a magic trick, cannons appeared on the

deck of the Black Angel. The bow of the Lancer exploded in a maelstrom of blood and body parts as the first volley of cannon balls tore across the deck.

A shrill chorus of screams cut through the air. Lothar looked up and saw a dozen men swinging from the masts of the Black Angel. They fell, like rain, joining their comrades on board the Lancer.

Archibald reached for the flintlock he kept in a ragged holster on his left hip.

A pearl handled dagger flew through the air and pierced Archibald's throat.

Bright red blood like a river made of scarlet erupted from his mouth. The stout man went to his knees as his jaw worked furiously. He died on his knees with his chest covered in blood.

Lothar slipped behind a barrel full of salted sardines as death stalked the deck of the Lancer.

The thirty-three members of the Lancers crew, most of them poor drunken deckhands who had gotten themselves in debt gambling in the ports, were overrun fairly quickly.

Lothar didn't have much experience in battle but to his young eyes this was not so much a battle as an execution. The men of the Black Angel slit throats and blew holes in heads with an efficiency that spoke to years of practice.

After the smoke cleared and the moans of the dying sailors drowned out the moans of the slaves in the cargo hold, Lothar witnessed two men from the Black Angel hold Captain March up by his arms.

The captain looked much worse for wear than any of the Black Angel's crew. His mouth bled and his eye was swollen shut. His hat had been knocked off his head and the sun beamed down on his bald pate.

The pirates killed or subdued every other member of the Lancer's crew, save for Lothar.

Whistling came from the stern of the ship. It rose and lowered in pitch and strength as the whistler made their way toward the bow of the ship.

Lothar, on hands and knees, peered around the weathered barrel. The whistler appeared, walking over bodies as he emerged from the cloud of gun smoke that hung over the deck.

Captain March looked up at the man. His white face grew paler.

The man stood in front of the captain. He was a giant, nearly seven and a half feet tall by Lothar's estimation. Black, twisted braids cascaded down his back and flowed over the long black coat he wore. Gold buttons ran up and down the front of the coat. An enormous sword rested loosely on his hip in a wooden scabbard. A gold lion's head served as pommel on the huge sword. He wore four flintlocks in four leather holsters and carried a blunderbuss on one of his massive shoulders. The man's braids were held back by a bright red scarf that was tied around his great shaggy head. His face was clean shaven and as smooth and black as a chunk of obsidian. He was shirtless and his expansive chest was dotted with scraggly scars and a strange pattern of what Lothar thought might have been ink, as if someone had drawn on the giant's chest with a quill . Suddenly, the man turned and pointed at Lothar.

"Come here little brother." he said in French. Lothar couldn't move. His body felt like it was forged out of rusted iron.

"Now, before the flies realize we have given them a banquet," the giant said, his voice rumbling out of his chest like distant thunder.

Lothar rose and walked toward the man on legs that felt as unsteady as a newborn calf's.

Blood ran across the deck in little mindless streams that were diverted here and there by gaps in the planking.

There is blood on my feet. Lothar thought.

The man peered down at Lothar. His black eyes were two pieces of coal on a field of white. He placed a paw of a hand on Lothar's shoulder.

"You are the one who speaks the many languages yes?" the man said.

Lothar nodded his head.

The tall man smiled. He pointed at the captain.

Captain March's lip quivered.

Captain March looked at the giant black savage with a mix of disgust and awe. His mind reeled with the enormity of what just happened to him and his crew. *Lothar stands next to the bastard, nodding his head as the creature speaks his monstrous gibberish,* the captain thought. *How could a group of savages best strong white men with English blood in their veins?*

"He wants to know how many times you have carried slaves as your cargo?" Lothar said.

Captain March spit a globule of blood and phlegm onto the deck. He licked his lips. "This is preposterous! I am a duly empowered Captain and representative of the Royal Crown!"

The giant held up his huge hand. He spoke to Lothar once more.

"He says who you are doesn't matter," Lothar said. "This will be your last trip. He says you have a choice – sail this ship back to the homeland of the people his men are now freeing in the lower decks or he will slit your back open and throw you overboard as chum."

Captain March's face turned a particularly bright shade of red. "You tell this darkie; this savage; this...monster that I will do no such thing and that if he releases me right now, I will ensure that the Crown only hangs him and doesn't draw and quarter him!"

Lothar glanced at the giant with eyes wide with fear.

"What did he say little brother?" the tall man

asked.

Lothar hesitated.

"Come now, I am sure I've heard worse," the tall man said.

Lothar let out a deep breath and told him.

The tall man leaned his head back and laughed and laughed.

He walked up to Captain March and spoke.

Lothar instinctively translated what the tall man said: "You don't understand. You are no longer in a position to bargain or threaten or intimidate. You are a mouse and I am a lion. You live or die at my discretion. So, again, I offer you a choice – sail these people back home or see what it feels like to kiss a shark."

Captain Marsh bit the inside of his cheek so hard blood squirted into his mouth. "Yes. Tell the bastard I said yes."

Lothar translated the captain's acquiescence.

"Yes what?" Lothar translated.

Captain Marsh hung his head. "Yes, Bandit King," he said weakly.

The Bandit King and his crew took half of the Lancers supplies and then applied leg irons to Captain

Marsh and the three surviving crewmen.

The Bandit King had Lothar ask the freed men if any of them were chiefs in their homelands. One held up a withered brown hand.

"I would keep a man up through the night and make sure that the good captain is not doubling back on the previous day's progress. " The Bandit King said. He jumped up onto the railing and grabbed a rope to swing back over to the Black Angel.

"Sir. May I come with you?" Lothar asked. The words were out of his mouth before he knew he was going to say them. The Bandit King stared at him for a long time.

"Little brother we don't spend most of our days freeing slaves, the Bandit King said. "Our's is a dangerous life and the grains of sand are always pouring through the hourglass. There are no old pirates."

Lothar looked around the deck of the Lancer.

"Anything is better than being a pet, Lothar said. "I can't go back to the homeland as you call it. I am a man without a country."

The Bandit King laughed.

"You are not a man at all. " he said.

Lothar took a step toward him. "I am more man than most of the men I have sailed with. I can be of use to you, sir. Please. I have nowhere else to go." He tried to keep his voice from cracking but he failed miserably.

The Bandit King ran a hand through his braids. At last he spoke. "Alright come on. But you have to earn your keep or you will be the one kissing a shark."

Port Royal was Heaven for devils.

Lothar had attended many fine dinner parties on the plantation. Well, attended was not the correct word. He had *served* and been put on display at many fine dinner parties in his seventeen years of life. In all that time, he had never seen such raucous revelry and unbridled debauchery like he witnessed his first night in Port Royal.

He was even more shocked by the sense of equality he experienced. Men of color fought, laughed and drank with white men. Black men ran taverns and were merchants throughout the port city. To his amazement, there were no chains in sight.

The crew of the Black Angel held court in the back corner of a bustling tavern called *New Babylon*. Lothar sat next to the Bandit King's First Mate, Black Tom Cracken. Tom's name was meant to be sarcastic. The man was whiter than any white man Lothar had ever seen. His hair was kinky, like Lothar's, but yellow, like corn meal. His strange pinkish eyes seemed to stare at things best left unseen.

A lusty woman, with as many teeth as Lothar had years, sat on Tom's lap, playing with the gold earring in his ear.

Lothar sipped a mug of something that stung his throat but strangely made him feel more jovial with every swallow.

Tom shoved his hand inside the woman's bodice and roared with laughter. "Eh, little brother, I do believe 'tis milk has soured! What say you?"

He pulled one of the woman's pendulous breasts from her garment.

Lothar swallowed more of the liquid in his cup and stared at the woman's soft, brown flesh. He was about to speak when the room started to spin and the contents of his belly emptied onto the wooden floor.

"Ho, now! No wasting of good, honest, stolen rum, little brother!" Black Tom said. He clapped Lothar on his back and nearly cracked his spine.

Lothar raised his head and looked up at the ceiling of the tavern. There was a cloud of female garments hanging from the rafters.

"Where did he come from?" Lothar blurted out.

Black Tom eyed him quizzically.

"The giant," Lothar said. "The Bandit King; where did he come from?" His head spun.

Black Tom shrugged, but the woman on his lap spoke. "He came from Hispaniola," she said. "He was taken from his home when he was twelve. At twenty, he killed his master and his master's family and escaped. He never accepted his slave name and he started calling himself 'Masterless.'

"No, no, you drunken trollop, you got it all wrong," A member of the Bandit King's crew said. "He was born in the Colonies. His father was an Apache and his mother was from the Khufu tribe. The Apache trained him to fight and he killed the bounty hunters who came looking for his mother since she was a runaway." The man fell out of his chair and straight into a drunken slumber under the table.

Black Tom laughed and slapped the woman in his lap on the rump.

"There are as many stories about his origin as there are drops of water in the sea," Black Tom said. "All I know is this: he is the bravest, toughest, wiliest man I have ever encountered. Make no mistake, he is a loyal friend but a pitiless enemy."

The crew member on the floor awakened suddenly, as if smelling salts had been waved under his nose. He spoke from beneath the table. "And he keeps us flush with rum, food, gold and loose women. Not always in that order."

Black Tom laughed again. He raised his glass and saluted the Bandit King.

The Bandit King raised his own cup and saluted his pale friend.

Lothar shuddered at the thought of having the Bandit King for an enemy. The Bandit King had his massive arm around two women. One was brown and one was pale as the sand on the beach just outside the window of the tavern.

Lothar raised his own cup and choked down some more of the rum.

"Which one of you is the Bandit King?" a voice demanded. Every member of the Black Angel's crew turned their heads and stared at a man standing at the end of the table.

Lothar had to squint to see him properly. His head was still swimming.

The man was of average size and build. His white face was dotted with a strange design that extended over his bald head. While he was not a man of enormous stature his hands were huge, with gnarled knuckles and thick serpentine veins.

Black Tom pushed the woman out of his lap and began to rise with his hand on his flintlock. The Bandit King raised his hand and motioned for Tom to sit.

"I am the man you seek," the Bandit King said. "If this is about business then we can take it outside. If this is about your woman, then I apologize."

The crew laughed.

The man standing at the end of the table laughed as well.

"This is about me cutting off your black head and taking it to the Governor," the man said.

Everyone stopped laughing.

The Bandit King stood. The women he was embracing quickly moved away from the table.

"Well that's a mighty bold statement," the Bandit King said. "Here is my retort."

He grabbed his mug and with more nimbleness than his large fingers would have suggested, he hurled the cup at his aggressor's head.

The heavy tin cup caught the man off guard. He was in the middle of reaching for his own weapon, a small pocket-sized version of a flintlock, when the cup careened into his forehead. A gash opened in his forehead like a child's smile. Blood poured down his face.

The Bandit King hopped onto the table and ran the length of it before his attacker could recover. Whistling, he kicked the man in the face.

The man nearly flipped over backward before landing on the floor in a heap.

"Now, can I finish my damn rum?" the Bandit King said with his arms wide.

The entire tavern erupted in gales of laughter. Lothar laughed too. The woman who had been sitting on Black Tom's lap kissed him on the mouth.

"Impressive," a soft feminine voice said.

The Bandit King whirled around. Standing next to the fallen attacker was a lovely woman. Her long black hair spilled down her back like a river made of midnight. Almond shaped eyes gave her a bemused look, as if she was giggling about the punch line of a jest she would never share. Her light, honey-brown eyes seemed to glisten in the light of the oil lamps in the tavern. She wore a modest white smock with loose fitting sleeves and a high sever collar.

"I certainly hope it was," the Bandit King said. "I aim to please." He dropped down to his haunches so he could look the woman in the eye. She smiled.

"He came highly recommended," she said quietly

.

The Bandit King cocked his head and gazed at her, as if seeing her for the first time. "Oh, did he now? And what was he recommended for?"

"He was recommended as one of the most vicious hired men in Port Royal," the woman replied. "He is a man renowned for his fortitude and ferociousness – the sort of man who would test a man like you. Apparently, his skills were exaggerated."

"Test me for what purpose, my lady?" the Bandit King asked.

"It's *sister*, actually," the woman answered. "Sister Abigail Hernandez and I wanted to test your skills because I want to hire you and your crew to rescue my sister...my *blood* sister...from a brothel."

The Bandit King, Black Tom, Lothar and Sister Abigail retired to a small room in the back of the tavern. A few candles that had seen better days offered a weak illumination against the inky darkness. Lothar found himself staring at Sister Abigail. He didn't need to search his memories to know she was the most beautiful woman he had ever seen in his entire life. Because of his skill with languages the Bandit King had insisted Lothar join them to alleviate any misunderstandings that might arise. Sister Abigail had spoken to the King in French but her native language was Spanish.

Lothar heard things scuttling in the dark that he did not wish to see in the light. He could hear the sea lapping against the shore through a window cut in the side of the stone and mud building.

The Bandit King sat on a half-barrel turned upside down. His great hands hung between his knees and his black eyes roamed up and down Sister Abigail's body. Not lasciviously, but with a genuine curiosity. Sister Abigail started to sit on a crate but Lothar offered her his seat, which was the only chair in the room.

"Thank you, young sir." she said primly.

Lothar just nodded.

"Well, Sister, let's get to it," the Bandit King said. "I have a lot of drinking and whoring to do. I hope you do not take offense to my choice of vices, but I have learned life is too short not to engage in activities that bring you pleasure."

Sister Abigail nodded.

"Yes ,well I am under no illusions as to what you

and your men are," she said.

Black Tom cleared his throat. "And just what are we Sister?"

"Brigands; corsairs; men for hire," Sister Abigail said. "But the situation I find myself in is dire and I do not have the luxury or the time to find men of good character and charity to achieve the ends I seek."

The Bandit King sat up straight and stared at her. "Yours must be a most vexing dilemma to have driven you down into this den of iniquity." He grasped one huge hand in the other and cracked his knuckles. The sound echoed throughout the room.

"When one battles demons, sometimes it is best to have a devil on your side," Sister Abigail replied. "The men who have my sister are demons, of that I have no doubt. My sister, Mia, was a servant girl at one of the establishments here in your city. She was kidnapped and taken by a man who calls himself Verpa. He is the master of an island off the coast of the Land of the Holy Cross in Brazil. It is a place that rivals Port Royal for debauchery and degradation. It is a place only the most vile of sailors and merchants seek out to satisfy their most perverted desires. Verpa and his family are abominations before our God. He lays with his own sisters and their abhorrent offspring are his loyal soldiers, enforcing his rule. My sister was able to get word to me through a vile merchant who used her for his own repugnant purpose. She is a prisoner there and is being forced to perform acts that even you may find atrocious."

The Bandit King placed his hands on his knees and, after a moment, he leaned forward. "Sister, I will not lie and say your story has not moved me, but in all frankness, your sister is not the first girl to stray too close to the flame and get burned. I am not so inclined to take my men into battle against the misshapen offspring of a mad procurer just because you say your sister is his prisoner."

Sister Abigail put her hands together as if to pray. "I have left my nunnery with a month's worth of alms and offerings. It includes one hundred gold coins, seventy silver coins, thirty pounds of myrrh and twenty pounds of salt. In addition, I have it under good authority that Verpa has a huge repository of gold and silver and dried goods taken in barter from the miscreants that frequent his island. The merchant that gave me my sister's message also gave me the coordinates of the island. If I cannot appeal to your Christian charity I will appeal to your worldly greed."

Sister Abigail's face was tight almost to the point of breaking.

The Bandit King stood and in two quick strides, was standing in front of the beautiful nun. He took her chin in and tilted her head up toward his. It looked, for a moment, as if he was going to kiss her.

"Sister, I know men, women and children who have been whipped and lashed under the name of Christian charity," The Bandit King said. "From where I sit, Christian charity is greed in black robes and fancy shoes. At least I'm honest about mine. I'll put this to the vote with my crew. You get some sleep. We will find you in the morning with our answer. Now I must bid you adieu for there are two young ladies who have promised me we will sin repeatedly and in new and fascinating ways. Au revoir."

The Bandit King let go of Sister Abigail's chin and grabbed her hand. He kissed her pliable skin with an exaggerated flourish and then he walked past her and left the room.

Black Tom and Lothar followed him.

As Lothar passed Sister Abigail, she reached out and touched his arm. "Please young sir," she said. "I need...my *sister* needs your help." Her voice was low and urgent. Lothar felt an ache stir in his loins. She smelled like lilacs and pine. Lothar touched her hand.

"Come on, little brother!" Black Tom yelled.

Lothar nodded again and ran after his crew mate.

Lothar awoke with a sour taste in his mouth. He heard someone snoring to his right. He cracked open his right eye and saw the woman who had been sitting on Black Tom's lap lying next to him on the rickety cot he barely remembered falling into. To his left was a half-full mug of ale. Lothar didn't know if the sour taste in his mouth was from the woman or the drink.

The woman moaned and turned her face away from the sunlight pouring through the window cut out of the wall.

Lothar winced as the light hit his face. He realized he was in a room above the tavern. The revelry had gone on long after they had left Sister Abigail standing in that dark room.

"Come on little brother. The crew has voted," a voice said from the doorway. Lothar looked up and saw Black Tom standing there with a curious smile on his face.

"Did I vote? " Lothar asked.

Black Tom chuckled. "No, you're not a member of the crew, yet. Come now, I know you are enamored of Lily Ann's charms but we have to prepare to shove off. We are taking the Sister to get her sister."

Lothar noticed that Black Tom was wearing his flintlocks, two short swords and leather wrist gauntlets. His strange yellowed hair was hidden under a black scarf.

"What do you mean I am enamored with her charms?" Lothar asked, pointing at the woman who slept beside him.

Black Tom chuckled again. "Well, let's say you made some rather extraordinary pledges of fidelity to her last night. But that is neither here nor there; time to earn your keep."

Black Tom turned on his heels and trotted down the stairs.

Lothar slid out of bed. He felt his world sway beneath his feet as he followed Black Tom.

Lothar had sailed on enough trips to have a relatively competent understanding of sail rigging and knot tying. However, the *Black Angel* had a few extra hatches and some rather unique accessories that tested his tenuous sailing skills. The cannons on the Black Angel were held in hatches below the deck that were operated by a complex block and pulley system that made his head hurt just looking at it.

He was sent to pack the gunpowder and muskets balls and load the cannon balls and carry crates of salted meat into the galley and a dozen other tasks that had him cursing ale and rum all morning.

At noon, Sister Abigail made her way down to the docks. Lothar watched her approach as he leaned against the deck railing taking a much needed break. She was no less gorgeous this morning than she had been last night. A heavy sigh escaped his lips.

"She *is* beautiful, but so is a hawk," a deep voice said behind him. "Both would tear your eyes out, I suspect."

Lothar whirled and their stood the Bandit King. He was shirtless and his braids were twisted into one large plait. Lothar noticed the markings on his chest were the crude outlines of a lion's head. In addition, a multitude of scars that ran up and down his massive arms. Two of them, one on each forearm, were curious symbols that looked like a horseshoe – a bit more round on the top, with a wider base on each leg.

"Sorry, Mr. Bandit King, sir," Lothar mumbled.

The Bandit King laughed.

Lothar noticed he laughed a lot.

"For what?" The Bandit King asked. "If we had to apologize every time we noticed a beautiful woman, a man's day would be filled with begging for forgiveness."

He clapped Lothar on the back.

Lothar coughed. He looked down to make sure his heart had not burst from his chest.

Sister Abigail sauntered over to where they were standing.

"Captain Masterless, I have a favor to ask of you," she said.

The Bandit King crossed his arms. "You are paying for the outfitting of our ship. "I think that earns you at least two commands and one favor. So what is it my lady?"

"I will require lodging for our trip to the Isle of Lamina," Sister Abigail said. "I wish to stay in a cabin alone."

The Bandit King scratched his chin. "You wouldn't be afraid of me and my men would you, me lady?"

Sister Abigail looked up into his eyes. "I will not trust the sanctity of my virtue to the moral fortitude of you or your men."

The Bandit King smiled. "Well, ma'am, far be it for me to spoil your virtue. I think we can accommodate you."

Sister Abigail pursed her lips then walked away.

A warm sense of melancholy filled Lothar's heart.

"She thinks we are awful men, doesn't she?" Lothar asked.

The Bandit King put his hand on Lothar's shoulder and looked the younger man in the eye. "We *are* awful men, little brother. We are corsairs and brigands but we are also free. Make no mistake, we exist in a world that would deny us everything, including freedom. I, for one, will embrace the life we live as I embrace the sea and then I will fill my cup with rum and drink to a good death, for when I die, it will be on my feet, not genuflecting and begging to be spared. I am the Bandit King. Never a bondsman will I be!"

His eyes blazed with a fire that made Lothar tremble. And then, like a summer squall, it was gone.

"Go and prepare a place to sleep," the Bandit King said. "We leave at a quarter past the hour. Do you have any experience with a flintlock?"

"I was trained in fencing by my former master," Lothar replied. "I have no experience with guns."

The Bandit King grabbed him by his collar and effortlessly lifted him off his feet. "You are a man. No other man is, or can be, your master, only your oppressor. I'll see that Black Tom gets you a cutlass. But first, answer me this? Why would an oppressor teach you to fence?"

Lothar smiled. "Well, it was with a wooden sword. He thought it was good sport. But one day I knocked his sword out of his hand. I was given ten lashes, but I enjoyed seeing the look on his face as his stick hit the ground."

The Bandit King returned his smile and lowered him to the deck.

"Lothar you might be a good fit for our motley crew after all," he said.

He turned and headed for the bow where Black Tom was going over the coordinates for their voyage as given to him by Sister Abigail. Lothar smoothed his shirt and let out a deep breath.

Three days passed before they caught sight of the island. Lothar was in the crow's nest when he spotted it – a large, rocky mass with a verdant peak that stretched toward the sky.

"Land Ho!" Lothar yelled down to the deck.

The Bandit King came out of his cabin. Black Tom approached him.

"What's the play here?" Black Tom asked, stroking the butt of his flintlock. "Go in with guns blazing?"

The Bandit King shook his head. "No, we entreat the lord of this island to let us partake of his particular brand of entertainment. Once we get a lay of the land, we make our move. I'll go ashore with Lothar and Horus and a few others. You stay on the ship with the rest of the boys. Once we know what forces oppose us, we will take the girl and the bounty. Never go in with guns blazing until you know how many guns are pointed at ya."

Sister Abigail emerged from below deck and stretched her arms.

Black Tom peered at her then looked at the Bandit King.

"Well, time to talk to the good sister," the Bandit King said. "Hopefully her lips are looser than her morals."

####

"The merchant who delivered my sister's message told me Verpa keeps his spoils in a guarded basement under the main..." she hesitated.

"Brothel my lady," The Bandit King said. "It's called a brothel."

"Yes, a brothel," Sister Abigail sighed. "I just cannot believe she is here."

"The spoils?" Black Tom asked.

"Yes the spoils," Sister Abigail said. "They are guarded by his misbegotten offspring. The room is said to be filled to bursting with goods – gold, spices, silver, whatever men deem worthy enough to part with to sully their flesh."

"How will we know your sister?" the Bandit King asked.

Sister Abigail smiled. "She looks just like me, except her hair is red; *blood* red and longer than mine. How do you propose to spirit her away?"

"Don't you worry about that my dear," the Bandit King said. "Just point her out and we will do the rest."

Sister Abigail leaned across the table and grasped the Bandit King's hand.

Black Tom raised his eyebrow.

"I have seen visions from my God," she said. "You are the one."

She stared into his eyes and he stared back at her. For a moment neither would drop their gaze. Then, Sister Abigail blinked and turned her head away. She stood and nodded. She hurried from the room without saying another word.

"What is her malady?" Black Tom said.

The Bandit King put his feet up on the table and pulled a jug of rum from under it. "I suspect she is second guessing her vows."

Horus chortled.

"Well, I for one want to have some fun before we take this Verpa off the board," Horus said. "Do you know how long it's been since I have lain with a woman?"

"Since you gave up your mother's milk?" Black Tom said with a smile.

Horus bit his thumb at him.

The Bandit King handed him the jug.

"Come now, fellows let us be jolly," the Bandit King said. "We are going to rescue a harlot at the request of a virgin. If there *is* a God, that has to qualify us for a double blessing."

The Isle of Lamina sat on the top of a volcanic caldera. Two rocky ridges shot out from the island parallel to each other like the legs of the letter 'U', forming a natural harbor.

Lothar could see other ships moored in those shallow waters as they approached the island. Some men from the two other ships splashed through the water and headed for shore with bags held high above their heads. Two hulking men waited on the beach with a thin woman between them. She was pale, with long, strawberry blond hair. The two hulking men were darker than the woman, with wide shoulders and sloped heads that sat on thick necks. The three of them were dressed like members of a royal court . The men wore red velvet frock coats and tight breeches and stockings. Identical powdered white wigs sat upon their massive heads. The woman wore a wide green dress with an elaborate bustle and a severe plunging neckline.

"Listen up gents," the Bandit King began. "Me, Horus, Liam, Octon, Lothar, Semi and the sister are going ashore. We will take stock of the situation then, after dark, we will signal the rest of you. We have discussed our plan, now I trust each of you to do your part. What is our motto?"

"We hang together, or we hang separately!" the crew said in unison.

"Good gents. Very good," the Bandit King said. "Alright, let's get in the dinghy. Someone rouse the sister."

"I'm here," she said.

Lothar turned his head toward Sister Abigail and his jaw dropped. The sister had traded in her habit for a pair of tight breeches and a close fitting white shirt. Her hair was twisted into two long braids that fell over her full breasts.

"Well, look what we have here," the Bandit King said, smiling. "Now you look like a woman ready to sin!"

"I still don't know why I have to wear this ridiculous attire," she said. Her face was pinched like a puckered wound.

"Sister, we want to go in like any other fellows looking for a bit of the good stuff," Back Tom said. "It wouldn't do to be seen bringing in a nun now would it?"

Sister Abigail said nothing.

"Let's go. The welcoming committee awaits," the Bandit King said.

Lothar had thought Port Royal was the height of hedonism. One look around the Isle of Lamina forced him to reevaluate that assertion. The brothel was decadent in a way nothing in Port Royal could ever hope to match. All around him men and women engaged in every manner of congress.

Horus dragged a stunning woman with slanted eyes over to a velvet covered couch and lay his entire bulk upon her back as he grunted and keened like a hog. The other members of the crew followed suit.

All, except the Bandit King.

He sat next to Sister Abigail and watched the proceedings with a strange impassiveness on his face.

A slight man plucked away at a harpsichord. The dulcet tones of the instrument seemed woefully out of place amid the grunts and groans that filled the hall.

The music ended abruptly. A dandy appeared on a raised dais that looked down upon the gyrating bodies. He wore a bright green frock coat and white stockings that bulged with his manhood. He had on a powdered wig and held a tankard in his hand.

"Gentlemen, I am your host, Verpa," the dandy squealed. "Please pause your exertions for a moment to join me in a toast!"

Verpa's monstrous associates moved through the crowd handing out earthen cups to only the men.

A brute with a face like a barnacle put a cup in Lothar's hand. After his previous encounter with ale and rum, Lothar had silently sworn off alcohol. The barnacle-faced man handed the Bandit King a cup as well.

"Now join me in a toast to your good health, to full pockets and to empty balls!" Verpa screeched in a high, womanish voice.

Each man in attendance threw back the cup; everyone, except Lothar.

The Bandit King dropped his empty cup. "What...did ...you ...do ...to me?" he mumbled. He rose from his seat and took two steps toward the stage before falling face first onto the table.

Verpa stopped smiling and hopped down from the dais. The other men in the room slid off the backs of their chosen mounts and collapsed onto the floor.

Two of Verpa's associates stared at Lothar.

Lothar rolled his eyes back and let his head hit the table in front of him. His heart was thudding in his chest hard enough to rattle his bones.

"Sister Abigail, are you sure he is the one?"

Lothar heard Verpa ask.

"He bears the marks," Sister Abigail replied. "What the Greeks called *omega*. The old tongue calls it *o'ski'ra*. He is the one. Take him to the grotto. Kill the others, then drain the harbor and kill the men on his ship. Take care, though, for they are men of great violence.

"As you wish, Sister," Verpa said. "Praise the God who sleeps beneath the Sea!"

"Praise the God who sleeps beneath the Sea," Sister Abigail echoed softly.

Lothar felt rough hands pick him up and throw him on top of his mates in a wooden cart. One of the misbegotten footmen rolled the cart out of the hall and turned onto a well worn path that cut through the lush verdant foliage of the island. Lothar kept his eyes closed and tried to quiet his fear, but his fear was a screaming baby in his head. That they had been betrayed was obvious. But to what end?

You will figure out a way to escape. You have to. Today is not the day you die a free man, he thought.

The Bandit King raised his head. His wrists were in shackles attached to chains that hung from the roof of a great cave. The air in the cave was cool. His chest was covered in goose-bumps. He kicked his feet and heard water splash. He craned his head and saw the opening to the cave behind him. In front of him was a gargantuan wooden door set in the very back of the cave. In the center of the door was a circular metal plate with bizarre etchings scrawled across it. The cave was a natural formation with some manmade additions. Torches ran up and down the wet limestone walls of the cave. Above the door was some type of balcony carved out of the rock. A pathway ran around the perimeter of the cave up to the balcony.

"He awakens," a female voice said behind him. Sister Abigail walked through the shallow water in the cave and stood in front of him. She was naked. Her long black hair was loose and fell across her full breasts.

"I take it you are not truly a virgin." the Bandit King said.

Sister Abigail threw her head back and howled. It was a wild sound, like a puma screeching in the dark. "No, my dear king, I am not. But let's not discuss what I am not and let us commiserate on what you *are.*"

Her eyes searched his face. He could almost feel the intensity of her gaze.

"I am a brigand remember," he said.

She touched his face. "Oh no, you are so much more than that." Her voice was tender. "Have you ever wondered what those marks on your forearms are? They are not made of ink like the marks on your chest. I heard tales of the great, Black pirate with the omega birth marks. The merchants who came to our island were in awe of you. But I wasn't sure until I saw you fight."

"Sure of what?" the Bandit King asked.

"The *shair 'vi corant*. The words slithered off her tongue. "The great warrior, whose seed will open the doorway for the God who sleeps beneath the Sea, so that he may return and wipe away all manner of false gods and reclaim his rightful place in this world. We are his last true subjects. We have searched for you for a very long time, my king. Your seed will open that door."

She pointed to the enormous door at the back of the cave.

"Sorry to disappoint you, deary, but I wouldn't touch you if you were last piece of cunny on earth," the Bandit King said.

"Oh no, my king, you will not plumb my depths," Sister Abigail said. "We will milk you like a maiden does a cow. And we will use that seed to open the door. Of course, the God who sleeps beneath the Sea will require nourishment after his long slumber. Unfortunately, you will be the first thing he sees, but I console you with the thought that you will have ushered in a bold new reign for our God."

A glassy sheen came over her eyes.

"I tell you what, my lady, when my men get here, I'll make sure I kill you quickly, and you can meet this god face to face without me losing my seed or my life," the Bandit King said.

Sister Abigail smiled. "Your men are dead, Bandit King. The ones who came ashore with you have had their throats slit and their bodies dumped in an old well. The ones you left on board your ship found themselves mired in a muddy whirlpool after we drained the harbor. We have been doing this for a long, long time my king. My family has lived here on the Isle of Lamina for over a thousand years. The Island of Tears is our home."

The Bandit King did not drop his head as she reported the deaths of his crew. He did not shed a tear. Instead he rolled his tongue a few times and then spit in her face.

Sister Abigail wiped away the spittle. "I will return with my sisters and my brothers shortly. The ceremony will begin."

She walked out of the cave.

This is all far from over, my dear lady, he thought.

Turgid water sloshed against his boots and the chains rattled.

####

Lothar felt every bump and every hole on the path as the wagon full of bodies was pushed toward its destination. Horus' inert form crushed him and sweat ran into his eyes, but he remained silent and motionless. He did not know what he was going to do or how he was going to do it but he knew his only advantage was the element of surprise.

Finally, the cart came to a halt.

The man with a face that looked like a partially chewed piece of meat put a rock under the wooden wheel of the cart and let out a deep sigh. Using only one hand, he dragged Horus's body out of the cart . The cart was wide enough for bodies to be stacked three wide and two deep. Lothar couldn't see what the man was doing but when he came back to the cart and grabbed Liam, Lothar could see his hands were covered in blood.

Lothar eased up onto his elbows and peered over the lip of the cart. The man stood in front of a stone well. He grabbed Liam by his tight, curly hair and without hesitating, drew a long dagger across his throat. Blood gushed from the wound. It still gushed as the man grabbed Liam under his arms and prepared to toss him into the well.

Lothar knew this would be his only chance. He hopped out of the cart. As he did the rock chocking the wheel moved and the cart careened down the pathway. Lothar screamed as he slammed into the man's lower back.

The force drove the man forward on the balls of his feet, sending him and Liam's body tumbling into the well.

Lothar sprinted into the lush jungle. Thorny vines and wide leaves slapped against his face as he ran. Fear no longer filled his heart. Anger had taken up residence there; anger for his crew and anger at being deceived; anger that became rage – a rage that blinded him.

So blinded by rage was he that he did not see the arm that snaked out from behind a palm tree and caught him in the chest.

Lothar's feet flew from under him. The air in his lungs exited his body with a whoosh. He landed flat on his back.

Black Tom stared down at him. "Where you off to in such a hurry, little brother?"

Lothar turned on his side and then hopped to his feet.

"She has the Bandit King!" Lothar said between deep breaths. "Liam and Horus are dead. The rest of the crew is in a cart rolling down the mountain! She said they were killing you fellows as well!"

Black Tom nodded. "Aye...as soon as I saw the water begin to drain from around our ship, we departed and made our way to land. We saw them take the King in one direction and the rest of you gents in another."

Lothar felt like he was going to vomit. When nothing came forth, he straightened his posture and looked Black Tom in the eye. "So what are we going to do, sir?"

Black Tom patted his flintlocks. "We go get our brothers. And we deliver a bit of Greek fire to this horrible witch and her ill-formed kin."

Lothar looked past him and saw the rest of the crew. They had bottles with cloth strips in the necks tied to their persons in make shift holsters made from some type of tightly woven yarn. Black Tom snapped his fingers and one of the crew handed him a cutlass.

"You with us, little brother?"

Lothar snatched the cutlass from Black Tom's hand. "Most assuredly, sir."

The Bandit King heard a cacophony of footfalls heading toward the cave where he hung like a fat goose in a butcher shop. The rumble of a multitude of voices singing in unison joined the footfalls as the procession neared the cave. He heard them come splashing through the water. By the sound, it had to be dozens of them.

Soft hands began to stroke his back and chest. Sister Abigail appeared in front of him like some strange phantom . She was still naked and every inch of her naked flesh was coated with some type of white powder that gave her a ghostly countenance. She walked through the rising tide until her face was mere inches from his. She smelled like charred wood.

"Now, my wicked king, it begins," Sister Abigail whispered in his ear.

She turned and walked along the rough steps of the parapet until she reached the stone balcony. She raised her arms. "Sai'kia, sai'kazan! Shi'kian et Kathullu!"

The Bandit King whipped his head from side to

side. Naked men and women filled the cave. The wanton women from the brothel and the twisted footmen that attended to them stood side-by-side, covered in the same ash as Sister Abigail. They repeated her strange mantra. The Bandit King felt soft hands reach into his heavy cotton breeches. The hands grasped his manhood. Despite not experiencing the slightest hint of amorousness, his manhood stiffened in the unknown woman's embrace.

Sister Abigail gibbered away on the balcony.

The crowd howled like lovers locked in an orgasmic embrace.

The Bandit King felt his arms begin to burn as he felt himself nearing the precipice of passion. His birthmarks were burning. They pulsed with a faint red glow. Sister Abigail screamed and the pain in his arms increased until it was unbearable. His body tensed, every muscle as taut as a piano string. He grunted as his seed exploded from his manhood and into the unseen woman's hand.

She released her grip and took off in an awkward run toward the gigantic door in the back of the cave.

Sister Abigail wailed as the ashen woman smeared his seed on the circular metal plate in the middle of the door.

"Good luck my dear," the Bandit King shouted. "I am a man among men but I doubt I have magic in my manhood!"

A flaming bottle sailed through the air and broke against the supple flesh of one of the ashen ladies. Flames coated her body like a second skin, running over her like quicksilver across a metal smith's bench.

The report of a flintlock roared twice in quick succession. The chains holding the Bandit King's arms fell to his sides.

He looked up on the stone parapet. Black Tom tipped an imaginary cap in his direction.

My brothers, he thought.

"Bandit King, I think you may need this!" Lothar shouted.

The Bandit King looked to his right. Lothar stood on the parapet. The young man hurled the Bandit King's broadsword through the air. As the bottles of Greek fire rained down, the Bandit King caught his broadsword with one hand.

"Oh yes, my dear cunny," the Bandit King whispered. "Time to pay all debts and the only currency I accept is blood!"

Whistling, he twirled his right arm and then his left until the lengths of chain were wrapped around his burning forearms. He pulled his sword from its scabbard and began slicing his way through naked bodies on his way to the stone balcony. The scent of gunpowder filled his nostrils as he whirled and jumped and slashed his way through the crowd. All around him bodies fell. Screams became dying gasps.

A misshapen footman jumped in his path. The Bandit King shoved his blade through the man's prodigious gut and then pulled hard to the side, freeing his sword and the man's entrails.

The man pitched forward.

The Bandit King hopped on his broad back then jumped onto the parapet.

Sister Abigail stood firm on the balcony. She did not run; she did not kneel. She faced the Bandit King with a haughtiness that seemed in contrast with the scene unfolding around her.

"Well, you truly *are* dangerous corsair," she said. "Come, kill me brigand. Run me through! It makes no difference now. The God that Sleeps Beneath the Sea has awoken. My life's mission is complete."

The Bandit King raised his sword.

"You put me in chains," he said. "For that alone I would kill you."

A thunderous crack filled the cave and stayed his hand. Another great crack split the air and all movement in the cave ceased.

Lothar froze in his tracks. He turned and peered at the large door. The circular metal plate was spinning – first, to the left, then to the right. The markings on the door glowed with a green, eldritch light. One more crack rent the air and then the disk fell from the door.

For a moment, all was silent.

Then, the door flew open, sending a wave splashing on the combatants.

A horrible roar assaulted Lothar's ears. A roar that emanated from somewhere he feared to envision.

"Oh my God," Black Tom gasped.

A figure walked out of the inky blackness beyond the door. It was twice as tall as the Bandit King. The shambling creature had greenish-black skin as slick as a seal. The thing walked on two legs but did not resemble a man. Its head was an undulating mass of muscular tentacles surrounding a raw, red gullet. Each tentacle ended with a twisted mouth filled with crooked yellow fangs. Its chest was covered with what appeared to be teats like one would observe on a nursing hound. It walked on legs that were as thick as tree stumps and its terrible hands each ended in wicked, green claws . Each talon was as long as a dagger.

"Run," Black Tom said, speaking in a low murmur at first. No one moved. "Run!" he screamed.

"Yes! He has awoken and now your time is at an end, sons of Adam!" Sister Abigail said. "He will destroy your cities and kill your babies and I will be his High Priestess. Now, he will...aaaaaagggrh!"

Sister Abigail ended her diatribe with a wail so full of agony, it made the Bandit King wince. As she spoke of her god one of his serpentine tentacles spilled over the balcony and enveloped her in a fatal embrace.

The appendage flexed and squeezed her rib cage, cutting off her scream in mid-wail.

"I'll take my leave of your island now, Sister Abigail!" the Bandit King said.

He ran down the parapet and then leaped over several bodies writhing in the final throes of death. He followed his men and the acolytes of the God that Sleeps beneath the Sea out of the cave. His lungs burned as he ran full speed through the jungle and away from the howling thing that devoured its followers.

The Bandit King reached the harbor and caught up with his crew. They stood on the shore, staring at their ship. The Black Angel sat in three feet of mud. The Bandit King could see that what he had taken for a natural formation was actually a man made trap. At the mouth of the harbor was a large wooden door. It was very similar to the door in the cave. The Bandit King deduced its purpose fairly quickly. A ship entered the harbor and the door was raised. Then through some form of machinery the water was bailed out of the harbor leaving the ship mired in muck.

"What do we do, sir?" Lothar asked. The crew stared at their captain with fearful, pleading eyes.

"We get on our goddamned ship," the Bandit King answered. "We use the cannons to blow the door. The sea will do the rest.

A mournful shriek escaped the jungle.

"Quick now gents!" The Bandit King said. "I fear

we haven't much time before that thing makes meals of us!"

He and his men slogged through the muck and the mud and boarded their ship.

"Fire the cannons!" the Bandit King commanded. The crew whirled the cannons on their rotating platforms toward the aft section of the ship. The charges were lit and the cannon balls hit their target with ferocious accuracy. Sea water poured into the harbor. Lothar held fast to the railing as the Black Angel was buoyed up and to the left before righting itself.

"Hard starboard, Black Tom! " the Bandit King yelled.

The sails unfurled and the strong southern winds began to the turn the ship until its bow pointed out of the harbor.

"Full speed ahead, Tom!" The Bandit King roared.

The sails of the Black Angel swelled with the winds rolling across the island as the ship left the harbor.

The Bandit King sat back in his chair on the bridge and laid his sword on the deck. He leaned his head back and closed his eyes.

He did not see the greenish black tentacle that wrapped itself around the railing.

"God save us!" Octon screamed.

The Bandit King leaped to his feet. He spotted a tentacle latching onto the rear of his ship. He looked back toward the island. The God that Sleeps Beneath the Sea was on the shore. His tentacles had reached out across the ocean and were coiling around the railings and rope cleats of the Black Angel.

"No more of this madness!" The Bandit King roared.

He picked up his sword and lunged toward the tentacles.

Lothar's words stopped him dead in his tracks.

"Shia'kazoan, shi'kali Kathula, si'donal!" Lothar said. He had climbed up to the crow's nest.

The wind carried his voice to the island.

The Bandit King watched in amazement as the tentacles uncoiled and slipped from the rails.

The creature on the shore fell to its mammoth knees. The Bandit King lowered his sword.

Lothar climbed down from the crow's nest to the cheers of his crew mates.

"What did you say to him?" The Bandit King asked.

"I told him to go back to sleep," Lothar said with a shrug.

The Bandit King laughed and laughed and laughed.

SEVEN THIEVES

Emmalia Harrington

Sweat escaped the turban Widow Edith Derosiers stuffed under her straw hat, dripping into her eyes. Any attempt to shake off the salty liquid sent droplets flying onto leaves and soil alike. Though a few dashes probably wouldn't harm her garden, she grabbed a corner of her neckerchief to swab her russet skin. Eyeing the pump bottle beside her kneeling legs, she considered applying some mist to her face.

The bottle was filled with the best insect repellent in the Virginia colony, a mixture of witch hazel, lavender and mint suspended extracts. She was only a third of the way through with this current batch; a quick spray on herself shouldn't be too wasteful.

Shaking her hands loose of cramps, Edith pressed her palm against her face. The action flattened her homemade mask, crushing the dried roses and lavender stuffed inside. Edith breathed deep, pulling the rose and lavender scent into her lungs, cleansing her innards. Even in her backyard kingdom, to travel unprotected was to court a painful death.

Rising to her feet, she beat dust off of her apron before picking up her tools and heading to her storage shed. Her knees and back complained only a little. Once everything was stowed away, she lingered at the doorway, taking in her treasures.

Herbs and flowers took up most of her land, planted as close together as she dared. Even with the air as still as it was right now, fragrance rose from every leaf and stem. Not one plant bore traces of browning, wilting or insects.

Nestled against her kitchen wall was a black canister large enough for an adult to stand with her arms outstretched. Edith didn't miss her childhood days of pumping water and hauling buckets to the kitchen until her arms and hands were one large burn. Using the sun to heat water was much more civilized, as was replacing firewood with mirror blocks. Her perimeter fence was constantly edged with glass bricks covered in dark cloth. While bare mirror slabs could absorb heat from sunlight, black coverings sped the process and prevented her and Widow Anker from blinding themselves as they worked outdoors.

Near the back of the property was a brick outbuilding outfitted with a shingled roof and a few tiny windows. Edith kept her still house cleaner than anything, discouraging rogue wisps of perfume.

If crouching for hours in direct sunlight in the height of summer was odious, entering her little laboratory made her want to scream. The only light peeked from around the locked shutters and oozed from mirror slabs. A place so dusky should have condensation on its walls and air that steamed with every breath. What she had was a reek so stale her floral mask was the only thing keeping her from gagging. Opening the shutters and leaving the door ajar risked contaminating her nascent work with outside miasma.

Giving the mirror slab by the doorway a double tap, more captured sunlight filled the room, illuminating slabs which supported large copper pears with drooping stems feeding fragrant liquid into a receiving flask. In one corner stood a device as tall as her, its round glass sides boasting layers of gravel, sand and charcoal. The bottom of the tube held a tap where she could help herself to all the purified water she could carry. Against a far wall were casks of *Seven Thieves' Vinegar* in the making.

A better world would have all her vinegar mature six months, allowing her ingredients to penetrate every drop of liquid. The current market demanded so much of the tonic, a single week had to do. Edith's culmination of breeding, composting, weeding and cultivating was hastened into the hobby of an idle housewife.

Stretching her arms over her head, working gardening induced knots, Edith headed to a corner filled with vats of spoiled wine and her shelves of distilled essences. All of her stocks were running low and camphor, peppermint and the other five thieves were nearly gone. Her customers would die or move on to a whiter, less experienced perfumer before her ingredients grew again.

Near the middle of the room sat a table filled with scales, vials and other instruments, scrubbed yesterday until her fingers bloomed angry red. Pulling down the necessary ingredients, Edith measured what she needed to make another vat of vinegar. Part of her wondered if she could pour the exact amounts with her eyes closed. The rest of her liked not being arrested or worse for selling faulty goods to whites.

The ground trembled beneath her in spurts. Straightening, a hand on the small of her back, she turned to find a familiar broad tawny body standing in the doorway. The newcomer was leaning against the frame, with heavy shadows under her eyes. Her gown and apron were rumpled, and her cap went askew as Edith barreled into Widow Marja Anker, delivering a rib creaking hug. The new woman returned the hug, the rumbling in her chest indicating a groan.

Edith stepped away, her eyes hardening as she took in the sweet woman's bare face and dried blood framing her nails.

Widow Anker caught the sweaty woman's glare. She mimed coughing into her free hand before turning the palm to Edith, revealing a lack of lung-generated pus.

Removing her mask, Edith rammed it into Widow Anker's open hand before pointing to their house. Widow Anker's lips moved, giving Edith a series of sounds tumbling into one another. Edith spun on her heel, returning to the table. Closing her eyes, she gave a small prayer that her Marja had enough sense to cover her nose at least until she returned indoors.

A small eternity later, with a flask of skin-cooling rosemary water in hand, Edith crossed her garden to the back door of her main house. The sun was finishing its peak in the sky, and the cramping in her stomach reminded Edith that she hadn't eaten anything since the morning light made its first forays into the day. Before food, she had to deal with more pressing concerns.

Inside her house, by the back door, rested a floppy paddle fan made of conductive wires and treated cloth.

Picking up her fan, Edith followed her nose to the kitchen, leading her to Widow Anker, back facing the room, scouring her medical gear with sand and water. Stomping the ground to alert the woman, Edith said "What were you thinking, being out all night?" Widow Anker wilted at the sound of Edith's voice, loud enough for the deaf to hear. "Do you want to give the City Watch a reason to lock you away? You of all people should remember the black's plague curfew."

Turning around, Widow Anker waited for Edith to bite her fan before slowly enunciating, "Mrs. Abrams was having a difficult birth." As her words hit the paddle, its cloth and metal hummed, passing the woman's message through teeth and bone. "I spent all night and a good part of yesterday making sure she and her babies would remain on this earth." Her muscles turned to rags, she slumped against Edith. Widow Anker said something Edith couldn't catch, prompting the woman to tap her Marja's shoulder and point to the fan.

Picking her head off from Edith's chest, Widow Anker told the fan, "She had triplets."

Edith blinked, then softly shoved her Marja towards the nearest chair. Widow Anker resisted the push, her mouth twisted into a thin smile. "Mr. Abrams closed his shop early. He refused to leave the hall outside his bedroom until the last of the afterbirth was delivered. With three new sons, he has no reason to have me jailed."

Opening her mouth wide and using her free hand, Edith mimicked Widow Anker's favorite praying style.

Stepping back to reveal her akimbo stance, Widow Anker said, "Do you think me a fool? I'm not going to witness if a woman and her babies look ready to die in front of me." Relaxing her arms, she added "Mr. Abrams is giving us a favor for this."

Edith raised her eyebrows.

Returning to the basin steaming on the counter, Widow Anker motioned for Edith to follow. Plunging her hands into the gritty water, Widow Anker said, "Mr. Abrams wants to pay me handsomely to spend the next fortnight looking after his wife and heirs. When I explained my other duties, he offered to pay me well and not report me to the Watch."

Filling her lungs with humid kitchen air, Edith yelled "It's not enough to go out into the plague air without protection? You want to be tossed into a cell again with only fleas for food and company?" Her shoulders sagging, she added "They won't let me give you perfume in jail."

As Edith turned away, Widow Anker caught the edge of her sleeve. A strong tug was all she needed to come free. When Widow Anker stomped the kitchen floor, trying to grab her attention, Edith kept walking.

Several minutes later she returned to the kitchen, a box in her hands. Moving with as heavy a step she could manage, she placed the box on the counter, pulled out a spray bottle and headed to the woman now at the table, busy drying a pewter enema syringe. It only took a few pumps to drench it and her Marja's hands with proper Seven Thieves vinegar.

Widow Anker leapt back, dropping the syringe. Her face was contorted into a "What's wrong with you?" look.

"I'm not taking chances," Edith said. Stopping for breath, she started to say more, but noticed Widow Anker's still perplexed visage.

Making a sigh large enough to move her arms and back, she picked up the syringe and walked up to her companion, showing her where droplets still shone on the metal. "You should have waited for it to dry first," she said into Edith's ear. "Wouldn't water weaken its strength?"

Her face burning, Edith hurried to her box, taking out a brass ball on a cord. The musty floral notes of chamomile seeped from holes punched into the metal. Edith turned to Widow Anker, eyebrows raised, holding up the pomander. The midwife lowered her head to give the perfumer an easier time fastening the chain and its pendant around her neck.

Edith made a point to leave the vinegar bottle by the still-wet midwifery tools.

When Edith wasn't working on Seven Thieves Vinegar, she was mixing, distilling, steeping and bottling to keep up with the wealthy's demand for protective fragrances. Some were liquids meant to be dabbed, sprinkled or sprayed onto the skin or clothes, while solid perfumes needed to be rubbed into place or carried around in pomanders, keeping their owners in a fragrant cloud that wouldn't fade within hours.

Vinegar wasn't as elegant as the scents she wore around her neck or peddled to the nicer shops in town, but her recipe was the nicest smelling available, and enough people could afford it. To keep her purse happy, she spent a better part of a week replenishing her stores.

In her still room, where none were around to look, Edith removed her shoes and stockings to give her feet room to swell. Her nose turned numb from the steam that escaped when she transferred distillations from one flask to another.

Preparing the vinegar itself required no heat, just a matter of clipping what she needed from her garden, drying the necessary herbs, layering them prepared containers, pouring over vinegar and leaving the mixture to sit.

As long as her hands kept busy, she never ground her feet into the earth, waiting for stomping that never came. She wouldn't keep scanning her surroundings, looking over her shoulder for traces of that kind tawny face. Edith would do everything in her power to make fragrances that were second to none in keeping disease away. Her pockets would grow so full she'd reinforce them with canvas. Widow Anker would never have to work for others ever again. Her Marja would stay out of prison, drinking all the tea and wine she pleased. There would be no praying that she could make a single flask last four days.

If the Abramses caught her Marja witnessing to their slaves, they probably wouldn't call the City Watch, but a judge to send her to the auction block.

It was every bit as likely that Widow Anker would remember to wear a mask or pomander locket, only to give it to a slave or beggar with no protection to speak of. Her Marja's lungs would fill with muck, forcing her to cough until her ribs cracked. No amount of Edith's perfume would bring her back.

These thoughts caused Edith's hands to shake so badly she dared not handle her perfumes and vinegar. She'd grab a spray bottle and stalk her garden, hunting for insects to blast into submission. By the time her bottle was empty her arms were usually steady enough to resume her work.

When Widow Anker didn't come home one night, Edith had to constantly remind herself that this wasn't the first time. Widow Anker was full of tales of missing curfew in her effort to save souls. She was only caught a handful of times.

The next day Edith worked her hands into blisters. From the afternoon onwards, her knees creaked with every movement. By that night, her feet were so swollen she feared having to take scissors to her shoes.

With the way her heart was pounding and her feet kept twisting against the floor, searching for the tale tell tremble of footsteps, sleep wasn't going to come. No matter, there was plenty to do. Taking the household supply of Seven Thieves vinegar, she swabbed it along every window, door, chamber pot and other areas prone to contamination. By the time she was finished, she couldn't stand, let alone walk without pain shooting up her soles through to her head.

Soaking her afflicted body in a bath of rose petals and lemon balm did wonders for her flesh. The fragrant water served as a reminder of how Widow Anker refused all protection for herself. For a while, Edith couldn't tell if her blood was boiling or if it was the bath.

It took three cups of wine to cool her enough to consider lying down. Sleep remained a stranger, forcing Edith to stare into the dark, captive to her thoughts. If the late Reverend Anker's followers could manage to sneak bread and small beer into the Ankers' cells, perhaps Edith could do the same for her Marja. She tried not to think of how easily guards could sneak up on her and succeeded. Thoughts of Widow Anker shoved before an audience, her mouth forced open to prove good health, crowded everything else from Edith's mind.

Her Marja's reputation as a troublemaker would likely get her sold to a sugarcane island. Burns and hunger were rampant, though most slaves took years to die. Edith should probably pray for a rice farmer to buy her Marja, where malaria would finish her off faster.

Edith might have stayed in her haze forever if a pair of strong hands hadn't shaken her out of it. She jerked upright and overshot nearly falling onto her bedding. The hands steadied her for a long moment before withdrawing.

Blinking the grogginess from her eyes, Edith felt for the mirror block on her bedside table. The other person beat her to it, awakening a flare that made

Edith wince. When her eyes stopped hurting, she made out a familiar shape gesturing with a free hand.

"I can't see you well," Edith said, causing her Marja to jump. Hauling her creaky body out of bed, she found her fan and bit it, turning to Widow Anker.

"I didn't want to wake you, nor did I to scare you," Widow Anker said, leaning to touch foreheads with Edith.

Edith stepped back, pointing out the window to the sliver of moon. Her Marja mimed slow, careful steps, stopping to look over her shoulder. Edith raised her arms and squinted as though aiming a pistol.

Widow Anker shrugged, motioning for Edith to bite her fan. "You shouldn't act as though it's my first time skulking about after curfew," the midwife said, "I've been practicing since before I married."

Edith held out her hand, pretending to give a speech before flipping through pages of an imaginary book. Then she hunched over, faking a coughing fit.

Widow Anker exaggerated a sigh, flopping her arms, before speaking into the fan. "That's not what happened. The triplets kept me busy until well after sunset, and Mrs. Abrams kept a close eye on me. I wasn't able to witness to her slaves." Her hands gathered bunches of her apron, twisting the fabric.

Edith pointed her head to the moon. Widow Anker looked away, mumbling. At Edith's prodding, she walked around the room in an exaggerated march, stopping every so often. When Widow Anker paused, she'd mimic opening a door and preaching the Good Word. A few times she paused by their bed, stroking the imaginary heads of the ailing.

Her vision turned grey before Edith remembered to breathe. Her arms trembling, she forced herself to back away before she did something regrettable. "Even if it's not at the Abramses, witnessing after curfew is still illegal. Why do you want to throw away this life you have?" she shouted, her throat rasping at the force of her words. "Is staying with me so awful, you'd prefer rotted lungs?"

Widow Anker had winced at Edith's initial outburst, but now stood at her full height, feet braced for whatever may come her way. She pointed to her heart and raised her hands heavenward.

Shoving past Widow Anker, Edith headed for the parlor. The cushions on the chairs were threadbare and starting to lose their stuffing, but a night sleeping on three seats pushed together wouldn't kill her.

Edith changed her mind the next morning. Her shoulders were full of knots, and her neck refused to straighten. Hobbling to the kitchen, she prayed that the water heater didn't cool too much overnight. A long steam over a basin of flowers followed by a massage with rose hip oil should turn her into a new woman.

Biting her lip and hunching, she stomped her foot. Nothing happened. Glancing about the kitchen and checking the pantry revealed the same amount of bread and clean dishes as last night.

It was impossible to run in her cramped state, forcing Edith to speed-limp to the front door, where Widow Anker kept a bundle of midwifery supplies. The bag was gone. Edith tried not to melt to the floor in relief.

After an endless stretch of time, where her heart refused to slow and she had to remember to breathe, Edith struggled upright. In the kitchen, she brewed some tea and sank into a chair, her mind whirring. She had every reason to be hard on her Marja, and yet... She started to shake her head, but still couldn't move.

What made Widow Anker Edith's sweet Marja was her devotion to Jesus. "'Under Christ, there is no man or woman, black or white,'" Edith quoted, "'There's only love.'" Edith traced her fingers along her cheek and lips, remembering Widow Anker's gesture as she first told Edith those words.

To block her Marja from offering freedom through Christ made Edith little better than a colony official, and every bit as stupid. If being locked up and left to starve couldn't stop Widow Anker, neither would harsh words. Edith cringed as she remembered last night's words. Was she trying to drive her Marja away? The idea of never sharing a home again with Widow Anker should be destroyed before it could take root.

Rising from the table, Edith checked the water in the heater before dragging out the bathtub. If she was going to act, it would be with a halfway working body.

Scouring every secondhand shop open to free blacks during the morning hours left Edith in her still shed well into the evening, working by the light of mirror slabs. When her neck cramped, she rubbed rose hip oil into the afflicted spot. If sweat dripped into her eyes, she shook it off. When exhaustion blurred her vision, she used her nose and fingers to find the right herbs and stuff them where they needed to be.

Years of handling trowels, shovels and uncooperative flasks gave Edith leather-hard hands. She gave thanks every night when her labor addled head caused the needle to slip, jabbing her flesh. A more genteel woman would have had more hole than finger by the end of the first night. Then again, a proper lady likely had more time to devote to needle work and make fewer mistakes, causing herbs to dribble out of half pinned hems.

It was two days before Edith found the time to voice her plan to Widow Anker.

When Edith entered the house that evening, her hands were cracked, her muscles were on fire and her joints were made of creaks. Turning into the kitchen, her eyes flicked to the spout that connected to the water heater, before settling on the cupboard where the tub lay, scoured clean and ready for another reviving soak.

Heading to the counter, she reached for the shelves that held her homemade blend of marigold, cornflowers and tea, along with the teapot painted with blue garlands her Marja loved. The hot water spigot helped to make a quick brew. In the pantry were rosewater Shrewsbury cakes that weren't too stale. Adding pitchers of milk and honey to the table, Edith screwed up her courage to seek her Marja.

Rather than stomp on the ground, Edith approached Widow Anker in the parlor, walking into her line of sight and waiting, twisting her fingers. The midwife's eyes remained fixed on her Bible. A thousand flurried heartbeats passed, but Widow Anker didn't turn a page. Clasping her hands together, Edith clutched them against her breast, drooping her head and shoulders.

The air hummed, reminding Edith of a string stretching to its breaking point. Looking up at Widow Anker would spell disaster, revealing a face creased with hurt. No, Edith would stand here all night and for the next week if she had to, moving only when her Marja signaled her thoughts.

Edith's knees screamed, wanting to know what on earth she was thinking. They'd swell and lock if she kept straining herself.

Widow Anker touched Edith's chin, guiding her face upwards. With trembling teeth, glittering eyes, reddening noses, it was like looking into a mirror. Placing her lips against Edith's ear, Widow Anker whispered her favorite verses before the two of them retreated into the kitchen.

Over tepid tea and Shrewsbury cakes, Edith outlined her plan, pausing and repeating herself with words and hands to make sure Widow Anker understood. Her Marja nodded, tracing notes to herself with her finger on the kitchen table. When asked if she could distribute scented fabric to more than just the Abrams' slaves, Widow Anker's smile threatened to crack her face in two. "Good news is to be shared with all," she said.

Widow Anker woke her up that midnight, full of fire in inspiration. Even biting the fan, Edith couldn't glean an ounce of sense from her companion. Daybreak and the brief night's sleep cleared Edith's mind enough to understand her Marja.

Though Edith was heading down the right path, setting aside time and resources to those who needed the most help, she could take greater steps. Why was she using her cast offs from making Seven Thieves' Vinegar, and dipping into her bumper crop of sage? Surely a slave's health would be better protected with flowers Edith reserved for her wealthiest customers. An elegant bouquet stuffed inside a kerchief would do wonders to protect someone's lungs.

No amount of Edith explaining that she liked to eat would convince her companion otherwise. Staving off a growing headache, Edith left for her garden before she could tell Widow Anker to grow her own herbs.

That night Widow Anker brought home bonus gifts from the Abrams, a basket of worn out cloth. Making a rude internal gesture at her joints, Edith settled by her Marja's side. Threading a spare needle, she followed her companion's lead.

MKONO YA MBAO

Steven Workman

Neema stands still, spear at the ready. I freeze behind her, worried she senses something alarming. She sniffs the air and nods. I inhale deeply too, and I smell it, a faint burning.

"It's close," I say, my eyes scanning the savanna. Everything is still, just long fields of grass with a few trees to break up the monotony.

Neema nods again. I admire her profile, how beautiful and majestic she is framed by the starry sky, how powerful her muscles are. I feel weak and clumsy compared to her, but she insists I'm improving in skill. Does she mean when I hunt or when we make love?

"Did you notice the animals?" Neema asks.

"No." My voice drops to a whisper. "What about them?"

"There aren't any." Neema sighs. "Come on, you have to start noticing these things for yourself. I can't do it all for you."

I look away, ashamed. "Sorry Neema..." What did she see in me? I mess everything up. All I can do is build moving wooden toys.

She takes my hand and squeezes it, smiling at me. "You're an excellent warrior and you make fantastic machines; I just need to help that potential along."

"Neema..." Her hand is so warm. I want to hold it all night, but a rustling in the grass startles us. We bring ready our spears and crouch down. Time passes and nothing more happens.

We continue on, the silence unnerving me. It shouldn't be this quiet. The lights that danced in the sky and the star that fell to Earth couldn't be good but we were determined to investigate.

Crawling down a slope, the burning smell grows stronger. I peek up over the slope and there it is, something dark and squat embedded in the ground surrounded by scorched grass, tiny fires lighting it up. It's like a huge spear tip, carved from smooth black stone, about half the size of our house.

"So that's what a star looks like up close?" Neema asks, unafraid. "I thought they'd be brighter."

Creeping up to the strange shape, the fires flicker out, and the air becomes much colder, leaving us shivering. I don't like it; this isn't natural at all. It's the work of evil magic.

"Neema, let's go back to the village!" I beg.

Ignoring me, Neema approaches the stone, poking it with her spear. The surface is smoother than anything I've seen before.

Something rustles behind us. I turn in time to see something lunge from the brush toward Neema. With a cry I rush to her defense, raising my spear to fight. It grabs my left wrist and cold shoots through my arm, forcing me to drop the spear. I stare, transfixed, at the thing rising before me, something burnt and black in the shape of a human swathed in dark rags, its face hardly more than a skull with bits of flesh still clinging to it. Its eyes stared nakedly without eyelids. Worst of all was its mouth, with a pair of long fangs curving from exposed upper jaw like those of the hyena. The quivering eyes gaze at me.

Neema's dagger buries itself in the thing's chest. It releases me and Neema's strong arms pull me away. I clutch my left arm, all feeling gone from it.

The monster sags over without a sound, trembling. Neema approaches cautiously but it stands up again, pulling the dagger out. No blood stains the blade.

The monster raises its head, and flesh now crawls along the skull, the dead tissue healing before our eyes. Skin as white as ivory forms in loose strips over the charred muscles. I can only stare in sick horror. What kind of evil spirit is this?

Neema brings her spear up. The monster's eyes flick in her direction, the pupils shrinking, and it flings the dagger out.

Neema stops abruptly. Blood runs from her lips.

My eyes lower and find her dagger now embedded in her stomach.

She falls backwards, her spear leaving her hands. I stare at Neema without comprehension. No, this can't be right. Neema can't die. She's the strongest of our village. This is some cruel trick the monster played! No one can defeat Neema!

The monster retrieves the dagger from Neema and turns to me. This time, blood drips off the blade, and that's when I fall to despair. Neema is dead and I'm very likely next.

Raising the bloody dagger up, the creature sucks at it with great relish. More skin grows over it, covering the face now. Straight, pale yellow hair falls from the head and long pointed ears spring out. It now resembles a woman, albeit a very unearthly one.

Taking the dagger from its mouth, it looks to me and smiles, saying something in a language unfamiliar to me. Before I can move, it springs forward, seizing my left arm again, that terrible cold filling me once more. With a single, swift chop, my left hand is freed from my arm, and I don't feel a thing. The creature leaves me to drop over as I clutch my maimed arm, my mind reeling at the horror. I can hear the monster mumble in its language.

I spot my spear lying beside me, and scramble to get it. Thankful it was my left hand gone and not my right, I pull it close. The monster says something behind me. Gripping the spear tightly, I roll toward the monster and thrust repeatedly. It throws its arms over its face, still holding my severed hand. It screams, some holes opening in its arms, the white flesh turning green and diseased. Shrieking, it turns away and runs faster than any big cat, vanishing into the savanna.

I crawl painfully to Neema's body, feeling retuning to my arm. I cradle her head and close her wide, startled eyes as I sob.

I have to tell the village. We will hunt this evil spirit and slaughter it. The village will not accept this insult, even from a monster like this.

I struggled to make it back, tearing some cloth off to tie around my stump and soak up the blood. Without the numbing cold, the pain is unbelievable and the blood loss leaves me dizzy, but I make it.

I soon wish I hadn't. Corpses litter the village, chunks of flesh carved out of them. The Stranger from the Sky stands at the center, cutting her arm open and forcing the bwana to drink from the wound. She smiles at me, and says in Kiswahili, "Thank you."

I adjust my left hand, flex the timber fingers, and test the complicated clockwork, all of it wooden. Everything is in order like the last thousand times I checked this night but I have to be absolutely sure; I can't allow anything to go wrong.

My only illumination a single candle, I poke my hand with delicate tools, adjusting the springs and gears within. The mechanisms make a soft ticking sound and every time I move my fingers there's a slight creaking. In the back of my hand is a small vial of explosive oil with a tiny pin attached to it for sticking onto clothes, a last resort weapon. I left the palm and fingers rough to better grip my implements. Everything was working perfectly; at this point I was stalling myself. I have a very good chance of dying tonight, but I can't die, not before avenging my village. Before avenging Neema.

Satisfied, I shut my hand and douse my candle. Donning a simple gray hooded cloak lined with pouches of herbs and chemicals, I creep away from the inn. London, even in summer, is so much colder and darker than my village. I can't wait to return to Kenya. The stench is unbelievable; human waste and dead animals rot in the wet streets and with so many people crammed together in small, hastily built homes, there isn't time for cleanliness. I wonder if my enemy enjoys these conditions, thriving in the filth and disease.

Navigating the dark, foggy streets, I am assaulted by a different odor, that of the grave and decay, and know my destination is close. I've seen her at night, crouched in the graveyard by the open communal graves, feasting on the dead when she doesn't feel like hunting. This place doesn't care what happens to the poor in life or death so no one officially investigates. Only eccentric monster hunters have shown any concern about the graveyard, a few of which disappeared when they set out at night.

Scaling the graveyard wall is no problem for me, my trained fingers finding uncanny purchase for me to climb them. I fall silently to the damp earth by the gate where I buried my sack a few nights earlier. Digging it up, I tear the rough burlap away to uncover my spear. I carved it myself, smooth, elegant, and made entirely of wood. A metal point would be more durable but wood was essential for my enemy.

Spear in hand, I creep toward the imposing church edifice, keeping alert in case my enemy is out in the graveyard. I wish I could take care of her during the day when she was more vulnerable but I have no idea where she sleeps, and killing her from a distance is too risky; I need to make sure she dies.

Even compared to the rest of London, the graveyard stinks and the open pit to my right is the reason. The poor who can't afford crypts are stacked together in flimsy coffins placed in open graves until no more can fit; only then is the hole filled in. It's amazing what people can get used to. It's useful to my enemy too; she has no shortage of food if hunting doesn't go well.

A low creaking reaches my ears. I draw my spear and crouch down, eyes on the grave pit. It's hard to see in the foggy night but I can hear wood prying and splintering and something scrabbling against earthen walls. With a grimace I realize my enemy has another use for the open graves. A shape rises from the hole, slow and clumsy, and the stench grows stronger. Two more shapes join the first, pulling out of the hole, loosened dirt raining upon suddenly vacant coffins.

Footsteps approach me. The things shamble in my direction, arms outstretched. During my time hunting the spawn of my enemy I learned that they could sense the life around them even when blinded, making it very difficult to hide from them. Did even these rotting puppets have that ability? If they did then it was likely they had the same weaknesses to wood and fire. My fingers tighten around my spear. This will be simple.

Springing up, I drive my spear through the eye of the closest creature with appalling ease, the tip piercing with a soft squishing sound. It twitches weakly on the end before I kick its chest as hard as I can. The thing slides wetly off and drops over.

Unsure if it's truly dead, I retreat a few steps back, away from the cold fingers. Up this close, I can see the puppets more clearly. The one on the left was once an African man. Its clothes are filthy with grime, eyes cloudy and mouth hanging open, its tongue pale and bloated like a huge grub. The other was an Englishwoman, in a dirt-stained dress, hair limp and her eyes as cloudy as the other. They stumble forward, moving over their fallen fellow. It hadn't moved so my blow must have finished it. Looks like they won't be a challenge.

I slam the butt of my spear into the woman's pallid face, knocking her off her feet. Without pausing, I puncture the chest of the man. It hardly reacted, reaching for me even as the spear tip sank further into its spongy breast. Recalling the techniques Neema taught me I spin around, avoiding gravestones, whirling the walking corpse until the spear dislodged. The corpse stumbled away, tripping over a gravestone behind it, which pitched it backwards. *So wood isn't enough, even to the heart.*

Before it can recover I plunge my spear up into the corpse's exposed throat, angling toward the skull. There's a sickening crack as I force the tip deep into what is left of the thing's brain, and it falls still at once. *So that was it.*

The grass rustles behind me as the remaining corpse creeps up from behind. I whirl around, striking through its eye like the first one. My stomach churns a little at how soft the thing is, how easy it is to pierce. It stops struggling soon enough, corrupted fluids pooling around the socket and my spear. I yank it out and try to wipe the tip on the grass.

No sooner had the last corpse fallen still then a soft clapping broke the silence. Gasping, I look up to the church. A figure now stands on the gray steps, applauding.

"Well done," the figure says in English but with an accent underneath unknown to me. I remember it all too well though. "The last ones who tried to sneak in here were torn to pieces by my guards. You're different though."

I grip my spear tighter, memories flooding back. My beloved Neema driving a knife into the Stranger's chest without effect. The Stranger taking my hand. Finding the village dead with the bwana and a few others turned into evil spirits like her...

The figure glides through the mist, inhaling deeply, her broad cloak fluttering. She hasn't changed in the three years since we last met, her skin as smooth and white as ivory, hair long and straight and a faint gold in color. She looks far more like the Europeans than she does my people, but some features mark her different from them too; no European has pointed ears, long fangs, or glassy claws.

She stops a few feet from me, a mild look of recognition crossing her smooth features before she smiles wider. "Ah! I thought you felt familiar!" she says, switching to Kiswahili. "The Kenyan village in 1772, yes? Remind me again who you are, exactly?"

Furious, I raise my left hand, knowing she sees in the dark better than any human. "I'm now Mkono ya

Mboa, and with this wooden hand I'll scoop the heart from your chest for killing the ones I loved!" I hiss through clenched teeth in Kiswahili too. A fire lights in my belly. All this preparation, all this travel, all this hate, all down to this one moment. My target is standing before me and all I need to do is end her.

The Stranger chuckles. "Oh yes, you. I must have made quite an impression if you renamed yourself after the deformity I gave you," she answers. "Your hand made a good little meal. I think I still have the bones. You must be here to avenge yourself and your tribe after you took care of me. Don't think me ungrateful for your hospitality."

She breaks into a wide grin, the teeth of a predator gleaming in her mouth. "Every time I eat one of these poor, diseased Englishmen, I think of how delicious your people were and thank them."

I pull my spear back as she begins laughing. My fury can't be contained any longer. Charging, I thrust my spear at her chest with enough force to pierce the hide of a lion, but it passes through nothing. The Stranger moves faster than any human ever has and is at my right in the blink of an eye. Her hand strikes my side, throwing me through the air like a leaf, the bitter cold of her touch shocking. I crash on my back, my spear jarred from my hand. I scramble to my feet; my side stings from the chilling blow but I'm grateful I missed the gravestones. I search for the spear. There is only a faint whispering sound as the Stranger darts between the gravestones, her movements a blur. She'll be on me in a moment.

I rip a pouch from my cloak, heavy as though filled with sand. Perfect.

The blur speeds toward me. Instead of running like she expects me to, I pour the contents of the pouch into my hand and with a deep breath blow it out in a wide cloud. The Stranger is too late to avoid it, grunting as it touches her, and she falls past me as the effects set in. She stops by a gravestone, coughing and sputtering. She raises a trembling hand that's turning green. I blow another pouch of herbs at her to keep her busy then ran off, looking for my spear. I practically trip over it in the darkness, but I keep my balance and retrieve it.

I whirl around, spear raised, but the Stranger is no longer by the gravestone. I let out a curse just before icy hands grasp my shoulders and slam me against a crypt wall hard enough to make me drop my spear. The Stranger's face peers into my own, the white skin now puffy and splotched with green, making her look as rotten as the walking corpses. She grins in spite of his pain, lips curling over long fangs.

"I underestimated you," she says, hands moving to my arms and squeezing. "You researched my kind thoroughly."

"The villagers you changed," I spit. "I observed them carefully before hunting them down, learning how you fear plants, fire, and wind!"

"Very good!" she laughs. "I trust you know that earth, water, and metal are useless against me. I can't sense any iron on you."

I closed my eyes, fingers grasping against the smooth wall, mentally begging my spear to return to my hand. "I saw you stabbed in the chest with a dagger and you pulled it out unharmed."

"And I stabbed the attacker with her own blade," she finishes.

She's powerful and smart but arrogant. We're cattle to her; what farmer expects his cattle to rise up against him? Yet there's always danger in herding, always a chance of being trampled. My arms slowly bend back, right hand reaching for the left. I can barely feel, they're so numb with cold.

"Who are you really?" I demand, fingers brushing the panel on the back of my hand. "What are you doing here?"

"Explaining that would be wasted on the likes of you," she sneers. "This poisoning you gave me will heal on its own in time, but if I eat your flesh I'll be fine by morning!"

Her mouth stretches, fangs extending. I crane my neck away as far as I can, death seconds away. I can't reach my hand in time; I need to keep her talking.

"Wait!" I cry. "I successfully tracked you down! Don't you think I'm more useful than meat?"

She stops, her mouth still open but curiosity in her inhuman eyes. "Go on," she rasps through her fangs. "Make it quick though."

I gasp for breath, looking for my words. I finally choke out, "You made some of the villagers into...spirits like yourself. Blood-drinkers and flesh-eaters that burn in the Sun. They weren't as strong but they still hunted humans just as you do."

She nodded. "My kind can't continue like the creatures here. One option we have is to select lesser beings and convert them to the darkness. They begin as degraded imitations but through rituals, can become full examples." Her eyes inspect me closely, and I remember when we first met. There's suspicion shining through but it grapples with...loneliness? She must not have had any companions for a long time. Maybe the Stranger's closer to us than she likes to admit.

"I certainly could use one as resourceful as you as an apprentice," she continues, "and despite your thorough education about my kind, it was only on those fledglings. You'd have to rely on me to survive until I perform the rituals to perfect you."

"But *what* are you?" I ask, shivering. Her touch is stealing all the warmth from me. "What would I be becoming?"

Her head leans back and her jaw pops back into place. "Death," she answers. She leans forward slowly to look me in the eye. "The cold darkness given hunger, forever seeking the warmth of life to devour."

I decline answering, instead struggling to comprehend what she means. The Stranger isn't really alive? Was she ever alive? She is an abomination beyond even her animate corpses, an affront to nature.

She sighs and peers up sadly at the starless night sky. "I never meant to come to these backward lands. I was in a war far away and happened to crash near your village. All I can do with these primitives is convert influential members and refocus your technology to suit me. One day I might be able to return home."

Home. The Stranger destroyed my home, my family, my friends, everything I ever knew. Of her home I know nothing beyond what she'd said, but I assume it's still out there somewhere, perhaps wondering if she will ever return.

The panel on my hand opens. I can feel the tiny glass vial inside. It's a good thing she's lonely. It could be a trick but she seems sincere. I hope she is.

She smiles at me. "If you accept, you'd...exist, I suppose the correct word is, forever more, with considerable wealth and power. This planet lacks unity, divided into their little warring tribes, ignorant to the bigger problems. With me, none of that has to matter. We can rise above and rule it!"

I ease the vial out, fingers curling around it tightly, my hands so numb that I'm unsure I really have it. I have only one shot at this. "Do it," I breathe. "Make me your apprentice." Good thing her process involves getting very close to me...

Instead of cutting her arm, her mouth drops open like a hatch, her fangs extending. So she's going to feed on me first. Even better. My heart races as she leans in, that repulsive mouth inching toward my throat. Her grip loosens a little and I make my move. My right arm whips out just as the fangs brush my flesh, the pin fastening the vial to the Stranger's cloak. Slamming my back against the wall, I swing my right leg up, driving my boot into the Stranger's upper chest as hard as I can. Stumbling back, her eyes grow wide in surprise. My foot finds my spear and flips it upright for me to retrieve. I slam the butt into the vial.

I throw my arms over my face just as the explosion goes off, protecting me from the blazing wind. The Stranger's unearthly screams fill the night, and I wish I could cover my ears too. Cautiously I lower my arms and see the Stranger sag to her knees, her cloak engulfed in flames, her face twisted in agony. Anguished moans escape her mouth as her flesh curdles and runs like melting wax. I watch as her dissolving hands claw at the earth, skin peeling off to reveal something black glistening in the firelight like mud. My stomach lurches at her grotesque destruction and even more at her pain, and the pain of my village returns to me, the pain of the people the Stranger was turning into her own. I had observed them, experimented in ways to kill them, and told myself it would be easier when I got to the Stranger.

Her eyes peel open, blazing with hate. Something's wrong though; her skin stops melting and slowly reverses, growing back in patches. I look down and see her hands totally restored, grave dirt moving up her arms and smothering the flames, filling in the damage. Even minor contact with earth was enough to heal grievous wounds?

Spear in hand, I ram it into her burning breast, the tip buried as far as I can force it. The Stranger gasps, black slime falling from her mouth. The flames strengthen and her skin sloughs off in blackened chunks that crumble into the ground. She looks just like when we found her.

"You can't...stop us..." the Stranger wheezes, smoke curling from oozing lips. *"We'll come...kill you...make you...cattle..."*

The flames overtake her entirely with unnatural speed, as though a predator consuming favorite prey. Her body crumbles away and the flames dissipate just as quickly. All that remains is a skeleton, still kneeling, human in appearance save for its long fangs and metallic sheen. No; something else is there. Something sparkles in the abdomen.

Wearily, I poke at the sparkling object and something round rolls out of the bloody ashes. A small jewel. Drawn to the bauble, I pick it up with my natural hand. A freezing pain shoots through it, and the Stranger's laugh fills my head.

I can never truly die, her spirit whispers to my soul. *With my core I'll make your body mine!*

No. Not now, not so close to finding peace. I can't let her win after all the suffering. I can't let my village, my Neema, be forgotten. I try to drop the jewel but she has control over my fingers, her presence sliding down my arm. In desperation I clamp my other hand around my forearm, trying to stop the spread. The rough wooden fingers squeeze my corrupted arm, the panel on the back still open. To my surprise, her presence weakens the moment I touch my arm. The wood!

Realization strikes me, and I tip my hand strenuously toward the slot. The Stranger tries make my fingers squeeze shut over the jewel but I feel her grip on me slipping; contact with wood is disrupting the Stranger's control. The jewel slips from my palm into the back of my wooden one, just the right size to replace the vial. Her control dissipates entirely, and I slide the panel over the jewel, the cold lessening in my arm already.

I drop to the ground, gasping, hoping my right arm isn't beyond healing. Warmth is slow to return to it and my hand is so numb I can't feel it, but the fingers move when I will them to. The Stranger's spirit is still there but now she howls and rages, simply a shroud over me. I laugh, clamping my hand over the panel.

"So that's why wood hurts you!" I point out. "It's not just poisonous to you, it disrupts your powers!"

You can't keep me like this! I'll regain my body and—

"Be quiet or I'll drop you into a bonfire," I mutter. The Stranger goes silent. Looks like that would be even worse than trapping her in wood. Perhaps even a permanent death?

Wait, the Stranger started, *we can help each other. I have some wealth stashed away. I can make you rich and powerful!*

"How likely are your kind to return?" I ask. "Are there any more of you here?"

The Stranger pauses for a moment. *I don't know. The chances of another ending up here are miniscule. Our power reaches far though; I've sensed something else on Earth, an ancient darkness that might call more of us here in the future. I'm not a soldier so any who come here looking for it will be far stronger than me.*

"How much stronger?"

You can expect far more than three animated corpses and they can rot wood with a glance. You'll need much more than some explosives and a spear.

I pondered this. If she's telling the truth then the world might be in terrible danger. Maybe not tomorrow or the day after, but someday...

"Then I'll just have to fight them when they show up," I say. "If it takes a long time then I'll train others, and they'll train more if they need to. It's not like I have a home to return to now."

I of course can help you! I know everything you need to know.

"I don't doubt it." I know she's just trying to save herself, but having just tried the same trick I don't blame her.

I lay in the dirt, closing my eyes and taking in the foul air. So I had my vengeance, just not the way I expected. I think of Neema, no longer dying but smiling. I smile too. Vengeance won't bring my love or village back, but I like to think she's satisfied with how this turned out. I won't forgive the Stranger but if she can be used to save the world then maybe I can learn to tolerate her.

I look at my wooden hand, rattling the jewel inside a little; the Stranger was foolish enough to risk me pulling a trick so she could have company. Well maybe I'm just as foolish, letting the Stranger stay with me for the same reasons. Or maybe we aren't as different as we think. Loneliness takes a toll, and I realized how lonely I've been the past few years.

Looks like we won't be lonely anymore.

THE CRAFTERS' COVE

D.L. Smith-Lee

Their chains rattled when the cabin rocked violently as the storm encroached. Buziba couldn't remember how many days it'd been since the Aldonians had taken him. The time he'd spent in the dark hold with the other Cayans seemed to meld together.

It didn't baffle him where they were being taken. This was a slave ship. They were headed for Lesthos, the major port city of Aldonia. From there they would be sold and separated from one another.

The people of the Cayan Isles were their most frequent choice to enslave, since most Cayan Isles had weaker lines of defense. Most were too poor and backwater to afford weapons, so their villages could hardly withstand a raid. Aldonian slave owners began to think of themselves as saviors of these poor, weak people as justification for their enslavement.

Buziba didn't feel rescued, he felt abducted. His hand traced the scab from the scar inscribed on his cheek. The sword that had made this mark was the same one that killed his brother as he tried to defend Buziba. He tried not to think of his capture, the final night he saw his brother.

His eyes had grown fond of the darkness. The cold chains cooled his skin, his only release from the sweltering heat in the hold. The vicious rocking hadn't been the only thing that woke him from his bare slumber. A loud crash against the bars of his cell startled him.

Glowing red eyes glared down at Buziba as he stared back awkwardly.

"I'll bet you want to be released from here," a deep and sinister voice whispered.

Buziba swore he'd heard it closer to him than where the red eyes glared at him. As if it was right in his ear.

"Yes," Buziba replied anxiously.

"Is that really what you wish?" the voice inquired.

He could only nod his head in response to the entity's question. This time Buziba was sure he'd heard the voice directly in his ear. The hairs on the back of his neck rose as a sudden chill shook his body. More than a chill, more like a blizzard.

Buziba could see his body shake but could not stop it. Regardless of the stifling heat he was cold, so cold he could barely feel his limbs as they thrashed about wildly. Buziba's mouth opened as the black shadow forced itself down his throat.

####

Buziba opened his eyes, now well-adjusted to the darkness. He stared at the ceiling, watching the water on the soggy wood sway back and forth. The storm was getting stronger. He stood and walked toward the iron bars of his cell only to be halted by the chains that bound his arms to the bulkhead behind him.

Heat burned within Buziba's chest. He'd never experienced rage like this before. Every vein in his body felt like a livewire, pumping energy through him viciously. Buziba shouted as he ripped the chains from the bulkhead, surely waking the other prisoners and alerting the guards.

The iron bars of the cell gave way as he bent them outward. The stampede of guards stormed the passageway, halting a few feet from Buziba. The sight of this great dark skinned man that stood before them was not the only thing that held them in shock.

The eyes in his head were not his own. They were as deeply crimson as the rivers of blood that ran through his hometown after these slave-peddling pirates attacked it. Rage consumed him again the moment he laid eyes on them. He charged forward as they brandished their muskets, diving for the first guard. He grabbed the man's throat and rattled him wildly as another stabbed the blade of his musket into Buziba's back. Buziba lashed out instantly, knocking the guard across the passageway, the blade of the musket still lodged in his back.

That is enough, the voice told him. His head swiveled over the four guards (the one flailing in his grip lifelessly, the one unconscious from the blow he'd struck to his head, and two who remained with their muskets pointed, cowering before him).

No, this voice he'd heard hadn't come from them.

Release the guard, the voice told him. He obeyed without a second thought. His eyes remained on the cowering guards as footsteps approached from behind. Buziba felt no fear, his resistance had waned.

The guards backed away slowly but were halted by two other Cayan men, who'd been released from their cells. Their eyes bore the same unearthly red glow as Buziba's.

Hold them down, the voice commanded. The Cayan men obeyed immediately, holding the guards as they thrashed about in their grip.

From his peripheral vision, Buziba could see multiple people walk around him, none of which were Aldonians. They stopped at his sides, nearly surrounding him as they watched a woman go ahead of them. She carried a small jar in her arms which she opened, screaming in a language which betrayed her obvious Cayan ancestry.

The two Aldonian guards' eyes grew large with fear as their mouths opened. They'd have screamed but the air was sucked from their lungs as the black shadows forced their way into their mouths.

Her voice, Buziba thought. It was her. She'd been the one ordering them.

The Cayan men dropped the guards, whose eyes had been changed almost instantly, as the woman returned the lid to the jar.

Her dark, knee-length dreadlocks and multi-colored garment she wore gave hint to her tribal heritage. But how was she able to use this jar as she could?

Buziba should have been horrified at the idea of being in the presence of a Crafter but he felt nothing. There were Crafters of fire, water, earth, air, spirit, ice, wood, and thunder but they had all died off. Those who didn't were hunted and slaughtered since their magic was sacrilegious to the will of the Twin Goddesses.

The woman turned to the men behind her, they were all under her influence. Their wills being taken away by their very spirits.

"I have freed you all." The woman announced proudly. "And now I have my very own ship and crew."

The men, Buziba included, all kneeled before this woman in a show of allegiance. They couldn't explain why they felt this compulsion. The woman smiled upon them with purpling stormy eyes.

####

The sun had finally broken through the infinite gray of the skies, beaming on the shimmering blue ocean. The sails of the *Damwedo* fluttered in the high winds. Kaba held the top of his tricorn hat securely to his head, counteracting the heavy winds.

Kaba had wept for days after the attack, not because of the severe gash left in his shoulder from the keen scimitar but because of his brother. He knew he'd never see him again. The people of his village were truly close-knit but that was nothing compared to the bond he shared with his brother. Their parents had been lost years earlier, taken by illness. Kaba only had his older brother to look after him. That had been nearly fifteen years ago.

Kaba descended below decks to see how his crew fared in the roughness of the seas. From the wooden threshold of the galley he watched as his pirates told tales by candlelight.

"The seas tell the tale of a Cayan witch who overturned a slave ship." Blaine, the newest addition to the *Damwedo*'s crew, told the men. "The high white sails turned ragged as she unleashed the spirits from a magic jar she carried with her. Using the spirits, she made slaves of her very own.

"She freed the captives aboard the ship and forced the spirits of the jar down their throats while holding their rightful souls imprisoned. Under the influence of the spirits, the slaves obeyed her every command. She'd ordered them to kill their captors, displaying feats of inhuman strength and speed. She spared but few, making them her slaves as well. That has been the story for years."

"I'd be willin' ta bet ye forty pounds o' gold that there ain't no witches," Simon said, his voice thick with laughter. "All sounds like a bunch o' spooky nonsense."

"That, good sir, would not be a false statement," Blaine said to the white bearded man of pink skin, clearly burned from long hours of sunlight like most lighter skinned pirates. "If I hadn't seen the witches myself I'd agree with you. But since my eyes have yet to betray me in my young age, I'll have to believe them."

"Aw, phooey," one of Simon's gang chimed. This one was called Leny, a younger man of his mid to late twenties. His fiery red hair was a dead giveaway to his North Aldonian ancestry.

"Well, my crew would've said otherwise, but they're all slaughtered, thanks to the witches and their henchmen." Blaine told them. The pirates laughed heartily at his words.

"And we're to believe this tall tale, why?" Simon asked, genuinely amused. The pirates stared amusedly at Blaine, a dark skinned Cayan descended man of smaller stature. They likely believed him to be an escaped slave or a convict. With his small stature, he could never have been a captain in their eyes.

"Because," Kaba's familiar voice rang across the cabin.

"Attention on deck!" One of the pirates shouted before they all shot upright, standing straighter than planks of wood.

"Carry on!" Captain Kaba yelled back as the pirates obeyed before continuing. "The seas also tell the tale of a great sea lord who ruled the ocean and all of its inhabitants. His most loyal subjects were wrathful witches, Crafters more than likely, who protected his kingdom. The Island Kingdom he ruled was protected by massive whirlwinds of water that flung wayward ships to the rocky shores and angry lightning that struck the topmost sails of ships, killing all aboard.

"One day the Order came and hunted down his witch servants, leaving his kingdom unprotected. Humans raided his island. Using their beasts and weapons, they destroyed the sea lord's kingdom. They say witches live on the remains of the island, inside a dark cove where they feed souls to a massive jewel."

"Cap'n sir, ye believe this one?" Simon asked in disbelief.

"If these witches are the same, then yes," Kaba said. "But I must know," he said to Blaine, "where did you learn this tale?"

"Word of mouth, Cap'n sir," Blaine responded.

It had only been a few days since he was allowed to board the ship. Kaba found the young man floating at sea aboard a plank of wood. He'd said he barely escaped with his life since the witches took his crew.

"Hmm, I suspect that the witches in the Sea Lord's tale and the Cayan witch are very similar. My hypothesis: they're the same witches, Crafters. Their jewel could mean massive fortunes for us all." Kaba said, aiming his words to the crew whose eyes lit up with revelation.

The cabin suddenly rocked viciously. Through the brass speaker horn, the helmsman, Alistair, yelled through.

"Cap'n sir, we've hit a massive storm out of nowhere!"

We must be close, Kaba thought.

"All hands on deck; that's not a request!" Kaba ordered.

Simon was his Bosun, in charge of all deck hands and deck operations. On the main deck, they immediately began fighting to steady the sails. The winds blew furiously as waves crashed against the ship's hull. Kaba squinted through the pandemonium and swore he could see a typhoon form ahead of them.

"All hands brace for shock!" He yelled over the storm.

Kaba awoke against the threshold of his cabin, the sunlight flaring his vision. His clothes were drenched. The crew laid strewn across the deck, most unconscious and some bleeding but all moving. Kaba strained to see through the blinding sunlight as he made his way across the deck to the lifelines. Looking over the side he could see the bed of rocks lined against the Damwedo's wooden hull.

The ship had run aground. The faint sway of the aft end told Kaba that all it would need was a little push to get it going again. Kaba looked out to the distance as the Island came into perspective. This had to be it. The cove that was the witches' home was surely nearby.

Kaba awakened his crew. The medic attended the injured and stayed aboard while Kaba readied the remainder of the crew.

"We go ashore before nightfall." Kaba ordered.

"Cap'n sir, I can lead the way in." Blaine said.

Kaba's eyes narrowed at the small dark man.

"Very well," Kaba answered.

Blaine nodded and swore Captain Kaba could trust him.

"Sir, are ye sure we can trust 'em?" Simon whispered to Kaba.

"I truly only have faith in one man. I'm speaking with him now," he said, looking Simon dead in the eye. He placed a hand on his shoulder. "He will lead us in, but you are my Commandant. I trust you."

Simon nodded.

####

The pirates disembarked the Island immediately. They treaded the rocky shore carefully as Blaine led the way to the deep, dark cove. The men lit torches and readied their swords. Kaba followed close behind Blaine.

The walls of the cove had grown thick with slimy algae that varied in color. Sea barnacles decorated the rocks they walked on.

From the distance, Kaba could hear low moaning noises.

"What was that?" Leny asked timidly, visibly shaking.

"That's the sound of death," Blaine whispered.

He turned to the pirates. Kaba had first thought it was the glow of the flames reflecting in his deep brown eyes but he was wrong. The deep umber of his eyes had been replaced with blood red irises that illuminated in the darkness. Kaba didn't hesitate for even a moment as he swung his blade, *Poisoned Steel*, but Blaine was swift. He ducked before the blade made contact and Kaba immediately came back with an overhead strike, slicing a piece of Blaine's finger away.

Blaine squealed a high pitched call, like a wounded animal calling for assistance. His reinforcements came, leaping from the darkness and squealing the same beastly outcry Blaine had unleashed. They were men with blood red irises that glowed in the steep darkness of the cove.

The pirates immediately took action.

Blaine fled from the chaos, holding the hand that *Poisoned Steel* had injured. Kaba chased after him, avoiding the ensuing battle.

Blaine led Kaba deeper into the cove. The rocky tunnel opened into a massive grotto where the walls shimmered blue from the clear waters as the sun shone through an overhead opening.

To Kaba's left, inside a colossal, dark cave that surely led to the outside, was a ship that was nearly as large as the Damwedo. Its sails had been tattered and torn and its wood was molded and darkened from years of neglect.

Blaine leaped across the deep, still river that separated the grotto where four women stood on the other side; one with skin and hair as pale as the midnight moon, one of tan brown skin and straight dark hair and two of skin and hair as dark and deep as Kaba's. Blaine sat beneath the women, whimpering as an injured animal would to its master.

Kaba could see the corners of the pale haired woman's mouth raise slowly.

"Well it seems as though he's come to us sisters," he heard the voice hiss behind him.

Kaba turned swiftly, swinging his blade simultaneously.

His steel rapier was caught mid-swing.

The ebon-hued hand that caught Kaba's sword latched on with an unrelenting vice grip. Dark blood oozed down its arm, decorating the stony grotto with its deathly red contrast. The shadows of the cave failed to conceal the face that the hand belonged to and the eyes that glowed red with brazen ferocity.

"Buziba," Kaba whispered, feeling the word echo in his mind. He stared into the eyes of the enormous minion that was once his own brother. He hadn't aged a day beyond the twenty-five years he had been on that fateful day fifteen years ago.

"I think he knows this one, sisters," the pale haired woman at Buziba's side uttered slyly.

Kaba's eyes couldn't tear away from his brother's, even to realize the pale witch had suddenly materialized.

"It would seem so," a second voice of smooth seduction whispered from behind him.

Kaba snapped from his trance and drew his revolver, simultaneously jerking *Poisoned Steel* from Buziba's grasp. Leaping backward, he swung his blade blindly at the witch he'd heard behind him, hitting only the air.

Kaba spun back to Buziba as he came charging at him, all four witches watching amusedly from behind. Kaba dived to the side, just barely escaping Buziba's crushing blow.

With calculated swiftness, Kaba fired a shot toward the Crafters.

The grinning, pale-haired Crafter fell lifeless,

assuring Kaba the enchanted bullets worked.

The Crafters' look of astonishment told him instantly that they hadn't expected this to happen.

The screeching howl of Blaine's high pitched voice from behind startled Kaba. Blaine was surely calling for help again, which made Kaba think back to his comrades. Had they fallen to the Crafters' zombies?

Kaba stood with his blade poised at Buziba and his revolver at Blaine as his head darted between the two. Across the grotto he spotted a glint, something so bright he couldn't ignore it. The glimmer of this object was not blinding, it was pleasant and almost hypnotic. For only a moment Kaba was dazed, entranced by the beauty of the radiance of this massive and beautiful object. But his trance was broken as the air in his lungs was stolen from him.

Two of the three remaining witches stood before him but something behind him had encased his throat in a death grip, lifting from the ground.

As the witches began shouting the ancient curse, Kaba felt his blood run cold. Regardless of the heavy gear he wore, he was freezing. From some last moment of desperation, he realized he had not dropped his revolver and began firing wildly.

No more than a moment later he was dropped to the rocky grounds, gasping for air.

"What have you done?!" One of the witches shouted.

"You fool!" Another screamed, terrified.

A furious, howling whirlwind raged through the grotto.

Kaba covered his head, peeking out as the Crafter women raised their hands in unison, as if in prayer, in an attempt to satiate whatever Kaba had angered. They shrieked in distress as the whirlwind lifted the three of them and their dead sister, tossing them through its currents violently.

Kaba could feel his body lift from the ground. He scrambled to grab something, anything that would stop him from being sucked into the vile storm. His arms searched wildly before a hand found his own, gripping him tightly. He braced the hand tightly for his life, squeezing it with both hands.

Kaba's eyes met the large brown ones that stared back at him, wide and alarmed. Behind him the storm had begun to subside as a flare of purple light sent Kaba flying forward, falling on top of the enormous person that rescued him.

"Brother!?" He said, his hands scrambling for the sides of Buziba's face. Buziba's wide, brown eyes were closed now. Kaba forced an ear to his mouth, listening for breathing. Nothing came. He rigorously tapped the side of Buziba's face in an attempt to wake him.

No, he thought. *No, no, no.* For the first time in fifteen years he'd looked into the eyes of his brother. He was sure he was dead, sure that the last bit of his family was gone forever.

"Cap'n, sir!" Simon called from the entrance of the grotto.

Kaba heard footsteps echo in the empty cave, surely the other members of the Damwedo's crew.

"No," he whimpered, his head falling against Buziba's body. All Kaba could pay attention to were the sounds of his own sobs and whimpers against his dead brother's chest.

He could feel the other men behind him but he didn't care if they saw this vulnerability. He had to release this, all of the anguish and hopeless expeditions. His brother had been avenged but that hadn't brought him peace.

"You squirt," a groggy voice said, vibrating his face.

Kaba's head shot up.

"Still crying," Buziba said weakly, forcing a grin.

Tears flooded Kaba's eyes as his brother attempted to sit up, opening his brown eyes.

The crew gasped behind Kaba as he flung his arms around Buziba. It was only when he brought his left hand up to hug him back that Kaba remembered the wound from him grabbing Poisoned Steel.

"What was that?" Buziba asked woozily.

Kaba looked over to the opposite side of the

grotto. The hypnotic shimmer met his eyes once more, only now he could see it more clearly. It was a massive jewel – larger than a cannonball and more purple than the night sky beneath the lights of an Aldonian metropolis.

"It was the jewel with which they trapped their captives' souls," Kaba uttered. "The source of their power."

Kaba could see a small hole in the side of the jewel, surely where his bullet had landed. He turned back to his crew, who was covered in blood and grime from their battle in the cove. He released his brother and stood, helping Buziba to his feet.

"Crew," he bellowed before them as they popped to attention. "This is my brother, Buziba. He comes with us, no questions asked."

"Aye, aye cap'n," the crew said in unison.

After pushing the Damwedo back to sea, they set sail from the haunted remains of the Island Kingdom. In his cabin, Kaba gazed into the massive shimmering jewel that had once belonged to the Crafters. Now the Crafters belonged to it, absorbed by its power. This would be worth a fortune on the market but its power was priceless.

"Can't believe all of this is yours, now," Buziba said, poking around the cabin.

"You mean *ours*," Kaba said from his desk. "You're my brother; what's mine is yours."

"So, where to from here?"

Kaba considered the question seriously for a moment, gazing back into the jewel.

"Cap'n sir," Blaine said timidly, poking his head into Kaba's cabin. He'd been forgiven, the crew understanding the influence that the Crafters had upon him. Kaba regarded him silently.

"I think I may know someone who might be able to tell us the origin of the jewel."

"And where might we find this person?" Buziba asked, crossing his arms.

"On my home Isle of Caris, in the Cayan Isles. My people called him a mystic," Blaine said.

Kaba considered Blaine's words. Perhaps they should have consulted the Order first. Perhaps he should have left the jewel where it was. But Kaba was all too curious of this new treasure to let it go that easily.

"What do you say Buziba?"

Buziba's wide eyes found his brother, a grin spreading across his face.

"I say we find out how to use this thing to our advantage; we'd be some of the most feared sailors on the waters," Buziba answered.

Kaba grinned at his brother's words. "My thoughts exactly."

MARCH OF THE BLACK BRIGADE

Balogun Ojetade

One

February, 1778

The snow that fell over New York City, like a gossamer curtain over a frost-covered window, was tinged pink by the bloody mist in the air, birthed by arquebus and caliver and tomahawk.

The Queen's Rangers – the elite of the British forces – charged the Patriots, weaving past burning corpses caused by the Patriots' *maple grenados* – apple-sized fragmentation bombs equipped with a small clockwork mechanism on top, above which sat a propeller that resembled the "wings" on the seeds of a maple tree. Wound up by hand, the maple grenado would then be released into the air, flying upward to a distance of sixty feet, then drifting down like a maple seed, exploding on contact with the first thing it touched.

The Patriots stormed forward to meet their red-coated foes, stumbling along the raised mounds of snow.

Exhausted, soldiers from both sides lost their footing on the icy, uneven ground and collapsed, never to rise again as they were impaled by bayonet or crushed by boot-heel.

Soldiers garbed in red and blue tumbled, tripped, cursed and crawled their way across the battlefield, taking and losing lives and quenching the earth's thirst for blood.

A frightening roar rose from behind the horde of Patriots.

The Queen's Rangers slowed their advance.

The Patriots retreated to their flanks, leaving space for a hulking figure that loomed in shadow in the distance.

Puffs of steam burst from its iron snout. The massive figure roared again; its huge, fangs flashed a glint of silver. The figure galloped toward the Rangers, leaving the shadows behind. A grizzly bear, with flesh of iron, came into view. A big bronze key protruded from the creature's back, turning slightly with each pounding step.

Captain James Youngblood, commander of the Queen's Rangers, raised his saber high. "A Franklin

Sentinel! Retreat!"

The soldiers turned on their heels and ran, careening across the snow and ice.

The Franklin Sentinels – clockwork monstrosities, given sentience by bits of Benjamin Franklin's sanity – were the most feared weapons in the Patriots' arsenal.

The iron bear closed on the Rangers, slashing with claws the size of short swords and gnashing with teeth the size of daggers.

Limbs, entrails and red cloth peppered the alabaster ground.

Ranger-upon-Ranger was left dying in the snow.

The Patriots charged forward again, fueled by the realization that New York City would soon be theirs.

There was an explosion. The Franklin Sentinel teetered, hopping on one leg and then fell with a loud crash.

The clockwork bear's left leg leaked oil from just below its hip.

The Patriots halted their advance, searching madly for the source of the blast.

The bear struggled to its feet.

Another explosion echoed across the frigid sky.

The Franklin Sentinel went down again.

Again, the automaton pushed itself up. Steam and bits of copper wire and gears poured out of large holes in its chest and back.

A rhythmic tick-tock – a din like the alternate tapping together of two immense spoons, one wood and one silver – came from a line of dead trees in the distance.

"Iron Horses!" A Patriot shrieked. "Scoot!"

Two black, metal vehicles, balanced on two spiked iron wheels, broke the tree-line. The vehicles were heavily armored. The metal plates at the front were bashed together to resemble a crude horse's head. The iron horses' sharp lines and large rivets made the machines look even more disconcerting and fearsome. With the thick armor that wrapped around the front and sides of the vehicle, a soldier would need incredible luck or unmatched skill to shoot the rider of an iron horse that was bearing straight down upon him.

Thus, the Patriots followed their comrade's advice and ran, scattering in all directions.

Behind them, a man of bronze and brass rolled. Its feet were similar to, but much smaller than, the spiked iron wheels on the iron horses. Its hands, however, were perfectly human-shaped; odd, as its maker had not bothered to give the creature eyes and only the rudimentary features of a Black man's face. The metal man stood as tall as the clockwork bear and its arsenal made it just as fearsome – five flintlock pistols worn around its waist, locked in place by either magnetism or magic, or perhaps a bit of both; it bore a blunderbuss on each thigh and in its perfectly formed hands, it carried an arquebus. Smoke billowed from the mini-cannon's muzzle.

The metal man fired the arquebus once more.

The Franklin Sentinel's head flew off its shoulders.

The clockwork bear's body collapsed and remained unmoving.

The iron horses ran down the fleeing Patriots, crushing them under their tremendous weight.

The few surviving soldiers scampered off, their cries of fear and agony resounding across the battlefield.

A cheer rose up from the Queen's Rangers.

The men on the iron horses and their metal companion rode up to the Rangers. The two men dismounted their "steeds."

One was a man of average height; a sturdy, rugged man, but so handsome, the women thought him beautiful, with his shoulder-length, silky, black hair and flawless russet, reddish-brown complexion.

The other man was a looming figure, who, when he was still, appeared to be a statue carved from onyx. As he approached, the Rangers chanted his name.

"Tye! Tye! Tye Tye!"

"Please, please," Tye said waving his hands before his chest. "Just call me 'Colonel Titus Cornelius;' or simply 'Colonel Tye.'"

The Rangers laughed.

Captain Youngblood thrust his saber into the air.

The laughter stopped.

"It took you long enough," the Captain spat.

Colonel Tye frowned. "Whatever do you mean, Captain? We were heading over to the *Velvet Kitten* when we saw you stumbling about in the snow, leaving a trail of yellow behind you and figured we had better help out."

Everyone laughed; everyone, except Captain Youngblood.

"I doubt the *Velvet Kitten* would serve a savage, a *black* savage and a...whatever the hell you are, Barbey."

"I am ut yuh eepuh caw 'automaton'," Barbey said. *"I am what your people call an 'automaton.'"*

The beautiful man with the silky black hair lurched toward Captain Youngblood. "Call me a savage one more time and..."

Captain Youngblood's hand shot to his saber.

Colonel Tye pressed the back of his hand against the beautiful man's chest, stopping him. "It is alright, Talako. The 4ᵗʰ Earl of Dunmore has requested our presence. We have to scoot."

"Aye, Colonel," Talako said, "Let us take leave. It's cold, after all; I am sure the Captain would like to change out of those wet knickers."

Laughter erupted from among the soldiers again.

"Shut up!" Captain Youngblood hissed.

Colonel Tye and Talako mounted their iron horses and rode off with Barbey cruising behind them.

Colonel Tye pulled into the winding station. Talako and Barbey pulled in beside him.

All clockwork devices needed winding up in order to work. The iron horses – and Barbey – were no exception.

With small, easily portable devices, a key was usually enough. Larger or more powerful clockwork technology however, required more than a simple key.

The power of the water in a watermill was transferred to the device needing winding through immense cogs that powered a large spindle that protruded from the side of the mill. This spindle was then fitted with a metal cap, designed to fit into the clockwork device.

Levers and gears were then employed to allow

the measured winding of the device.

The iron horses would take five minutes to "charge;" Barbey, fifteen.

"Hey, Talako," Tye said, tapping him on the shoulder. "Let's grab a bowl of stew at Mrs. Wilkes' before we meet with Governor Murray; I'm famished."

"That's Royal Governor, John Murray," Talako said. "Fourth Earl of Dunmore. And we can't be late for a meeting with an official again."

"Royal, my dilberry maker," Tye said. "That cock robin is only alive because he provides us with the iron horses and the opportunity for runaways to go free *and* to kill white folks without getting hung."

"That's a lot," Talako said.

"We wouldn't need freedom if they had let us be free like we were in the first place," Tye replied.

"Well, we can kill him after the war," Talako said with a shrug. "Right now, we have to be on time."

Yeah, yeah," Tye sighed. "We'll be back in about half past the hour, Barbey."

"Yekkir," Barbey replied. *"Yes, sir."*

Tye and Talako trudged through the muddy brown slush along Broad Way Street to the intersection of Broad Way and Dyes. There, they approached a large building where there stood a pair of young British soldiers, whose carnation faces told Tye the men had been on guard for several hours. The guards snapped to attention. Tye nodded as he passed them, pushing the door open. He stepped inside with Talako close behind him.

Soldiers bustled about a capacious hallway, moving in and out of rows of offices on each side.

Tye and Talako strode to the end of the hall, where two more young soldiers stood at a pair of red oak doors trimmed in brass.

One of the soldiers rapped on the door with his knuckles.

The door opened a crack and a thin, angular face peeked out. The door closed. A few seconds later, the door opened wide. The man with the angular face stood in the doorway, his nose in the air. His gray hair showed around the edges of his brown, horsehair wig; his green coat and breeches smelled new.

"Looks like a leprechaun," Tye whispered.

Talako snickered.

The man spoke. "The Royal Governor John Murray, Fourth Earl of Dunmore, will see you now, Colonel Tye. Your man may enter, too."

"My man?" Tye hissed. "My Captain! Captain Talako. He's chewed more dirt than any of you in this place."

"Apologies, sir," the man said.

"Timothy, let the gentlemen in," Governor Murray said.

"Yeah, Tim," Tye said. "Step aside."

Timothy's eye twitched as he stepped out of the way.

Tye and Talako walked past him.

Talako stopped and then pointed at Timothy's eye. "You should get that checked out."

Tye and Talako stood before the Governor, who sat behind his desk.

"Have a seat, gentlemen," the Governor said, pointing at three chairs opposite him.

Tye and Talako sat down.

Tye glanced at the empty chair beside him. "Who's the third chair for?"

"For me."

Tye peered over his shoulder. Standing in the doorway was a tall, athletically built woman with skin as black and shiny as the curly knots of hair all over her head.

She was stunningly beautiful to Tye, even though she was dressed in men's clothing – a waistcoat, breeches and stockings; the only somewhat feminine article of clothing was a lace jabot she wore on the front of her shirt.

"Well, hello," Tye crooned.

The woman sat beside him. "Hello," she said.

"Colonel Tye, isn't it?"

"Yes," Tye replied.

"I'm Ngozi Edochie," the woman said. "Pleasure."

"The pleasure is all mine," Tye said, scanning Ngozi with his eyes. "I assure you."

Talako rolled his eyes.

"And my friend here with the condition is Talako," Tye said.

Ngozi frowned. "Condition?"

"Yes," Tye said. "His eyes roll about uncontrollably. The doctor said if he keeps doing it, his eye muscles might spasm and eject his eyeballs."

Ngozi laughed.

Talako started to roll his eyes again, but thought twice and did not.

"Alright, alright, enough twaddle," Governor Murray said. "I have an assignment of utmost importance for you, gentlemen. Ngozi will assist, providing her services as your tinkerer and weapon-smith."

Tye turned his gaze to Ngozi. "Are you any good?"

"Ngozi is Britain's Chief Tinkerer and the inventor of the iron horse," Governor Murray chimed in.

"What *he* said," Ngozi said.

"Impressive," Tye said. "We've got us a bonafide bigwig to keep us clods in line. So, what's the work, Governor?"

Governor Murray leaned forward in his chair. His perused the room as if searching for some spy hiding in the shadows of the corners.

"This mission requires the utmost discretion," he whispered. "No one is to know except for those in this room and those directly involved."

"Go on," Colonel Tye said.

"I want you to put together a small force – twenty soldiers at the most – men as hard as iron with the dark stain of war on their souls," Governor Murray said. "Train them in your...unorthodox fighting methods and when they are ready, you and your unit will destroy a base erected by the rebels in Monmouth County, New Jersey. Ngozi will supply you with any weapons and transportation you need."

"Obviously this base is a threat," Colonel Tye said. "Why?"

"The rebels are manufacturing a vapor there," Governor Murray replied. "Intelligence reports say this vapor eats the flesh of men, stripping skin and sinew from bone."

"And where, exactly, am I allowed to pull the soldiers who will join me on this perilous mission?" Colonel Tye asked.

"From any company, with the exception of the Queen's Rangers," Governor Murray said. "And, of course, not a company's best; we need them on the front lines."

"I figured as much," Colonel Tye sighed. "So, I get the dandy prats, the chalkers, the cock robins and fart catchers, then?"

"Well, yes," Governor Murray said. "But I am confident that you and your merry band will be able to whip them into shape in no time."

"You can keep your whip," Tye said. "And how much time is 'no time?'"

"Six weeks," Governor Murray said.

Ngozi snickered.

"You have a deal," Tye said. "Under one condition."

A blast of air rushed from Governor Murray's nostrils. "I figured your freedom would be condition enough, but what is it?"

"Ngozi here is my first recruit," Tye replied. "Her skills can be quite useful during the training and on the mission."

Ngozi's smile faded. "What? I have much work to do in..."

"Agreed!" Governor Murray said, interrupting her. "I will have an escort show you to the area I have set aside for the training and housing of your men.

Good day, gentlemen."

Two

A platoon of soldiers stood, in four rows of five soldiers per row, in the middle of a great expanse of land that was blanketed in snow. Piles of logs surrounded them. Atop the logs sat several axes, hammers and small boxes.

All of the soldiers, except for Ngozi Edochie, were men. Their expressions ranged from curious to unconcerned, but they all bore a hardness; a hardness only forged in war.

One soldier, a bullish man named Hawkins, stood in stark contrast to the others; even more than Ngozi. Unlike the rest of the soldiers, who were Black, Private Hawkins had long, blond hair and a complexion that looked as if he had run a mile – a constant tinge of pink under his milky skin.

Colonel Tye, with Talako and Barbey flanking him, sauntered toward the formation.

"Welcome to Casa Incognegro, you rogues and whip-jackets," Colonel Tye said.

Snickers rose from among the platoon.

"I see some of you looking around, taking it all in," Tye continued. "Maybe you're looking for the tea pot, or the piss pot, depending on your mood."

Tye a big step forward, stopping within less than an arm's reach from the soldiers in the front row.

"Well, guess what?" He said. "We ain't got either one! What we *do* have is three acres of land and a fartleberry feast of lumber. So..."

"Twaddle!" Private Hawkins spat.

Tye shot a glance toward him. "What did you say?"

"I said 'twaddle'," Private Hawkins said. "This is complete and utter nonsense. It's colder than a witch's teat out here. Where are our bunks?"

"Watch your mouth!" Talako said. "You are addressing a superior officer."

"Superior? Officer?" Private Hawkins chuckled. "You ain't a real officer. Not in this white man's army, you ain't."

"Real enough," Tye said. "Step forward."

Private Hawkins tromped out of the formation and walked up to Colonel Tye. "What is it?"

Colonel stared into Private Hawkins' eyes. His expression was stone. "How many people have you killed?"

"What?" Private Hawkins said, scratching his head.

"I am speaking English, I believe," Tye replied. "How many people have you killed?"

"Thirteen," Private Hawkins said, thrusting his chest outward and raising his chin.

"I have personally killed 878 men while looking them in the eye; more with my musket and my long bow," Colonel Tye said. "I have hiked thirteen days straight without sleep or food and stuffed four feet of my own intestines back into my stomach. That's why I wear the rank of colonel. That's why you *will* respect it."

Private Hawkins spit a glob of mucous into the snow. "Why are we here?"

"I can tell you why *I'm* here," Tye said. "To teach."

"What are you going to teach me?" Private Hawkins said with a smirk.

"Nothing," Colonel Tye replied. "*You* are going to teach *them*."

"Me? Teach this lot of bucks and belly-warmers?" Private Hawkins grunted. "What could I possibly teach them?"

Colonel Tye slapped Private Hawkins across the jaw. A loud *crack* echoed across the field. "That what I say, goes."

Private Hawkins stumbled sideways. He pressed his palm against the red spot on his face. "I'm gonna kill you, nigger!"

Private Hawkins drew his saber.

Colonel Tye drew a pair of small daggers from the cuffs of his sleeves.

Private Hawkins charged forward, his cutlass whistling as he slashed away in an x-pattern.

Colonel Tye evaded each blow, delivering a slash of his own with each duck, weave and fade.

While each of Private Hawkins' blows missed, all of Colonel Tye's connected, opening several chasms of flesh on his arms.

Blood poured down Private Hawkins' sleeves and pooled at his feet.

The private lunged forward with a deep thrust toward Colonel Tye's chest.

Colonel Tye side-stepped the blow and then darted forward, jabbing the knives repeatedly into Private Hawkins' throat, neck and face.

Blood sprayed into the air.

Private Hawkins collapsed onto his face, unmoving.

Colonel Tye stood on Private Hawkins' back. "Anyone else think what I have to say is nonsense?"

He perused the faces of the soldiers.

They answered with silence.

"Good," Tye said, smiling. That was your first lesson, courtesy of Private Hawkins. Your second lesson is this: all muscles, because they depend on blood, depend on breath. Before you are any good to me, you will first learn to breathe."

Tye pointed at a pile of logs. "Around you are five piles. On top of each pile are three axes. Grab one. Come back without an axe and Barbey here gives you a new fundament hole right between the eyes. You have two minutes. Go!"

The soldiers scrambled toward the hills of wood. Nineteen soldiers fought for possession of one of the fifteen axes. As one soldier neared the top, another grabbed his ankle and then yanked him into the snow.

"Fall in!" Colonel Tye commanded after two minutes had passed.

The soldiers reformed – four rows; three, with five soldiers per row; one, with four soldiers, who stood at the rear, shrinking into each other's shadows.

Ngozi Edochie stood in the middle of the front row, her axe resting against her thigh.

"Well done, Captain Edochie," Colonel Tye said. "You get to live."

Ngozi smiled.

"This time," Tye said.

Ngozi's smile faded.

"You four in the back...front-and-center!" Tye commanded.

Three of the men plodded toward the front of the platoon. The fourth bolted in the opposite direction.

Colonel Tye craned his head, peering over the soldiers at the running man.

"Barbey," he said after nearly a minute, letting the man sprint several hundred yards.

Barbey drew the arquebus from his back.

"This, lady and gentlemen, is *Nomo*," Colonel Tye said. "As in whatever she hits is no *mo'*."

Barbey opened his chest plate and then reached inside with a perfectly formed hand. He withdrew an iron ball about the size of a man's fist and slid it into *Nomo*'s open breech. He then closed the breech portal and sealed it.

The soldier continued to gallop across the ankle-high snow.

Barbey fired.

A moment later, the soldier was gone. Only his boots, with his feet still in them, remained.

Barbey pressed *Nomo* against his back, where it remained. With lightning speed, he drew a pair of flintlock pistols. He fired, hitting two of the soldiers who had no axe between the eyes.

The soldiers fell. Wisps of smoke rose from their foreheads.

Barbey hurled one of the pistols at the third

man with no axe. The barrel pierced the man's brow, sinking into his head up to its trigger guard.

The soldier shook violently, but remained standing until Barbey snatched the pistol out of his skull. He then fell onto his back.

"That was lesson number three," Colonel Tye said. "We complete our mission at all costs."

Colonel Tye pointed at the piles of wood again. "When you climbed those piles, I am sure you noticed the hammers and boxes of nails resting up there with the axes."

"Yes, sir!" the soldiers replied.

"Outstanding!" Colonel Tye said. "You are going to build our encampment – the barracks; the privy; the mess hall; the officers' quarters – all of it. You don't eat; you don't sleep until you do. Understood?"

"Yes, sir!" the soldiers shouted again.

"And by the way, since we have a lady among us, you will have to build a small barrack for her, too," Colonel Tye said. "I told you, this is a lesson in breathing. Captain Talako will take it from here. I will see you all in the morning.

Colonel Tye sauntered off.

The soldiers became ants, working together to erect a shelter against the cold and snow.

"Press down the breath," Talako ordered as the soldiers swung their axes and hammers. "Pull it down into your loins, behind the fundament, where the emotions reside. Calm yourselves. Calming your emotions makes a calm *soldier* and a calm soldier feels no fear. As you breathe, clear your mind of thoughts and impressions from outside you. Then the thing inside you...your mission...can receive all your attention."

The soldiers, spurred on by Talako, worked on, until even the stars were in need of respite from the observance of their toil.

####

March, 1778

The soldiers crouched low, huddling together in a clearing in a forest. Colonel Tye and Captain Talako squatted among them. Barbey stood watch a few feet away.

"A week ago, I leaked word to the seediest dives in New York, New Jersey, Delaware and Pennsylvania that a cache of the Queen's gold was hidden in these woods," Colonel Tye whispered. "Last night, I leaked the gold's exact location and that a platoon of Black soldiers is securing it, but is relieved by the Queen's Rangers from dusk until dawn."

"We're securing gold now, Colonel?" A young soldier asked.

"Talako, I thought you said this boy had sense," Colonel Tye said.

"Normally, he's sharp," Talako said, glaring at

the young man. "Didn't have your coffee this morning, Robinson?"

"No sir," Robinson lied.

"Drink three cups when we get back," Colonel Tye said.

"Yes, sir!" Robinson said.

"For the rest of you who have not had your coffee yet," Colonel Tye sighed. "There is no gold; I used that to draw pirates, thieves and rapscallions for this exercise. Talako..."

Talako nodded. "There are about forty men searching this forest right now; men who would slit their own mother's throat for an ounce of silver. You have each been given a knife. They have swords, guns and maybe worse. Kill each and every one of those bastards before they kill you. None of you leaves this forest until they are all dead."

The soldiers nodded in unison.

"Now, go!" Talako hissed.

The soldiers leapt to their feet and then crept into the forest.

"Forty men?" Talako whispered in Tye's ear. "There's more like *sixty* men out there."

"Nothing like the unexpected to test a man's mettle," Colonel Tye said.

"Or to make him soil his breeches," Talako said.

The men laughed.

Let's get up in the trees, so we can get a bird's-eye view of this shindig," Colonel Tye said. "Barbey."

Barbey thrust his fingers into a thick oak tree. He then scaled the tree until he found a thick branch strong enough to hold his comrades' weight. He then climbed back down. "Ig ah yog – *"It's all yours."*

Colonel Tye climbed the tree, using the gashes made by Barbey's fingers as hand-and-footholds. Talako followed close behind him. They sat on the large branch and observed.

Barbey pulled branches from the tree and then covered himself as best he could with the wood and dying leaves.

There was no cover for the soldiers, however, except for the thin mist and the shadows of the trees that shifted with each howl of the wind.

The soldiers advanced, stepping carefully across the snow with their shoulders hunched low and the points of their knives trained on the flickering shadows in the forest that grew more distinct all the while.

The wind died. The platoon split to either side, crouching and blending their bodies with the outlines of the trees and hills of snow.

A beefy man, dressed in a thigh-length black robe and bicorn hat, darted out of the shadows and hauled himself onto a boulder with a meaty slap of flesh on stone. The man wore no shoes, or trousers. He perused the area down the barrel of his musket.

Robinson stalked the man at his rear, bounding across the snow without making a sound.

He crept up right behind the shoeless man and then, with a powerful thrust, he drove the tip of his blade into the base of the man's spine.

The shoeless man opened his mouth wide, but could produce no scream.

Robinson twisted the knife, withdrew it and then ran the keen blade across the man's throat.

Blood erupted from the man's neck.

Robinson lowered him to the ground and then snatched the musket from the man's hands. He searched the man's pockets and found several small balls of iron. Robinson stuffed the ammunition into his pockets and then crept back to his comrades.

Again and again, others clambered into the area. In moments, the thugs outnumbered the soldiers.

Finally, one of the thugs – a lanky man dressed in the fine clothes of a sea captain – pointed toward the trees and snow mounds behind which the soldiers hid.

"Over there," he shouted. "I spotted the tip of a boot protruding from behind that tree!"

The criminals charged toward the hiding

soldiers, parting the mist like rotting silk.

"Damn it!" Ngozi snarled. "Go, go, go!"

The soldiers bounded across the snow. One of them, a man in his early forties whom the platoon dubbed "Gramps," peered over his shoulder.

The thugs were closing on them.

Gramps opened his mouth to say something. Before he could speak, the muted crack of a rifle shot smothered his words. His face erupted in a spurt of gore. Robinson stopped and then whirled on his heels to face his pursuers.

"Those bastards got Gramps!" He wailed.

Robinson dropped to one knee and then fired, carving a trench through the top of a pirate's skull.

The pirate crumpled into a moist mass in the snow.

The other thugs took cover behind the trees.

"Cover me!" Ngozi shouted.

Robinson reloaded and took aim.

Ngozi sprinted toward the dead pirate.

A dirty faced man dressed in several layers of buckskin and fur stepped from behind a tree, aiming a crossbow at Ngozi's head.

Ngozi leapt toward the dead pirate.

Robinson fired.

The bullet zipped over Ngozi's back and struck the fur-covered man in the chest.

Ngozi landed on top of the pirate. She grabbed his flintlock pistol and fired it as a thug peeked from behind a tree. The thug fell onto his back. One eye was gone, replaced by a black pit.

The soldiers charged, cursing and screaming, toward the thugs.

The thugs, believing the soldiers to be armed, remained behind cover for a few moments, until they realized no more shots had been fired.

The thugs stepped from behind the trees, but the soldiers had already closed on them.

It was over in seconds. Blood and flesh littered the forest, and clouds of gun smoke, thick and light gray, filled the air.

Three dozen bodies lay in twitching, leaking heaps. Black soldiers lay alongside white thugs, but thugs had suffered the worst of it.

The surviving soldiers, twelve in all, were now in possession of flintlock pistols, muskets and blunderbusses.

"Reload," Ngozi ordered. Her voice was calm, but her hands shook.

"I'm bleeding," one soldier cried, pressing his hand against a gaping wound in his side.

"Bleed on your own time," Ngozi said.

The words were barely out of her mouth when the forest around them erupted.

The next wave of thugs – about forty of them – rushed toward the soldiers.

The soldiers ran, adrenaline and purpose kept them moving.

They reached a fallen tree and took cover behind it.

They fired in unison, reloaded quickly and fired again, killing scores of thugs.

But more thugs came; and more after them, their pale skin nearly blending with the snow.

A soldier the others called "Booker," because he read a book every three or four days, howled, stepped from behind cover and fired, his blunderbuss rending a thug into mincemeat.

Booker kept firing.

Ngozi joined him.

Robinson joined her.

The surviving soldiers joined them.

"Looks like the team has bonded," Colonel Tye said.

"They are willing to kill together; to even die together, so they are surely willing to live together,"

Talako said, almost pleadingly.

Colonel Tye nodded. "Barbey!"

Barbey burst from between the sticks and dead leaves and sped toward the battle. He fired Nomo.

Five thugs fell.

Barbey sped past the soldiers and rolled straight toward the thugs.

Several thugs fired. The bullets ricocheted off of Barbey's steel hide.

The thugs ran.

Colonel Tye and Talako ran toward the soldiers.

"Give chase!" Colonel Tye commanded. "Do not let one thug leave here alive!"

The soldiers ran beside Colonel Tye; beside Talako, killing thugs.

They slew their enemy with zeal unmatched, for they knew that they were no longer their instructor's subordinates, they were brothers...and sister.

####

Colonel Tye paced back and forth before his platoon. Talako and Barbey stood a few yards from the formation.

"Every advanced culture on earth has their own naming ceremonies, practices, or manner in which names are given," Colonel Tye said. "Many of us were given names, quite unceremoniously, by men who would have the unmitigated effrontery to claim human beings as their property – Jones; Culpepper; Robinson."

Colonel Tye stopped, front and center before the soldiers. "But your name – all names, in fact and all titles – represents your mission, your power and your challenge. Do you understand?"

"Yes, sir!" The soldiers replied sharply in unison.

"It is not the mission of any man to be a slave to anyone or anything," Colonel Tye continued. "The enslaved hold no power and their challenges do not serve to build, only to destroy. Do you understand?"

"Yes, sir!" The soldiers said again.

"Talk back to me!" Colonel Tye said, pounding his chest with his fist.

Yes, sir!" The soldiers boomed.

"What name should be worn by men and women black of skin and blacker of blood and bone?" Colonel Tye said. "What name should be worn by men and women who, though they be few, have the power of many, yet move as one?"

Colonel Tye looked from soldier to soldier, locking eyes with them.

"Today and forever more," he said, raising his saber high above his head. "We shall be called the *Black Brigade*. Let Earth and Heaven tremble!"

A cheer rose from the platoon and shook the morning sky.

"Who are we?" Talako asked, as the soldiers rallied around their Colonel.

"The Black Brigade!" They shouted.

"Who?" Talako asked again.

"The Black Brigade!"

"Who?"

"The Black Brigade! The Black Brigade! The Black Brigade!"

Three

Ngozi sat, one leg draped over the other, at Governor Murray's desk, sipping tea.

The governor sipped from a mug filled with hot buttered rum.

Behind the desk, at the Royal Governor's window, stood a strongly built man. He was of average height, with a large head and square, deft hands. His balding, light brown hair was long, hanging a bit past his shoulders. His clothing was as clean as it was plain. The man stared out the window, his bespectacled gaze focused on the evening sky.

"Finally, Tye gives his soldiers leave," the governor said. "I thought I would never get a report."

"Colonel Tye maintains a short tether on his dogs of war," Ngozi said.

"And what do you think of the Colonel and his officers?" Governor Murray asked.

"Who is that?" Ngozi said, nodding toward the man at the window.

"He is a man of no consequence to you," Governor Murray replied.

"Then I am a woman of no words," Ngozi said.

The man at the window whirled around. His face was a mask of rage. "Impertinent, Black bi..."

"Ngozi, meet Mr. Benjamin Franklin," Governor Murray said, interrupting him. "Former Postmaster General of the United States of America."

Ngozi sat bolt upright. "America? Wait...the chronomancer who fathered the *Franklin Sentinels*? Here?"

"Worry not," Governor Murray said. "Benjamin is a friend."

Ngozi studied Ben Franklin's face. His eyes were gray and steady; his mouth wide and humorous with a pointed upper lip. His visage bared his brilliance, his hubris, his madness. She thrust her hand toward him. "Friend."

Franklin took Ngozi's hand in his and kissed the back of it. "Apologies for the outburst. It would seem that the stresses of this war have caused me to forget my manners."

Ngozi replied with a nod.

"So, Tye's soldiers...are they ready?" Governor Murray asked.

"They are," Ngozi said. "They are sharp, fearless and so full of piss and vinegar they would kill a brick, choke a stick and drown a glass of water."

"And what of Tye?"

"He is a brutal, but effective teacher," Ngozi said. "His men admire – and I dare say, love – him because he trains and fights right beside them and regards them as brothers, not subordinates."

"So, they would follow him anywhere?" Ben Franklin inquired.

"Right into perditions flames, if he asked them," Ngozi replied.

"Even into a chamber filled with flesh-eating vapors?"

Ngozi's eyes darted back-and-forth between Governor Murray and Ben Franklin. "Wait...you plan to use that vapor on the Black Brigade?"

"Black Brigade...is that what he calls them?" Governor Murray snickered.

"*Us*," Ngozi said. "That is what he calls *us*. You expect me to step into that flesh-eating vapor, too?"

"Of course not," Governor Murray said. "You are too valuable to the Crown. I will send for you just before I send Tye and his men to Monmouth. From here, you will be sent back to England."

"And our deal?" Ngozi said.

"You will be given an estate in London and the release of your parents, as promised," Governor Murray said. "Just keep making us those weapons and vehicles of yours and all will be fine."

"It seems you have another Master Weaponsmith under your employ," Ngozi said. "One with knowledge of vapors and poisons."

"That title belongs to me," Franklin said with a slight bow.

"I am still perplexed why a Continental is working with us," Ngozi said.

"He is working with me," Governor Murray said. "When King George ordered that any slave who joined in this war would be given his freedom, I knew it was the end – the end of the Continentals and the Crown. Give hundreds...perhaps *thousands* of Blacks guns and training in war and soon we will be overrun by pickaninnies out for white blood."

"And what does any of that have to do with the vapor?" Ngozi asked. "Does the vapor only target Black flesh?"

"That would be divine," Governor Murray replied. "But, unfortunately, no. It is no secret that

Colonel Tye and, especially his man, Talako, were born with certain...gifts. They are much heartier than most. If the vapor kills them, killing everyone else would be easy as pie."

"Killing *any*one," Ngozi said.

"Excuse me?" Governor Murray said.

"You said killing *every*one; you meant *any*one."

Governor Murray just stared at Ngozi. His expression was stone.

Ngozi shifted her gaze to Benjamin Franklin. He smiled broadly.

"Oh, good Lord," Ngozi gasped. "You plan to kill every soldier in this war – on both sides."

"Yes," Governor Murray said. "Is that a problem?"

"Not at all," Ngozi said, leaning back in her chair. "Two armies of white men dying is not a problem at all...and well worth the thousands of Black men who will die, too. I am just in awe of the genius of it."

Governor Murray laughed. Ben Franklin's smile broadened.

"Very good," Governor Murray said. "Now, tell me all about this Black Brigade. Spare no details...we need to know exactly what we are dealing with."

####

The *High John Clockwork Theatre* was a wonder to behold. A collection of automatons that performed a show in a makeshift tent. The show was presented by John De Conquer – showman, raconteur and entrepreneur.

Some of the mechanical devices were basic and aged; others bore the mark of a more sophisticated designer.

The newer automatons possessed fine movement, were solidly constructed and had a seemingly militaristic bent.

De Conquer's four daughters darted about, winding up the old devices as De Conquer charged up the new ones with small bits of his own sanity – the common fuel for such constructs of metal and magic.

Colonel Tye, Talako and Barbey sat in the front row; Tye and Talako in the velvet covered chairs and Barbey on the floor beside them, as there was no chair in the theater strong enough to hold his weight.

"Do you miss it?" Colonel Tye asked.

"Oh", Barbey said. "I ah oh-ik. A oh-ik ohg ahk ayk ig hig oh-ig agga ag eggy oggah." *"No. I am a shootist. A shootist should not waste his skills shooting apples and empty beer bottles."*

"Agreed," Colonel Tye said. "And thank you, for the tickets."

Barbey nodded. He raised his iron arm and pointed a perfectly formed finger at the stage. The show was about to begin.

The show itself consisted of a risqué dance performed by buxom female automata, accompanied by mechanical drummers and trumpeters; a tap dance to the accompaniment of a four-armed automaton who deftly played a fiddle and hamboned at the same time; and a jaw-dropping battle at the end, the climax of which was the destruction of several life-like wax dummies.

Midway through the show, Ngozi joined them, taking a seat directly behind Colonel Tye.

"What is the good word, Captain Edochie?" Colonel Tye said, smiling.

"As you suspected, Governor Murray is up to no good," Ngozi said.

"When is a white man not?" Colonel Tye said.

"The mission is a trap," Ngozi said. "Meant to kill the entire Brigade."

"We will talk at length later," Colonel Tye said. "Murray does not suspect where your loyalties actually lie, does he?"

"I imagine I would be dead, if so," Ngozi replied.

"Indeed," Colonel Tye said. "But let's worry about the Governor later, for now, just sit back and enjoy the show!"

Four

April, 1778

Colonel Tye, Barbey and Ngozi stood before their brothers of the Black Brigade. Colonel Tye inhaled, taking in spring air and the smell of sycamore and wild leeks. He paced before his soldiers for a while before he spoke.

"If war is the father of us all, king of us all, a battle is the mother; the queen," Colonel Tye said. "This war will make some of you men; some it will make slaves again; some free. But this battle will, as mothers are wont to do, birth us anew and make us all *gods*!"

The soldiers roared.

"There is no blasphemy in this," Colonel Tye said, with a wave of his hand. "Is it not the Christian's bible – the first book most of you ever read – that says 'Ye are *gods* and *all* of you are children of the Most High'?"

"Yes, sir!" The soldiers replied.

"Today, we face the might of both the Royal *and* the Continental Armies," Colonel Tye said. Today, we walk into the trap they have set for us. But, do gods tremble in fear?"

"No, sir!"

"Do gods die?"

"No, sir!"

"Well, the mummy-daddy, big God of gods can," Colonel Tye said. "In fact, all God does is watch us and kill us when we get boring. So today, at least, whatever you do...be Blacktastic!"

The soldiers laughed.

"Black Brigade!" Colonel Tye boomed.

"Yes, sir!" The soldiers boomed back.

"Black Brigade!"

"Yes, sir!"

"Mount up!"

The soldiers pounded their chests in unison. "Yes, sir!"

Roaring, they sprinted off in single file.

Colonel Tye turned to Ngozi. "Is the other vehicle ready, Captain Edochie?"

"Almost, sir!" Ngozi replied. "She's been at the winding station all night. It won't be long now."

"Good," Colonel Tye said. "Pick up Talako on your way. He is at the *Velvet Kitten.*"

"Had to get one in just in case it was his last?" Ngozi said, shaking her head.

"No," Colonel Tye snickered. "Well...yes, but his main purpose was to...sluice his gob."

Ngozi scratched her head, frowning. "Take a

hearty drink? Of rum?"

"Of humor," Colonel Tye replied.

Ngozi's face paled. "What?"

"Humor," Colonel Tye said again. "Blood, lymph, bile...or worse."

"Yes, yes, I know what humor is, thank you," "But drinking it? Captain Talako is some kind of...Ossenfelder?"

"Ah, you are familiar with the poem," Colonel Tye said with a slight bow.

He danced around the room as he recited the poem:

> "My dear young maiden clingeth
> Unbending. fast and firm
> To all the long-held teaching
> Of a mother ever true;
> As in vampires unmortal
> Folk on the Theyse's portal
> Heyduck-like do believe.
> But my Christine thou dost dally,
> And wilt my loving parry
> Till I myself avenging
> To a vampire's health a-drinking
> Him toast in pale tockay.
>
> And as softly thou art sleeping
> To thee shall I come creeping
> And thy life's blood drain away.
> And so shalt thou be trembling

For thus shall I be kissing
And death's threshold thou' it be crossing
With fear, in my cold arms.
And last shall I thee question
Compared to such instruction
What are a mother's charms?"

Barbey clapped.

Colonel Tye bowed toward the four corners of the room, his arms sweeping in exaggerated movements.

"And no, Talako is not a vampire by definition," Colonel Tye said. "He is something altogether unique. He is quite alive and, as I said, his diet is not limited to blood, but any bodily fluid."

"Is he the only one of his kind?" Ngozi asked.

"He has been ostracized by his own people due to his condition of birth, so I would imagine so," Colonel Tye said. "Now go. Talako can explain much better than I."

####

Women bustled about the *Velvet Kitten*, flirting with men in the parlor or leading them upstairs.

A burly man dressed in a white tuxedo met Ngozi just beyond the door.

"We don't hire cargo here," the man said, smiling broadly. The smell of rancid meat wafted from between his rotting teeth.

Ngozi exploded forward. Her left knee slammed

into the big man's liver.

The man collapsed onto both knees.

Women screamed in horror.

Ngozi drew her flintlock pistol and pressed its muzzle against the side of the man's head. "What is your name?"

"Ma'am?" the man croaked.

"Your name," Ngozi said. "What is it?"

"Reed," the man sputtered. "Bernard Reed."

"Bernie, I don't know what is more insulting...you calling me cargo, or you assuming I have the slightest desire to be a whore," Ngozi said. "Bernie, Bernie, Bernie...what are we to do with you?"

"Please, ma'am," Bernie cried. "I'm so, sorry."

Ngozi pushed hard against Bernard's head with her pistol, pressing his ear toward his shoulder. "The trouble with you, Bernie, is that you lack the power of conversation but not the power of speech."

"If you blow his head off with that shot, drinks are on me,"

Ngozi snapped her head in the direction of the voice. Talako stood before her, tucking his shirt into his pants.

"By drink, I hope you mean water or wine," Ngozi said.

Talako laughed. "Tye told you."

"He did," Ngozi replied.

"Well, you are my sister," Talako said. "There should be no secrets between us. So, are you killing him, or what?"

"Later," Ngozi said, slipping her pistol into her belt. "Right now, we have more pressing issues to attend to."

Talako picked up a suede bag sitting at his feet and then tossed its strap over his shoulder. "Okay."

Talako thrust his leg forward, driving his boot-heel into the back of Bernard's neck.

The big man fell onto his face, unconscious.

Talako turned toward the parlor. "Attention, everyone!"

The bustling and screams stopped. Silence fell over the brothel.

"When we walk out the door, you will forget we were ever here," Talako said. "Carry on."

The bustling began anew.

Ngozi and Talako sauntered out the door.

"That was amazing," Ngozi said. "Is that one of your abilities as a..."

"As a priest," Talako said. "Imbibing humor enhances my strength, speed, heartiness and ability to sense the physical world. The spiritual world is a different matter, altogether."

"Your priests have much in common with those of my homeland," Ngozi said. "However, they avoid war. How do you reconcile the two?"

"Many will argue that there is nothing remotely spiritual in combat," Talako said. "Consider this: mystical or religious experiences have four common components – constant awareness of one's own inevitable death, total focus on the present moment, the valuing of other people's lives above your own, and being part of a larger religious community such as the ummat al-Islamiyah – the collective community of Islamic peoples – or the church."

Talako reached into his bag and withdrew two tomahawks. He slipped them into his belt; one beside each pistol. "Those same components exist in combat. The big difference is that the mystic sees Heaven and the warrior sees Hell. I see – and reside in – both."

"When this war is over, what will you do, then?" Ngozi asked. "Will you finally choose the spiritual over the militaristic; priesthood over warriorhood; Heaven over Hell?"

"Most of us, including me, would prefer to think of a sacred space as some light-filled wondrous place where we can feel good; where we can find a way to shore up our spirits against death," Talako said. "We do not want to think that something as ugly and brutal as war could be involved in any way with the spiritual. However, would not every devout Christian say that Calvary Hill was a sacred space?"

"Point well taken," Ngozi said. "Hopefully we will get a chance to discuss such things again."

"We will," Talako said. "In this world or in the one beyond the veil."

"So, you think there is a chance we will die?" Ngozi asked.

"There is always a chance," Talako answered. "Thankfully, that chance is a minute one."

"How so?" Ngozi inquired.

"Out of every one hundred soldiers in any war, ten should not even be there; eighty are just fodder for arquebus and musket; nine are the real fighters and we are lucky to have them, for they make the battle," Talako said. "But there is one...one who is a *warrior*, the one who the enemy prays that when he dies, he comes back fighting on their side. *That* is Colonel Tye. He is why we will come out of this alive."

"I look forward to fighting beside him," Ngozi said.

"Well, then, let's get to that winding station before we miss the battle!"

####

A ticking din echoed across the township of Shrewsbury.

The residents of the town stood on both sides of

Thornebrooke Road, staring – in awe and terror – at the dozen iron horses that sped up the road like an iron wave upon an embittered sea.

Colonel Tye, who rode in the center of the front row, controlled the vehicle with one hand and scanned both sides of the road with the pistol in his other hand.

At the end of the dirt road, atop a hill, loomed a huge, box-shaped house. The wooden house was covered in clapboard painted alabaster. Its tall, central chimney belched white smoke into the sky.

The double doors in the center of the house flew open. A moment later, men dressed in red and blue stormed out of the house, like ants fleeing a burning anthill.

"Forward!" Colonel Tye commanded.

The iron horses built up speed until, to the people standing on Thornebrooke Road, they looked like nothing more than a black and crimson blur.

Such high speeds would deplete nearly all of the iron horses' energy, but that was fine with Colonel Tye; he had no intention of the Black Brigade returning to New York on them.

The Black Brigade closed on the hill under a storm of pewter shot. The balls bounced harmlessly off the iron horses, falling to the ground before them.

"Break left! Break right!" Colonel Tye shouted.

"Break left! Break right!" each squad leader shouted in unison.

Colonel Tye veered off the road to his left. Barbey and half of the Brigade followed him. The other half veered to the right.

Smart move, Colonel Tye thought. *They knew they could not penetrate the iron horses' armor with their muskets, so they intended to cause collisions by making the wheels slip on the pewter that covers the road.*

Townsfolk leapt out of the way of Barbey and the iron horses as they left the road and then zipped just behind the tree line.

The vehicles' spiked wheels sent chunks of grass and dirt flying into the air. The vehicles stormed toward the house on the hill concealed in the shadows of the trees.

The British and American armies fired desperately toward the trees, praying to get lucky and hit something, but their God was obviously busy elsewhere for luck was not on their side.

Both lines of iron horses darted back onto the road simultaneously and reformed with amazing speed and precision.

"Battles are won by slaughter and maneuver," Colonel Tye shouted. "Great leaders contribute more in maneuver and demand less in slaughter and the greatest leaders win with equal portions of both. So, my only orders to you now are maneuver wisely...and kill 'em all!"

To the inexperienced troops who faced this well-disciplined unit, the shock was devastating. On both sides – Red Coats and Blue – entire units simply melted away, some without firing a shot. The men who stood their ground discovered they could not reload quickly enough to hold off the terrifying sight of so many iron horses coming toward them. From a distance, it was the iron ball – from musket, blunderbuss, flintlock and Barbey's Nomo – that did horrible work; from up close it was the blade – from sword, dagger and bayonet. Governor Murray's men, traitors to both Crown and Continent, tried to hold their ground, but they were soon overtaken by the rapid advance of the Black Brigade's well-disciplined attack. Murray's men turned toward their one sanctuary, the safety of the house that manufactured the flesh-eating vapor.

Colonel Tye sat upon his iron horse at the end of the road, a couple of hundred yards from the factory and watched, through gaps in the drifting gun smoke, men scurry into the house.

Barbey came to a stop beside him. The rest of the Black Brigade lined up, in three columns, behind their leader.

"Are you ready to burn this wretched place down around them?"

"Yes, sir!" The soldiers roared.

Then let's finish this and..."

The sound of rolling thunder erupted from the house and tore across the sky.

The ground shook violently.

A moment later, the house vomited a stream of strange and fearsome creatures out of its doors.

"Hessians!" Colonel Tye shouted.

Colonel Tye set his eyes on the Hessians. They were men from the waist up, astonishingly broad and muscular, with brooding expressions. One had the body of a silver horse; the rest were chocolate brown. On their human torsos, they sported a dolman – a close fitting, short-cut black coat, with heavily braided gold buttons and loops. Over the dolman, they wore a pelisse – a similar coat, but with fur trimming – slung over their left shoulders. The creatures wielded Hellebardes – two-handed pole weapons with two whirring steel axe blades. The blades resembled a circular saw as they whizzed around. The Hellebardes were topped by a steel spear point.

"Centaurs?" Robinson said, squinting and craning his head toward the incredible sight.

"They call themselves hussars," Colonel Tye said. "But yes."

"Ever fought one?" Robinson asked.

"No," Colonel Tye said.

"Ever wanted to?" Robinson said.

"They are as strong and swift as a horse, with

the intellect, training and skill of a cavalry soldier," Colonel Tye replied. "What do you think?"

"Yes?" Robinson said.

"Damned right!" Colonel Tye bellowed. "Come on, brothers! Let's have some fun!"

The Black Brigade spread out into a semicircle, firing their muskets and flintlock pistols at the hussars.

The fast moving horse-men were hard to hit, but a few fell under the volley.

Barbey fired *Nomo*.

Three more hussars fell.

The hussars were now close enough to slash and thrust at the Black Brigade with their Hellebardes. Coupled with the hussars' amazing strength – about five times that of the strongest human – the keen, hard blades ripped through the metal hide of the iron horses and tore into flesh behind the armor. Several brigade members were knocked from their horses this way and then trampled to death under might and weight of hussar hooves.

A hussar leapt over Robinson's iron horse and then thrust downward with the Hellebarde, piercing his skull with the spearhead.

Robinson's eyes rolled up into his head. His mouth moved, but no sound came out. Whether it was reflex or will would never be known, but Robinson pulled the trigger of his blunderbuss one last time.

The weapon spat a cloud of iron shrapnel that hit the leaping hussar square in the gut. The hussar fell to the ground on its side. Its entrails poured from the gaping hole in its torso.

Barbey stomped on the wounded hussar's head, flattening it.

A slash across Barbey's arm drew oil.

Barbey whirled around to face his attacker.

The silver-bodied hussar stood before him. The creature, standing nearly eight feet tall at the shoulder, was bigger than its brethren.

"Ich bin Aldo Ulz," the silver hussar said. "Kommandant der Husaren." – *"I am Aldo Ulz, Commander of the Hussars."*

Barbey answered with a swift kick to Ulz's knee.

The bone made a sickening crunch as it bent inward toward the other leg at an impossible angle.

"Verdammt!" Ulz screamed as he collapsed onto his pulverized knee.

The Commander of the hussars slashed upward with his Hellebarde, carving a chasm in Barbey's face.

Barbey staggered backward. Tiny gears oozed out of his face on rivers of oil.

Barbey charged, pointing *Nomo*'s muzzle at Ulz.

Ulz slashed with the Hellebarde.

Barbey blocked Ulz's attack with *Nomo* and then thrust the arquebus into Ulz's chest. The muzzle burst through the back of Ulz's dolman.

Ulz gurgled and sputtered as his heart and a chunk of lung fell to the ground behind him.

Barbey lifted Ulz before him and charged toward the hussars, firing Nomo with one hand, reloading with the other, as he kept Ulz aloft as a shield against the whirring Hellebardes.

Within a few seconds, Ulz was carved to pieces by his comrades' Hellebardes.

Within those same few seconds, a dozen hussars fell to Barbey's arquebus.

Colonel Tye leapt from his iron horse and then rolled across the dirt between a hussar's legs. The creature was busy trying its best to carve through an iron horse's armor.

Colonel Tye stopped, lying flat on his back beneath the hussar. He drew his pair of knives and thrust upward, with blistering speed, into the creature's abdomen and girth as he scooted on his back toward the hussar's tail.

The hussar's guts rained down upon him as he scooted.

Colonel Tye hopped to his feet just before the hussar collapsed onto its face.

Tye took a moment to peruse his surroundings. The field was bathed in smoke and blood. A fresh wave of iron ball volleys came from the left. His surviving comrades – six in all – fought on against the hussar hordes.

A deep buzzing din came from high above the battlefield.

Colonel Tye gazed skyward. High above him was what looked like a giant creature, with a cigar-shaped body and 40' long wings like those of a condor. The creature's body was carved from African black-wood. Whirling brass rotary blades were protruded from both ends of the thing and the wings flapped up and down.

An *ornithopter* Ngozi had called it. An invention she had kept from the Crown as she planned to use it to carry enslaved Africans to freedom.

The ornithopter's panel door slid open. Talako kicked a score of grenados out of the vehicle into the open air. The grenados, wicks burning, rained down upon the hussars, blowing chunks of horse flesh all over the battlefield.

The ornithopter circled, dropping more grenados.

More hussars fell dead.

"Rückzug!" A hussar cried. "Retreat!"

The surviving few hussars galloped into the house. The doors closed behind the last one.

A cheer rose from the battlefield.

Talako lowered ten thick ropes. He then shimmied down one to the ground. He sprinted past the cheering Black Brigade soldiers to Colonel Tye's side.

"She is amazing," Colonel Tye said.

"Captain Edochie or the ornithopter?" Talako asked.

"Both," Colonel Tye said. "When this is all over, I'm going to ask her to marry me."

Talako raised an eyebrow.

"The ornithopter," Colonel Tye replied.

The men laughed.

"Everyone, give me your grenados and then gather up those of your fallen brothers," Colonel Tye ordered.

"Yes, sir!"

The soldiers did as their leader commanded, laying the clay grenades at his feet.

"Talako, tie them all together on one wick," Tye said.

"Tye..." Talako said, shaking his head.

"Do it!" Tye said.

"Yes, sir," Talako sighed.

Talako deftly, and with great speed, braided the wicks of over thirty grenados into one long wick her drew from his shoulder bag.

"Good job," Colonel Tye said, inspecting Talako's handiwork. "Now, all of you...climb those ropes and get the hell out of here! Barbey, you go east, to the shore. The rest will meet you there."

"Yes, sir!" The men said in unison. Barbey nodded.

Ngozi brought the ornithopter back around. The soldiers sprinted toward the dangling ropes. Barbey sped off.

Talako hugged Tye. Tye slowly brought his arms up and embraced his brother.

"We will circle around to get you," Talako said.

"I know you will," Colonel Tye said. "I'll be there."

"I know you will," Talako said.

"Go." Colonel Tye said.

"Yes, sir!" Talako said, clicking his heels and pounding his chest. He turned from his friend, sprinted toward the ropes, leapt onto one and climbed up into the ornithopter.

The wings of the ornithopter flapped faster. The airship rose high above the trees and then flew off.

Colonel Tye draped the connected grenados all

around his iron horse and then mounted it. He held the long wick that connected the grenados in one hand and then with the other, he drew a striker – a tool that looked like scissors, but with flint on one 'blade' and steel on the other – from the pocket of his coat. He rubbed both sides together, producing sparks, which he used to light the long wick. Then, he took off, racing toward the double doors of the house where the vapor was made; the house full of hussars and Murray's men.

The iron horse crashed into the door, shattering it.

Colonel Tye disappeared into the darkness cast by the shadows within the house. He rolled off the iron horse and then scrambled toward the frame where the door once stood. He could hear howls, screams and the pounding of hooves behind him.

He sprinted out of the house and up the road toward the bodies of his comrades and the hussars.

A massive explosion rocked the battlefield and knocked Tye onto his face. He got to his knees and crawled toward the hussar he gutted earlier. He snatched open the chasm he rent in the hussar's belly and then crawled inside. He quickly gathered entrails from the ground and pulled them inside with him. He then pressed down on the slit, closing it the best he could.

A yellow haze rose from the rubble that was once the house. Carried by the wind, the thick mist floated across the battlefield. As it traveled over the corpses, they blistered. A moment later the flesh turned into mush and melted off the sinew and bone.

The cloud was a carnivorous predator, ravenous for meat and consuming all in its wake.

Five

June, 1778

Tye sat next to Ngozi, chuckling at Talako and Barbey as a crowd of small children climbed all over them, demanding that Talako teach them to wrestle, or that Barbey give them a ride on his back.

"You picked the perfect locale," Ngozi said. "Madagascar is lovely at this time of year."

"You sold me on the place," Tye said. "After we finish building the winding station, we can get up in the air again. There are a few places on the mainland I would like to visit – Kemet; Luongo; Oyo."

"We have to move carefully in Oyo," Ngozi said. "British slavers visit regularly and in abundance. King George has issued a two hundred-pound reward for the return of each soldier in the Black Brigade, with an additional six hundred pounds for *your* arrest and return. A slaver would do well to add us to his cargo."

"Someone should put an end to the slave trade in Africa," Tye said.

"Tye...you promised our days of fighting battles

were over," Ngozi said. "And you promised *me* a go at a normal life."

Barbey zoomed past their table with three overjoyed children clinging to his back.

"Well, normal for *us*," she said.

"I know, I know," Tye sighed. "Forget I mentioned it.

"Wait, you're giving up that easily?" Ngozi said. "No trying to convince me?"

"No," Tye replied.

Ngozi's eyes narrowed. "You're up to something."

"No, I'm not," Tye said.

Ngozi leaned forward in her chair. "Alright; look…promise me marriage and two children afterward and I'm in."

Tye beamed. "Fine."

"A boy and girl."

"Fine."

"Alright, then," Ngozi said.

Tye leapt to his feet.

"Black Brigade!" He called. "Gather around, brothers…we have a mission!

ABOUT THE AUTHORS

Cane

Milton Davis is a research and development chemist, speculative fiction writer and owner of MVmedia, LLC, a micro publishing company specializing in Science Fiction, Fantasy and Sword and Soul. Milton is the author of *Meji Book One* and *Meji Book Two*; *Changa's Safari Volumes One, Two* and *Three*; *Woman of the Woods*; *Amber and the Hidden City*; and *From Here to Timbuktu*. He is co-editor of six anthologies; *Griots: A Sword and Soul Anthology* and *Griot: Sisters of the Spear*, with Charles R. Saunders; the *Ki Khanga* Anthology with Balogun Ojetade; the *Steamfunk!* anthology, also with Balogun Ojetade; *The City* cyberfunk anthology; and the *Dark Universe* space opera anthology. Milton Davis and Balogun Ojetade recently received the Best Screenplay Award for 2014 from the Urban Action Showcase for their African martial arts science fiction script, *Ngolo*. Milton resides in Metro Atlanta with his wife Vickie and his children Brandon and Alana. You can find Milton online at: http://www.mvmediaatl.com/.

Sea-Walker

Carole McDonnell is a Jamaican-American writer who has spent most of her years surrounded by things literary. Her writings appear in various anthologies including but not limited to, *So Long Been Dreaming: Post-colonialism in science fiction*; *Fantastic Visions III*; *Jigsaw Nation*; *Griots: A Sword and Soul Anthology*; *Steamfunk*; *Life Spices from Seasoned Sistahs: writings by mature women of color*; *Fantastic Stories of the Imagination*; and *Lost Trails: Weird Western*. Carole McDonnell's novels are *Wind Follower*; *The Constant Tower*; and *My Life as an Onion*. Her collections of short stories, *Spirit Fruit: Collected Speculative Fiction*, and *Flight and other Stories of the fae*, are available on Amazon and Kindle. Her Bible Studies include *A Fool's Journey through Proverbs*; *Scapegoats and Sacred Cows of Bible Study*; and *Blogging the Psalms*. Her reviews appear in print and at various online sites. Carole is a columnist for several Christian and African-American magazines. She lives in New York's Hudson Valley with her husband, two sons and their pets.

Fool's Errand

Gerald L. Coleman is a Philosopher, Theologian, Poet, and Author residing in Atlanta. Born in Lexington, he did his undergraduate work in Philosophy and English at the University of Kentucky. He followed that with a degree in Religious Studies and a Master's degree in Theology at Trevecca Nazarene University in Nashville. His most recent work appears in, *Pluck! The Journal of Affrilachian Arts & Culture*, *Drawn To Marvel: Poems From The Comic Books*, and *Pine Mountain Sand & Gravel Vol. 18*. He is a speculative fiction author, including short stories, the most recent having been published in the Science Fiction, Cyberfunk, Anthology: *The City* by MVMedia. He is the author of the Epic Fantasy novel *When Night Falls: Book One of The Three Gifts*. A co-founder of the Affrilachian Poets, he has just released a collection of poetry entitled *the road is long*. You can find him at geraldlcoleman.co or follow him on Twitter @Iconiclast.

Bloodline

D.K. Gaston was born in Detroit, Michigan. His first book, *XIII* was published in 2007. D.K. is the author of mysteries, thrillers, science fiction and fantasy, including the wildly popular Urban Fantasy novels, *Taurus Moon: Relic Hunter* and its sequel, *Taurus Moon: Magic and Mayhem*. D.K. is a devoted husband and father and when not enjoying time with his family, he is always working on his next novel. Check D.K. Gaston out at: http://www.dkgaston.com/.

An Omnibus Ride in Scarlet

Nat Turner was an enslaved Afrikan who led a rebellion of enslaved Afrikans and free Afrikans in Southampton County, Virginia on August 21, 1831 that resulted in the deaths of at least 60 Caucasians. Nat Turner lived in one of the most repressive regimes in the history of the world during its most oppressive time. He was passionate, energetic, committed, and dedicated to the eradication of slavery. Nat Turner remains elegantly and elaborately wrapped in the fabric of resistance to domination, earning his place in the panoply of revolutionary icons such as Boukman, Dessalines, Zumbi, Touissaint L'Ouverture, Delgres, Yanga, Harriet Tubman, Nanny, Denmark Vesey, Gabriel Prosser, and John Cavallo.

The Adventure of the Silver Skull

Deanna Baran lives in a remote part of Texas where cowboys may still be seen in their natural habitat. A librarian and former museum curator, she writes in between cups of tea, playing Go, and trading postcards with people around the world. Her work may most recently be seen in *The MX Book of New Sherlock Holmes Stories* and the *2015 Young Explorer's Adventure Guide*.

Fury

Zig Zag Claybourne's short fiction and essays have appeared in *Fiction Fix*, *Vex Mosaic*, *Alt History 101*, *The Wayne Review*, *Flashshot*, *Reverie Journal*, *Stupendous Stories*, *The City* anthology and numerous other publications. He is the author of the novels *The Brothers Jetstream: Leviathan*, *Neon Lights*, *By All Our Violent Guides* (as CE Young) and the story collection *Historical Inaccuracies*.

Traveler's Song: A Pulse Prelude

Born in Iowa, but later relocating and raised in Alton, IL and St. Louis, MO, **Kai Leakes** was an imaginative Midwestern child, who gained an addiction to books at an early age. The art of imagination was the very start of Kai's path of writing which lead her to creating the *Sin Eaters: Devotion* Books Series and continuing works. Since a young child, her love for creating, vibrant romance and fantasy driven mystical tales, continues to be a major part of her very DNA. With the goal of sharing tales that entertain and add color to a gray literary world, Kai Leakes hopes to continue to reach out to those who love the same fantasy, paranormal, romantic, sci-fi, and soon, Steampunk-driven worlds that shaped her unique multi-faceted and diverse vision. You can find Kai Leakes at: www.kwhp5f.wix.com/kai-leakes.

The Adventure of the Black Star

Jeff Carroll is a writer and a filmmaker. He is pioneering what he calls Hip Hop horror, Sci/fi and fantasy. He has written and produced 2 films, *Holla If I Kill You* and *Gold Digger Killer*, which won Best Picture at the International Hip Hop film festival. He has published 4 books: the novelization to *Gold Digger Killer*, *Thug Angel: Rebirth of a Gargoyle*, It Happened on Negro Mountain and *Sci-Fi Streetz: The Book of Hip Hop Sci-fi Stories*. His short stories have appeared in *Genesis: The Black Science Fiction Society's anthology*, *Genesis: the magazine* and in the Cyberfunk anthology, *The City*. Jeff Carroll is also the author of the non-fiction book *The Hip Hop Dating Guide*. He studied African History in college and his stories always include lots of action and a social edge. Jeff writes out of South Florida where he lives with his wife and youngest son. Connect with him at his blog http://hhcnf.blogspot.com/ and on Facebook, Instagram and Twitter.

The Bandit King and the Island of Tears

S.A. Cosby is a writer and poet originally from Mathews County, Virginia. A fan of fantasy and science fiction since an early age, S.A. started writing in high school and continued during his studies at Christopher Newport University, where he majored in English. His short story *The Rat and the Cobra* is published by Thug-Lit.com in their tenth online issue and his story *The Green Eyed Monster* features in the anthology *Sound & Fury: Shakespeare Goes Punk*. He is also author of the novel *The Brotherhood of the Blade: The Invitation*. S.A. lives in Gloucester County, VA with his pug, Pugsley.

Seven Thieves

Emmalia Harrington is a writer with a deep love for speculative fiction. Though the bulk of her work is non-fiction, she has short stories published in the podcast magazine *Cast of Wonders*, and in Simmons College's *Sidelines* magazine. When she isn't making Occidental clothing, she is cosplaying or making Japanese style outfits. Aside from sewing, Emmalia enjoys knitting, dyeing, academia and especially writing. Her Master's thesis combined several of her loves, explaining the political context of women's clothing in the early United States.

Mkono ya Mbao

Born in California in 1986, **Steven Workman (S. J. Fujimoto)** developed a love of fantasy through a childhood filled with reading books and dreams of publishing his own series. Traveling around East Asia and Europe made those dreams even bigger. "Nkono ya Mbao" is his first published work and he hopes there will be many more.

The Crafters' Cove

Currently residing in the Pacific Northwest, **D.L. Smith-Lee** is a natural born Midwesterner. He has published short stories of horror and dark fantasy with Sirens Call Publications, Forgotten Tomb Press, Dreamscape Press, The Were-Traveler and J.A. Mes Press. Always diligently at work on his next piece, he writes for escape from reality and the love of writing.

March of the Black Brigade

Balogun Ojetade is the author of the bestselling non-fiction books *Afrikan Martial Arts: Discovering the Warrior Within, The Afrikan Warriors' Bible* and *The Young Afrikan Warriors' Guide to Defeating Bullies & Trolls*. He is screenwriter / producer / director of the films, *A Single Link, Rite of Passage: Initiation* and *Rite of Passage: The Dentist of Westminster*.

Balogun writes about Steamfunk, Rococoa, Dieselfunk, Sword & Soul and the craft of writing at http://chroniclesofharriet.com/.

He is author of nine novels – the Steamfunk bestseller, *MOSES: The Chronicles of Harriet Tubman (Books 1 & 2)*; the Urban Science Fiction saga, *Redeemer*; the Sword & Soul epic, *Once Upon A Time In Afrika*; a Fight Fiction, New Pulp novella, *Fist of Afrika*; the gritty, Urban Superhero series, *A Single Link* and *Wrath of the Siafu*; the two-fisted Dieselfunk tale, *The Scythe*, the "Choose-Your-Own-Destiny"-style Young Adult novel, *The Keys* and the Urban Fantasy epic, *Redeemer: The Cross Chronicles*. Balogun is also contributing co-editor of two anthologies: *Ki: Khanga: The Sword and Soul Anthology* and *Steamfunk* and editor of the *Rococoa* anthology. Finally, Balogun is the Director and Fight Choreographer of the Steamfunk feature film, *Rite of Passage*, which he wrote based on the short story, *Rite of Passage*, by author Milton Davis and co-author of the award winning screenplay, *Ngolo*.

You can reach him on Facebook at www.facebook.com/Afrikan.Martial.Arts; on Twitter at https://twitter.com/Baba_Balogun and on Tumblr at www.tumblr.com/blog/blackspeculativefiction.